ALSO BY [

Oblivion's Grasp
Book Five of
Immortality and Chaos
by
Eric T Knight

Copyright © 2018 by Eric T Knight
Version 2.1 8/2016
All Rights Reserved
No part of this book may be used or reproduced in any manner whatsoever without
written permission except in the case of brief quotations embodied in critical articles
and reviews.

ISBN-13: 978-1986174398
ISBN-10: 1986174395

Author's Note:
To aid in pronunciation, important names and terms in this story are spelled
phonetically in the glossary at the end of the story.

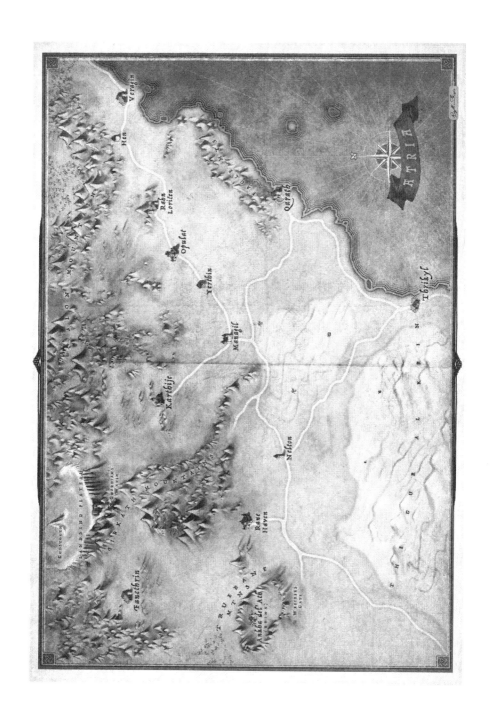

FOR KIM
MY COMPANION ON
MY SPIRITUAL JOURNEY

ONE

Wulf Rome and Quyloc were jerked off balance by the hunter and before either could recover they struck the glistening web of the Veil. It was like plunging into an icy lake, a sudden, freezing, heart-stopping cold. The hunter jerked again and then they were through the Veil, gasping on the other side.

Quyloc fought to stay upright, but one leg was still dead from where he'd been touched by one of the Children and his arms were pinned to his sides. He fell onto his face.

As he was pulled through the Veil, Rome let go of Quyloc. Once on the other side, he charged the hunter. Before he took two steps the hunter flung its free hand at him. There was a hissing sound and four black lines shot from its fingertips, striking Rome in the chest with enough force to knock him backwards. As Rome tried to regain his balance the lines wrapped around him, snaking out to wrap around both of his arms and pin them to his sides. The hunter yanked on the lines and Rome fell to the ground.

Quyloc made it onto his knees and from there he looked up, into the shadowed face of the hunter. There was no way to read emotion in that alien countenance, but he sensed triumph radiating from it and in the burning red eyes was the knowledge that this time he would not escape.

Quyloc went cold inside. He fought briefly against his bonds, but it was hopeless. Four black lines—like thin ropes but somehow knobby, as if jointed—were wrapped around him, and when he struggled, they tightened as if they were alive. He still had hold of the *rendspear*, but it was pinned to him and he could do nothing with it.

Gathering all the lines in one hand, the hunter crouched and slapped the ground with its palm twice. Then it stood. After a few moments Quyloc felt a rumbling from deep in the ground. It grew stronger, closer. Quyloc looked over at Rome, who had gotten onto his knees as well. The big man was staring at the hunter. It was a thing of blackness and shadow, the outlines of its body shifting, as if not completely there.

Then the ground beside the hunter broke open as something pushed up from below.

A large, hooked beak appeared, dirt cascading from it. Huge, silver eyes opened, fixing on the hunter. Legs ending in paws as wide and flat as spades, with thick, blunt claws, emerged from the dirt and it used these to lever the rest of its body free. It was broad and squat, its head tapering smoothly to a thick neck then down to a sinewy body rippling with muscle.

The hunter held out the bundle of black lines and the squat thing bit down on them. The hunter spoke to the squat thing, its voice the sound of glass being smashed by stone. The squat thing blinked.

The hunter turned and strode away, walking with a smooth, sliding gait toward a thick fog bank in the distance. It moved quickly and soon disappeared into the fog. The squat creature settled to the ground, turning so that its silver eyes fixed on Rome and Quyloc.

There was movement beside him as Rome struggled and managed to get to his feet. His movement caused the squat thing to growl, but it stayed where it was. Rome gave it a glance, then ignored it.

"I take it that was the hunter?" Rome asked. His voice sounded peculiar. Some of the sounds were truncated, others elongated. It made it difficult to understand him.

Quyloc didn't respond. He couldn't. Despair had folded its black wings around him and there was no escape. He'd been trapped in this dread land before, when they were on their way to Guardians Watch. Against all hope, Rome had saved him, using the black axe to cut him free. But that wasn't going to happen this time. No one knew they were here. There was no hope of rescue.

Every night since then he'd had nightmares about being pinned to that rocky butte, the filaments that hung down from the sky draining his life away. Every night he experienced the pain and horror of that time once again and now the nightmares had turned real as he'd somehow always known they would. He was trapped in this place forever, just as Lowellin had warned him so long ago when he first showed him the *Pente Akka*. That realization paralyzed him.

Rome looked down at his bonds. "What are these things? They're strong, whatever they are. I can hardly move my arms at all. I think they're alive. They get tighter when I try to move."

Quyloc knelt there, staring at the ground, wishing he could die.

Rome shook his head and scowled. "I can't believe I let myself get caught off guard like that. After all you told me about the hunter and how many times it's tried to trap you, I should have known it would take this opportunity. I should have been ready."

That was Rome, always shouldering the responsibility. And this time he should be, Quyloc thought, feeling a spark of anger. He'd been opposed to the attack on Melekath, had thought they should at least let Tairus and the others know what they were doing, but Rome had ignored his advice and bulled forward like he always did.

Rome looked over his shoulder at the Veil. Just visible on the sands beyond it was the black axe, lying where he'd dropped it while trying to save Quyloc. "If I just had my axe. Between it and your spear we could kill this damned hunter and be done with the thing." He looked at Quyloc. "At least you have your spear. Can you move at all, maybe work it free?"

Quyloc turned an angry glare on him. "No, Rome, I *can't* move. I *can't* get it free."

Rome gave him a surprised look, then nodded. "I get it. You're angry."

"Really, Rome? What makes you say that?" Quyloc said bitterly.

"You were against attacking Melekath but I made you do it anyway."

Quyloc slumped, the energy required to be angry draining from him suddenly. "None of it matters now anyway. We're doomed. We'll never get out of here."

"Don't talk like that," Rome said sharply. "We'll figure something out. We always do."

"Not this time," Quyloc said dully.

"There's always hope. You were trapped here before and I managed to free you."

"No one knows we're here, Rome. Even if they did, they don't have the axe like you did, remember?"

"Someone could go fetch it."

"Who? Lowellin? I wouldn't bet on it. I think we've seen the last of Lowellin. His last hope was infecting the *sulbits* with chaos power and now that's gone, I think he's running." The one *sulbit* Lowellin had infected with chaos power had gone berserk. Rome and Quyloc had been lucky to kill it before it did serious damage. "I think he's more afraid of Melekath than we are."

"I don't know why. Melekath seemed pretty weak to me."

3

"You should have left me, Rome."

"What?"

"When the hunter caught me. You should have let it take me. It wasn't after you. You'd still be free."

"I'd never do that."

"And that's your weakness. You don't know how to cut the dead weight before it drags you down."

Rome was looking at him in bewilderment. "Is that what you think you are, dead weight?"

"It's not what I think. It's what I know. It's true." The words came out heavy and laced with bile, but this time all the bile was directed at himself.

"Then you're a damned fool." Suddenly Rome was angry. "Gods, can you really be that thick, as smart as you are? Have you forgotten what kind of war we're fighting?"

Quyloc didn't answer. He stared at the ground, wishing Rome was far away, wishing he'd kept his mouth shut.

"This is no normal enemy we're fighting. It's...I don't what it is. I'm way out of my depth." Rome stopped, seemed to be struggling with the next words. When he spoke again the anger was gone. "You really don't get it, do you? The only way we're going to beat the Children is together. That's what's always counted. We're a team. I've known it since we were kids, since we took down Dirty Henry together. I knew then that we could do anything together, that nothing could stop us. I don't...I don't know if I would have made it through these dark days without you."

Quyloc turned his head and gaped at him. "You really...? *You* took down Dirty Henry. He was already dead when I showed up. All these years you've been telling that story like I was instrumental but the truth is I did nothing. I hate that story. I hate when you tell it. It's a lie, nothing but a damned lie. Just like me, just like my whole life." He ran out of words and knelt there, panting. He'd wanted to say that for a long time.

Rome shook his head. "It wasn't like that at all. I don't know where you got that idea. Dirty Henry had me backed into a corner when you came in and hit him from behind. I cut him, but my blade broke and I had nothing. He would have killed me if it wasn't for you."

"Why do you keep telling it like that?" Quyloc yelled. "It didn't happen that way at all. He was on the ground, nearly dead. I didn't do anything! I've never done anything!" The squat thing perked up at his shout, looking expectantly from one man to the other. A long, gray tongue came out and swiped across its face.

Rome's eyes grew very wide. "Where is this coming from, Quyloc? How'd you get it so backward in your mind?"

Suddenly Quyloc experienced a moment of extreme disorientation. For just one moment, he remembered the death of Dirty Henry differently. He remembered it like Rome said. But he knew it was false and he savagely pushed the memory away. "Because it's true. It happened like I said. The way you tell it…you're just putting me up, like you always do. You don't care for what others think of you. It's too easy for you. It's always been too easy for you. You don't understand what it's like to be a coward. You don't know what it's like to live your whole life in fear, waiting for others to figure it out. Well, I won't do it anymore. I'm sick of hiding. It has to be said. I'm a coward. I've never done anything but walk in your shadow. I thought that here, in this place, I could finally get past it. I thought that here I could finally be my own man, but instead I've failed again. But this time I didn't just bring me down, I brought you down too and everyone in Qarath. I'm a failure and a coward and it's finally caught up with me." His words died off. He was choking on his own self-loathing. But at least he'd finally said it. That had to count for something. *Didn't it?*

Rome was looking at him as if he'd gone insane. "You, a coward? But…you're the bravest person I know. You're not a failure. I'd never have taken the crown without you. *You* led us to the axe. *You* led us out of the Gur al Krin."

"Stop it," Quyloc said feebly.

"No. Not until I've said what I have to say. You think you're a coward because you live your life in fear? Is that what you think? Then you don't know anything after all. A coward is someone who runs from his fear. You've never done that. Dirty Henry caught you. I can't imagine how terrifying that must have been. But still you found the courage to follow me into his lair and kill him. *That's* bravery. Gorim's balls, Quyloc! Lowellin told you the *Pente Akka* would probably trap you, that you had no real chance against the hunter, but you came anyway. Over and over. How is that not courage? Tell me that."

"You make it sound like…"

"Like what? Like the truth? I'm a soldier, Quyloc. I've seen a lot of cowards in my life. I don't even hold it against them. Some men just can't seem to help themselves. But you aren't one of them. I'd stake my life on it."

The disorientation had returned. Old memories surged within him, some of them colored completely differently. Quyloc could make no sense of them. "This isn't a good time to talk about this."

"Why not?" Rome challenged him. "You got something else to do? Maybe you were planning on taking your dog for a walk?" He gestured at the squat thing, sitting there staring at them with its silver eyes. Its tongue came out again and slid over its face.

Quyloc was about to reply when the squat thing turned its thick head and looked toward the fog bank.

The hunter was returning.

Two

The hunter strode rapidly across the stony plain toward them. Briefly, Rome fought against his bonds, then gave it up. Escape would not come that way. Better to conserve his strength and wait for his chance. He tried to make a fist with his right hand and was gratified to see that his fingers responded with a twitch. It wasn't much, but it meant that the deadness caused by the Children's touch was temporary.

He watched the hunter closely as it approached. From the smooth, flawless way it moved, Rome could tell that the thing would be deadly in combat. Other than its knife-like claws, the hunter carried no visible weapons, though Quyloc had said it could manifest some kind of shadowy sword blade when it was fighting. The thing had to have a weakness. Everything did. The eyes maybe?

All too quickly it reached them. It stopped by the squat creature and held out one hand. The creature growled and so the hunter struck it on the side of its head, causing it to yelp and spit out the black lines. The squat creature made an eager sound, its toothy jaws opening wide as it leaned toward the two men. The hunter shook its head. The squat creature gave a last, hungry look at the two men, then burrowed back underground and was gone.

Without looking at the two men, the hunter turned and headed back towards the fog bank, pulling them along after him. Quyloc tried to come to his feet, but his numbed leg betrayed him and he fell on his side. Rome, already on his feet, fared better for a while, but then the hunter jerked on the lines and he fell also. The hunter exerted no discernible effort in dragging them.

It hurt, being dragged along over the stony, uneven ground. It was humiliating too. Rome had never felt so helpless in his entire life. He felt like a doll being dragged around by a child.

The fog closed in around them, so thick that Rome could barely see Quyloc, bouncing along beside him. He thought he heard Quyloc's voice once, but it was muffled, distant. Iridescent green flying creatures about the size of his hand, with four wings and bulbous eyes on the ends of stalks, began to appear out of the gloom. One landed on his face and he jerked his head around, trying to scare it away, to no avail.

It bit him and he grunted with the pain. He redoubled his efforts, twisting this way and that and was finally able to flip himself over far enough that it had to fly away or be smashed on the ground.

More appeared and he thrashed wildly, trying to keep them off him. So engrossed was he in his private war that he didn't at first realize it when the fog began to thin. As it did, the creatures faded away as well.

Their surroundings had changed. The sky overhead was the color of brass. There was no sun, no clouds, and no indication of where the light came from. The ground had changed to solid black rock, smooth as glass and radiating heat.

A minute later the hunter stopped. Rome breathed a sigh of relief, but his relief was short-lived. The hunter hoisted the two men into the air where they dangled, heads down, like chickens waiting to be slaughtered. As Rome slowly twisted in the air, he saw that they were on the edge of a high cliff. At the base of the cliff was a broad river, greenish-brown and turgid. The far side of the river was cloaked in thick greenery, huge trees trailing vines, bright spots of clustered flowers. Far in the distance was a low mountain that slumped like a candle left in the sun to melt. Smoke drifted in a steady stream from the top of it.

Rome was starting to get a bad feeling about this when suddenly the hunter hurled the two of them off the cliff.

THREE

The fall hurt. Rome thought he might have broken a rib, although how that could be since his body wasn't actually in this place he didn't know. He just knew that the water felt hard as a rock when he hit it. He went down deep, far enough that he had time to wonder if he was going to float back to the surface. He tried to kick with his legs, but without his arms he was mostly helpless.

In time he did bob to the surface, though. Surprisingly, he didn't gasp for air like he thought he would. He didn't even feel out of breath. Was he actually breathing? Floating on his back, he lifted his head to look around. Quyloc was floating a short distance away. "You okay?" Rome asked him.

"No. I'm not okay."

Rome lay back and just floated then. The pain in his chest was subsiding. The water was a lot more comfortable than being dragged over rocks. "Well, at least we got free of the hunter," he said, trying to lighten things up a bit.

"We didn't get free. It threw us off a cliff."

"Still, it's a start. Where do you think we're going?"

"Did you see that low mountain in the distance?" Quyloc asked. "It's a volcano. That's where the *gromdin* lives. I think that's where we're going."

"Is the *gromdin* that thing you told me about that's trying to break into our world?"

"Yes."

"That sounds bad."

"It is bad."

"This *gromdin* thing, you think you could kill it with your spear?"

"What?"

"Do you think you could kill it with your spear?"

"I don't know, maybe. The thing is huge."

"But you've killed other things in here with it."

"That doesn't mean I can kill the *gromdin*."

"I bet you can. We'll just have to wait for our chance. When it comes, I'll distract the *gromdin* and you stab it."

"Just like that."

"More or less."

"What if the *gromdin* never releases us from these bonds? What are we going to do then?"

"It's not a complete plan."

"It's not a plan at all."

"It's a start. We'll make up more as we go along."

"You're unbelievable. You know we have basically no chance of surviving this, right?"

"I wouldn't say that. It's a bit of a long shot, I'll admit. But something will come along. It always does."

Quyloc twisted around so he could look at Rome. "What's my job?" he asked him.

"What?"

"What do I do?"

"Well, I don't know your actual title. You know I'm not good with that stuff. But you're my main adviser."

"And what does an adviser do?"

"Is this a trick question?"

"Just answer it."

"You advise me. Right? Is that what you're looking for?"

"And *do* I advise you?"

Rome gave him a funny look. "Did you hit your head?"

"Just answer the question."

"Yes, you advise me all the time. You're the best adviser a man could have. What's your point?"

"The point is that I can't see any reason why you have an adviser *when you never take my advice*!" Quyloc shouted the last words.

"That's silly. I take your advice all the time."

"Name one time."

"Well, there's that time when…no, that's not a good example. How about when…? Do we need to talk about this right now? I'm having trouble thinking."

"Why not talk about it now? As you pointed out recently, we don't exactly have anything else to do right now."

"It's just hard to concentrate. I'm thirsty."

"You can't be thirsty. You're not really here."

"I'm going to drink some of this water."

"I advise you not to. Water is power on this world, but it's also poison. We probably won't live long enough, but eventually that poison is going to seep into us and kill us. Last time I only got a little bit on my skin and I would have died if Lowellin hadn't drained it out of me."

"What can it hurt? You said we're not really here."

"Go ahead, then. You're just proving my point."

"Which is…?"

"That you never take my advice!"

"That's not true."

"You're right, Rome," Quyloc said, his voice returning to normal levels. "You do follow my advice. Why, for instance, there's the time I advised you not to pull the black axe out of that wall…oh, wait, you ignored me and released Melekath and his Children. Or there was the time when I advised you not to attack Melekath. Let me see. How did that go again?"

"Okay, okay, so I don't take your advice very often—"

"Ever."

Rome winced. "Ever?"

"Promise me one thing. If we somehow get out of here, just listen to what I have to say once in a while. I'm not saying you have to listen to me every day. But every now and then, instead of running off like a difficult child and just doing the first thing that pops into your head, stop and listen to me. Okay?"

"Am I really that bad?"

"You're like a dog that gets a bone in its teeth. You get an idea and you just won't let go."

"Things mostly work out though, don't they?"

"I'm not answering that until I see what happens with the *gromdin*."

"I promise," Rome mumbled, feeling chastened. "When we get out of here I'll start taking your advice more often." Was he really that bad? He had to admit, he couldn't think of any times when he'd actually taken Quyloc's advice. He remembered asking for it…and then just doing what he'd meant to do anyway. Still, things *did* mostly work out. Didn't they? He looked at the strange, thick greenery sliding by on the bank as they floated down the river, the weird bronze sky overhead. Maybe Quyloc was right. A lot of where they were right now *was* his fault.

They floated for a while in silence, then Rome said, "I can move my left hand a little bit. If I can work it free a bit more I might be able to get a hold of my belt knife… Hey, my knife's gone."

"That's because you're not really here. What's here is more like a thought of yourself. I don't really understand it. Anyway, even if you had your knife on you, it wouldn't be your knife. It would be nothing more than a mirage."

"But your spear is real."

"It *came* from here."

"And that bone knife you used to have, that you killed that monster with?"

"It probably came from here also."

Rome thought about this for a time. "Didn't you tell me that when you want to leave this place you kind of picture the Veil in your mind and it appears?"

"Yes."

"So, can't you do that now?"

"No, I can't. I couldn't do it the first time the hunter caught me either. Even if I could summon the Veil, I'd still have to cut it and I can't get my arms free to do that."

Rome pondered some more. "You said that my body, what I'm looking at now I mean, is like a thought of me."

"Yes."

"So, if I'm just a thought, why can't I just think myself out of here?"

At that moment something appeared in the sky, heading toward them.

FOUR

Opus hurried out of the palace. Tairus was waiting for him at the foot of the front steps. Opus didn't need to say anything; his appearance said it all. For once the small man's perfect decorum was broken. His hair, always neatly oiled and combed, was in disarray. His jacket had a smudge on it. Even his thin mustache seemed to droop. Clearly, he'd had no luck finding Rome or Quyloc either. It was midmorning. They'd been searching for Rome and Quyloc since shortly after dawn, when the two men failed to show for a meeting with Tairus and Naills.

"I turned out the entire staff," Opus said. "We searched every room."

Tairus cursed under his breath. Melekath and the Children would be here in two days and their macht and his chief adviser were missing. Tairus didn't have to look around the courtyard to see what was on the face of every soldier, every servant, every man, woman and child. He'd had men search every inch of the palace grounds and sent others into the city, to every spot either man was known to frequent. There was no way to keep such a search quiet. By now the entire city knew. Rome was the glue holding them all together. Without him, Tairus feared the whole city would fall apart.

The palace gates opened and a carriage carrying the FirstMother Nalene and the Insect Tender Ricarn entered, answering Tairus' summons. Tairus didn't particularly like either woman, but he was happy to see them right now. This was a problem that was clearly beyond his ability to solve.

"How long have they been gone?" Nalene asked in a peremptory tone as she got down out of the carriage. She sounded like she was addressing a servant who had burnt supper, rather than the general of Qarath's army.

Tairus bit back his angry reply. This was no time for it. "No one has seen them since last night."

"You checked the taverns and the brothels?" Nalene demanded. She had lost weight and the stubble on her head was mostly white. She looked like she'd aged twenty years since all this started. But she had not lost her arrogance or her haughtiness. "Likely Rome simply drank too much and is sleeping it off."

Then Tairus did snap. "*Macht* Rome is not in a tavern or a brothel. You'll do well to watch how you refer to him."

Nalene drew herself up—she was actually taller than Tairus, who was short and stumpy—a scathing reply coming to her lips, but Ricarn forestalled her by holding up one hand. Nalene wavered, then backed down and closed her mouth. Ricarn had that effect on people.

"Can you find them?" Tairus asked her, turning away from Nalene, deliberately excluding her. "Use your bugs or something?"

"My sisters are searching as we speak," she replied. "If the two men are within the city, we will know. But they will not find anything. This I know already."

Tairus felt like he'd been punched in the stomach, her words reaffirming his worst fears. In truth, he'd already known Rome wasn't in the city. If Rome was in the city nothing would keep him from turning up. "Do you think they're…dead?" It was hard to say the words.

Something crawled out of Ricarn's long, straight black hair and disappeared into her red robe. She was staring at Tairus, but he had a feeling she wasn't seeing him. For long seconds she stood motionless. She might have been carved from alabaster, so unearthly white and flawless was her skin. A butterfly landed on her shoulder, its wings waving slowly.

"No," she said at last. "They're *gone*."

"But where? How?"

A servant came tentatively down the stone steps toward the little group then. She was in her middle years, hands red from hard work. She had hold of the hand of a little boy, probably about five, and she was pulling him along behind her. He was trying desperately to get away, clearly terrified.

"Begging pardon, Chief Steward, sir," she said.

Opus turned to her.

"You said we were to tell you at once, if we learned anything about the macht, however so small."

14

"What is it?" Tairus barked, louder than he'd meant to. The woman shrank back and the little boy gave a small shriek. Opus held out a hand to stay him.

"What is it?" Opus asked, crouching and speaking directly to the little boy. "Come, no one will hurt you. But you must speak up and quickly."

The woman pushed the boy in front of her. Something about Opus seemed to give him courage for he pulled his hand away from his mother and stood straight, looking Opus in the eye.

"I saw the macht, sir. Before dawn. He was going into the tower. He had the black axe."

"You're sure it was him?"

The boy nodded.

"That's no help," Tairus said. "We already searched the tower."

"Not everywhere," Opus replied, tapping himself angrily on the temple as he stood. "I should have thought of it sooner. I must be an idiot."

"What are you talking about?"

"Quyloc has a secret chamber under the tower that he likes to go to. Part of an old escape route for the king, I think."

"If it's secret, then how do you know of it?"

Opus gave him a look as if he was a slow child. "This is my world. I pay attention."

Opus led them around the edge of the palace and to the tower, calling for a servant to bring a lantern as they went. They entered a store room on the ground floor. In the corner of the room, hidden behind some crates, was a trap door. He pulled it up, revealing iron rungs set into the wall of a shaft that led down into the stone.

"His chamber is down there." Opus handed Tairus the lantern and Tairus started down, followed by the two Tenders. A few minutes later they were standing in a small room with a small window that looked out over the sea. Against one wall was a cot, a chair sitting beside it.

On the cot, lying on his side, was Rome. Slumped in the chair was Quyloc.

Tairus ran to them. "Rome! Wake up!" He shook Rome but there was no response. He put his fingers to the large vein in Rome's neck but could feel no pulse.

"They're not dead," Ricarn said. "They're gone. There's nothing inside."

"What do you mean they're gone?" Tairus asked. "I can *see* them."

"You see their bodies. The essence of who they are is elsewhere."

Tairus remembered then: Quyloc lying motionless on the stone, while at the same time he was across the battlefield, fighting Kasai.

"But why? Where would they go? Especially now, with Melekath so close."

"The boy said Rome was carrying the axe," Ricarn mused. "Maybe they went to attack Melekath, surprise him like Quyloc surprised Kasai."

Suddenly it all made sense and Tairus sat down heavily on the desk. "Yeah," he said wearily. "That sounds like Rome, damn him. It's just the kind of thing he would do."

"It's an idiot thing to do, that's what it is," Nalene said harshly, suddenly angry.

"I'm sure he had his reasons."

"Yes, I'm sure they seemed like good reasons after a night of rum with his whore," she shot back at him.

Tairus came off the desk, his fists clenched. "You will *not* speak of the macht this way," he growled.

"Why are you defending him? Look what he's done. Just when we need him the most he runs off on a fool's mission and gets himself killed. Gets them both killed." Her *sulbit*, sitting on her shoulder, crouched as she spoke and hissed softly, opening its mouth, which was filled with fine, needle-like teeth. It was the yellow of old ivory and the size of a cat, its head blunt and rounded, its eyes black and deep set. Its hind legs were thicker than its front legs, and the toes on its front paws had grown longer, more fingerlike.

"Ricarn just said he's not dead, only gone," Tairus snapped. "He'll be back."

"Stop deluding yourself. If he was going to come back, he would have already. He's been gone for hours."

Ricarn raised one hand. She didn't say a word or make any other motion, but both of them ceased at once. "There is another possibility. They might be in the *Pente Akka* itself."

"The place where Quyloc got his spear?" Tairus asked, feeling sick at the thought.

Ricarn nodded. "There is no way to know for sure, of course. Not without help. Though I believe you can help us with that, can't you, T'sim?"

Tairus looked around. "Why are you talking to T'sim? He's not..." His words trailed off as T'sim entered the room. He was dressed as

16

always, in his long, brown coat with the polished silver buttons. He looked like a small, slightly built man of middle years, a completely unremarkable man. And yet, his face was curiously unlined and just a little too symmetrical, with none of the flaws that make faces human. His eyes were different too, a blue that was sometimes startling and clear and other times cloudy and almost gray, like the sky. He stood with his hands clasped behind his back.

"You wish my assistance, Insect Tender?" T'sim asked, giving a slight bow.

Ricarn gestured toward the still forms of Rome and Quyloc. "We are missing two of our leaders."

T'sim nodded. "They left in the early morning, before the sun."

"We need to know if they are anywhere under the sun, or if they are in the *Pente Akka*."

T'sim frowned slightly. "You want me to look into the *Pente Akka* and see if they are there. I confess, I do not like to go near that place."

"It would be a great help."

T'sim blinked, considering this. "It is not our way. My kind have never involved themselves in the world. We have always stayed above the endless conflict."

"Listen, T'sim—" Tairus began, but again Ricarn stopped him with the slightest gesture.

"However," T'sim continued, "the prospect of a future without those two is a considerably less interesting one. Fascinating events seem to revolve around them."

Now Tairus just couldn't hold it in any longer. Ignoring Ricarn, he burst out, saying, "That's all you have to say? You know, if we don't stop the Children they'll devour everything, even you and your brethren. Doesn't that mean anything to you?"

"Actually, I find the prospect somewhat enticing," T'sim answered, unperturbed by his outburst. "I have long envied your kind the ending that awaits you at the end of your lives. This world has grown very old for me." His brow furrowed slightly. "My only concern is that the end offered by the Children may prove to be even duller than what I now experience. The last time I sought a change, when I moved into this form—" he indicated his body "—and took up residence within the Circle known as Life, it did not, admittedly, turn out the way I thought it would. Some decisions, once made, cannot be undone."

Tairus just stared at him. "I have no idea what you are talking about."

T'sim looked at Ricarn. "I will look for them."

A sudden gust of wind blew into the room through the window, whirling around T'sim. It was as if T'sim were made of sand. He just seemed to blow away and then was gone.

They were left there looking at each other. Finally, Nalene said, "How long will this take? I have a great deal to do. The *sulbits* are not nearly strong enough. They need to feed more and it is better if I am there when it happens. Sometimes it does not go…well."

That made Tairus shudder. Nalene and the rest of the Tenders who had *sulbits* had been letting them feed on the citizens of Qarath for the past few days, the idea being that the *sulbits* needed to grow as strong as possible before Melekath and his Children arrived. Even though the citizens who were fed on were volunteers, and even though Rome had given his approval and Tairus knew it was necessary, he still hated the idea. It felt horribly wrong. Several people had already died during the process, when the Tenders were unable to pull their *sulbits* away in time. He only hoped it was worth it in the end.

"He will not be gone long," Ricarn responded. "Time and distance do not mean much to him."

It was only a few minutes later that T'sim returned. "They are there. The hunter caught them and is turning them over to the *gromdin*."

Alarmed, Tairus asked, "What does *that* mean?"

"In some ways it is good, because the *gromdin* needs them alive for its purposes," Ricarn said. "It will keep them so for as long as it can, so that it may draw off as much of their Song as possible."

"What's it keeping them alive for?" Tairus already knew he wasn't going to like the answer and in his mind he cursed Rome again for leaving him here to deal with this on his own.

"It will use their Song to shred the barrier between our worlds," Ricarn replied calmly.

Nalene paled at her words. Tairus felt sick. "We have to get them out of there." To T'sim he said, "Go back. Get them out of there."

T'sim shook his head. It was Ricarn who spoke. "He cannot go there. No Shaper can. It is why Lowellin needed Quyloc in the first place."

"It is a place formed of chaos power," T'sim said. "Any power from our world, whether LifeSong or that which inhabits the Spheres of Stone, Sea, and Sky, is instantly annihilated when it comes into contact with chaos power."

"Then how is it Rome and Quyloc are there?"

"They are not really there," Ricarn said. "Only their spirit bodies are."

Tairus rubbed his temples. "You know that doesn't make any sense, right? None of this does."

"Nevertheless," she replied. Ricarn was watching him closely, as if waiting to see how he would react.

"Can't *you* get them out of there?"

"Without an item from that world I cannot pass through the Veil," she replied.

"You know what this means, don't you?" Nalene said to Ricarn. Ricarn nodded slightly.

"Well, I don't," Tairus growled. "Enlighten me."

"Soon the *gromdin* will begin stealing their Song. Regardless of the cost, we cannot allow that to happen."

"Hold on there," Tairus said, putting one hand out. "You better not be saying what I think you're saying."

"That's exactly what I'm saying."

"Forget it. You'll have to go through me."

"Do you have any idea what will happen if the *gromdin* makes it into our world?" Nalene blazed. "Did you even listen to what T'sim said? We won't have to worry about what Melekath and the Children do. We'll already be dead."

"We don't know that will happen," Tairus said stubbornly.

"Talk to him will you?" Nalene asked Ricarn. "Maybe you can get through his thick head."

"She is correct," Ricarn said. "However, it has not begun yet and when it does, it will not happen instantly. We will probably have at least a few minutes."

"Then there's still time," Tairus said.

"She said *probably*!" Nalene snapped. "No one really knows."

"It's good enough for me."

Nalene gritted her teeth. "Understand, I don't *want* them dead."

"Is that true?" Tairus. "Maybe you want Rome out of the way so you can make yourself queen."

"That's ridiculous!" Nalene snapped. "It's true that I have no love for either man, but I'm not stupid. We need them against Melekath. He's the enemy here."

"But you're quick to talk about killing them."

"Just think for one minute, you stupid little man!" she rasped. "Think about what you're saying. This is the abyss we're talking about.

19

If the *gromdin* steals enough Song from them, it will shred the Veil. That Veil is the only thing protecting our world from the abyss. If the abyss spills over into our world… Would you really risk the whole world for two people?"

"I would and I will."

Nalene put her hand on her *sulbit*. "And if I decide to just kill you right here, right now? What will you do then?"

"I'll die with my fingers in your throat," he grated. "Whatever you do to me, you won't survive it."

"This does not benefit us," Ricarn said smoothly. "There is still time. When the *gromdin* begins, we will be able to *see* it," she said to Nalene. "Action can be taken then."

"No one touches them until that happens," Tairus said, staring at Nalene. "No one touches them without my permission. *I* decide when it happens, *if* it happens. Do you understand?"

Nalene crossed her arms, her thick jaw set in a harsh line. Her *sulbit* was standing up on its hind legs, its tiny teeth bared at Tairus. "People die in war. Even one as thick as you understands that. *I* will not sacrifice an entire city, an entire world, because you cannot handle the thought of your friend dying. When the time comes, I will see them dead, regardless of what you say or do. Do you understand *me*?"

They stood there staring at each other for a long moment, neither backing down, until Ricarn said, "We are wasting time here."

A short while later Tairus summoned four of his most trusted soldiers, including Nicandro, Rome's aide, to the secret chamber. When they saw Rome and Quyloc lying there, seemingly lifeless, they paled. Nicandro looked to Tairus.

"I know what it looks like, but they're not dead," Tairus told them.

"What's wrong with them?" Nicandro asked.

"They're…gone. You've seen that spear Quyloc carries. They went to the place where he got that."

"Why?"

Tairus hesitated. He was tempted to tell them to shut up and follow orders. This was the army and he had many duties to attend to. But he also knew that these were not ordinary times. They needed answers. They needed hope. He made a sudden decision to give them part of the truth. "They went there to attack Melekath."

"Has the enemy captured them?"

"Yes."

"Will they return…?"

Tairus gave a harsh laugh. "You know the Black Wolf. Have you ever known him to lose? He probably has Melekath by the tail right now." He gestured at the bodies. "Pick them up. We need to move them into the tower where we can keep a better eye on them."

They carried the two men up and put them in a room on the second floor of the tower. "You four stay here and guard them," Tairus told them. "A Tender is coming. She is the only one you are to allow in. She's coming to watch over them, to let us know if things are starting to go wrong." He stared hard at Nicandro. "This is very important. If she sees anything, reacts to anything, send someone to get me at once. I'll send a squad to hold the entrance to the Tower. No one enters until I say so. Not the FirstMother, not anyone. Is that clear?"

Nicandro and the others saluted.

The door opened. All five men reached for their weapons. A tall, young Tender entered. She looked at the five men arrayed before her, but her expression betrayed no fear or surprise. To Tairus she said calmly, "I am Bronwyn, sent by the FirstMother." Her *sulbit*—about the size of a small cat, its skin ivory with hints of crimson, its body sleek and narrow—crouched on her shoulder, its beady eyes fixed on Tairus. It seemed eager.

"You will do nothing without my permission," Tairus told her. Turning to Nicandro he said, "Bar the door behind me."

21

FIVE

TWO large, winged things had appeared against the bronze sky, flying towards them. As the creatures drew closer, Rome and Quyloc could see that they were twice the length of a man, their long, slender bodies covered with iridescent green skin. They had huge, bulbous eyes and two sets of transparent wings, flapping so fast they were only a blur. A high-pitched whining came from them. They flew up and hovered over the two men.

"I think this is our ride," Rome said. "What took you two so long?" he called.

The creatures dropped down and one landed on each man. They had six legs, each ending in hooked claws. They took hold of the men, their wings buzzed faster, and they lifted into the air.

The river had brought them close to the volcano and once they were airborne, the creatures headed toward it. They were finally going to come face to face with the *gromdin*. Quyloc remembered the first time he'd seen the creature, the night he'd killed the assassin with the bone knife. Just that one glimpse had terrified him. The thought of coming face to face with the creature was immeasurably worse. Panic welled up inside him, pure animal fear, bleak and unreasoning. It would be so easy to give in to it.

But Quyloc knew fear. Fear was his oldest companion, riding his shoulder while he fought to survive on the streets of Qarath as an orphan and right on through every day of his adult life. He woke up with fear and he went to bed with fear.

It would not get the better of him.

He forced himself to calm down, noting distantly how much taking deep breaths helped, even here where he had no body. In time the urge to panic subsided and he was once again his own master. Probably there was nothing he could do. Probably all was lost. But he would face it on his own terms, with his wits about him.

22

The volcano was jagged, black rock, an angry fist thrusting its way up out of the jungle. Its slopes were bare of vegetation, but they were not empty. Scores of misshapen creatures were crawling, running and slithering up its sides, heading for the top. Quyloc stared at them, his fingertips on his *rendspear*. Just let his arms be free for a moment before his death and he would take a number of those creatures with him. They, too, would know fear.

Standing atop the volcano, on a shelf of rock surrounded on three sides by lava, was the *gromdin*. It was a mottled, gray-green color and it was huge, big enough to kill a man simply by stepping on him. It stood on two legs. Its head was a swollen lump on top of the bloated mass of its body. When it saw them its cavernous mouth opened and it barked a command at the winged things carrying them. They brought Rome and Quyloc closer.

It reached greedily for them and Quyloc had to fight a new tide of panic as huge, clammy fingers closed around his body. The thing brought them in close and stared at them as a man will stare at a great prize. Then it held them up and roared in triumph. Quyloc thought that he had never felt so helpless.

The *gromdin* set the two men down on a raised slab of raw stone. Lying on the stone, Quyloc caught motion from the corner of his eye and turned his head. The first of the creatures racing up the sides of the volcano had reached the top. They perched on the jagged black stones that ringed the molten lake, leering faces, slavering jaws, hungry eyes. They knew the time had come. The new world awaited them. Quyloc turned his face away from them and stared up at the sky, again willing himself to stay calm. He needed to be ready. If there was a chance to escape, to fight back, he had to be prepared to seize it.

The *gromdin* raised both its arms to the sky and bellowed something in its harsh language. As it did so, a hard wind began to blow and the sky began to churn. Waves appeared in it, growing larger by the moment, until it looked like a storm-tossed sea. The creatures clinging to the sides of the volcano howled and squealed with delight. The storm built higher. Quyloc thought he could feel the stone under him shaking.

The *gromdin* bellowed again and made a slashing motion with one massive hand. Instantly the wind and the waves stopped as if frozen. There was a loud ripping sound and the bronze waves peeled back, revealing what looked like a massive pane of thick, purple-black glass. The gathered creatures went silent, all of them staring up at it.

Another bellowing command from the *gromdin* and hundreds of thin, black filaments spilled from the purple-black pane of sky. They arrowed down, heading straight for the two men. Quyloc tensed, knowing how much this was going to hurt.

Rome grunted in pain when they struck him. Quyloc bit his lip to keep from crying out. It felt like fiery worms were burning their way through his flesh. It was worse than he remembered.

The black filaments started to pulse as Song from the two men flowed through them. The far ends of the filaments clustered together on the purple-black glass. They sprouted smaller, finer filaments that writhed across the glass and, finally, pierced it.

The glass cracked.

Bronwyn was sitting on a chair, facing Rome's and Quyloc's bodies, a distant, glazed look in her eyes. Suddenly she tensed and sat bolt upright.

"What is it?" Nicandro asked. Bronwyn didn't answer. She seemed to be holding her breath. Nicandro exchanged a look with the other soldiers. They arrayed themselves around the Tender, hands resting on their weapons.

All at once Bronwyn came back to herself. She looked at the soldiers standing around her, as if just noticing them for the first time.

"What's happening?" Nicandro asked again.

"It's starting," she replied, standing up. One hand moved toward the *sulbit* on her shoulder and the soldiers drew their weapons.

"Keep your hands away from that," Nicandro warned her.

Slowly, Bronwyn moved her hand away from the creature. "I meant no threat."

"See that you don't."

"I have to inform the FirstMother. Will you allow me to leave?" Nicandro nodded and she left the room hurriedly.

"You two follow me," Nicandro said after she was gone. To the other soldier he said, "Bar the door behind us. Don't open it unless it's me or General Tairus. Understand?"

At the door of the tower, Nicandro told the other two soldiers "Close this door behind me and bar it. I'm going to get the general."

Six

The black filaments burrowed deeper into the two men and the pain increased. Rome's heels drummed on the stone and a harsh cry came from him. Quyloc screamed. It felt like he was being torn in half.

In the sky, the ends of the filaments probed blindly into the pane. The cracks grew wider. Sunlight shone through.

All at once a whole section of the purple-black pane seemed to shatter and fall away. Jagged pieces rained down around the two men and the *gromdin*. Through the hole could be seen the palace grounds.

The *gromdin* howled in triumph.

The pain was unbearable. With all his heart Quyloc begged for death. Anything to stop the pain. Choking sounds came from Rome…

Quyloc blinked. He was standing on a flattened area on top of a mountain, a strange yellow sky overhead. Far below was a wide valley. The floor of the valley was covered with plants of brilliant hues, unlike anything he had ever seen. He raised his hands, looked at them, wondered if he was dead.

"If you keep fooling around it will be too late," a voice said.

Quyloc spun. The speaker was nearly as tall as he was, slightly built, but with faded yellow skin. He was completely hairless, with large, bulbous eyes and a wide, lipless mouth. There were gills on the sides of his neck and his hands and feet were webbed. "What? How did I get here?"

"You're not here," said another voice behind him. Quyloc turned. There was another of the strange creatures, sitting cross legged on the ground. This one was clearly ancient, so old that her skin had turned mostly white. A sparse clump of hair grew from her head, scraggly and long enough to reach the ground. She turned her head to look at the first speaker. "They're not very smart, are they?"

Quyloc struggled to regain himself. His sense of disorientation was so complete that he could barely form words. "Who...who are you? Where am I?"

"We are Lementh'kal," the first speaker said. He inclined his head slightly. "I am Ya'Shi. She's an Ancient One. They don't have names." In a conspiratorial whisper he added, "She's so old she forgot her own name." He dodged a rock that the Ancient One threw at him. "As for your second question—I imagine you are lying somewhere in the pile of dead stone you call Qarath with your friends gathered around wringing their hands in worry. Though I haven't checked, so I can't be sure." Very seriously he added, "I really can't keep up with everything, you know. I'm very busy."

"You don't *do* anything!" the Ancient One shouted.

"Be quiet!" he shouted back at her. "You're making me look bad in front of our guest."

Quyloc struggled to get his thoughts under control. Too many questions, too much remembered pain. Part of what Ya'Shi had said came back to him. "They found our bodies? They know where we are?"

"Hey, it's thinking," the Ancient One said. "That's a good sign."

"Soon they will kill him and his friend," Ya'Shi said.

"To close the hole into the abyss before it is too late," she replied. She turned her head and fixed unblinking eyes on Quyloc. "Unless you go home. Now."

Quyloc looked at her, confused. "I can't. I don't know how."

"Oh look, it's being stupid again," she said.

"Stop it!" Ya'Shi snapped at her. "You're not helping."

"You're the one who came up here and disturbed my meditation," she said crossly.

"You weren't meditating. You were sleeping."

"That's an outrage! I am a respected Elder of the Lementh'kal!" she spluttered.

"Will you two shut up!" Quyloc yelled. "I have to get home. I don't have time for this."

"What *do* you have time for?" Ya'Shi asked, his tone calm and reasonable. He stepped up very close to Quyloc and examined him carefully. His eyes were very luminous. "Be careful before you answer. Time is harder to save than you think."

Quyloc's head was spinning. None of this made any sense. How did he get here? Had he gone crazy?

"Yes, you are crazy," Ya'Shi said, as if reading his thoughts.

"Completely crazy," the Ancient One added.

"I brought you here," Ya'Shi said, stroking Quyloc's shoulder and upper arm in a soothing fashion. "I hoped we could talk some sense into you."

"*You* brought me here? You have the power to...?" Quyloc felt dizzy. The world seemed to be spinning around him. "You have to help us."

"Like a rescue?" Ya'Shi asked.

"Maybe we should fight the *gromdin*," the Ancient One said. "I imagine that would be quite an epic battle."

"Too bad you're too lazy to go anywhere," Ya'Shi said with a snicker.

"I'm not lazy!" she shouted. "I'm busy meditating. It's harder than it looks. Watch." She sat very straight and closed her eyes. A few moments later she was snoring softly.

"What's going on here?" Quyloc sputtered, backing away. "What's wrong with you two?"

"Hey, we're not the ones bound in the *Pente Akka*, having our life sucked out of us because we're too stupid to leave." Ya'Shi patted him on the cheek and shook his head sadly.

"I've tried to leave!" Quyloc yelled. "Just tell me how and I will!"

Ya'Shi shrugged. The gesture looked very odd on him, one shoulder coming up and then the other, a ripple running down his entire body. "I don't know if there's any getting through to you, but I will try again. I will speak slowly so that you can keep up. Are you ready?"

Quyloc wanted to shake him. He wanted to lie down and curl up in the fetal position. He wanted to cry. "Yes."

"Okay." Ya'Shi beckoned him close. Quyloc hesitated, then leaned in. "You're not really there," Ya'Shi said in a whisper, then nodded sagely. "Just like you're not really here."

"*What*?"

"I think this one is dumber than the other one," the Ancient One said without opening her eyes.

"You're not really there," Ya'Shi said emphatically. "You can leave any time you want."

"But that's crazy! I've—"

"The *gromdin* has only trapped the thought of you. You said it yourself. Just leave. That's all you have to do."

"It's not going to do any good," the Ancient One intoned flatly. "Just like it didn't do any good with Netra. It's sad, really, that the fate

27

of our world is in the hands of such as these. We never really stood a chance."

"You haven't stood in a hundred years," Ya'Shi shot back.

The Ancient One nodded and tugged at a few of her hairs, which seemed to have grown into the ground. "True."

"Are you ready?" Ya'Shi asked Quyloc.

"What? No! I'm not—"

He was cut off as Ya'Shi pushed him off the edge of the mountain. He fell, tumbling wildly…

And found himself looking up at the *gromdin*, the broken sky overhead.

SEVEN

Tairus was standing in front of the tower when the FirstMother arrived, fifty armored soldiers in rank behind him, weapons drawn. On either side of the armored soldiers were a dozen archers, arrows nocked. The FirstMother came hurrying around the side of the palace, three other Tenders in tow, and she pulled up when she saw the way was closed.

"Stand aside, Tairus," she warned. "You know what has to be done."

"If any of them lays a hand on her *sulbit*, open fire," Tairus told the archers.

The other Tenders looked questioningly at the FirstMother. Nalene's eyes flashed with rage. "Now, with Melekath and his Children nearly at our gates, with the *Pente Akka* threatening to overwhelm our world, *you would have us turn on each other?*"

"I will not stand by and see Macht Rome slain with no chance to defend himself."

"You would sacrifice everyone in this city, in the whole world, for *one person*," she snapped.

Tairus thought about it, then nodded. "I would."

"You're a fool," she hissed.

"No. I'm a believer. I've spent too many years around Rome. I've seen him come through impossible scrapes before. *And* he has Quyloc with him. Quyloc and I don't like each other all that much, but I know what he's capable of. I *know* those two will figure a way out of this."

Nalene started to reply when there was a sizzling, popping sound from overhead. Everyone looked up and several of the soldiers cried out in alarm.

Outside the window of the tower room where Rome and Quyloc lay a jagged rent had appeared in the air. Through the rent could be seen a seething mass of pulsing black filaments.

"What is that?" one of the Tenders cried.

"It's the abyss," Nalene replied, her voice loud enough for all to hear. She turned the full force of her gaze on the soldiers behind Tairus. "This is happening because of you," she thundered. "If you don't let me stop it, it won't matter what Melekath does. We'll already be dead."

Many of the soldiers exchanged uncertain looks. There were nervous mutters from their ranks.

"Stand your ground!" Tairus barked. "Protect your macht!"

A foul wind blew through the rent, which was growing larger by the moment. Sparks popped along the edges of the opening and electricity filled the air. The black filaments appeared to be attached to the edges of the rent, seemed almost to be gnawing at the edges, chewing the hole larger.

Four more Tenders arrived and took their places behind Nalene, sharing anxious looks, waiting for the command from their FirstMother to attack. Behind them a crowd of servants and soldiers began to gather. Many of the soldiers had their weapons drawn, but they looked uncertain.

"I can see Macht Rome!" someone shouted, pointing.

Through the rent, small in the distance, were two figures, lying bound on top of a smoking mountain. Each man had a large number of the filaments attached to him.

"What in Gorim's hell is that?" one of the soldiers behind Tairus muttered.

A huge, rubbery creature with mottled, gray-green skin was standing beside the two bound men. Motionless until now, no one had paid it much attention. But now it looked up and right at them and bellowed, the sound shocking in its brutality. Soldiers and Tenders alike took an instinctive step backward. Only Tairus and Nalene held their ground.

The thing grabbed hold of the filaments and began to climb, moving swiftly toward them. On the edges of the volcano a seething mass of bizarre creatures leapt and howled.

"It's the *gromdin*!" Nalene yelled, turning on Tairus, her face twisted with rage and fear. She seemed to be seconds away from physically attacking him. "We have to close that opening now!"

For the first time Tairus began to seriously doubt. Rome and Quyloc didn't look like they were about to escape. The *gromdin* looked like trouble and it would be on them soon. His loyalty to Rome and faith in his leader could not hold up against his responsibility to the city of

Qarath and its residents. He knew what Rome would say if he was there. Part of what made Rome who he was was his willingness to sacrifice himself to protect his followers.

Tairus yelled, "Open the door, Nicandro!" He looked Nalene in the eye. "Don't try and follow me. If this must be done, I will do it."

Nalene bared her teeth. "If you fail…"

"I won't." The soldiers pulled back, opening his path to the door, which was swinging open. Tairus ran through the door and up the stairs, yelling for the door to the room to be opened as well. It opened just as he got there, the lone soldier in the room staring at him white-faced. Tairus ran to the window and looked out.

The *gromdin* was about two-thirds of the way to the rent, climbing fast. Behind it the other bizarre creatures had begun to swarm up the filaments as well.

Tairus turned to the still forms of Rome and Quyloc and drew his belt knife. "I am sorry, old friend," he whispered as he raised the blade.

"Wait, sir, one of them's moving!" the soldier cried suddenly, pointing at the rent. "It's Quyloc!"

Rome and Quyloc could see the standoff before the tower, soldiers and Tenders poised at each other's throats. The rent had grown rapidly, big enough now that a whole squadron of men could run through it. Rome was thrashing against his bonds and yelling, "Stand down, Tairus! Kill us, kill us!" even though there was no way anyone on the other side could hear him.

We've lost, Quyloc thought.

Hard after that: *No.*

NO!

He started to fight against his bonds but then stopped.

Just leave. You're not really there.

The *gromdin* began climbing the filaments. Tairus was still facing off against Nalene. Rome and Quyloc would have front row seats to the destruction of Qarath. And they would be the instruments of its destruction. Other creatures started to climb the filaments as well, scurrying up like misshapen rats.

I'm not really here.

Quyloc closed his eyes and tried to get his breathing to slow, his muscles to relax.

But the chaos all around him made it impossible to concentrate. The pain was increasing. Making it worse was the awareness of how close the *gromdin* was to the rent. He had to hurry. He had only seconds left.

Quyloc tried again to clear his mind, to push away all distractions and reach for the calm in the center of the storm.

Then, all at once, he found the calm. The pain, Rome's shouting, the howling of the creatures, all faded into the background. Time stopped.

In his mind, a faint light appeared.

It was the remains of a small fire. He was in a decaying building, the smell of rot in the air. A man stood with his back to him. The man seemed very large. Beyond the man was a boy, several years still from manhood, staring at him defiantly, a broken knife in his hand.

Quyloc looked down. In his hands was a heavy chunk of wood.

He screamed his hatred and fear and charged the man, hitting him as hard as he could. With the first blow the man stumbled forward. Before he could recover himself, Quyloc hit him again. And again. The man went down, bleeding from his head…

Quyloc opened his eyes.

He was standing beside the stone slab, the *rendspear* in his hand. The black lines which had bound him were squirming on top of the slab. The filaments that had been attached to him were shriveling away, crumbling into dust.

As the filaments crumbled away, the *gromdin* looked back over its shoulder. Seeing that Quyloc was free, it howled and pointed at him, then increased its pace.

One of the creatures perched at the edge of the volcano turned toward Quyloc, its multifaceted eyes reflecting dozens of images of him. Its toothy maw opened and it rushed him.

Coolly, almost slowly, knowing he had all the time in the world, Quyloc jabbed the spear into its open mouth. The spear cut through the thing with ease, coming out the back of its head. He snapped the weapon back and the creature dropped.

Rome stared at him, bug-eyed. "How did you…never mind. Leave me. You have to stop that thing."

"I can't leave you," Quyloc replied. "You're not here either."

The *gromdin* had reached the rent. Panic on the other side as people scrambled to get back.

With a flick of his wrist, Quyloc severed the filaments attached to Rome with the spear. The *gromdin* howled with rage as the filaments shriveled away. It started to fall, then caught itself on the edge of the rent.

But Nalene had not been idle. She threw out one hand and from it leapt a jagged Song bolt. The bolt struck, not the *gromdin*, but the edge of the rent, which crumbled away. The creature howled again, lost its hold, and began to fall.

"Time to go," Quyloc said. He grabbed the front of Rome's shirt and effortlessly pulled him free of his bonds. More creatures had reached the top of the volcano and they charged the two men in a wild mass.

Quyloc ignored them. He drew the Veil in his mind, blinked and saw it before him. A quick slash from the spear and the Veil tore. Still holding onto Rome, Quyloc leapt through the opening.

On the dunes, Quyloc turned back and saw clawed hands reaching through the hole in the Veil. Another blink—see the Veil whole—and the opening in the Veil closed, severing the reaching limbs.

Rome was looking around. *The axe*, he said. Pulling away from Quyloc, he went to it and scooped it up. Quyloc followed, and as soon as Rome had the axe, put his hand on his shoulder. Another blink and they were lying on a table in the Tower, a stunned soldier staring at them.

EIGHT

"God*damn*," Rome said, sitting up and looking at Quyloc in awe. "I can't believe you just did that."

When Quyloc sat up the delayed adrenalin hit him and he started to shake all over. "I can't believe it either," he admitted.

Rome climbed off the table, but his legs failed him and he would have fallen if Tairus hadn't caught him. For a long moment the two men stared at each other, then Tairus whooped and wrapped Rome in a hug.

Quyloc climbed off the table too, waving away the soldier's offered help. He stood there, leaning against the table, trying to get the shaking under control.

Tairus let go of Rome and turned to Quyloc. "That was the most amazing thing I have ever seen," he said. "Thank you. With all my heart, thank you."

Using the spear as a cane, Quyloc was able to let go of the table and stand on his own. The gratitude in Tairus' eyes was painful for some reason and he had no idea how to reply so he turned away and walked to the window. Tairus patted him on the shoulder as he went by.

To Rome, Tairus said, "I can't tell you how glad I am you're back."

"Probably not as glad as we are to be back," Rome told him, a broad smile splitting his bearded face. "It looked to me like you were about to go to war with the Tenders."

"I was," Tairus admitted.

Rome's smile disappeared. "I should bust your rank right here and now, you know."

Tairus drew himself to attention. "You'll get no fight from me."

"No one is worth sacrificing the entire city for, hell, the entire world."

"You're right, sir."

Rome gave him a curious look. "And you'd do the same thing again, wouldn't you?"

"Without hesitation."

"Wool-brained fool," Rome said.

"My mam always said so."

Nalene entered then, a knot of soldiers and Tenders following her. Beside her was Nicandro, who looked at Rome apologetically and said, "I tried to stop her, Macht."

"It's okay," Rome said, waving him off. He sat down heavily in a chair and laid the black axe on the table, keeping a protective hand on it.

Nalene stood over him. "Of all the reckless, idiotic things you could have done…"

Rome looked up at her wearily. "There's no need for that. Quyloc already made the same point. You're both right. It was a stupid thing to do."

That surprised Nalene. Some of the fire went out of her and for a moment she looked a little off balance. Her *sulbit* slunk from one shoulder to the other. She looked around the room and her eyes fell on Quyloc, then went to his spear. "It is good you are back," she said, the words seeming to pain her. "Later I would like to know how you freed yourself from your bonds."

"Later," Quyloc agreed. He turned away and looked out the window, not wanting to meet anyone's eyes just then. He noticed that there were some soldiers and servants gathered around something on the ground at the base of the tower. They shifted and he was able to see what it was.

A chill went through him.

"You need to see this," he said.

Rome, Tairus and Nalene moved to stand beside him. Nalene stiffened when she saw what it was. Rome swore softly.

On the ground was a small orange and red sand dune.

Rome turned to Quyloc. "Where did *that* come from?"

"I don't know," he said.

"It looks like the sand in the Gur al Krin," Tairus said, his words trailing off as the implications sank in.

"It is," Nalene said sharply, turning on Rome, one hand raised in a clenched fist. It looked like she wanted to strike him. "Do you have any idea what you've done?" she demanded. He looked at her blankly and she continued. "Maybe this will help: The Gur al Krin was caused by chaos power leaking through a rip into our world."

Rome winced. "You're saying there's a rip here now too?"

She nodded.

"And I caused it."

"Yes, you did. Congratulations, Macht Rome, you just doomed Qarath."

As Rome was starting to leave the room, Quyloc stopped him.

"What is it?" Rome asked him.

"We touched the water in the *Pente Akka*," Quyloc replied. "Last time I touched the water there, it poisoned me. I would have died without Lowellin's intervention."

"So we need to find Lowellin."

"If we can."

"T'sim!" Rome called "Where are you?"

"I'm here," T'sim said from behind Rome.

Startled, Rome spun around. "We need Lowellin right away."

T'sim cocked his head to the side, a question in his eyes. Then he nodded. "You were in the water. There is a great deal of residual chaos power lingering on you."

"That's why we need Lowellin."

"He is not close. It may take me some time."

Just then a spasm of pain washed over Quyloc and he staggered to the side. Rome was turning to him when the pain hit him as well.

"We're running out of time," Quyloc gasped.

"If I may?" T'sim asked. "I may be able to help."

Rome bent almost double as a new spasm hit him. "We'll take it," he choked.

"Follow me to the ground floor," T'sim said calmly. "The closer we are to bedrock, the better."

NINE

Jimith stopped at the servant's door and looked around. It was late at night and the corridor at the back of the palace was deserted, as he'd known it would be. But it paid to be extra sure. Opus had expressly forbidden the servants to go out and look at the sand dune that had appeared in front of the tower, and he'd made it clear that the consequences for disobedience would be severe. As far as Jimith knew, no one had disobeyed Opus yet, though it had been all the servants talked about the entire day, and plenty of them had found excuses to go into rooms on upper floors that overlooked the area. He'd been one of them.

But he wanted to see it up close.

Jimith was young and possessed of a curiosity that knew no bounds. There wasn't a room in the whole palace he hadn't snuck into at least once, including the macht's personal quarters. He'd never been caught either, which was a source of real pride for the boy. No one was better at sneaking around, better at hiding or moving quietly, than Jimith. He figured if he ever put his mind to it, he could be the greatest thief this city had ever seen—when he was grown a little more—the kind of thief that got sung about in the taverns.

All of which meant there was no way he wasn't going out to look at the dune close up, no matter what Opus said.

He opened the door carefully. He already knew it didn't squeak. He knew exactly which doors in the palace squeaked and which ones didn't. His eyes had already adjusted to the darkness and he could easily see the soldier that had been posted at the corner of the garden to keep people away from the dune. The man was sitting on the stone bench there, leaning on his spear, snoring softly.

This was going to be too easy. Maybe he should swipe the guard's helmet, just to make it challenging.

On cat feet Jimith crept through the garden on the paved path, passing within a couple steps of the sleeping guard as he did so, and made his way toward the tower. The moon was only a sliver but there was easily enough light to see the dune.

He crept closer. It looked bigger than it had looked from above and for the first time he felt a shiver of fear. Maybe he should have stayed in the palace. What if the thing was dangerous?

But that was silly. It was only sand. And he wasn't going to touch it anyway. He just wanted to get a closer look at it.

He stopped a few paces away from it and stared at it. Where had all that sand come from? The palace servants were rife with rumors about it, but no one had any real idea. Just as no one had any real idea what had happened that morning, with the strange window to another world opening up and some kind of creature trying to get through, only being stopped at the last second by Quyloc and the FirstMother.

There was a rustling sound from the dune and goosebumps suddenly rose on Jimith's skin. He almost ran off right then, his mind full of images of clawed things crawling out of the sand and reaching for him.

But he was braver than that. He stood his ground and told himself it was just leaves blowing across the sand, never mind that there was no wind that he could feel.

The sound came again, from the other side of the dune, he was sure of it. He took a look over his shoulder, making sure the guard hadn't stirred, half hoping he had. But the guard still snored.

He made his way around the dune, careful to stay well back from it, and came to an abrupt stop as he rounded the end.

There was something on the dune, something dark and sprawling and multi-legged.

His heart started pounding wildly and he almost, almost bolted. But he saw that it wasn't moving and he fought down the fear. He peered closer. Those weren't legs at all. It looked like some kind of plant, some kind of vine with broad leaves that reflected silver in the moonlight. The leaves were bigger around than his head, growing up on stalks that were waist-high on him. The vine covered about half of the dune and as he watched, one of its tendrils grew visibly, rustling over the sand as it did so.

This was bad. He had to tell somebody.

He started to back away, then paused. There were flowers growing on the vine, great big things, the most beautiful flowers he'd ever seen.

He had to see them closer.

He inched closer, wishing it wasn't so dark, sure that the colors were gorgeous and vibrant, colors that would put the most expensive lady's gown to shame. He took another step forward and the flower moved. He was looking right down into it now, almost within arm's reach.

There was a sudden breath of air on his face and a cloud of pollen puffed out from the flower.

It settled on his skin and he began to scream.

"At least it seems to have stopped spreading for now," Rome said. It was the next morning and he and Tairus were standing in front of the tower, looking up at it. The vine that was growing out of the dune had almost completely engulfed the tower. The leaves of the vine were bright green outlined with crimson and about an arm's length across. Here and there were huge, bright orange flowers.

"It's not bad enough that we have to fight an enemy you can't kill," Tairus said glumly. "Now we have to worry about some monster plant eating us in our sleep too."

"Now, don't get all worked up," Rome replied. "We don't *know* that it eats people."

"Yeah, you're right," Tairus said sarcastically. "It probably *doesn't* eat people. It probably just kills people for no reason. Hooray. Finally, some good news. I won't be able to stop smiling the rest of the day."

"You're grumpy today," Rome observed.

"Good of you to notice."

"You need to stay positive."

"Oh, I am. I'm positive things are going to get a lot worse and look," he said, waving at the giant plant, "I'm right!"

Quyloc, who had been standing off to the side staring at the vine, spear in hand, eyes unfocused, came walking up then.

"What did you find out?" Rome asked him.

"It's definitely from the *Pente Akka*," Quyloc replied. "I think I remember seeing those same flowers in the jungle along the river."

"How do we kill it?"

"I don't know," Quyloc admitted. "If I could get to the main stalk I could probably cut through it with this." He held up the *rendspear*. "But that's a big if. And it might be it would still live even then."

"Why don't we just dump a bunch of lamp oil on it and burn it?" Tairus asked.

Quyloc shrugged. "It's worth a try, but somehow I don't think it's going to be that easy."

"Of course it isn't," Tairus groused. "Why should it be easy? Nothing else is."

"He's in a bad mood today," Rome said to Quyloc. "What do you think we should do?"

Quyloc gave Rome a surprised look, then said, "I think we should leave it alone. We have bigger problems right now."

"I agree," Ricarn said from right behind them, causing Tairus to jump. He spun on her, spluttering with anger, then saw who it was and clamped his mouth shut on whatever he'd been about to say.

"The Children will be here before the end of the day," Ricarn continued. "That is the more pressing danger."

"Melekath's wound didn't slow them down at all?" Rome asked.

"No."

"That doesn't make any sense. I know we hurt him. I think we hurt him bad." Rome looked to Quyloc for confirmation, but Quyloc's expression remained neutral. A thought occurred to him then. "You don't think they just left him behind, do you?"

TEN

"This should be interesting," Reyna said. The tall, red-haired woman was standing on the road, watching as a number of the Children slowly closed in around Melekath.

Heram—huge, blocky and muscular—was standing nearby, flanked by two of his followers. "He is badly injured," Heram said. He sounded surprised.

"Do you think he will die?" asked Dubron, one of his followers.

"Father can't die," the other follower said, a man named Leckl. "He's Nipashanti." Leckl had been badly injured in a fire while in the prison. He had used Song stolen in Thrikyl to mend much of his injury—his arm, which had been burned down to the bone, was once again whole—but he'd had no luck with his face, which was still mostly covered by angry red scar tissue.

"You know what I mean, Leckl," Dubron growled. "Will he stop, never move again?"

"Shut up, the both of you," Heram said and they both went quiet. They knew how fast Heram's temper went volcanic.

Melekath was on the road, struggling to sit upright. There were numerous stab wounds in his chest, from where Quyloc had struck him with the spear. He also had several gashes from Rome's axe, including one that cut down through his shoulder to his ribcage. There was no blood, only a curious sparking blackness revealed in the wounds. Melekath started to topple over and only just managed to catch himself with one hand.

Around him were probably a dozen of the Children. Other Children were arriving in ones and twos as word of what had happened spread through their numbers. They were still cautious, none of them with the courage to make the first move yet, but anticipation and hunger marked their faces and they were steadily inching closer, drawn by the power that leaked from Melekath. They had fed on that power for three thousand years while trapped in the prison. It didn't have the sweetness of LifeSong, but they were ravenous and beyond caring.

"If they have more of those weapons we will have to move carefully," Heram said. The big, bearded man in the black armor had cut Heram's leg nearly off with the black axe he carried. Heram had enough stolen Song in reserve to reattach the leg, but it was still weak and he had broken off a tree limb which he was using as a crutch.

"If they had more, they would have used them," replied Reyna, her gaze fixed on the Children. There was a hint of a smile on her lips. "It was a desperate gambit and it failed. In fact, they helped us. With Father out of the way there will be no one to hinder us. We'll hit Qarath tomorrow and there will finally be enough Song for everyone." She glanced at Heram and saw him looking at her latest prize hungrily. "You just never seem to plan ahead, do you?" she said mockingly. "That's why you're always so hungry."

Heram glared at her with his red eyes, but said nothing. Instead he motioned to his two followers and they moved off a short distance to talk. No doubt they spoke of plots against her, but Reyna wasn't worried. The two men who had attacked Melekath had done her more than one favor: weakened by the axe blow, Heram was no real threat to her now, even with his two followers to help him. It occurred to her that she could take him out now while he was weak and be rid of him once and for all. But doing so would weaken her more than she cared. There were others who might see that weakness as an opportunity to band together and try to bring her down. Best to wait.

Reyna's attention fell to her prize. The woman was on her knees. Attached to her ribcage was what looked like a gauzy, gray-white tether. The other end of the tether was attached to the middle of Reyna's palm. A small, but steady, flow of Song trickled down the tether and into Reyna.

The woman's eyes were fixed on Reyna. To Reyna's surprise, she did not see despair in those brown eyes, but rather a smoldering rage and a hunger to strike. "You're not like the rest of the shatren, are you?" Reyna said. "I think I'm going to be glad I kept you alive, and not just for food, either. I think I want to know more about you. Let's start with something simple. What's your name?"

The woman didn't answer.

"Oh good," Reyna said, smiling, "you're going to make this interesting. I like that. It will give me something to occupy myself on the walk to Qarath. I think training you will be very entertaining. Who knows? Maybe I'll even keep you as a pet for some time. Would you like that?"

No answer. Only a steady glare.

"The first thing you need to learn," Reyna said, "is that when I ask you a question, I expect an answer, and I expect one right away. Patience, as you will also learn, is not a trait I have ever bothered to cultivate, being one of those traits that I believe only the weak and powerless require."

Suddenly, without warning, she gave the tether a savage jerk. The young woman allowed a small scream to escape her before she could bite it off. Her face went very pale.

"What do you think?" Reyna asked her. "Is patience a trait that I should acquire?" She gave the tether a small twitch as she finished the sentence and was gratified to see the young woman shake her head.

"That's a start," Reyna conceded. "But I expect you to speak when you are spoken to and I expect you to address me as Mistress. Is that clear?"

When the young woman didn't respond right away she gave the tether another jerk, eliciting another cry of pain.

"Well?"

"Yes," the young woman gasped. Another tug on the tether and another sound of pain. "Mistress," she added.

"There. See? You're learning already. Now, let's try your name again. What is it?"

"Netra," the young woman said, a second later adding, "Mistress."

"Two in a row!" Reyna said. "We're on a roll now. I think you'll find that it will get easier and easier for you the more you do it. Who knows, if you do well enough, I might even keep you alive for a long time. I'm going to need servants, you know. I don't plan on eating everybody. Would you like to be my servant?"

She frowned and twitched the tether when Netra didn't respond immediately.

"No, Mistress."

"Really? I don't understand. Wouldn't being a servant be preferable to death?" Actually, Reyna understood completely. She would rather die than be a servant to anyone. She found herself somewhat liking this stubborn young woman. She was nothing like those two sniveling, crying sisters she'd taken from Thrikyl. Weak, fearful people disgusted her more than anything.

"No, Mistress," Netra replied.

The reply was dutifully subservient, but the look in her eyes was anything but. This was an unusual young woman she had captured. How had she gotten this way? Why was she so strong? She would enjoy prying the answers from her.

"Where are you from?"

Netra hesitated, not enough to give Reyna an excuse to punish her, but just enough to show she was still rebelling. It was just what Reyna expected her to do. She liked her better and better.

"Rane Haven, Mistress."

"Never heard of it," Reyna said. "But then, I guess there's a lot of places now I've never heard of. That's what happens when you go away for a few millennia. So, did you learn how to steal Song at Rane Haven?"

Reyna saw the slight flinch from Netra and sensed that she'd hit on a sore spot. Was Netra ashamed of her power? Why?

A commotion drew Reyna's attention away before she could pursue the questioning further. Melekath was still huddled on the road. He had ceased trying to stand and seemed to be expending his efforts in staunching the puncture wounds in his torso. Though the gouges left by the axe looked more fearsome, they were not leaking like the punctures were. Reyna could *see* the Stone power spilling through Melekath's hands. He was getting weaker by the minute.

The spear that had caused those wounds—where had it come from? She looked at her arm where she'd been cut by it. For some reason she hadn't been able to heal the wound, not all the way anyway. There was still a purple-black gouge there. A whisper of doubt crossed her mind, just a suggestion that maybe Melekath was right to be cautious, that they had no way of knowing what they were up against, but she ignored it. However powerful that weapon was, there was only one. As she'd told Heram: if the defenders had more of the same, surely they would have struck with them. Why tip their hand with such a weak attack otherwise? Still, it would be wise to make sure other Children led the attack when they got to Qarath. Let them bear the brunt of any surprise defense. She would lose no tears over any of them. Maybe Qarath's defenders would even take down Heram for her and save her the trouble.

Melekath raised his head as the first of the Children reached out and touched him. He looked so pathetic Reyna almost felt sorry for him, just one bedraggled old man, a shell of what he had once been. The woman—a bent over, hairless thing of indeterminate age, her skin bleached-bone white—put her hand on Melekath's cheek…

With a soft cry, Melekath jerked back from her, his eyes wide.

All at once she threw herself on him, grappling him like a berserk lover, mouth straining for one of the puncture wounds in his chest. He threw her off, but she threw herself at him again, and then it was like the fragile dam holding the others back broke. Maddened by their hunger, they charged Melekath with howls and cries of eagerness. He went down, buried under them.

Reyna walked closer, Netra stumbling along behind her. She took her time. There was no rush. She was curious what Melekath would do. Would he finally turn on his Children? Certainly he had shown far more forbearance than she ever would have. She would have broken the necks of most of them hundreds of years ago. Impaled them on stakes and left them to writhe in torment.

She watched them scramble frantically, like piglets fighting for a teat, then after a minute decided it was time to intervene. She wanted Melekath still conscious. She hated him, but she had questions she wanted him to answer. Last night she'd been there when he emerged from traveling through the Stone. He'd said that the Guardians weren't coming? Why? What had happened? Were they now enemies of the Children?

"Get off him," she snapped, grabbing one of the flailing mass of bodies by his ankle and jerking him back out of the pile. He squirmed in her grip and tried to bite her—his lips were loose and black, barely covering the two large teeth that were all he had in his mouth—and she tossed him aside with a curse.

She grabbed another one off the pile, tossed her aside, then another and another, cursing at them steadily as she did so. Then she was at the bottom of the pile and what she found was curious. Very curious.

Where Melekath had been there was only a lump of vaguely man-shaped stone. She peered closer. It was stone all right. She kicked it and it shattered into pieces. Underneath was a tunnel bored into the ground.

"He ran away," she said, disbelievingly. "I never thought I'd see that."

Heram came up then. "Where did Father go?"

Reyna pointed and Heram came closer, then bent to look down into the tunnel. "He went back to the Stone," Heram said, sounding surprised. He turned to look at her. "What do we do now?"

"Now," she replied, "we go to Qarath. We've wasted too much time already. I'm hungry."

ELEVEN

Netra was freezing. She shivered and wrapped her arms around herself as she walked along behind Reyna, but it did no good. The cold she felt had nothing to do with the temperature. It was the tether that tied her to Reyna. Her warmth, her vitality, her very life, were leaching away down that line.

At most she figured she would live only a few days with this thing attached to her, even if Reyna didn't suck her dry like a spider devouring its prey before then. There was a vast, bottomless emptiness inside Reyna—inside all the Children—and it pulled at her, trying to drag her in. It was like standing waist-deep in a flooding river. It was all she could do to keep her balance, to keep the current from sucking her down and carrying her away. But she knew that eventually she *would* lose her balance, and then she would die.

She wondered where Shorn was, and guessed he was probably close by. It made her feel better to know she wasn't alone, but at the same time she worried that he would get himself killed trying to rescue her. She didn't want anyone else to die because of her.

Netra looked down at the tether. It had struck her on the left side, low on her ribcage, tearing a hole in her shirt. From the spot where it was attached, angry red lines like swollen veins radiated outward, wrapping halfway around her torso. She touched the tether experimentally with one fingertip, jerking back at the sudden burning pain. What was it made of? How could she get it off? Even if she could withstand the pain, she wasn't sure what would happen if she ripped it out of her. She might bleed to death. If she had a knife, she might be able to cut it, but her knife was still in her pack, which was either lying back where she'd left it when she set out to get a closer look at the Children or in Shorn's possession.

They'd been walking for an hour already. The rest of the Children were strung out on the road behind them, the closest a few hundred paces back. Reyna had set a fast pace from the beginning, and she'd told Netra right off that if she couldn't keep up, she would be happy to drag her.

Reyna seemed to be lost in her thoughts, so Netra decided to take a chance. Maybe she could learn more about the tether *beyond*. It took only a few moments—breathe in, breathe out, breathe in, catch hold of the outgoing flow of Song in her breath and let it pull her out of herself—and then she was *beyond*.

Immediately, the day changed. The normal world faded into the background. Laid over it was a new world, one that she used to find so comforting, so peaceful. It was in the depths of *beyond* that she had always felt closest to Xochitl.

But *beyond* was different here, so close to the Children. Gone were the gentle mists, shredded by the shrieking winds of madness that swirled around the Children. She felt wraithlike, insubstantial, and for a moment thought the winds would blow her away, never to return. She fought to keep the madness out, but felt herself slipping, and knew she needed something solid to hold onto.

What came into her mind's eye was Shorn. Solid, immovable, loyal, dependable. She latched onto the thought of him as tightly as she could, clinging to him to save herself.

When she felt steadier, she turned her attention outward once again.

What she saw shocked her.

A normal person's *akirma* glowed with a gentle, diffuse, white light, but Reyna's *akirma* looked nothing like that. Her *akirma* looked scabbed over, the gentle glow almost completely concealed by dark, interlocking patches. The small amount of light that escaped between the scabs was clouded, dirty.

What had happened to her *akirma*? Was that what the Gift had done to her?

She looked away from Reyna. Now was not the time. The tether was almost black and she could barely *see* it, wouldn't have seen it had it not been for the faint glow as her Selfsong trickled down its length. The swollen veins that extended from the end of the tether appeared thicker, angrier in here. As she watched, they extended a little deeper into her, reaching for the brighter glow in the center of her being. That was her Heartglow. If the veins reached that…

She had to do something to slow them. But what? An idea occurred to her. Maybe she could try healing it, treat it like an ordinary wound.

Summoning Selfsong, she focused it on one of her hands. The *akirma* around that hand began to glow more brightly. Then she placed her fingertips at the end of one of the veins and began releasing the Selfsong, focusing it directly on the vein, in her mind picturing it as white fire burning the vein away…

And was knocked out of *beyond* by a solid, stinging slap to the side of her head. Her ears ringing, Netra looked up at Reyna, blinking her eyes against the involuntary tears that flowed.

"I felt that." Reyna had stopped and was glaring at her, her hands on her hips.

"I wasn't doing anything, Mistress," Netra protested.

Reyna slapped her again. "Now you're angering me. I thought you understood what a bad idea that is."

Netra touched the side of her face, which was stinging from the slap. "I'm sorry, Mistress," she said.

"I don't think you are. Not yet." She jerked hard on the tether and Netra cried out and staggered, the pain so intense she couldn't see for a second.

Reyna took hold of Netra's chin and tilted her face up, squeezing hard enough that Netra's jaw began to ache. "Are you going to behave now?"

It was hard to speak, but Netra managed to say "Yes, Mistress."

Reyna let go of her and patted her cheek. "I don't believe you, you know that? I think you'll never behave. But that's okay. It's only what I expect of you. Now let's move on again. I'm hungry and Qarath isn't getting any closer."

As they started off again, Reyna said, "Walk up here beside me. I want to keep an eye on you." When Netra didn't obey immediately, she twitched the tether, causing Netra to gasp.

"So, enough about me," Reyna said lightly, when Netra was alongside her, "tell me about you."

"What do you want to know?" Netra asked. Reyna shot her a look and she added, "Mistress."

"Let's start with where you learned how to do that."

"Do what, Mistress?"

Reyna gave her another look, her eyes narrowing. "You know what I hate? I hate when someone treats me like I'm an idiot. People who treat me that way get hurt."

Hastily, Netra said, "I'm a Tender. Or at least I used to be, Mistress."

Reyna stopped suddenly and turned on her. There was a frightening, feral look on her face and Netra suddenly realized how very fragile her situation was.

"A Tender of Xochitl?" Reyna said in a very cold voice.

Netra swallowed. "Yes, Mistress."

"You probably shouldn't have told me that."

Netra said nothing, afraid that anything she could say would only make things worse. Reyna thrust her face very close to Netra's. There was a twitch in her eyes that spoke of how close she was to the edge. "Do you have any idea how much I hate Xochitl?"

"No, Mistress," Netra said in a very small voice.

"Much, much more than you can imagine. I swore that when I got out, I would find a way to destroy her. Her and everything she cares about." The coldness in her voice was truly terrifying. Netra started shaking. "Where is she?"

"I don't know, Mistress," Netra said desperately.

Reyna grabbed her by the throat, lifting her up onto her toes, her grip horribly strong. "Don't lie to me," she hissed.

"I'm not, Mistress," Netra choked out. She could barely get the words out. "I swear. Xochitl left us long ago. No one knows where she is."

At first she thought Reyna would just kill her anyway because her grip got even tighter. Netra clawed at her hand, but it might as well have been made of stone for all the good it did. Darkness began to crowd her vision.

Suddenly Reyna let her go. Netra collapsed to the ground, gasping for breath.

"I *will* find her," Reyna said, bending over her, shaking with suppressed rage. "Do you hear me? No matter where she is hidden, I will find her and I will..." Her words trailed off and she stood there, her hands curled into claws and her face twisted with hatred.

She straightened and stood for a long moment with her eyes closed. Gradually the shaking eased and she opened her eyes. She brushed at some flecks of dirt on her dress and straightened it. It was a gesture so normal, and so incongruous, that Netra almost doubted what she was seeing.

Reyna looked up and saw that the others were getting close. She bent, took hold of Netra's arm and lifted her to her feet.

"Come on. We need to go. I've already spent way too much time with those idiots."

They walked in silence for some time after that, then Reyna said, "Walk up here beside me. Talk to me."

Dutifully, Netra hurried up beside her.

"You think I'm a monster, don't you?"

Netra, surprised by the question, at first couldn't say anything. Then she said, "No, Mistress."

"Don't lie to me," Reyna replied. There was no heat in her voice, only resignation. "Lying, deceiving, manipulating, those are my games. No one's better at them than I am. Tell me the truth."

Netra swallowed. "Yes, Mistress."

"Yes, what?"

"I…I think you're a monster."

"You may be right. Probably you are. But I wonder. Was I a monster when I went in, or did I become one in there? I know I wasn't a very nice person before the prison." A raw laugh came from her. "I believe the words 'conniving' and 'bitch' applied most frequently. But I don't think I was a monster. I was just a survivor. I lived in a world where if you weren't eating the others, they were eating you." She looked at Netra. "You have no idea what I'm talking about, do you? You probably grew up in some backwards village. Let me tell you what my world was like.

"My father was very wealthy. My mother died when I was just a child and my father doted on me. He was my world." Her voice went soft as she spoke of him and for a moment she paused, remembering. "I was sixteen when he died." Her voice caught just a little bit as she said the words. "Overnight my whole life changed. I went from being sheltered and protected to easy prey with lots of money. His body wasn't even cold before the predators started circling. I didn't know they were predators, of course. I believed they were actually trying to help me.

"There was one young man. His name was Damin. He had golden curls and strong arms. He was the most beautiful man I'd ever seen. I'd met him several times at balls and danced with him, but my father said he was beneath us and wouldn't let him court me. Damin showed up that first night after my father died. He was kind and gentle and understanding. He held me all night as I cried, whispering to me that he was there, that he would protect me. It was he who took care of arranging my father's burial and dealing with the legal details of his estate.

"We were married within a month. I stood next to him and made my vows and thought I was the most fortunate woman in the world.

"As soon as we were married, he changed. He became distant, cold. He was gone all the time in the city, leaving me alone at my father's country estate. Most nights he didn't come home. When I complained, he told me he was doing it for us. He was taking care of my father's business and it took all his time. When I cried he became angry and told me I was nothing more than a spoiled child.

"I tried to control myself. I tried to just be happy with the times when I got to see him, even if he hardly spoke to me. I loved him so much. I thought if I just tried harder I could please him, but nothing I did worked.

"One night when he didn't come home I just couldn't take it anymore. I had to see him. The servants tried to talk me out of it, but I was desperate and I shouted at them until my carriage was made ready.

"When I arrived at my father's house in the city, the servants there tried to stop me too. They told me Damin was working and couldn't be disturbed but I pushed my way past them.

"I found him in bed with three women."

Reyna stopped talking for a minute. When she started again her voice was filled with old rage. "When I walked into that room and saw him there, like that, I experienced a moment of utter clarity. I suddenly realized the truth about the world. I saw how young and foolish I was. I saw how easily he had preyed on my weaknesses and taken advantage of me." She made a fist. "And I knew I could not rest until I had crushed him.

"I knew in that moment that in order to do so I had to make him believe I was no threat to him." She gave a bitter laugh. "It wasn't even that hard. I ran from the room crying hysterically and screaming. I took to my bed and wept, but inside I was plotting.

"When he came and made his excuses I pretended to forgive him. I let him think I was the empty, weak person he thought I was. As soon as he was gone I began to gather information. I had money at my disposal, money he did not control, and I used it to find out everything I could about him. I learned every detail of his business dealings, many of which had been outlawed by the king. I learned who his enemies were and then I learned everything I could about them, looking for the one I could use.

"The one I chose was a few years older than Damin, a man named Harald. Harald was a brutal, vicious man and a great many people were afraid of him. It was easy to seduce him and use him. He saw exactly what I wanted him to see: a weak young woman that he could use to strike at a foe. I became his lover.

"In time I uncovered what I was looking for. Damin had a large shipment of outlawed goods coming in. I told Harald that I had overheard Damin talking about it with a partner, that he'd been complaining about having to take delivery in person. I knew Harald wouldn't pass up the chance to crush his rival and that he'd want to be there to see it happen with his own eyes.

"It all worked perfectly. The appointed night came and Damin left for the meeting. I hurried to Harald and told him the time had come. Harald took a handful of his hired swords and hurried after him. Neither of them suspected a thing. They walked right into a trap. I'd tipped off the king's tax collectors. They were both arrested and several days later they were publicly executed."

The look she turned on Netra was fierce and exultant. "After that there was no turning back. I couldn't go back to being a child. I had wealth and I had beauty and I learned how to use both. I rose high and I rose fast. None were better at the game than I was. Nothing seemed out of my reach.

"Then one day I looked in the mirror and I knew there was one foe I couldn't beat. There was gray in my hair and lines on my face. I was getting old. Getting old meant getting weak and I knew once I was weak the predators would be at the gates and they would tear me into little pieces.

"Melekath's arrival seemed like a miracle. He offered eternal youth. I would never need to fear getting old and weak." She gave Netra an appraising look. "You have no idea what I'm talking about. You're still young. You think you'll never get old. If you were older, you'd understand why I did what I did. If you'd lived through the prison, as I did, you'd understand why I am this way now."

Netra said nothing, only wondered where this was going.

Reyna's expression changed then, some light dawning on her. "Maybe you do understand. At least a little. I felt your hunger when you attacked me this morning. You know there is nothing sweeter than Song. You know the power of your hunger."

"No," Netra protested. But she knew Reyna's words were true, that what she said had in fact already occurred to her. Even then she could feel the hunger lurking inside her, waiting to get free. They were not so different after all. The thought horrified her.

"You can lie to me, but you can't lie to yourself. That's something else I've learned," Reyna said.

They walked in silence for a while then, while Netra grappled with the truth of what Reyna had said. She wondered if her hunger would ever go completely away. She wondered if she would ever be free of the stain of what she had done.

At one point Reyna looked around and said, "Not a bad day, is it? I'm guessing it's late summer, right?"

Netra, surprised by the randomness of the comment, could only murmur her assent.

"It's nice to see seasons again. We didn't have any in the prison. It was always cold. There were no plants. Not living ones anyway. You know, I never cared for plants. I never even thought of them at all. But once they were all gone I really missed them. I really missed a lot of things." There was a note of sorrow that was almost childlike in her voice and Netra looked at her, surprised.

"When I was a child I nearly drowned," Reyna continued. "I fell into the pond at my father's summer estate and I got twisted up in my dress and I couldn't get free. I was sure I was going to die. It was a horrible feeling." Her face twisted suddenly. "But drowning was nothing compared to how it felt when the prison closed over me. I couldn't breathe. I felt utterly alone, utterly abandoned. I wanted so badly to die. But I *didn't* die. I *couldn't* die."

The emotion behind her words struck Netra like an almost physical blow. For a moment she was there in the prison, reliving the feeling with Reyna.

"I thought when I got out of the prison those feelings would go away. I thought that once I could see the sun again everything would be different." She turned a bleak look on Netra, then looked quickly away. "But I don't. I still feel like I'm drowning. I still wish I could die."

Abruptly Reyna's face just crumpled. She began shaking and she hunched forward, odd gasping sobs coming from her. Strangely, there were no tears.

Netra wanted to reach out to her. She wanted to do something to ease her pain. Hesitantly, she moved closer and touched Reyna on the forearm.

Reyna jerked away. "Don't touch me!" she shouted, swinging one fist wildly. The blow caught Netra on the shoulder and sent her sprawling.

Reyna took off walking again and Netra had to get to her feet and run after her. Reyna's legs were longer than hers and she set a pace that was nearly impossible for Netra to match. She couldn't do it by walking. She had to jog to keep up. Her whole torso began to ache horribly and each breath caused lances of pain in her chest. She grew more and more exhausted until finally she tripped on something and fell. When Reyna hit the end of the tether, the pain was so excruciating that Netra screamed.

Reyna stopped and looked back. "Get up," she said.

Netra struggled to her knees. "Can we just...can I rest for a moment? I'm so tired."

She expected Reyna to say no, or maybe just to jerk on the tether again, but instead she shrugged. They waited there for several minutes until Netra got her strength back and then they continued on.

The sun was nearing the horizon. Netra stumbled along behind Reyna, so exhausted she could hardly think straight. It was all she could do to pick up one foot after the other and continue on. Her life was steadily draining away from her down the tether and soon there would be nothing left of her. Reyna hadn't spoken in hours and Netra had the sense that she regretted her earlier lapse of vulnerability.

Where was Shorn? she wondered. She hadn't sensed his presence all day. Though she could not believe he would abandon her, still she could not completely relinquish the thought that he had done so. Maybe it would be best if he had. Even if he was able to defeat Reyna, it wouldn't do any good. There was no way to break the tether.

Netra lifted her shirt. The area around the tether had turned purple. The veins that radiated from it were swollen to the size of her little finger. Every step caused new pains. She was alternately freezing cold and burning with fever. She could feel that the veins had almost reached her heart. Several times she'd tried to muster Song and use it to build a barrier around her core, to at least slow the veins down, but she'd had no luck. She was just too weak.

She realized she wasn't going to live much longer. At most she would make it through the night.

Have I really come this far, gone through so much, to die like this? she asked herself. It didn't seem possible and yet at the same time she couldn't escape the feeling that she deserved what was happening. What Reyna was doing to her and what she had done to those Crodin nomads was fundamentally no different. Perhaps it was fitting that she pay for her crime this way.

Why not give up now? Why keep fighting?

In the midst of her despair, she suddenly felt something. Was it Shorn? Wearily, she raised her head. The road they were on had just crested a low ridge and in the distance was a town built on several small hills beside the ocean. It looked like a fairly prosperous town, its buildings made of stone and many of them two story. There was a strong stone wall around it and a tower overlooking the gate.

She felt it again. It *was* Shorn. The feeling was too faint to figure out what direction it came from, but she guessed he was ahead, in the town. That probably meant that he planned to try to rescue her there.

She looked at Reyna's back. Strangely, she had mixed feelings about the woman. She feared her, of course, but after the things she'd shared about herself Netra couldn't quite find it within herself to hate her.

If I had gone through what she's gone through, would I be the same? she wondered. All she had to do was look at how she'd acted after she found Siena and Brelisha dead at the Haven. There was her answer.

She wished there was some way to reach out to Reyna, to get her to see that…

To see what?

That she should give up? And then what? She couldn't be killed. Should she let herself be cut into pieces so she couldn't harm anyone else?

It was a futile line of thinking. At that moment everything seemed futile to Netra. As if through a thick fog she glimpsed a future in which she escaped from Reyna and made it to Qarath. Even if that happened, it still would not change the fundamental problem of the Children.

They could not die.

Short of once again imprisoning them, Netra could see no way to defeat them. And after what she had learned about the prison, she didn't think she could once again condemn them to that place, even if it were in her power to do so.

Netra almost gave up and laid down in the dirt right then. It all seemed so pointless, all her running, all her struggling, the pain, the sorrow—all of it to fight a war that was lost before it ever began. Dimly a part of her mind knew that some of her despair was due to the tether and its corrosive effect on her, but she just couldn't seem to help herself.

As they approached the town, Netra's sense of Shorn grew stronger. He was definitely waiting within its wall to ambush Reyna. She was tempted to call out, to warn him away. There was nothing he could do anyway.

But she also knew there was no way she could convince him to leave her in Reyna's clutches. Turning his back on her like that simply wasn't within the realm of who he was. All she would accomplish would be to warn Reyna and doom Shorn.

For her part, Reyna seemed completely oblivious to the possibility of attack. Whether it was because she considered herself invulnerable or whether it was something else Netra couldn't have said. Regardless of the reason, Reyna walked through the town's open gate without the slightest effort to look around for danger.

The shadows were growing long as they entered the town. The buildings were mostly stone, with red tile roofs and large gardens. The place showed signs of being hastily abandoned. A door that hadn't been latched properly banged in the breeze that blew in off the ocean. The street was littered with small personal items that had been dropped and there was a cart that had overturned, spilling an ornate rocking chair and a wooden chest on the cobblestone street.

Their footsteps echoed hollowly as they made their way down the main street toward the center of town. A crow perched on a wall stared at them with beady eyes and then flew away squawking. There was a large plaza in the center of town, with a small park in the center of it, containing two stone benches underneath two large maples.

On the far side of the plaza, beside a wide street, a large, stone building of some type—probably a temple—was under construction. Scaffolding ringed the structure, which was already three stories tall. Large, cut stones were still sitting on the scaffolding, waiting their turn to be set into the wall.

Netra looked at the temple and knew immediately that Shorn was there. She couldn't see him, but she could feel him.

They had only just started across the plaza when Reyna stopped abruptly. Netra had a momentary panicked feeling that she had somehow alerted her to Shorn's presence. But instead Reyna turned to her.

"Maybe we should stop here for the night. I confess to being sick of sleeping on the ground. A soft bed would be a nice change." She looked Netra over and shook her head. "You don't look so good, you know. You could probably use the rest."

"I'm actually not that tired," Netra said desperately.

Reyna snorted. "That's the worst lie I've ever heard." Her eyes narrowed. "Why would you say that? What do you hope to gain?"

"Nothing. I just...I didn't want to anger you."

Reyna wasn't convinced. "What are you up to?"

Netra cast about for something to say that would assuage her suspicion. "It's the tether," she said. "It's killing me. If you don't remove it, I won't last through the night anyway. I'd rather just keep going and get it over with."

"Giving up so easily?" Reyna said. "That doesn't sound like you."

"Does it matter?" Netra blurted out. "Aren't I just food to you anyway? Why would you care? What threat could I possibly pose to you?"

Reyna stared at her for a bit, judging her words. Then she turned and surveyed the plaza slowly as if looking for something. "You're right. It doesn't matter. We are stopping here for the night. I'm going to sleep in a real bed and see if I can't find another dress to wear. This one is filthy. A bath would be nice too. Maybe I'll let you off your leash and let you draw me one. Now, I just need to find the right house."

She looked back down the street they'd come in on. "There were a couple houses that looked promising down there, but I hate the thought of going backwards." Making a sudden decision, she turned around. "There's sure to be something up ahead. Come on." She twitched the tether, and Netra gasped with pain and tottered after her.

As they crossed the plaza Netra tried not to look at the temple, tried to avoid even thinking about it, as if somehow her thoughts would tip Reyna off. But it was difficult. She wanted to see Shorn. She felt as if the sight of him was the only thing that would give her the strength to continue on another step.

They reached the far side of the plaza and entered the wide street. The temple loomed over them on their right. Netra fought to keep her head down and her thoughts empty.

All at once she had a terrible feeling that she'd been wrong, that Shorn wasn't here at all. She looked up just in time to see Shorn rise to a standing position on the scaffolding two stories up, one of the cut stones held over his head.

Reyna never saw the attack coming.

Shorn dropped the stone and it struck her square on top of the head, driving her down onto the cobblestoned street with a sickening crunch. Netra gasped and fell to her knees as a strong jolt of pain traveled through the tether from Reyna to her.

As Reyna struggled feebly to rise, Shorn jumped down beside her. The stone he'd struck her with had cracked in half and he grabbed the larger piece and began slamming it into the back of her head repeatedly.

Each blow seemed to be hitting Netra as well and she collapsed onto the street, choking on the pain.

Somehow Reyna was still conscious. Netra could feel her reaching through the tether. It was like a vacuum was opening beneath Netra and she knew she only had moments to live, that Reyna was grabbing for her Selfsong and planning on draining her so she could use the extra power to fight off Shorn. As she tried feebly to resist what she knew she couldn't, Netra whispered to Shorn.

"The tether. Hurry."

He glanced at her and somehow understood what she was trying to say. Dropping the stone, he grabbed the tether in both hands, wincing as he did so, and quickly wrapped it around his hands so it wouldn't slip through them.

Netra's life began to race down the tether.

He stepped on Reyna's arm with one foot and gave a mighty tug.

The tether ripped free of Reyna's hand. Netra screamed.

As she fell into unconsciousness, she saw Shorn bending over her. The last thing she knew he was lifting her and carrying her away.

TWELVE

Drawn by Reyna's screams, Heram and his two followers hurried into the town, the rest of the Children struggling along behind them. Still limping on his damaged leg, Heram got there just as Reyna sat up. Her skull was caved in, her face a pulpy, unrecognizable mass. Half of her scalp had torn away and it hung down over the side of her face. Her neck was broken, her head flopping to the side.

Heram came to a halt and stared down at her, a broad smile filling his crude face. "You don't look so good," he observed.

Using her hands, she lifted her head so that she could look up at him with her one functioning eye. The other had come out of the socket and dangled uselessly. Her mangled lips worked and she spit broken teeth out of her mouth. "Stay away from me," she said brokenly.

Heram nodded to Dubron and Leckl and without warning they jumped on Reyna, tearing at her with their bare hands, greedy mouths closing on her.

Reyna screamed in pain and rage and all at once there was a silent explosion of power. Heram's followers were thrown back like rag dolls. Reyna came to her feet, stumbling and almost falling as she did so. She held onto the wall of the temple for support and faced off against Heram, her head lolling bonelessly to one side. "Come on," she croaked. "Here's your chance."

Heram shook his thick head. "Not yet."

She turned to look at the other Children who were arriving. "Anyone else?" They edged backward at her words.

Reyna lifted her head in her hands. Power surged within her. With a series of pops and crunches her skull began to return to its normal shape. The bones in her neck fused and when she moved her hands away her head stayed upright. She pushed the mangled eye back into its socket and lifted her torn scalp, setting it back into place.

In less than two minutes she was done. Her face was still a mess and her neck was crooked, but she was, once again, mostly whole. She drew herself up and patted dust from her dress. She surveyed the gathered Children.

"Stay away from me," she warned them, and turned and walked away.

THIRTEEN

It was nearly dark when Netra regained consciousness and opened her eyes to find herself cradled in Shorn's arms. Her hand went automatically to her side, feeling for the tether. But it was gone, leaving only a sore spot that made her wince when she touched it.

"What happened to it?" she asked.

"It crumbled away," Shorn said.

Netra sagged back in his arms, a huge sense of gratitude and relief rising up inside her. She felt weak, but she was alive. "Thank you for saving me again."

Shorn didn't answer, only continued walking, his long strides eating up the distance between them and Qarath. She sensed that he was angry and wondered at it.

After a few minutes she said, "You can put me down now. I think I'm strong enough to walk on my own."

Shorn kept walking as if he hadn't heard her.

"Aren't you listening? I said you can put me down."

"No." His voice was harsh with suppressed emotion.

"What do you mean, no? I don't need to be carried." No answer. "You're not going to carry me the whole way." Still nothing. "Put me down!" She tried to fight him. It did no good at all. "What's wrong with you?"

The glare he turned on her made her recoil. "You ask me that?" he rumbled. She got the feeling he was close to shaking her.

"Can we stop for a minute and talk about this? Just put me down. I feel ridiculous trying to have a conversation with you like this. I'm not a child."

Shorn never broke his stride. "I will put you down when we reach Qarath."

"That's enough," she said, struggling some more. Compared to him, she was no stronger than a kitten. She gave it up. "What are you so angry about?"

At first she thought he wouldn't answer. Then he fixed his almond eyes on her, piercing her with his intensity. "I cannot watch you kill yourself." Behind the anger she felt real anguish.

His words struck her like a physical blow. She tried to speak, swallowed, then tried again. "I'm not trying to kill myself," she said in a small voice.

"Aren't you? Alone, you threw yourself at the prison. Alone, you walked into the camp of your enemy. What else should I think?"

Again she had to take time to recover before she could speak. "I can't...I have to make up for what I've done. It doesn't matter what happens to me."

"It does to me."

Netra felt her heart stop.

"I was dead," Shorn said. "I had lost everything but my life and I wanted only to lose it too. You...showed me there is still something to live for. Now do you understand my anger?"

"I never meant to hurt you."

He looked down at her. Slowly, he said, "I believe you."

"Then you'll put me down?"

"No."

FOURTEEN

Shorn walked nonstop through the night. Despite her protests, Netra slept much of the night. After all the running and the conflict, it actually felt good to just let go, to let herself be carried and not try to do anything. They reached Qarath the next morning, about an hour after sunrise. Shorn stopped when they were close and set Netra down. She held onto his arm while regaining her balance. "Not my favorite way to travel," she told him with a faint smile.

"Nor mine," he rumbled, rubbing his arms.

Surprisingly to Netra, even though the Children were close, the city gates were open. A small but steady stream of people and animals issued from the gates, taking the road that led north. As Netra and Shorn approached the city, a wagon drawn by a pair of horses emerged, a man and his wife sitting on the wagon seat. The back was piled with possessions and supplies, two children clinging to the pile. Behind the wagon were a handful of people on foot, likely servants, each carrying a bundle.

The husband's attention was fixed on the road so it was the wife who saw Shorn and Netra first. Her eyes grew very big and she gripped her husband's arm and said something to him. He looked up, saw Shorn, and started. He snatched up a sword that was lying beside him on the seat, holding it up with one shaking hand. The servants clustered together in a nervous huddle, looking like they might dart back inside the city walls. Even the horses shifted uneasily, nostrils flaring as they took in this strange creature which confronted them.

"I think we should get off the road and let them go by," Netra said. Wordlessly Shorn moved to the side.

The couple stared at them suspiciously. The woman whispered something to the man and he flicked the reins, urging the horses forward. All of them stared nervously at Shorn as they passed by, moving as far over to the other side of the road as possible.

By that time a handful of soldiers had spilled out of the gatehouse and formed ranks in front of the open gates with their weapons drawn. There were shouts and running footsteps as archers took up positions in the towers flanking the gatehouse. Arrows were nocked and bows were drawn. From the far side of the gatehouse came a clanking sound as the portcullis was lowered.

"Stay here," Netra said. She walked forward with her hands up. "It's okay! We're friends. We only seek shelter."

"It's not you we're worried about," one of the soldiers said, stepping out in front of the others. Clearly he was an officer. The hand holding his sword was steady. Shorn was not the first abnormal thing he'd seen recently. "It's that thing following you."

"What the hell is it?" another said, a young man with black hair, barely more than a boy.

"It's not one of the Children," a third said, an older man with gray in his beard. "That much I can tell you."

"Is it Melekath?" asked the black-haired one.

"That's a damn fool thing to say," the officer said over his shoulder. He was middle-aged, his uniform stiff and clean, his face freshly shaved.

"I'm a Tender," Netra said. "This is Shorn. He's my friend. Let us in. We can help. We have information about the Children that the FirstMother will want to know."

"A Tender you say?" the officer said, his expression becoming slightly less suspicious. He lowered the sword fractionally.

"Kinda late, ain't you?" the gray-bearded soldier said.

"Shut your mouth, Clet. Show respect." To Netra the officer said, "Begging your pardon, but can you prove it? I mean, that you're a Tender?"

Netra held up her hands. "How do I do that?" She still had her *sonkrill* in her pack—Shorn had retrieved it after she was captured—but she doubted the soldiers would know what it was.

"Ask her if she's got one of them *sulbits*."

"Shut up, Clet," the officer said. The way he said it made it clear it was something he said often—and something he didn't expect to have any real effect. To Netra he said, "Well, do you?"

"I don't know what a *sulbit* is." An idea occurred to Netra. "I think some of the Tenders from my Haven are here. You could send word to them. They'll vouch for me. But you need to hurry. The Children aren't that far behind us."

At her mention of the Children all the soldiers looked to the south. Then the officer looked back at her. "Could be you'd be a lot smarter following those people north." He gestured at the wagon with his sword. "Could be this is a death trap." The other soldiers looked grim at his words and the young, black-haired one paled somewhat.

Netra looked at Shorn, then back at the officer. "I appreciate the warning, but no more running. This is where I need to be."

The officer considered this, then abruptly sheathed his sword. "Archers, stand down!" he called. The archers in the gatehouse towers released the tension on their bows, but they kept arrows nocked. "Lower your weapons," he ordered the men behind him.

"You're letting them in?" Clet asked.

"I am."

"But—"

"Look at him, Clet," the officer said, gesturing at Shorn. "You telling me you don't want him on our side in the fight to come?"

"If'n he don't turn on us," Clet said sullenly.

"I'm not explaining myself to you. Stand down. Let them pass." Grumbling, Clet sheathed his weapon and stood aside with the rest. Every eye was fixed on Shorn and every hand was near a weapon as he and Netra approached the gatehouse. Awed murmurs came from the soldiers. The tallest came up to Shorn's shoulder, but with only a fraction of his breadth.

Netra and Shorn passed through the outer gates and into the gateway passage, which was almost a dozen paces long. She looked up and saw dark murder-holes above them in the arched stone. Netra held her breath. She could feel the tension that radiated from the soldiers manning the murder-holes. They were frightened, beset by an enemy they didn't understand, one they had no real hope against. Though ordered to stand down, she could feel how little it would take to cause one of them to lose his nerve and attack.

Compounding her fear was the fact that the portcullis at the far end of the gateway passage was still down. Had they walked into a trap? She felt Shorn's tension and knew that he had noticed the same things.

It was a relief when the chains rattled and the portcullis slowly rose as they approached it. They walked under it and out into the broad, open square beyond.

The square was several hundred paces across and there was a large statue in the middle. Bordering the square on all sides were tall, stone buildings that had clearly been designed to provide a second layer of defense in case the outer wall was breached. The buildings had been built together and there were no windows on the bottom three floors. Only one narrow street led from the square into the rest of the city and it had heavy, iron-bound wooden gates to close it off.

Two squads of soldiers stood facing them when they emerged from the gateway passage. There were a few dozen civilians in the square as well, people fleeing the city with what possessions they could carry. They stared at Shorn with wide eyes.

One of the soldiers came forward. He looked askance at Shorn, then faced Netra and told her he would escort them to the Tender estate. They passed through the narrow street leading from the square and then turned onto another, wider street, that led up the hill toward the palace, visible at the highest point of Qarath.

As the street climbed, the buildings lining it grew larger and more opulent until giving way to large, walled estates. The soldier led them to an estate that had forty or fifty people standing in line outside it.

"I wonder what all those people are here for," Netra said.

"They're feeding the *sulbits*," the soldier replied.

"They're feeding what?"

"You'll see," the soldier replied, leaving them and heading back down the street.

The people waiting to get into the estate were lined up next to the wall along the uphill side, most of them fidgeting nervously, lost in their thoughts enough that they didn't notice Shorn as he and Netra approached. The few who did gaped at him and seemed to be seriously considering running away.

Manning the gates was a woman dressed in a white robe. She had severely short hair and she was flanked by two armed guards. Neither she nor the guards noticed the approaching pair: She was turned half away, talking to the first person in the line, and the two guards were staring at the ground.

As they got closer, Netra sensed something strange, something that she couldn't identify. Whatever it was, it was radiating a great deal of energy, but the energy was different in a way she didn't understand.

Then something crawled out of the woman's robe and onto her shoulder and Netra stopped, grabbing Shorn's arm as she did so.

"What is *that*?" she whispered.

It was unlike anything Netra had ever seen. About the size of a rat, it stood on its hind legs. Its tail was fairly long and was curled around the woman's neck as if to help it balance. Its head was blunt and rounded, its mouth a sharp gash, its eyes black and deep set. It was a milky white color with hints of light brown or yellow in its skin, though it was hard to tell for sure. The thing was difficult to focus on, as if she was seeing it through cloudy water.

It was staring at her.

"The guard asked to see your *sulbit*," Shorn replied.

"You think that's what it is?"

"There is only one way to find out." Shorn started forward once again.

Netra followed hesitantly. The *sulbit* made her uncomfortable. The energy radiating off it made her skin itch. It seemed unnatural. It was also clearly powerful. Large quantities of Song swirled within it, far more than should have been possible for something so small.

But the most disturbing thing about the creature was its stare. There was hunger in those black eyes. Hunger for her.

The woman was clearly a Tender. Did all the Tenders have them?

All this and more went through Netra's mind as she followed Shorn up to the gates. When they got close, one of the guards suddenly looked up and saw Shorn. The man went pale and backed up against the wall, choking out a warning to his partner. The other guard looked up and was so shocked he dropped his sword after drawing it. Picking up his sword, he tapped the Tender on the shoulder.

"What is it?" she asked querulously without turning. "Can't you see I'm busy?"

"Begging your pardon, Tender, but...but..." He was pointing his sword at Shorn and the tip was wavering badly. The first guard seemed paralyzed, backed up against the wall, staring at Shorn.

Making a disgusted sound, the Tender turned. When she saw Shorn her mouth dropped open. "What in the Mother's name is that?" she whispered. The *sulbit* on her shoulder was now crouching, its mouth open in a soundless snarl.

"His name is Shorn," Netra said.

The Tender's gaze flicked to her, then back to Shorn, who had come to a halt and was standing with his thick arms crossed over his chest.

"Who are you? What do you want?"

"I'm Netra. I'm a Tender. I need to speak to the FirstMother."

When she said she was a Tender, the woman relaxed fractionally. She put one hand up and stroked her *sulbit*, murmuring to it as she did so. Her *sulbit*'s mouth closed.

"The FirstMother is very busy. Come back later."

"Please…" Netra began, but she got no further because Shorn, clearly deciding he'd been patient enough, simply started walking forward.

The Tender's eyes grew very wide and for just a moment she stood her ground, but when it became clear that Shorn wasn't slowing, she scurried out of the way. The guards had already moved and though she hissed at them they made no effort to impede Shorn in any way.

"Thank you," Netra said to the startled Tender, and followed Shorn through the gate.

"You sure know how to make friends," she said to him when she caught up.

"We don't have the time," Shorn grunted.

Netra had to agree with him. Even from this distance it seemed to her she could feel the Children, could feel Reyna especially. Several times during the night she'd awakened with a certainty that some trace of Reyna's tether was still buried within her, waiting to flare to life. But when she looked within, she found nothing.

Shorn pointed. "I believe that is the FirstMother." Then he headed that way.

They were on a broad, paved drive that led up to a large mansion, several stories tall. The drive was circular in front of the mansion, with a fountain in the middle that was surrounded by flower beds. But now the fountain was dry, the flowerbeds fallow with only a few yellowing weeds in them. To the left was a row of four long, low, wooden buildings that looked cheap and recently constructed. To the right was an open, grassy area, where a group of people waited apprehensively. Near them were a dozen Tenders in a line, each bent over a kneeling person, one hand resting on their shoulders. Overseeing them all was a stern-looking Tender wearing a large, gold Reminder, the many-pointed star inside a circle that was the symbol of the Tender faith. A thin Tender with narrow features and a long face stood beside her.

As she got closer, Netra realized that the Tenders' *sulbits* were crouched on the shoulders of the people who were kneeling. But what were they doing? She took two more steps before suddenly it hit her.

They were feeding.

She could *feel* the Song they were drawing from the people. It gave her an unpleasant sucking sensation in the pit of her stomach.

The feeling of revulsion was so strong that Netra stopped, grabbing onto Shorn's arm as she did so.

"How can this be?" she whispered, more to herself than to him. "How can they *do* this? Why?"

But did she really need to ask why? After what she had done? After what she'd seen?

Shorn gave her a questioning look and she nodded. "It's okay," she said.

The FirstMother was a large woman whose robe hung on her loosely, as if she had lost quite a lot of weight recently. Her *sulbit* was larger than any of the others and she held it in the crook of her arm as if it were a baby. She didn't see the two of them approach, her eyes fixed on the Tenders as they fed their *sulbits*.

Her *sulbit*, however, was staring fixedly at Netra. It chittered and she looked down at it, then up to see Shorn and Netra approaching. She did a double-take when she saw Shorn and her free hand went to her *sulbit*. She muttered something to the Tender attending her and when the woman looked up she gave a startled squeak and fell back a step.

"Who are you?" demanded the FirstMother. She was staring at Shorn, but her *sulbit* was still staring at Netra. Netra felt her heart beat a little faster.

"I'm Netra," she said. "This is Shorn."

But the FirstMother didn't seem to be listening. "How did they get in here, Velma?" the FirstMother demanded of the Tender standing beside her, as if she had personally let them onto the estate.

Velma waved her hands helplessly. "I don't know, FirstMother."

"I wonder why I bother to have guards at all. They're almost completely useless."

Velma shrugged, then nodded vigorously.

"What do you want?" the FirstMother asked. "I'm busy."

"I can see that, FirstMother, but this is important." The FirstMother's expression said more than words could have about how doubtful she found that. "It's about the Children."

That got the FirstMother's attention. "What about them?"

"I can help you against them."

The FirstMother looked her over. "I seriously doubt that." She measured Shorn up and down. "Though I suspect Rome could find a use for that one on the wall. Go up to the palace and talk to them." She turned her attention back to the other Tenders, clearly dismissing Netra.

"I'm a Tender," Netra blurted out.

The FirstMother looked irritated that she was still there. "Without a *sulbit* you're useless to me. Go away." Again she looked away.

70

"I was captured by the Children. I can tell you things about them."

That got her the FirstMother's attention again, but she looked skeptical. "A bold claim, child, but one I seriously doubt. The Children leave no survivors."

"It is true," Shorn interjected.

The FirstMother looked mildly surprised that Shorn could speak. She turned to Velma. "Go with her. Hear what she has to say."

"Me?" Velma squeaked.

"Do you see anyone else standing here?"

Velma looked around like a trapped animal. "Right now?"

"Yes, *now*."

Velma nodded furiously, but the FirstMother had already dismissed her and turned back to the Tenders she was overseeing. Velma came hesitantly over to them, making sure she didn't come within arm's reach of Shorn. She looked worried he might try to bite her. For his part, Shorn didn't even look at her. He was busy looking around, assessing possible threats, establishing the layout of the estate.

"Uh, follow me, I guess," Velma said. She led them back over to the paved carriage way then looked around, as if unsure where to take them. Uncertainly, she turned to them. "So..." she said, biting the corner of her lip. After a long hesitation she ventured, "I'm not really sure what I'm supposed to ask you."

"Does it make any difference?" Netra asked. "No offense, but I don't think she's going to listen to you."

Velma hung her head. "You noticed."

"I did."

"Were you really captured by the Children?" Velma asked, looking up at Netra with big eyes.

"Yes, I really was."

"How did you escape?" She glanced sidelong at Shorn. "I bet it was him." Now that Velma had accepted that the FirstMother wasn't going to expect a real report from her, she seemed to be getting over her fear somewhat.

"It was him," Netra said. She rubbed her face. She suddenly felt really tired. She'd put so much into getting her and now she was here and it didn't seem to make any difference. She just wanted to lie down and sleep. "Maybe you can help me. There may be some Tenders here from the Haven where I grew up."

"If they're here, I probably know them. I know a lot of the Tenders," Velma said proudly.

"One of them is Cara. She has long, blonde hair…" Netra trailed off, realizing that all the Tenders she'd seen had very short hair and so that description probably wouldn't help. But Velma brightened right away.

"Of course I know Cara!" she said excitedly. "She was a great help when the FirstMother went off to Guardians Watch and left me here in charge."

Netra doubted the last part. Who would leave this apparently simple woman in charge of anything?

"She is wonderful at the morning services," Velma continued. "Everyone loves her. That was the greatest help, when she took them over. I was awful at them," she confided to Netra. "I never had anything to say."

"Okay," Netra said, cutting in before the woman spent all day talking. "Do you know where she is?"

"Not right now," Velma admitted, peering around at the estate grounds. From the way she was squinting, Netra thought she probably couldn't see all that well. "But it shouldn't be hard to find her. Come on. Let's go look."

She led them around the side of the house along a tiled path through gardens that had been neglected for some time. As she walked, she kept up a steady stream of commentary, but Netra heard none of it. She was thinking about the *sulbits*. What *were* those creatures? Where did they come from? She remembered the Musician she and Shorn had encountered on their way back to the Haven. He'd seemed surprised that she didn't have a *sulbit*, but never answered when she asked him what they were. Apparently they fed on Song, but why were they being fed on people?

"There she is," Velma exclaimed, stopping and pointing.

Netra looked and saw a woman sitting on a stone bench, her hands folded in her lap. Even at a distance, even half turned away, Netra knew at once it was her and she cried her name and ran to her.

FIFTEEN

"Oh, oh, oh, I can't believe it's really you. I can't believe you're back," Cara kept saying as she cried and hugged Netra to her as tightly as she could. At least that's what she thought she was saying. She was so surprised and so overwhelmed that she couldn't be sure. It didn't seem real. She'd dreamed of this moment, but deep down she'd been terrified it would never happen, that she'd seen the last of the woman she considered her sister.

At length they pulled apart and looked at each other, still holding hands. "It's really you, isn't it? I'm not dreaming?"

"It's really me," Netra replied, tears streaming down her face as well.

"I'm so glad you're back. I've been so frightened." Cara remembered then, why Netra went away. "Did you find your mother?"

"No, I didn't. I think I was close, but then the Plateau…it kind of blew up and I had to leave."

"You were on Landsend Plateau when it exploded?" Cara's eyes went wide. "We could see the smoke from here."

"It's where I met Shorn." Netra gestured. Shorn was standing nearby, watching, waiting.

Cara started when she saw Shorn. "Oh," she said, in a small voice. "He's awfully big."

"He's the reason I'm here," Netra said. "He saved me more than once."

Cara put her hand on her heart. "Thank you for bringing my friend back," she told him.

Shorn did not reply.

"He's not much of a talker," Netra said.

Cara turned back to Netra. "Please, sit down. I want to hear everything." She noticed Netra's wince as she said the words and she wondered at it.

"It's a long story," Netra said, sitting down on the bench beside her. "I've…been through a lot."

Cara looked at her worriedly. Her friend looked so tired and worn. She seemed so much older. She reached over and squeezed her hand. "You can tell me when you're ready."

Netra leaned back on the bench. "It feels so good to just sit down. I feel like I could sleep for days."

Cara noticed that she moved her body gingerly, as if she were wounded. "Are you hurt?"

Netra put her hand on her left side. "I'm all right. It's going away."

"Are you sure? We have a really good healer…"

"I don't think she could help me. It's not an ordinary wound."

Now Cara was really worried. "I don't like the sound of that, Netra. Let me see it." Netra tried to protest, but Cara wouldn't have it. "If you won't let a healer look at it, you at least have to let me. I didn't just get my dearest friend back only to have her bleed to death on me."

"It's not bleeding."

"Then let me see it."

"Okay, if it means you'll leave me alone about it. What happened to you? When did you get so bossy?"

Cara considered this. It hadn't really occurred to her before, but now that Netra mentioned it she could see the truth of it. "Ricarn's been working on me," she said.

"Who's Ricarn?"

Cara shook her head. "Stop trying to distract me. Let me see your injury."

Reluctantly, Netra lifted the edge of her shirt. There was an angry red blotch on her lower ribcage and red lines radiating outward from it.

"That doesn't look like nothing to me," Cara said. "You need to see a healer."

"Trust me. It's much better than it was."

Cara looked at her suspiciously, then turned to Shorn for confirmation. "It is true," he said after a moment.

She turned back to Netra. "That's no ordinary bruise. What caused it?"

Netra pulled her shirt back down. "One of the Children. She hit me with some kind of…I don't know what it was. It looked like a big, thick spider web. I couldn't break free and she was draining my life with it."

"She *what*? You were captured by the Children? How did that happen? How did you get away?"

Netra gave her a wan smile. "That's too many questions at once."

Cara looked at her friend closer. "You didn't just go to the Plateau, did you?"

Netra looked away, but not before Cara saw the sudden shame in her eyes. "No, I didn't," she said in a small voice.

"It's okay," Cara said, taking hold of her hand. "Whatever happened, it's okay now."

"I wish that were true."

Cara swallowed, the reality of their current situation falling down on her. Seeing Netra again so unexpectedly had pushed it out of her mind for a brief time, but now it was back.

The Children were coming.

The threat of the Children's approach hung like a cloud over the city. Sometimes Cara woke up in the middle of the night choking on that fear. At least half the residents of Qarath had fled the city. How many times had she laid there in the dark and wished she could go with them?

"How come you don't have a *sulbit*?" Netra asked, pulling Cara out of her thoughts.

Cara clasped her hands in her lap and looked down. She bit her lip. "I said no." She was surprised at how guilty she still felt by that decision, even while she absolutely felt it was the right decision and would do the same thing again. It was just more proof of what Ricarn was always telling her, that she spent too much time being sorry and not enough time just being herself. She looked up at Netra. "When we got here all of us were told to go with Lowellin and receive our *sulbits*. But when the FirstMother told me to go I said no."

"Really? You said no?"

Cara caught the surprise in Netra's voice and smiled. "I know. It surprised me too."

"You said no to that scary woman." Netra seemed like she was trying to convince herself.

"Does she scare you too?"

"Yes."

"I think she scares all the Tenders. Except Ricarn. Nothing scares her."

"She must have been furious."

"She was. I thought she was going to kick me out into the streets."

"And yet you didn't back down."

"I wanted to. I just couldn't. It just felt wrong."

"Well, I'm proud of you."

"Of me? Really?" Hearing those words from Netra meant so much to Cara. She'd always had a deep, secret fear that Netra looked down on her for being so weak.

"I'm sorry," Netra said suddenly.

"For what?"

"I never thought…I always thought that…" Netra stumbled, unsure what to say.

"It's okay. Neither did I."

They sat there for a minute, then Netra said, "The Children will be here this afternoon I think."

Though the news wasn't surprising—Ricarn was tracking the Children's progress through her insect spies—still it brought a shudder from Cara.

"I have information I think the FirstMother should have. It's about the Children and it might help," Netra continued. "But she wouldn't listen to me."

"We should find Bronwyn. She'll be able to help. The FirstMother will listen to her."

"Bronwyn's here?" Netra asked, her eyes lighting up. "Who else?"

"Just Owina, Karyn and Donae. Jolene disappeared before we left and Siena and Brelisha chose not to come. They're still at the Haven." She saw the sudden pain on Netra's face and said, "What is it?"

"Siena and Brelisha…they're dead. Tharn killed them."

"Oh." Cara put her hand over her mouth. Those women had been all the parents she ever had. She wiped at her eyes. "It seems unimaginable to me. I always thought they would live forever."

"Me too."

"And yet, every morning when I go out into the city for morning services, I cannot help but think that every person I see will probably be dead in a few days, and I will be also."

"I found some," Cara said, walking into the room where Netra was just finishing her bath. She was carrying a pair of wool trousers and a plain, cotton shirt. It was midafternoon. "Jemry, he's one of the guards, is about your size. You should have seen the look on his face when I asked him for his spare clothes." She set the clothes down on a small table and handed Netra a towel. Wrinkling her nose, she nudged the small pile of dirty clothes lying on the floor beside the tub with her foot. They were the clothes Netra had been wearing when she arrived. They were little more than tatters and dirty beyond any hope of cleaning. "I can't believe you had these hidden outside the Haven and that you put them on when you were out roaming around in the countryside. Brelisha was already furious with you for dodging your lessons. If she'd known you were wearing men's clothes her eyes would have popped out of her head. You'd have been doing kitchen cleanup until you were an old woman."

"Which is why I never told you about them," Netra said with a small smile, picking up the shirt. "You're the worst liar ever. The second Brelisha looked at you, you would've cracked and told her everything."

"I know. I never could stand up to her. I was always a little afraid of her." Her words trailed off as she wiped a sudden tear from her eye. Then she said, "But you're back now, where you belong. I don't understand why you don't just wear a robe like the rest of us."

"I've been wearing pants for so long I'm not sure how to wear anything else," Netra replied, wringing water out of her hair.

"Really, Netra? Or is it that you prefer wearing pants?"

Netra pulled the pants on and turned to her. "There's a fight coming, Cara. I need to be able to move around. A robe will just get in my way."

As if triggered by her words, horns began blowing in the distance. The Children had been spotted. Netra began putting her moccasins on.

"But you don't have a *sulbit*," Cara protested. "The FirstMother said only Tenders with *sulbits* are to go anywhere near the wall. The rest of us are supposed to stay here."

"I'm sorry, Cara," Netra said, standing up and putting one hand on her shoulder. "But I've gone through too much to just sit here and do nothing."

Cara opened her mouth to argue with her, then closed it. "You're right, of course. It was selfish of me to try and keep you here with me. We need all the help we can get. I'm just afraid of losing you again."

Netra pulled her in and gave her a hug. "You're not going to lose me that easily. Remember, I have Shorn to look out for me."

They left the room. Shorn was waiting in the hall and the three of them hurried outside. Tenders and guards were scurrying everywhere. The FirstMother was yelling orders. Soon there were a couple dozen Tenders lined up on the carriage way in front of the FirstMother. The rest of the Tenders and their guards gathered behind them. A woman dressed in a red robe walked up to stand next to the FirstMother. She alone seemed completely calm and unhurried.

"Who's that?" Netra asked.

"It's Ricarn. She's an Insect Tender."

"But I thought they were…" Netra began, then broke off. "Forget it. We'll talk about it later."

"It's time," the FirstMother said, walking along the line of Tenders. "I know you're frightened. But we've been through the fire before. We faced Kasai and Tharn…" She broke off. Her *sulbit* was acting very strange, scurrying from one shoulder to the other and making frightened noises. All the *sulbits* were doing the same.

"Quit that!" the FirstMother snapped. "Settle down!" She tried to grab her *sulbit*, but it eluded her and jumped to the ground. It chittered to its brethren and they chittered back. Then they began abandoning their Tenders and running for the estate gates.

"Shut the gates!" the FirstMother yelled, but the guards, stunned by what was happening, were slow to react and before the gates were halfway closed the *sulbits* had streamed out into the street.

The FirstMother cursed and ran after them, everyone else following. When Netra got into the street, she saw that the *sulbits* were standing on their hind legs in a tight circle, chittering and shifting from one foot to the other.

"Enough of this," the FirstMother snarled, striding over to them.

"Don't," Ricarn said, but the FirstMother ignored her. She bent down to grab her *sulbit*, but before she could get a hold of it, it turned on her, hissed and spat something at her.

At that moment Ricarn pushed the FirstMother, not hard, but just enough so that she staggered to the side.

The *sulbit*'s attack missed the FirstMother's face and struck her in the shoulder. There was a sizzling sound and the fabric of her robe dissolved. The skin underneath blistered instantly. The FirstMother clutched her shoulder and stared at her *sulbit*, her face gone white.

The *sulbits* tilted their heads to the sky and began to wail, a strange, unearthly sound that made the hair rise on the back of Netra's neck. The air around them began to blur.

"What are they doing?" Cara whispered.

"I don't know." The blurriness grew stronger and then mists appeared, rising out of nothing. Netra rubbed her eyes in disbelief. "Can you *see* that?" she asked Cara, who nodded. From the noises around them, Netra realized that she and Cara weren't the only ones who *saw* what was happening. "It can't be," Netra murmured. "The kind of power necessary to pull all of us *beyond*…there's no way those things have that much inside them. To do that they'd need the power of…"

She and Cara exchanged looks.

"They're summoning the River," Cara breathed.

"But how is that possible?" A realization struck Netra. "Those things *come* from the River, don't they?" Cara nodded.

Netra turned back to look and was shocked at what she *saw*. Inside the circle of *sulbits* the street was gone. In its place was a dark hole.

Something was rising in the hole, something that glowed with a powerful, golden brilliance, that thundered with silent power. It spilled up out of the hole and rose into the air, a wild, foaming mass like a small geyser. The *sulbits* were still wailing, tiny forelegs raised up as if in supplication.

"They're going home," Cara said.

The FirstMother must have realized the same thing, because she turned to Ricarn. "Do something," she said, an unusual pleading note in her voice.

Ricarn moved forward. The FirstMother's *sulbit* turned its head and hissed at her. She crouched, holding out her hands, palms outward. Then she chittered.

The FirstMother looked stunned. "You can *talk* to them?"

Ricarn ignored her, all her attention focused on the *sulbit*. She chittered again. The FirstMother's *sulbit* responded. To Netra it sounded wary.

Ricarn moved closer. The River was now a churning, glowing mass twenty feet tall. She made a motion as if she were wiping a window clean, and when she pulled her hand away a horrified murmur arose from the Tenders. The *sulbits* fell back, tiny voices rising in alarm.

There was a streak of purple darkness in the River.

Ricarn chittered again. The *sulbits* hesitated, looking from her to the River and back.

"What is *that*?" the FirstMother asked Ricarn hoarsely.

Without looking at her, Ricarn replied. "It is chaos power. I am showing them that their home is no longer safe."

"Did the Children do that?"

"No. This taint comes from the abyss. I believe it was done by one of the Guardians."

"Mother help us," the FirstMother whispered, low enough that Netra barely heard her.

The *sulbits* were now chittering amongst themselves. They seemed to be arguing. Then the one belonging to the FirstMother made a loud rasping sound and the others went quiet. It chittered at them. None responded.

The River began to recede, sliding back down into the ground. In moments it was gone, along with the hole and the mists. The *sulbits* began to return to their Tenders.

"How did she do that?" Netra asked Cara.

Cara shrugged. "I have no idea. I can't figure that woman out at all."

SIXTEEN

"What took you so long?" Rome yelled at Nalene as the wagons bearing the Tenders arrived. He was jumpy. Everyone was. He couldn't see the Children from here, but he could feel them and they were getting closer. They made him feel…unbalanced. It was like he was standing on the edge of a massive cliff and a great wind was trying to push him over the edge.

"We had a problem with the *sulbits*," she snapped, getting down from the wagon.

"What's wrong with them?" The *sulbits* were clearly agitated. Nalene's was making a mewling noise and scurrying back and forth from one shoulder to the other. A couple of the Tenders' *sulbits* were crouched on their shoulders, tiny claws locked into the cloth of their robes, teeth bared. On some of the Tenders he couldn't see the creatures at all, but he could see them moving underneath their robes, trying to find a place to hide.

"What do you think is wrong with them?" she retorted. "They're afraid of the Children." With some difficulty she managed to get a hold of her *sulbit* and tucked it into the crook of her arm. One of the other *sulbits* squirmed away from its Tender, jumped down and ran underneath the wagon.

"We don't have time for this," Rome said. "We have to have that barrier."

"You think I don't realize that?" she barked. "You think I can't feel them coming?"

Rome bit back the angry comment he'd been about to make. Standing here fighting wasn't going to do anything but waste time. He saw Quyloc hurrying up and turned to him. "Do you still think this is going to work?"

"It's all we have," Quyloc replied.

"I'll try to buy you as much time as I can."

81

Rome took off at a trot for the wall. He ran up the stone steps and gained the top of the wall. It made him feel a little bit better to see that his soldiers were ready. They looked pale, but they looked resolute as well. Most of them were veterans of the battle of Guardians Watch and he knew he could count on them.

About half of the soldiers held bows and the rest, except for those manning the ballistae, were armed with long spears.

"That doesn't look good," Tairus said, looking down at the Tenders.

"It seems those things are afraid of the Children too," Rome said grimly.

"Where's their guards?" Tairus asked. "Where are they going to get the Song they need to put up the barrier? They're not going to use my soldiers, are they?" There were several squads of soldiers formed up in the square, waiting orders.

"No, they're not going to use soldiers," Rome replied. "From the way the FirstMother explained it, they don't need to use people like that anymore." In the first battle of Guardians Watch, the Tenders bled the Song they used for their attacks from their guards' flows. Later they bled that Song directly from the enemy. "That's part of the reason they've been feeding those things so much recently. It's not just to make them stronger, it's to build up a reserve of Song inside them. The Song for the barrier is going to come straight from the *sulbits*."

"You think it will work, the barrier? When they practiced it yesterday it didn't work."

"It better work," Rome said.

"They better hurry," Tairus said, glancing over his shoulder at the advancing Children. They were less than five hundred paces away now.

For the tenth time, Rome shifted his armor to a more comfortable position. It was always like this before battle for him. His armor chafed and pinched everywhere and nothing he did ever made it right.

Tairus sighed. "Why can't things ever be easy?" He pointed at the advancing Children. "I take it that's the one you were talking about, the big, red-skinned brute?"

"That's him."

Tairus cleared his throat and spat. "I thought you were crazy when you told me he could probably smash down the gates with his fists."

"And now?"

"I wish you were crazy."

"Me too. If anything, he's bigger than I remember. Oh well, if it was easy, it wouldn't be any fun, would it?"

Tairus fixed him with a gimlet eye. "I don't like your idea of fun at all."

"You're just getting old, that's all."

"I'd like to get a whole lot older."

Rome turned to his aide, Nicandro, who was waiting nearby. "Go down the line. Remind everyone to concentrate fire on the big guy. Whatever it takes, keep him away from the gates."

It was the ballistae Rome was counting on the most. They were huge things, mounted on iron stands and bolted to the top of the wall, armed with iron bolts fully as long as man was tall. They could knock down a charging horse. They should be able to slow the big guy.

Rome heard his name called from the foot of the wall and he turned and walked to the inside edge of the wall and looked down. At the foot of the stairs stood a tall, young woman wearing men's clothes. Beside her was a hulking, copper-skinned figure wearing roughly-made, tanned leather. Before them, blocking their way, was a soldier. He'd retreated to the bottom step, his sword held out in front of him. It looked insignificant compared to the huge figure in front of him.

"They want to come up on the wall, macht!" the soldier yelled.

"That's the pair who came into the city this morning," Tairus said. "She claims to be a Tender. I don't know *what* he is."

"Let them up!" Rome called down. He watched as they started up the stairs and to Tairus he said, "See the way he moves? He looks like a fighter to me."

"How come he's got no weapons then?"

"Look at the size of him. I bet his fist is as big as your head. Maybe he doesn't need any weapons."

Tairus made a sound that indicated what he thought of a fighter without any weapons, but he made no other comments as the two climbed the stairs. When they stepped onto the top of the wall, Rome walked over to them, Tairus following.

"I'm Wulf Rome, macht of Qarath," Rome said. "Who are you?"

"I'm Netra," the woman replied. "And this is Shorn."

Shorn was even bigger up close. Rome wasn't used to feeling small, but he felt small looking up at him. He saw the way Shorn looked him over—his gaze lingering for a moment on the handle of the black axe sticking up from behind Rome's back—the way he noted the positions and weapons of all the soldiers on that section of wall, and knew he'd been right in his assessment of him. He was definitely a fighter. Rome realized he was smiling. Their odds of survival just got a little bit better.

"We want to help," Netra said.

Rome shifted his attention to her. She was younger than he'd first thought, deeply tanned by the sun and worn to the hard edge a person gets through a lot of walking on short rations. In her face he read experiences far beyond her years. She'd clearly traveled some hard roads.

"We can use all the help we can get," he told her. "I heard you're a Tender." She nodded, reluctantly it seemed to him. "You have one of those things on you somewhere, a *sulbit*?" he asked.

"No."

"What can you do?"

"I know the Children. I escaped from them yesterday. With Shorn's help."

That surprised Rome. He glanced at Tairus.

"I saw you and another man attack the Children yesterday."

"You were there?"

"We were following the Children. You hurt Melekath badly. He's not with them anymore."

Rome shifted his armor and scratched. "I heard as much from Ricarn. That's why we're trying to get the barrier up. Without him, the only way they can come in is through the gates." It was good to know that his ill-advised plan to attack Melekath had actually produced some benefit.

"What else can you tell me?" Rome asked Netra. "What weaknesses do they have?"

"I don't think they have any," she said grimly, looking out at the Children. "You see the tall one, with the red hair? Shorn smashed her head with a rock. Smashed it to a pulp. Look at her now."

"It slowed her down though, didn't it?"

"It did. But not for long. And she'll get stronger with every person she feeds on. All of them will."

"So I've heard."

"She—her name is Reyna—she can shoot something at you, like a big spider web, and feed on you from a distance."

"How far?" Tairus interjected.

Netra shook her head. "I don't know for sure. I was a few paces away when she did it to me." Rome noticed that her hand went to her side as she spoke. "But I don't think she can shoot it far. Especially not now, after she had to use some of her strength to heal herself."

"That's good to know. I'll pass the word to the troops," Rome said.

"Thrikyl's city gates were ripped off their hinges. I think the big, red-skinned one did it. I think he might be able to do the same to these gates."

Rome exchanged looks with Tairus. "Is that it?" he asked Netra.

"Reyna and Heram hate each other. As soon as the opportunity comes, they'll turn on each other. Reyna hates all the Children. She won't hesitate to sacrifice any of them."

"That's good to know," Rome said. "Maybe we'll find a way to use that." He glanced over at the Children. They were getting close. To Shorn he said, "You need a weapon?"

Shorn looked disdainfully at the weapons the soldiers were carrying and shook his head. He held up his hands. "I have these," he rumbled. His thick fingers ended in blunt claws that looked like they'd have no trouble tearing through wood. His forearms were as big around as a man's leg. Rome saw no point in arguing with him.

"Then let's see if we can buy the Tenders the time they need," Rome said. Nicandro had returned and Rome turned to him. "Tell the men to watch out for the tall woman with the red hair. She can shoot some kind of web and kill a man from a distance." Nicandro saluted and ran off.

"What's your plan?" Heram asked Reyna as they approached the city. He casually backhanded one of the Children who tried to run past him, sending the woman sprawling. "I told you no one rushes the city until I say so," he growled. Another one of the Children was starting to inch by, but when Heram glared at him he put his head down and backed up.

"Why would I have a plan?" Reyna replied. "Don't *you* have a plan?"

"My plan is to keep an eye on you."

Reyna gave Heram a crooked smile. It was all she could manage. She didn't need a mirror to know that her face was still a shattered mess. Her jaw hurt terribly and her mouth didn't seem to close right. "It bothers me that you still don't trust me."

He ignored her comment. "It would be better if we still had Melekath to make a hole in the wall for us."

"Well, then you shouldn't have let them attack him."

"I didn't see you trying to stop them."

"*I* don't think we need him. *I* think we're better off without him." She spoke confidently, but the truth was that she wished Melekath were there too. After the beating the big copper-skinned one had given her, she had developed a healthy respect for her enemies. But there was no way she would ever admit that to Heram. She would rather die than admit any weakness to him.

"We have to concentrate on the gates," Heram said. "That's their weakness."

"Excellent plan," Reyna replied. "I knew you had it in you. I knew you couldn't be as thick as you look. Not that there was ever any possibility of that."

Again Heram refused to rise to her jibe, only fixing his small, deep set eyes on her for a moment before looking away. He really frustrated her sometimes. He was simply no fun to poke at all. She longed for a foe who was a real challenge, one who plotted and counterplotted the way she did. What she wouldn't give for a real test of wits.

But then, that was why she'd teamed up with Heram to bring Melfen down all those years ago, wasn't it? Because Melfen was too smart. He'd been a real threat to her. If she hadn't eliminated him with Heram's help when she did, she might be the one lying crushed and paralyzed under a massive pile of stone back in the prison.

In truth, Reyna did have a plan. Her plan was to let the rest of the idiots charge the city walls, while she stayed back out of harm's way and watched. That way, if the defenders had any more nasty tricks, she'd be able to find out at no risk to herself.

"You'll be able to knock those gates down, won't you?" she asked Heram. "Like you did at Thrikyl?"

"They'll come down," he replied.

"You're not too weak now, after healing that terrible cut the little man gave you with his little axe?"

Heram turned a heavy frown on her and she saw with satisfaction that finally one of her jabs had landed. Heram hated being bested, and the fact that he'd been beaten by a foe no more than a third his size had to rankle.

"You'll see," Heram said.

"I'm sure I will," she told him lightly.

They walked in silence until they were just about at the edge of bowshot, then Reyna turned to Heram. "Time to let them loose?" she asked. He nodded. She raised her voice. "All right. Go get them."

With a shriek, the Children raced for the city. Heram hesitated for a moment, looking at Reyna. She shook her head and then he joined the rush. Reyna bit her lip. It was agony, standing here when all that Song was so close. She wanted to fling reason to the winds and charge the city too.

She didn't have to wait long to see what the defenders' response would be. A rain of arrows began falling on the Children almost immediately. The arrows couldn't stop any of the them, but they did hurt. Most importantly, they distracted the Children from what was coming next.

There was a series of low, heavy thumps as the ballistae fired, all of them within a second of each other. Heram had a half dozen arrows sticking out of him and he was yanking them out as he lumbered forward, so he didn't see the heavy iron bolts flying toward him. The first one struck him a glancing blow on the shoulder, tearing through desiccated flesh and ricocheting off. The force of the blow spun him completely around, causing most of the other bolts to miss.

But not all of them.

As he spun, one bolt struck Heram square in the middle of his back, knocking him down on his face. A cheer went up from the defenders.

The cheers died off quickly when Heram came to his feet a moment later. Grimacing, he grabbed the shaft of the bolt and pulled it the rest of the way through him. He turned toward the wall. Holding the bolt in one hand, he reared back, and flung it at the defenders. It sailed high, missing the soldiers on the wall, but one unlucky soldier in the square looked up too late and the thing hit him in the hip, sending him crashing to the ground, screaming.

One of the bolts that missed Heram struck an older man who was behind him. The force of the impact was such that he was lifted off his feet and flung backwards. The bolt stuck in the ground and he dangled there, arms and legs flailing uselessly, screaming with pain and frustration. Finally, his thrashing loosened the bolt enough that it worked its way loose and he toppled to the ground. Laboriously, he stood up. But he wasn't strong enough to pull the bolt out of him. Eventually he just gave up and resumed his charge, the huge bolt making him weave and trip as he stumbled forward.

As Reyna had expected, most of the Children just ran blindly at the walls, which of course they were completely unable to climb. They tried to scramble up, but none got more than a little way off the ground before they lost their grip and fell back down. While they were trying to climb the walls, they were easy targets for the Qarathian defenders, who dropped stones on them. One stone hit a woman square in the head, and she lay on the ground twitching, her head cracked open like an egg, dusty, withered gray matter showing inside. But the lure of all that Song drew her inexorably and moments later she sat up and began trying to climb the wall once again.

Heram ran for the gates. By then the ballistae had reloaded and they fired another round, but Heram was watching for them this time. He ducked one and another only lightly scored his side. The rest missed. Once he made it up to the gates the ballistae could no longer swivel far enough to fire at him.

The gates were iron-bound wood nearly two feet thick and Heram planted himself before them, his feet spread wide, and began hammering them with double-fisted blows. The gates shook in their frame with each blow. Archers rained arrows down on him until he was bristling with them, but he simply ignored them. The stones the defenders dropped on him just bounced off.

It was an awesome physical display and even Reyna was impressed. She reminded herself not to take him too lightly.

"Those gates aren't going to hold for very long," Tairus said. He and Rome had moved to stand on the wall just above the gates, and were looking down at Heram. Each time Heram struck the gates, flakes of stone broke off around the hinges. The hinges were noticeably bent already.

Rome crossed the top of the wall and yelled down at Nalene. "FirstMother! We need that barrier!" His voice easily cut through the din of the battle and Nalene spared a moment to look up at him. But it was clear she couldn't deliver the barrier yet. She had her own *sulbit* calmed down, but most of the other Tenders were still struggling to control theirs.

Rome hurried back to where Tairus was still looking down at Heram and drew the black axe from its sheath on his back. He started climbing onto the battlements. "Someone get me a rope!" he yelled. Under his breath, he said, "I'm going to cut his leg completely off this time. See if that slows him down."

A soldier came running with a rope, but before he could get it tied off, Shorn was moving. He snatched up a half dozen ballistae bolts, climbed up on the battlements and jumped off the wall.

When he landed, two of the Children ran at him, but he easily knocked them down using the bolts, then began running toward Heram.

"Give him some cover!" Rome yelled. A fresh barrage of stones and arrows rained down on the Children, making it hard for them to pursue him.

Engrossed as he was with pounding on the gates, Heram didn't notice Shorn's approach.

Shorn ran up behind Heram and stabbed one of the bolts into his back, with enough force that it went all the way through him. Heram howled, and as he turned Shorn rammed another bolt into his gut. Heram howled again and grabbed the bolt, ripping it free. As he did so, Shorn quickly backed off a dozen steps.

Heram bellowed like a maddened bull and charged Shorn. Rome gripped the haft of the black axe tighter, fearing that this would be the end of the strange fighter. As big as Shorn was, Heram loomed over him and could probably tear him to pieces with his bare hands.

But then he realized that Shorn was expecting Heram to charge and was ready for it. He still had four of the ballistae bolts. As Heram charged, he jammed their butts into the ground and set himself in pike position. Heram was so enraged he didn't try to dodge around the bolts or even slap them aside. The bolts took him in the chest. They bent visibly, but held. Heram ended up skewered on the bolts, still bellowing, swinging his mighty fists at Shorn. But he couldn't quite reach him.

Rome scanned the battlefield and saw that a new danger threatened Shorn. Two of the Children, men bigger and stronger-looking than most of the rest, were circling around behind him. Focused as he was on Heram, it didn't look like Shorn had noticed them.

"Behind you!" Rome yelled.

Shorn glanced over his shoulder just as they ran at him. At the same moment, Heram suddenly changed his tactics. He stepped back, the bolts tearing free from his chest. Then he charged Shorn again.

But Shorn, instead of running away, ran at Heram. It looked like pure suicide.

At the last moment, Shorn ducked to the left, under Heram's outstretched right arm. Heram tried to react, but he was too big and had too much momentum. As he went by, Shorn kicked him hard in the side of the knee. Heram's knee bent sideways and he went down.

Shorn spun to meet the first of the attackers coming up from behind him, but the leg he'd kicked Heram with betrayed him and he stumbled. The first man managed to hook an arm around Shorn's arm and Rome could see the way Shorn immediately wilted under that devouring touch. All too well he remembered what it had felt like when one of the Children touched him.

Shorn clubbed the man on the side of the head with his other fist and the man went flying. Then he shook his arm, as if trying to will feeling back into it.

The next man was close behind the first and Shorn had no choice but to backhand him.

Heram had gotten unsteadily to his feet by then, but before he could reenter the fight one of the ballistae fired. The bolt struck him in the side and knocked him staggering sideways.

More of the Children were converging on Shorn. The city's defenders rained arrows and spears down on them and ballistae bolts flew every few seconds, but the Children, maddened by their hunger, ignored it all and kept coming. Shorn was backed up nearly to the gates, the Children spread out in an arc before him, coming from every direction.

Rome pounded on the battlement, hating how helpless he felt. There was no way they could risk opening the gates to let Shorn in. Ropes could be dropped to him, but Rome knew they couldn't lift him up fast enough before the Children got a hold of him.

Shorn slapped his next attacker aside, but three more came running up behind him. Shorn kicked the closest one, who fell back and tangled up the other two, all of them falling down.

Shorn bent and snatched up one of the stones that littered the battlefield, raised it over his head and threw it into the midst of another knot of Children that were rushing him. The stone, as big as a man's torso, tore through them and sent them flying.

But it was clear that Shorn was weakening fast. The next stone he reached for slipped from his grasp and while he was trying to pick it back up, a woman darted forward and dove at his legs, catching hold of one ankle. The ankle buckled and he fell against the gates.

Righting himself, Shorn kicked the woman away, but there was no real force behind the kick and she threw herself at him again almost instantly. He punched her, but his blow was weak and she was able to latch onto his arm. While he was trying to dislodge her, four more converged on him with gleeful shrieks and behind them came still more. He slapped weakly at the first with his free hand, but that left him open and the other three got their hands on him. Shorn went to his knees, more Children pouring over him.

Meanwhile, Heram had gotten back to his feet and was tossing Children out of the way as he tried to get to Shorn.

That's when something completely unexpected happened.

There was a flash to Rome's left and a kind of shockwave, but one that threatened to pull him toward the flash instead of knocking him away.

Standing a dozen paces away, leaning over the battlements, reaching down toward Shorn, was Netra. All around her lay the unmoving forms of a half score soldiers.

The air blurred around her hands, there was a hissing, crackling sound, and a brilliant blaze of light flashed from her down to Shorn.

The effect was immediate and electric.

Shorn roared and came to his feet, shaking off the Children like a bear shaking off wolves. He was shining so brightly it was difficult to look at him.

Heram lunged at him.

Shorn grabbed one outstretched hand, pulled and turned simultaneously, flipping Heram over his shoulder. Heram slammed headfirst into the gates.

While Heram was getting to his feet, Shorn broke through the ring of Children. Once free of them he stopped, grabbed up a stone, and threw it at Heram.

Heram looked up just as the stone struck him on the shoulder. With a roar of fury, he charged at Shorn, trampling the Children who didn't get out of his way.

But Shorn was no longer backed into a corner. He had room to maneuver and he made the best of it. He dodged Heram easily, picked up another stone and threw it at him. Then he was moving again.

Over and over he did this, taunting Heram, letting him get close but staying out of his reach. And as he did it he slowly but surely lured him away from the gates, along with many of the Children.

Rome looked over as Netra slid down the wall and sat down. What just happened? he wondered. What did she do? Did she kill all those men?

Rome started toward her, but stopped when Tairus yelled.

"We've got a new problem!"

Rome turned to look. Reyna was entering the fight.

SEVENTEEN

"Unbelievable. They're even dumber than I thought," Reyna grumbled to herself. "Isn't there a complete brain among the lot of them? Can't they see what he's doing?" Most of the Children were chasing the big, copper-skinned man when anyone could see that he was deliberately luring them away. The few who weren't chasing him were about as effective as rabbits, hopping up and down at the base of the wall. Every minute a couple more fell to stones, limbs and heads crushed.

Did Netra just do what she thought she did? she wondered. Was she really that strong? Despite herself, Reyna was impressed. She was also intrigued. She hoped she'd get a chance to capture Netra again. This time she'd make sure she didn't get away. She'd keep her alive until she learned everything that girl knew.

But that was for later. Now it was time to act.

She'd seen enough that she was reasonably sure the defenders had no new weapons. The bearded one with the black axe and the lean man with the spear could present problems, but she was confident they'd never get close enough to trouble her.

It was time to show them all who they really needed to fear.

She headed for the wall. She hadn't gotten very far before several ballistae bolts came flying her way, but she was ready for them. She released the slightest breath of her power, letting it radiate out from her. It was as if the bolts hit an invisible shield, deflecting away before they could strike her. Arrows followed, with the same results.

That was the problem with Heram—one of the problems anyway. He thought of power in only one way: brute strength. He didn't realize that power came in many different forms and had many different uses. It was a weakness many men had, and one she had exploited many times.

The storm of arrows and bolts increased as she neared the wall, but she ignored them. She strode calmly, regally, toward them, head up, looking steadily at them, taking her time. She walked like a queen crossing her throne room. Let them see their doom approaching and despair. The soldiers on the wall were shouting to each other. So far none of them had broken and run, but she could tell they were close. It wouldn't take much. She liked this feeling, the abject terror she inspired.

She was a dozen paces from the wall when she stopped and flung out her hands.

When Rome saw Reyna stop and put up her hands he yelled, "Get down! Now!"

The soldiers were ready and they reacted quickly, ducking down behind the battlements—except for one man to Rome's left. Rome saw him jerk back as something snapped through the air and struck him, knocking him back a couple of steps.

The man looked down in horror. What looked like a dirty spider web, but about as big around as a finger, was stuck to his chest. He grabbed at it and then jerked his hand away with a cry, as if it had burned him. He half turned toward Rome, his mouth working, and took one step, one hand coming up, reaching. Then a stricken look came into his eyes. The color leached from his skin until it was like wax and then he began to visibly deflate. In moments he was on the ground, withered and desiccated, the skin split open along his cheekbones and across his scalp.

The soldiers nearest to him drew back in alarm and one lost his nerve, jumped up and ran for the stairs. Another web shot through the air, striking him in the back. A scream came from him as he tried to reach back for it. Then he stiffened, his eyes rolling back in his head. He spasmed and went down.

"Stay down!" Rome yelled. "She can't get you if you stay down!"

After a moment, Rome peered over the battlement. Reyna was standing motionless with her eyes closed. As he watched, her facial features started to melt and flow, then reform. When the flesh solidified once again, the ruin of her face was healed. The missing patches of hair grew back. Her limbs straightened, withered flesh filled out. It was both awesome and horrifying to watch and it brought home to Rome just how hopeless this war was. How could they defeat an enemy who could do that?

The transformation complete, she opened her eyes and saw Rome looking at her. "Do you like what you see?" she called to him. She did a slow twirl, showing off.

"I'd like it better if you were leaving," he yelled back.

"Yes, I'm sure you would. But we both know that isn't going to happen." She glanced off to where Heram and the rest were still chasing Shorn. "Sooner or later that big idiot is going to realize just how stupid he is and..." She shook her head. "I take that back. That is something he'll never realize. But he will give up eventually, and then he'll come back. When that happens, your gates will come down. You know that, right?"

"And when that happens, we have a little surprise waiting for you," he replied under his breath, hoping that it was true.

"I'll just assume from your silence that you agree with me. So let me offer you a deal. Save us all this trouble and just open the gates. Do that and I give you my word we'll spare some of you...let's say half. After all, I'm going to need servants, right? I don't want to kill you all. What do you say?"

"No chance," Rome called back.

"Really?" She seemed genuinely surprised, or she was just a good actor. "I assure you that you and those you choose will be among those left alive."

"The answer is still no."

"So you choose to fight, to anger me and then suffer the consequences, rather than take my deal and save a great many of your people? Is that right?"

"That pretty much sums it up." Rome had an idea. "The problem is, Reyna, that I don't know if I can trust you. Why don't you come closer? Let me look in your eyes. Let me see if you can be trusted." He hefted the axe as he said this. Let her come to stand below him and he would jump off this wall onto her. He just might be able to take her down before she could kill him.

Reyna shook her head. "I don't think that would be a very good idea. I've seen you with that axe of yours. I saw what you did to Father with it."

"It was worth a try," he yelled.

"Of course it was. And I don't blame you for it. You've seen how pathetic my companions are. Any reasonable person would assume that I'm the same. Unfortunately for you, I'm not." She turned and saw that

Heram and the others had finally given up chasing Shorn and were returning.

"Oh look, here they come now." She looked back up at Rome. "One last chance to reconsider."

Rome didn't answer. There was nothing, really, to say.

"The gates, Heram," she said when he arrived. "Stop fooling around and bring them down."

Heram glared at her for a moment, then walked to the gates and resumed pounding on them.

The wall shook and stone dust sprinkled down.

Nalene looked over her shoulder when the thudding resumed. She could see a sliver of light between the gates each time Heram struck them. She exchanged a look with Quyloc, who was standing to the side, the *rendspear* in his hand, and in that look was the same shared knowledge.

How long would it be before the gap was big enough for him to get his hand in there? Once he was through the gates, how long would the portcullis last?

She turned back to the Tenders. They were formed up in three groups of seven, each group a diamond pattern. Bronwyn stood at the head of one group, Perast and Mulin at the head of the other two. Only Bronwyn's and Perast's groups were ready, the air around them hazy with pent-up energy waiting to be released. Mulin's wasn't. One of the Tenders in that group was still struggling with her *sulbit*. As Nalene watched, the creature got out of her grasp and scurried up her arm.

"Control that thing, Owina!" Nalene yelled.

Ricarn put a hand on her arm. "It won't help to yell at her," she said calmly. "She is already afraid."

"Not as afraid as she will be when those gates fall," Nalene snapped at her, her own fear, as always, coming out as anger.

"You are afraid too."

Nalene started to deny it, then looked away. The truth was that she was terrified and so was her *sulbit*. The creature was standing on her shoulder, pressed against her neck, trembling. "We're almost out of time," she said.

"We are," Ricarn agreed, turning to look at the gates. She sounded so calm, almost uncaring. How many times Nalene had wished she were as detached as Ricarn?

"Maybe we should just go ahead and put up the barrier with what we have," Nalene suggested.

Ricarn gave her a look, one thin eyebrow arching slightly.

"I know, I know," Nalene said. She knew as well as Ricarn how that would probably work out. They'd practiced this barrier yesterday, once they learned that Melekath was no longer with the Children and so they didn't have to worry about them coming through the wall. Nalene wished they could have practiced it a dozen times, but the Song they burned each time was so great that if they had, the *sulbits* would have been too depleted to be effective. They were strong enough now to hold a great deal of Song, but it wasn't an unlimited amount.

This wasn't going to be like the impromptu barrier Nalene had thrown up at Guardians Watch to protect the Tenders from the wall of gray flames. That had been a temporary thing that only remained up as long as she held it in place with her will.

This barrier had to be much stronger and it needed to be static. The plan was for the Tenders at the head of the three formations to feed Song into the gatehouse opening, where Nalene would weave it together in such a way that the Song, instead of rushing off and diminishing, would constantly flow back through the barrier. That way the barrier could be maintained by minimal additions of Song, rather than by constantly replenishing the whole.

What they'd learned when they practiced was that the flows coming from each formation had to be close to the same strength. If one of the three was significantly weaker than the other two—say by the loss of one Tender—it would be like making a chain where every third link was forged of inferior steel.

Nor could the barrier be built initially by two flows and the third added in later. The structure of the barrier was such that adding a third flow after it was complete would cause the whole thing would fall apart.

Nalene spun around as a loud cracking noise came from the gates.

One of the gates was sagging noticeably. Thick fingers reached into the gap between the gates. The fingers curled, found their grip, began to pull. The gate cracked again.

"Look away," Ricarn said. She had not turned to look. "You must focus on the task at hand. If you are not ready, you will not be able to control the flows when they deliver them to you."

Nalene forced herself to look away, to look instead at Owina. The older woman's face was pale as she pulled her *sulbit* down off her shoulder and cradled it in her arms. She bent her head, whispering to it, stroking it with a shaking hand.

"Come on," Nalene said through gritted teeth, trying to will Owina to get her *sulbit* under control. "Come on…"

There was another crack, louder than the rest, and Nalene couldn't control herself. She turned to look just as one of the gates was ripped away from its hinges and thrown off to the side. Instinctively, she fell back a step. Her *sulbit* cowered against her. She could sense how close it was to bolting. She was moments away from it herself. She could hear gasps from the other Tenders.

Heram stepped into the opening. His cold, hungry eyes met hers and Nalene flinched. Something like a smile came onto his harsh visage. He took hold of the other gate and ripped it away as well.

"Look at me!" Ricarn hissed. The force of her words was such that they penetrated Nalene's fear and she turned to her. "You must forget about him. Forget everything. Block it out."

Ricarn turned her attention to Owina. "The creature is feeding on your fear. Until you get yourself under control, you will never get it under control."

Owina nodded and took a deep breath.

As Heram stepped into the gateway passage, Quyloc moved up to the portcullis and raised his spear.

"Do you remember this? Do you remember what it can do?" Quyloc challenged him.

Heram's eyes went to the spear and the smile left his face. "It won't make any difference. I don't care how much you hurt me with that thing. It won't stop me from killing you."

"We'll see about that," Quyloc replied, settling himself into a fighting stance. He was surprised at how steady and confident his voice sounded, because the truth was that he believed what Heram said.

Before Heram had gone two more steps, other Children surged into the passage and charged forward with wild yells and howls. A few were struck by stones dropped through the murder holes, but most made it to the portcullis untouched and they hit it like a flood. Faces pressed up against the metal latticework and grasping hands reached through.

Quyloc felt the Tenders' fragile control slip. They were only moments from breaking.

He stepped forward and stabbed, then stabbed again and again, as fast as he could. Those he struck screamed and purple-black wounds appeared in their flesh. They fought madly to pull back, but there were too many behind them, pressing forward in their desperate eagerness, and they couldn't get away.

Dimly, Quyloc heard Nalene yelling something, but her words did not register. His only thought was to keep attacking, to hold them off as long as he could.

Heram waded into the crush of Children, grabbing them and throwing them back out of his way. "Get out of my way!" he yelled. "Get back!"

His bulk was immense, seeming to fill the gateway passage. He was too tall to stand upright completely. The Children were like puppies in his hands.

Then he was through them and standing at the portcullis. He looked past Quyloc at the Tenders. "What is this?" he asked. "Are you trying to make a shield out of Song?" He smiled. "It won't work, you know. I like Song. It will just make me stronger."

"We'll see about that," Quyloc replied grimly. "We might have a surprise for you."

Heram grabbed hold of the portcullis and Quyloc slashed across his fingers. He winced as the dried flesh of his hands was peeled back, but he didn't let go. Instead he smiled, the harsh smile of a predator about to kill his prey.

"It is only pain," he said. "I know pain. And I know hunger. Hunger is stronger."

He began to pull on the portcullis, while Quyloc attacked again and again, reaching through the openings to stab his forearms.

The portcullis held. It bent slightly, but that was it.

Heram let go and began banging on it. Quyloc moved closer, trying to reach further through and stab Heram's face or his body. Suddenly Heram snatched at the spear. For one heart-stopping instant he had hold of the weapon. Quyloc jerked on it desperately and just managed to yank it away before he could snap it.

Heram changed tactics. He bent and grabbed hold of the portcullis near the bottom with one hand. With the other he fended off Quyloc's renewed attacks as best he could. Some got through, but they were not enough. His mighty legs flexed and he began to pull. The metal bent.

"When it is open, I go through first," he warned the other Children. "Anyone who runs past me, I will tear you in half."

He pulled and the portcullis bent more. There was now a knee-high opening. Quyloc darted forward and stabbed at his feet.

"It's not enough," Heram told him. "I told you."

He shifted his position, took hold of the portcullis with his other hand, and gave a savage jerk.

There was a scream of tortured metal and Quyloc knew they were all dead. There was no way he could hold this monster off, but he knew he would die trying. He had to attack now, while Heram was still off balance.

Just as he started to leap forward, Ricarn grabbed his arm. "Get out of the way."

Without hesitating, he jumped to the side, then turned to look at the FirstMother. The air around her was glowing so brightly that he couldn't see her.

Heram leaned back, his mighty muscles flexed, and he tore the portcullis completely away with a triumphant yell.

At that same moment three thick bands of light shot forward into the gatehouse opening. He saw the FirstMother step forward, her hands thrown out, fingers bent as if trying to grab something only she could see. Her jaw bunched and the tendons stood out as she grappled with the Song.

The bands of light began to move, weaving around each other, faster and faster. By the time Heram tossed the portcullis behind him and turned around, there was a glowing latticework of Song covering the gatehouse opening.

"You made a terrible mistake," he grunted, and reached for the barrier.

But Ricarn was already moving. Moving with quicksilver speed, she stepped up to the barrier and struck it with her right hand. In the fraction of an instant before her hand struck, her arm changed.

Her flesh seemed to flow and reform and where the flesh of hand and forearm had been, there now was segmented, chitinous exoskeleton, tapering at the end to a curved point, like a scorpion's stinger.

The stinger bit into the barrier and from it flowed something scarlet that spread instantly to the whole thing, so that it was now a deep, burnt-red color.

"Now," Ricarn said in Quyloc's ear.

Heram slammed into the barrier…

And fell back, howling with pain. Huge blisters covered most of his arms.

Right behind him came the Children. Sizzling noises came from them as they hit the barrier and they also fell back, howling and screaming.

Breathing hard, his heart pounding, Quyloc lowered his spear. "What do you think now?" he said to Heram.

"It will not be enough," Heram said. Then he turned and walked away.

X X X

Once Heram had the gates down, Reyna moved forward along with everyone else. But as she reached the entrance to the gateway passage, she felt the buildup of power at the other end and stopped. Then she stood there and watched. The creatures the Tenders had surprised her. She'd never seen such things before. What were they? What were the Tenders doing with them?

When Heram tore down the portcullis, she stepped into the passage, then stopped again as a strange light filled the other end.

When Heram roared in pain, she quickly backed out of the passage, bewildered by what had just happened. How had they possibly managed to do that? The barrier was made of Song, that much she could tell, but the woman in red had changed it somehow. She'd poisoned it.

Xochitl or one of the other Shapers must be helping the defenders. She looked around. How come they hadn't shown themselves? What other traps did they have planned?

She heard muted cheering from the defenders and looked up at the top of the wall, wanting to see if any of them were foolish enough to show themselves. When none did, she hurried away.

It was time to reevaluate. The possibility that Qarath harbored one or more Shapers was a troubling thought.

She passed the road leading north and it occurred to her that they could simply leave. There were other cities. Surely they weren't all as well-defended as Qarath.

But she rejected the idea almost immediately. She would not admit defeat so easily. There had to be another way into the city.

She stopped outside missile range and turned to wait. A minute later Heram approached. The blisters on his hands and forearms were leaking fluid. Black streaks ran up his arms. His face was twisted with rage. He stomped up to her and stuck his face close to hers.

"When are you going to start helping?" he growled.

"What did you want me to do?" she retorted. "Should I have gone with you to chase the copper-skinned man around? Or maybe you wanted me to help you break gates down? Is that it? Did you want help breaking down the gates?"

Heram clenched his huge fists and for a moment she thought he was going to strike her.

"I almost had them," he replied through clenched teeth. "If you had done that web thing, killed even one of those Tenders, they wouldn't have gotten the barrier up in time and we would be feeding right now."

A number of the other Children had gathered around and they added their voices to his then. Not liking how this was going, Reyna fought the urge to take a step back. She couldn't show weakness now. If she did, they'd swarm all over her. A memory of what they'd done to Melekath surfaced.

"How could I?" she said, forcing herself to meet Heram's glare. At least she was nearly as tall as he was, though a fraction of his bulk. "You and the rest of these fools were in the way. I couldn't get a clear shot."

"Because you stay back and let us take all the risks." A growl from the others greeted his words.

"I hang back because I'm planning strategy. Have you heard of strategy? Do you know what it is?"

Heram crossed his thick arms. "So? What have you planned? Tell us of your grand strategy to get us into Qarath."

Reyna gave him her best look of disdain. "Not yet. I'm still working on it," she said.

Heram grunted. "I think you have nothing. I think you cower in the back and let us take all the risks." His eyes narrowed. "Maybe it is time for a change."

Reyna glanced around. More of the Children had gathered and they were all listening raptly. Most of them looked hostile. What would happen if they all attacked her at once? Could she survive that?

"No more talking," Dubron suddenly chimed in. He was standing on Heram's right, his gaze fierce and feral. "She's fed recently. I can smell the Song on her. Let's take it from her."

"You'll never get into the city without me," she warned.

"You're lying," Dubron cried. "You don't have a plan."

"You will *not* speak to me this way," Reyna blazed, outrage overcoming her trepidation. Dubron flinched, but he did not back down.

"Then tell us your plan," Heram rumbled.

Desperately, Reyna cast around for something to stall them. How else *could* they get in? Then she saw something she hadn't noticed before and she turned to them and smiled.

"You want to know my plan? I'll tell you then. We have to wait until after dark, but here's how we're going to get in to Qarath…"

EIGHTEEN

Rome was crouched on the inside edge of the wall, the black axe in his hands, when Heram tore through the portcullis. He tensed, ready to leap on Heram's back the moment he stepped out of the passage.

Then the barrier went up and Rome sagged down onto his knees, his relief so immense that all the strength ran out of him in an instant. *That was too close.*

"What do you know?" Tairus said from beside him, wiping his brow with the back of his hand. "It worked. I thought for sure we were all dead."

"Yeah, you and me both."

Turning, Rome crouch-walked back across the wall to the battlements, where he peeked over to see what was happening. Tairus followed. Reyna was walking away. A moment later, Heram emerged from the passage and followed her, along with many of the Children.

Rome stood up the whole way. All along the wall, soldiers looked to him, questions on their faces. He knew they were looking to him for guidance and he knew that he had to provide it, regardless of how he felt. He raised his fist in the air and gave a shout. All up and down the line soldiers came to their feet and echoed him, but the cheer was short-lived and lacked any real enthusiasm. Every person there knew all they'd done was buy a little time. They'd all seen, up close and personal, a foe that could not be defeated.

Rome knew how they felt. He'd known all along that the Children couldn't die. He'd known all they could do was buy time and hope for a miracle. But somehow he'd convinced himself that it couldn't be that bad. He'd convinced himself that they'd have some hitherto-unknown weakness that could be exploited.

We can't win.

The truth of it was like a lead weight lying on his chest. He put a hand on the battlements to steady himself as he sheathed the axe.

103

"They look like they're going to attack her," Tairus said, pointing.

Most of the Children, Heram at their head, were gathered in a half circle around Reyna. They were too far away to hear what was said, but it was clear that Reyna was on the defensive.

Along with most of the army on top of the wall, the two men stood there and watched as the drama unfolded in the sunset. Rome felt a sense of disorientation. It was a surreal scene, unlike any siege he'd ever witnessed. Where were the ranks of soldiers, defensive embankments, rows of tents? Instead there were less than a hundred people, none of them carrying weapons, all of them in rags. They looked like a disorderly mob of beggars and cripples. Nothing like an army at all. There was no order, no discipline, no plan.

The tension passed and the knot of Children began to break up. A few of them started picking up pieces of firewood.

"I don't think they're going to attack again today," Tairus said.

Rome had to agree with him, but it didn't make him feel any better. Part of him wanted to continue the battle, to just get it over with.

"Make sure we keep a good eye on them," he told Tairus, and headed for the stairs. He felt Tairus looking at him as he walked away, felt the unspoken words the man wanted to let out, but he did not turn back.

Once he got off the wall, he went over to the FirstMother. She was sitting on a crate, her head in her hands. Her *sulbit* looked like it was asleep. Only two of the Tenders were still standing near the barrier, thin streams of Song flowing from their *sulbits*, sustaining the barrier.

"That was well done, FirstMother," Rome said.

The FirstMother looked up. Her face was haggard with exhaustion. Her *sulbit* seemed drained of substance, almost translucent. "It was too close," she said.

"Your Tenders will be able to keep it up?" he asked.

"So long as we keep feeding the *sulbits* we can."

Rome stuck out one hand. "Take from me," he said softly.

Nalene's eyes widened. There was a hiss of breath from Quyloc and he said, "Macht Rome, is this wise?"

Rome ignored him, keeping his gaze fixed on the FirstMother. Her *sulbit* stirred itself and stood up, its black eyes on him. He could feel its hunger.

"Are you sure?" she asked him.

"I will not ask my people to do what I will not," he replied.

104

She nodded once, then leaned forward. She took his hand in hers and whispered something to her *sulbit*. It moved sinuously down her arm and balanced on her palm. Once again its black eyes went to Rome, just for a moment, then its head dropped to his hand.

Its mouth did not actually touch Rome's skin, but still he could feel it touching him. A sudden pressure, not on him, but near him and then, deeply, painfully intimate.

Something vital—something he'd never known he had until this moment—began to drain out of him. Coldness started in his extremities and moved toward his center. His vision narrowed. The sounds of people and animals grew dull and distant. He felt himself drifting away.

Then she pulled the creature away. Rome felt hands on him, holding him upright. His knees were weak and he was terribly dizzy. Dimly he heard himself say, "Bring my horse."

Quyloc said something in response, but Rome seemed unable to process it. He turned and blinked. Instead of his horse, there was a carriage there, the driver looking at him with worried eyes.

"That's not my horse," he said.

"It will do," Quyloc replied, and guided him to it.

"Maybe just this once," Rome said, and let himself be helped into it. There was the slap of reins, the voice of the driver, and the carriage took him away.

"Lady?"

Bonnie opened the door and saw Opus standing there, as neatly groomed as ever. He was dressed in his black livery, the wolf's head embroidered on his breast. Spotless white gloves covered his hands. His thin mustache was perfectly trimmed, his shoes shined to a high gloss. The world was ending, but Opus would face it with every hair in place.

"I'm no lady. You know that," she said.

"You are Macht Rome's lady. That is all I need to know," he replied calmly.

Bonnie put her hands on her hips. "Well?"

"The Macht is on his way. I thought you should know."

Bonnie was instantly alarmed. She'd heard the horns blowing and knew what it meant. She would have gone down to the main gates herself, but the guards on the palace gates wouldn't let her leave, telling her it was the macht's orders. "What happened? Is he okay?"

Opus held up one white-gloved hand. "He is fine. Only…a little drained."

But Bonnie was already pushing past him, heading down the hall, holding up her skirts in one hand so she could move faster. Opus hurried to catch up. He was shorter than she was. "What do you mean, drained?" she demanded as he caught up to her.

"He let a *sulbit* feed on him."

Bonnie gave him a sharp look. "He let a *sulbit* feed on him? How do you know this?"

"Lady Bonnie, it is my job to know. I have those who keep me informed. And they have informed me he is on his way here…" He trailed off, giving her a sideways look. "In a carriage."

That surprised Bonnie. "A carriage? But Rome won't ride in a…" Now it was her turn to trail off. "That's why you came to get me."

"I thought it best."

"Thank you," she said simply, touching him on the arm. They walked in silence then. In truth, Bonnie was glad for something to do. She'd spent the whole afternoon pacing Rome's chambers, fretting. A lot of the time she'd spent questioning her decision to move to the palace. She felt so useless and out of place here. She didn't know anyone. There was nothing to clean. Opus' staff saw to that. The Grinning Pig wasn't exactly homey, but it was the closest she had to a home.

They moved into the main palace halls and she noticed that there were quite a lot of servants hurrying about, sweeping, dusting, carrying linens. There were workmen as well. A small team of them were working on an arch, chipping old paint off it, readying it for a new coat. It struck her as odd.

"What's going on?" she asked Opus.

Opus made a negligent gesture as though it were nothing, though the whole time his eyes were moving, surveying the servants and workmen like a general inspecting his troops. "Merely some cleaning and overdue repairs."

"In the middle of a siege?"

Opus gave her another sideways look and a tiny shake of his head. At the next intersecting hallway, he led her to the right. This hall was deserted. When they were out of earshot of the servants he said, "Everybody's scared. Give them time to think on it and the whole lot of them…" He made a fluttering motion with his hand.

"Oh." Bonnie looked at Opus with new eyes. "I see."

A few minutes later they were at the front doors of the palace. A carriage was just pulling up. Rome was inside, slumped against the door, his eyes closed. Her heart opened up when she saw him and she ran to the carriage, was pulling at the handle before it stopped.

Rome sat up and blinked at her. A smile split his bearded face. "I fall asleep and wake up to an angel. No one could be luckier than me."

Bonnie wanted to kiss him. Instead she took hold of his arm and helped him down from the carriage. He leaned heavily on her. "What were you thinking anyway?" she asked, a bit more sharply than she intended.

"I can't ask my people to do it if I'm not willing to."

"And what good will you be for your people if you can't stand up?"

"What difference does it make? There's nothing I can do anyway."

There was something in his voice she'd never heard before and she searched his eyes, afraid suddenly. "I don't believe that, and neither do you."

"I don't know what I believe anymore." Unable to meet her eyes, he turned his face away. It was something she'd never seen him do.

"Are you okay?" she asked him.

"I don't know."

Not knowing what else to say, she asked, "The barrier is holding then?"

"For now." He looked like he was about to say something else, but Bonnie was suddenly aware of too many people nearby, listening. She took him by the arm and led him away before he could get started. She led him back to their rooms and closed the door firmly behind them. Rome walked across the room, unbelted the black axe and dropped it on the table. Then he flopped down in a chair with a sound like a groan and closed his eyes.

"They'll find a way past it. Eventually they're going to come in. There's nothing we can do."

Bonnie pulled up a chair and sat down beside him. She took one of his hands in hers.

"I'm sorry," Rome said, opening his eyes. He touched her stomach gently. "I wanted to raise a child with you."

"Don't be so sure we won't."

He slumped back in the chair. "I'm sure."

She was suddenly angry. She came to her feet, her fists on her hips. "Then we'll die!" she snapped at him. "But don't apologize. Not for something you can't control."

He looked up at her, his gaze haunted. Then he looked away. "You don't know…I never told you."

"No, I don't know. Tell me." Her words were sharper than she'd intended, but she couldn't seem to stop them.

"This is all my fault. I never listen, I just charge ahead and now…and now…"

"What are you talking about? What's your fault?"

Rome put his face in his hands. "Quyloc told me not to do it. I should have listened to him. I never do."

She knelt beside him. "You're not making any sense."

"I pulled it out of the wall. That's what made the prison crack. I didn't know what it was, just a weird thing sticking out of a wall, but Quyloc knew. He said no, but I did it anyway. I brought this on. I've killed you both. I've killed everybody."

The despair and self-hatred in his voice hurt to listen to. Bonnie felt tears in her eyes. She tried to pull him to her, but he resisted. "What are you talking about? What was sticking out of a wall?"

Rome gestured vaguely at the black axe.

"That was stuck in the wall of the prison? *Melekath's* prison?"

Rome nodded. "When I pulled it out, I cracked the prison. That's how Melekath and his Children were able to escape. I should have listened to Quyloc, but I wanted it so badly. I wanted revenge on King Rix and I ignored everything else."

There was nothing for Bonnie to say. She knelt there beside him, clinging to his arm, afraid they would both drown.

NINETEEN

Netra heard the cheering and felt the pressure inside her ease as the Children retreated, but she was too tired to stand up and see for herself. Instead she just sat there with her eyes closed, leaning against the battlements, wrestling with the mix of relief and shame that roiled within her.

What did I do to those soldiers? Are they all dead?

She felt hollow, empty.

She felt hungry.

She tried to focus on Shorn. She did it for him. She would do anything for him. She could still vividly picture that moment when he went down under that mob of Children. She'd been sure he was going to die and she just lost it. The thought of him dying—the one bit of stability in a world gone crazy—pushed her over the edge.

She still wasn't entirely sure what it was she did. It had all happened so fast.

She remembered that from *beyond* she'd *seen* the scabbed-over *akirmas* of the Children converging on him. His alien *akirma* held against them for a moment, but it was soon pierced in numerous areas and his Heartglow began to flicker dangerously.

That was when it happened. She would have unflinchingly given every scrap of Selfsong within her to save him, but she knew instinctively that it wouldn't be enough, that the Children would consume it as fast as she gave it to him.

But hers was not the only Song in the area.

Aided by the hunger that lurked always inside her, she'd simply reached out and *taken* it. She'd ripped it away and dumped it into Shorn.

She'd saved Shorn's life, but at what price?

She opened her eyes, fearing she would see herself surrounded by the shrunken husks of her victims. Soldiers pointing their weapons at her, faces filled with mixed hatred and fear.

But there were no bodies. She saw a soldier being helped down the stairs, and one who was unconscious being carried, but no bodies.

A vast sense of relief rolled over her.

She was trying to stand up when someone approached.

"You want a hand?"

She looked up and saw a soldier, an older man with curly brown hair and a leathery face, bending over her, his hand outstretched.

She looked at his hand, surprised. Had she heard him right? The hand wasn't withdrawn. Cautiously, she reached out. "Yes. Yes, I would."

He pulled her to her feet. Her legs were unsteady and she had to hold onto his arm to stay up. "Let me help you down the steps. They're steep and we wouldn't want you pitching off the edge. It's a nasty fall."

"Why are you helping me?" she asked.

"You're on our side, aren't you?" He sounded confused by her question.

"But…after what I did."

He stopped and looked at her. "Honestly, I don't know *what* you did. But I guess it was no more than you had to."

"I could have killed those men."

"True," he conceded.

"Aren't you afraid?"

"Yep. But it's not you I'm afraid of." He hooked his thumb over his shoulder. "It's them. C'mon now. Let's get you off this wall."

Still holding her arm, he guided her over to the top of the stairs and there he stopped once again. She followed his gaze and saw he was looking at Rome, kneeling before the FirstMother. Her *sulbit* was bent over his hand.

"I don't see how what you did is any different from that," he said. "Except some of who've given to those things have died." He shrugged. "It's war. People die in war. If they didn't, we'd have to call it something else."

But do we have to become like those we're fighting against?

The words were on her lips, but she kept them in. She couldn't bear to say them aloud. She couldn't bear to acknowledge her fear out loud. Because the truth was that she was not so different from the Children. She could steal someone's life and she didn't even need to touch them to do it. The difference was that for them it was a compulsion, while for her it was a choice.

The soldier helped her down the stairs. Netra let go of his arm and discovered that she could stand on her own.

He looked her over. "You're not going to make it far on your own. I'll get you a ride." He walked away before she could respond.

She stood there, weaving slightly. People, soldiers mostly, hurried around her, going about their various duties. It seemed to her that they were all giving her a wide berth. She suddenly felt very alone.

The soldier returned. Behind him came an old man leading a pony pulling a small cart, of the sort used to haul firewood or vegetables about the city. "I'm sorry," the soldier apologized. "This is all I can find."

"It's fine, really." She felt embarrassed, ashamed even, by his solicitude. She was a fraud. The feeling grew worse when the old man pulled off his hat and touched his forehead in a gesture of respect. She wanted to run away, but she was too weak so she allowed the soldier to guide her to the back of the cart and help her in. He saluted her, the old man chirped to the pony, and the cart started away.

She sat on the back of the cart and wished the cart could just keep on going and take her far away from everything. There were a fair number of people in the streets. None of them seemed to notice her. She took some comfort from that.

At some point she felt Shorn's presence and looked up as the big warrior came jogging out of a side street. The pony sidestepped fearfully as he came running up, but the old man calmed it with a word and a touch on the animal's head.

"I was scared," she said, close to crying with relief. "I thought you were…you were going to…" She couldn't say the words.

"How many died?"

She flinched before his words. His voice sounded accusatory. "None. I think."

"And you? How are you now?"

She lowered her head. "I'm okay." She could feel his eyes on her. She took a deep breath. "I'm hungry. But it is under control, I promise you."

"Are you sure?"

Suddenly she was angry. She looked up at him. "Why are you doing this? I saved your life. Doesn't that count for something?"

"It does," he said. "But not if the price is losing you."

Her anger evaporated. "I'm afraid, Shorn, and I'm so tired."

He put his hand on her shoulder. "I do not think this will last much longer."

His words chilled her, but they were no more than what was already in her heart.

The cart stopped outside the gates to the Tender estate and before Netra could move Shorn had picked her up out of the cart. "Put me down, Shorn," she told him. "I don't need to be carried."

At first she thought he was going to ignore her, but then he set her down reluctantly. She thanked the old man and, followed closely by Shorn, walked through the gates. The guards stared at them, but neither said anything. Word of how Shorn had fought Heram singlehandedly was going to spread fast throughout the city.

The sun had set and Netra stopped on the broad carriage way, wondering where she should go. She'd seen the barracks where most of the Tenders slept, but no one had actually told her she could stay there.

Then Cara came hurrying up. "Oh, I'm so glad you're safe!" she exclaimed, throwing her arms around Netra. "I was going to come looking for you." She pulled back and took in Netra's haggard look. "What happened? Are you okay?"

"I don't know. I need to sit down. I need to rest. I don't want to see anyone right now."

"I have just the place," Cara said, taking her hand. She led her to the back of the estate. Set just back in the trees was a small hut. Cara opened the door of the hut and pulled out two old, wooden chairs. Netra sat down gratefully. Cara looked at the other chair and then at Shorn, a doubtful look on her face. "I'm not sure if it will hold you, Shorn, but you are welcome to it. I don't have anything else."

Shorn shook his head and walked off a short way, where he sat down with his back against a tree trunk.

Cara pulled the chair close to Netra and sat down. "What happened?"

Netra leaned back and rubbed her eyes. "Heram was breaking down the gates, but the FirstMother didn't have the barrier up yet. So Shorn jumped down off the wall and attacked him. But there were too many of them. They almost killed Shorn. I thought they were going to. I lost control…" Her words trailed off.

"Are you saying *you* were able to stop the Children somehow?"

"No. That's not it. I gave Shorn some extra Song, enough that he could fight them off."

"I don't understand. You *gave* him Song? How?"

"I don't exactly know," Netra admitted. "It was something like what happens in healing, but it was more than that."

"So you shared *your* Song with him?"

Netra didn't want to talk about this. She knew where it would lead. She just wanted to sleep. But she also needed to let it out and Cara deserved to know the truth about her. "No. I took…I took from the soldiers around me and gave that to him."

Cara's eyes grew very wide. "Where in the world did you learn to do that?"

"It's just something I learned along the way. I've been through a lot since I left the Haven."

"You didn't take enough to kill them I hope?"

"I don't think so."

Then Cara reacted in an unexpected way. Her eyes grew very bright and she leaned closer.

"This is amazing!"

"What?"

"You just proved what Ricarn has been saying all along. She keeps telling me that Tenders don't need *sulbits* to manipulate Song. We don't need anything. The ability is naturally within us." Cara squeezed her arm. "And it proves what I've been saying all along: You're special. I always knew you were special. I always knew—"

Netra cut her off. The words were like knives. "Stop. Please don't say that."

"Say what? The truth? You *are* special."

"I'm not special. Really, I'm not."

"But you are!" Cara cried. "Why, even with their *sulbits* I bet—"

"Stop saying that!" Netra snapped, more harshly than she'd intended.

Cara sat back, dismay on her face. "Why…what's wrong?"

Netra bit her lip. She wanted to say nothing, because she knew that once she started, she wouldn't be able to stop the words from pouring out of her. "Because believing that I'm special is what caused all this." Her voice broke and she angrily fought the tears that threatened. "I believed I was chosen by the Mother. I believed that I was her champion. That's why we're all in danger right now. Because I was arrogant and stupid and…" She had to pause to get control of herself. "It would have been better if Tharn had killed me at Treeside."

"How can you say that?" Cara's look was one of total confusion. "I don't understand why you would say that."

Netra looked down at the ground, trying to get up the courage to say the words. "I freed Melekath," she said in a small voice, wrapping her arms around herself.

"You…" Cara frowned, unable to wrap herself around the idea. "You *freed* Melekath?" She swallowed visibly. "How is that even possible?"

"I broke the prison. It was cracked, but he couldn't get out until I took hold of a trunk line and I used the power within it. It's because of me that Melekath and his Children are free. All those people in Thrikyl, they're all dead because of me."

Cara shook her head. "No. I still don't believe it. No one could do that."

And then Netra told her the rest of the story in a rush of words and emotions. How everywhere she turned she saw only death and destruction until she thought she might go mad from it. Then the final straw came when she arrived at the Haven and found Siena and Brelisha killed by Tharn.

"I went crazy when I found them," Netra said. "That's when I really began to hate." Her voice took on an edge. The hatred was not gone. "The next day I met Jolene. She told me of her visions. She was convinced that Xochitl was being kept prisoner by Melekath." More anger filled her. Some at Melekath, most at herself. "That's when I knew *I* had to free her. And why did I believe that?" she asked mockingly. "Because I was convinced that I was special. *I* was the chosen one. *I* was the one who would save Xochitl so that she could save the world."

Shorn had stood up, and looked like he might approach the two women, but then he stayed where he was, watching.

"I still don't see how you were able to take hold of a trunk line," Cara said.

"I did it with stolen Song." Netra was shaking now. She drove her fingernails into the palms of her hands, trying to use the pain to get hold of herself. "I'm no better than the Children."

"You stole Song?"

"The first time was on the Plateau. I took some from a deer. I did it to save Shorn. After I met Jolene and started heading for the prison I stole some more, just animals at first. I told myself it couldn't be helped, that sacrifices had to be made for the greater good."

"Only animals *at first*?" Cara had her hand over her mouth.

"I found a Crodin camp at the edge of the Gur al Krin. I drained them. Every one of them." Netra was panting. She couldn't bear to look into her friend's eyes, knowing what she would see there. "That time I didn't even bother to justify what I'd done. I did it because I was crazy and because it felt good. I *liked* it. I still do."

Cara had pulled back and Netra was perversely glad of it. She didn't want Cara stained by what she'd done. At the same time, she felt as if her heart would break. More than anyone else in the world, she cared what Cara thought of her.

Shorn took a step closer, then hesitated, indecision on his rough features.

Netra risked a glance at Cara and was surprised at what she saw. Cara no longer had her hand over her mouth. She was sitting up very straight and there was pain in her eyes, pain *for* Netra. Where was the revulsion? Where was the condemnation?

Netra got to her feet and loomed over Cara, grim and terrible. "Don't you understand? I *killed* an entire camp. I drank them dry and I left them dead." She spoke the words harshly, lashing Cara with them, wanting to drive her away and at the same time crying out for her to stay.

Still Cara didn't look away. She didn't wring her hands. She didn't cry. She just stared up at Netra.

"Then I used the life I had stolen from them and I broke the prison. I freed Melekath and the Children. *I* did it. *Me*. Now you know. Do you still think I'm special?"

All three of them hung there then, frozen in some terrible tableau. Netra waited for what had to come next. Cara would pull back from her in horror. It was only what she deserved.

But Cara refused to cooperate. She stood. She started to pull at the braid that was no longer there, then dropped her hands to her sides.

"No. You're not special."

Netra felt herself collapsing inside. She thought she might fall down. So much depended on Cara.

"You're just Netra. My oldest, dearest friend."

Netra put her hand on the chair, trying to keep herself upright.

"You made terrible mistakes. People have died. More will die."

Netra sagged down onto the chair. It was too much. She could not survive this.

Cara moved closer, and put her hand on her shoulder. "You're my oldest, dearest friend," she repeated. "Nothing can change that. I can't imagine what you went through. So I wouldn't dare to judge you. All I can do is keep saying that you're my friend and I love you." She took hold of Netra's chin and turned her face up. "I forgive you, Netra. I forgive you for being lost and afraid and desperate. I forgive you for being human."

Then she knelt and drew Netra into a hug. She did not let go for a long time.

TWENTY

"So what is your plan?" Heram demanded. Darkness was falling. Reyna had a small hand mirror that she'd recovered from a wagon with a broken axle that had been abandoned beside the road and she was staring into it. A few of the Children huddled miserably nearby. The rest were wandering around near the city gates. Now and then one of them tested the barrier and yelped in pain. They were watched warily by a handful of soldiers on top of the wall.

"See the river over there?" She pointed. A line of trees—except near the city walls, where they'd been cut down—marked the banks of the Cron River as it exited the city and made a lazy curve through the countryside before dumping into the sea.

Heram looked at the river, then back to her, no comprehension showing on his face. "So?"

"How does it get under the wall?"

He swung his head—he had very little neck so turning his head required turning most of his body—back to look at the river again. "There is an opening under the wall." He started to go take a closer look, but she stopped him.

"Don't go over there right now, you idiot."

He glared at her.

"If you go now, while it's still light, they'll get suspicious. Maybe put up a barrier?" she said, exasperated. Was there anything besides muscle in that thick head of his?

"We wait. Hit them after dark."

"Exactly. They won a small victory this afternoon. We'll let them celebrate it. Let them think that maybe they will survive this."

"I can't wait anymore," one of the nearby Children said plaintively. "I'm so hungry."

Reyna ignored her. "We'll wait until after midnight, when most of them are asleep." She went back to looking in the mirror. She'd been

117

working on her face for the past half hour and she was quite pleased with the results. Her lips were red and full. Her eyes were larger now, tilted, with an almost feline look to them. Her teeth were longer, sharper, her cheekbones more pronounced. She wanted to do more, but the light was failing.

"How do you know there isn't a barrier there too?" Heram asked.

"Because I have a brain, that's why!" she snapped. She couldn't wait until she had no more use for this idiot and could rid herself of him. "If they had a barrier up, we'd be able to feel it." What passed for a brow on his lumpy face furrowed as he struggled to follow her. She gestured at the front gates. "Focus. Can't you *feel* the barrier there? Can't you *hear* it?"

After a moment he nodded. "It's like a swarm of hornets in the distance."

"*That's* how I know there isn't one blocking the river entrance."

He looked over at the river, then back at the city wall. "It could take time to break through. We need a distraction. Some attack there." He pointed with a thick finger at the main gate. "While we go in by the river."

She had to admit that wasn't a bad idea. To herself anyway. She didn't have to admit anything to this walking lump of stupid. "Fine. We'll do that. You pick the ones for the distraction. I'll let you know when it's time."

He turned back to her. His face betrayed none of his thoughts. Maybe he didn't have any. That would explain why he'd survived the prison so much better than most of the others. It was their thoughts that drove them mad. "It must be terrible for you," he said slowly.

"What is?"

"That you still need me." He reached out and flicked one of her long, red tresses. "Maybe you should have spent more power on muscle, less on this junk."

"Don't touch me!" she hissed. "Don't ever touch me!"

"We will see, I guess." His face was as flat and blank as ever.

"There is nothing to see. Muscle or no, I am far more powerful than you. You should be thinking about how you will placate me, rather than angering me further."

He rubbed his broad jaw and said again, "We will see."

"Quit saying that."

"They fear you," he said, gesturing at the other Children. "But they hate you more."

His words chilled her. Reyna had to struggle to make sure her sudden fear didn't show on her face. "If I even think you are rousing them against me, I will destroy you first. Be sure you understand that. Whatever else happens, you will not survive it."

He nodded. "We will see."

"It's time. Are you going to explain your brilliant plan to them, or do you want me to?" Reyna asked Heram. It was an hour after midnight. The city was quiet.

"I'm not sure," he replied. "Maybe I'm too stupid."

"We both know the answer to that."

"I will try." Earlier Heram had told those Children who could still move to gather and wait for his orders. Now he stumped over to where they were waiting. Excited murmuring rose from them. They knew something was about to happen, but not what it was. Heram named a dozen names, then said, "Dubron, you lead them over to the main gates. Give us a few minutes to get into place, then attack the barrier."

"What?" Dubron demanded. "Why?"

"Because I told you to," Heram growled. Dubron subsided, but some of the others whose names had been called continued to complain.

"I'm not going to do it," Karrl said. He hadn't fed in some time. Large flaps of his newly-grown skin were peeling off, showing gray underneath.

"Me either," Linde, his wife, said. "I'm going with everyone else." She and her husband moved over to stand with the larger group.

Heram made no reply. He simply charged them. They shrieked and tried to run but they weren't fast enough. He picked the two of them up by their necks, dragged them over to Dubron's group, bashed their heads together twice and threw them on the ground, where they lay whining and moaning.

"Anyone else unhappy?" Heram asked. There was no reply. "Now go. Hit the barrier hard, so they believe it is a new attack."

Reluctantly, the ones Heram had chosen moved off in the direction of the gates, arguing amongst themselves. Linde slapped Karrl and he cursed at her.

"You have quite a way with words," Reyna said. Heram grunted.

The rest of the Children followed Reyna and Heram excitedly. One of them began talking loudly. Heram turned and growled at him. "Shut up." He did.

119

They entered the line of trees bordering the river and moved through them toward the wall, stopping when they reached the area where the trees had been cut back. They were still a couple hundred paces from the wall and there was no cover to approach closer. Torches flickered on top of the wall, illuminating the sentries. Near the wall, the banks of the river were steep and rocky. The grate the river flowed through was dimly visible. It was made of thick interwoven bars of iron set into stone.

"Do you think you can rip that out?" Reyna asked.

In answer, Heram flexed his thick shoulders and cracked his knuckles.

Several minutes later there were yells from the distance, followed by flickers of light and cries of pain as Children threw themselves at the barrier. On top of the wall, the sentries began to move that way, weapons in their hands. Soon there were only two left, both turned toward the disturbance at the front gates.

"I have to get closer," she whispered. "Wait here." She crept forward along the bank of the river, feeling surprisingly exposed. Again and again the defenders had proven they were not helpless. What other defenses did they possess? Were they readying an attack even then?

One of the sentries froze, as he caught movement from the corner of his eye. He turned, hesitated, not sure what he was seeing in the poor light.

His hesitation cost him his life.

Reyna ran forward, throwing up her hands as she did so. Gray-white webs shot from her palms and struck the men. A yank and they were dragged over the battlements, hitting the ground with solid thumps. The other Children rushed forward, drawn to the two fallen soldiers like moths to a flame.

Reyna was just finishing off the soldiers when the first of the Children fell on them. Reyna released the webs and they dissolved into nothing almost instantly. Then for a moment she just stood there, basking in the feel of the Song coursing through her. Truly, nothing else could ever compare with this feeling.

Heram reached the wall and slid down the river back. He walked out to the grate and stood in the swirling waters of the river like a boulder. He took hold of the thick bars and set his feet.

Reyna reached the river and splashed down into it, a handful of the Children right behind her.

Heram began to pull. At first nothing happened. He reset his feet and pulled again, the muscles knotting and bunching under his red skin.

All at once the grate gave way with a squeal of metal and cracking stone. Heram turned and threw the grate to the side with a grunt.

The underbelly of Qarath lay open.

TWENTY-ONE

Treylen was jolted out of his sleep the instant Heram set foot in the Cron River. He straightened, every sense coming alert. He was sitting on one of the low footbridges that spanned the river, not far from the wall, his feet dangling in the water. He'd been there since sunset, certain the Children would try this way into the city and determined to be ready. Yet still he'd somehow managed to fall asleep, not even awakening when the Children attacked the barrier at the main gates. It took Heram's presence in the river to awaken him.

Another shock traveled through the water, stronger even than the one caused by Heram. This one was almost painful. He knew instantly it was Reyna. A normal person wouldn't have felt either shock, but Treylen wasn't normal. He was a Sounder, part of an ancient, nearly extinct order dedicated to the Sea and its denizens. He'd kept his allegiance hidden his whole life: the people of Atria feared and distrusted the ocean and those who worshipped it were not well treated.

Another shock, then a dozen more in short order. All of them drawing closer. He'd been right about the attack.

He wished he'd been wrong.

There wasn't much time. From inside his coat he fumbled out a hollow, wooden tube, about as long as his arm and as big around as his thumb, nearly dropping it in the process. He put one end in the water. From a pocket he took a reddish fossil that looked like an eel curled into a tight ball, its tail in its mouth. With the fossil, he began tapping on the tube. He tapped, paused. Tapped. Paused. A short, repeating pattern.

By then Heram had reached the gate and was tightening his muscles. All this the water told Treylen. The water told him a great deal, attuned to it as he was. With one finger in the water he could sense the presence of a person standing in the water miles away, could tell if the person was male or female, even sense emotions, if they were strong enough.

The rage and madness coming off Heram was strong enough to leave a foul taste in Treylen's mouth and cold fear in his chest. He tapped faster, with more urgency. Where were they?

They weren't going to answer. They'd fled.

Heram tugged on the iron grate. The stone cracked.

Still there was no answer from the *li-shlikti*, the creatures that dwelled in the water, mostly in the sea. For them the rivers were too confining. The *li-shlikti* were not creatures born of Life. They were lesser Shapers, of the Sphere of Sea. For days Treylen had been calling to them, warning them of the danger posed by the Children, danger that would eventually reach them. He didn't know if they were listening, but he kept trying anyway. What other choice did he have?

Heram yanked again on the grate and suddenly the stone holding it in place broke away. He tossed the grate aside.

Treylen scrambled to his feet, adrenalin pumping. In the dimness under the wall he could just see a dark, bulky shape coming through. Other shapes crowded behind.

Treylen ran off the bridge. On the bank he stopped and looked back. Every instinct told him to run, but he knew it would do no good. If the Children got in now, no place in the city would be safe. There were shouts from the top of the wall and the sound of running soldiers, but they were too late. The Children had breached the wall and Qarath would fall.

Heram emerged from beneath the wall and straightened. His bulk nearly blocked the opening. He looked bigger close up than he had from a distance, masses of slab-like muscle covered in reddish skin. Heram looked around and when his eyes fell on him, suddenly Treylen realized how quickly he would die.

Heram waded toward him. Other Children spilled out behind him, led by the tall, red-haired one.

On legs that felt like dead stumps, Treylen began to back away. He saw the red-haired one raise one hand toward him and felt the power within her gather.

The water in the river suddenly rose. At the same time, the water around Heram's feet began to boil madly. He looked down in confusion. The disturbance spread until it surrounded all the Children. Several cried out. There were dim shapes in the water, pale blue and silver, long and slim like eels.

Treylen almost cried out in relief. The *li-shlikti* had come.

The *li-shlikti* raced faster and faster, racing in circles around the Children, more of them arriving every second. Heram bellowed his rage and slapped at the things as they wrapped around his legs, but they had no real physical form, being creatures of the water, and his blows had no effect. He grabbed at them, tried to yank them off him, but there was nothing to grab onto.

Heram turned to the nearest river bank, realizing he had to get out of the water. More of the *li-shlikti* swarmed over him, wrapping around his torso, several getting onto his arms. Reyna was yelling, stabbing at the water with bolts of power, none of which had any effect. The other Children added their impotent yelps as they were engulfed by the creatures.

The river rose higher, becoming a raging flood, though upstream from the Children it was as low and placid as ever. Being smaller and weaker, the rest of the Children succumbed quickly. The *li-shlikti* covered them completely, binding their legs together, pinning their arms to their sides. Unable to maintain their balance, the Children began to topple over and were soon swept away, disappearing under the wall.

Reyna held out a little longer, but it wasn't long before she fell over and was swept away too.

Heram made it almost to the riverbank before he could go no further. He stood there, bent at the waist, every muscle engaged as he fought to break their grip on his legs and take that final step. The river raged around him as scores of *li-shlikti* wrapped around his entire body except for his head.

Heram turned his head and fixed Treylen with his cold gaze. "Still this won't stop me," he said.

Heram toppled over. More of the creatures swarmed over him and, slowly at first, then with gathering speed, he was dragged back to the opening under the wall. Just before he disappeared under it, he got one huge hand free and grabbed the bottom of the wall. There he hung, his great strength too much for the creatures to overcome.

Then the stone he was holding tore away and Heram was flushed under the wall.

Treylen walked into the river—the flood was already beginning to recede—and stood there with his eyes closed, reading the currents. He felt it as the Children were dragged out into the sea, then out to the deep water, and sucked down.

With dismay he realized that the *li-shlikti* were already loosing their holds on the Children and swimming away. Treylen could feel their pain and confusion and he went cold inside as he realized something:

The *li-shlikti* had to let go because the Children were absorbing Sea force from them.

Treylen slumped to the ground, exhausted. How long he sat there he did not know, but at some point people walked up to him, carrying lanterns. He looked up and saw Macht Rome, Quyloc and the FirstMother looking down at him.

"What happened here?" Rome asked him.

Treylen tried to stand, then gave it up. "They broke in, but I called the *li-shlikti* and they dragged them away. They're in the sea now."

"You did what?" Rome asked.

"He's a Sounder," the FirstMother said.

"What is a Sounder?" Rome asked.

"They worship the Sea," Quyloc added.

Treylen wanted to correct him. His kind didn't worship the sea. They felt an affinity for it. It was not the same thing. But he was too tired.

"I thought they were all gone," the FirstMother said. "Our order hunted them mercilessly during the days of the Empire."

"You didn't get us all," Treylen said, finding a bit of defiance left in him.

Rome was looking at the gap under the wall. There were soldiers on top of the wall, talking excitedly. "It's a good thing they didn't," he said. "You just saved us all."

"This is my home too," Treylen said.

"We need to talk some more," Rome said. "Once you're recovered. You look ready to drop. For now though, you have my gratitude for what you did here tonight." He extended his hand and helped Treylen to his feet. "Get a cart over here and help this man to his home," he ordered.

"One more thing," Treylen said. "The Children…they hurt the ones I called to help."

Rome blinked at him, not understanding, but Quyloc got it. "They can absorb power from the Sphere of Sea now too."

"Mother preserve us," Nalene whispered.

TWENTY-TWO

It was predawn the next morning when Cara arose. Though she moved quietly, Netra woke up almost immediately and sat up. She'd slept on the floor in Cara's hut, Shorn sleeping outside.

"You should go back to sleep," Cara said.

"Where are you going?"

"I lead the morning services," Cara said, casting her eyes down.

"You do? For the other Tenders?"

"No. For the whole city. Those who are interested anyway."

Netra got up, rubbing her eyes and trying to process this new information. "You lead services for the whole city?"

Cara shrugged modestly. "It's nothing, really. The FirstMother just has me do them because she's too busy since she got back."

"That's not true at all," a new voice said. "They're not nothing. Her services are beautiful, that's what they are."

They both turned. A Tender was standing in the doorway. She was a bit odd looking, one shoulder lower than the other, an unusual cast to her eyes. Those eyes looked angry right then.

"Oh, Adira," Cara said. "How long have you been standing there?"

"Long enough." Adira came into the tiny hut and stared defiantly at Netra, as if she was somehow to blame. "When she said no to the *sulbit* I hated her. But I was wrong. She's a Tender, a real Tender. Like the olden days."

"I agree with you," Netra said, which didn't seem to soften Adira's anger at all. She stood there looking at Netra darkly. Netra realized then that Adira had taken hold of Cara's robe and was clutching it with one hand. Without saying anything, Cara pulled her robe away from the woman.

"What do you want, Adira?" Cara asked gently.

Adira turned, blinked at her. "It's time for morning services."

"I'd like to come too," Netra said.

"Are you sure?" Cara asked. "Shouldn't you rest?"

"I've rested enough. I want to see you lead the service."

"Well, okay," Cara said reluctantly and turned toward the door.

But Adira didn't move. She just stood there staring at Netra in that unnerving way she had. Finally, she said, "What makes you so special?"

That surprised Netra. Surprised her and made her feel a little guilty for some reason, as if Adira had said something aloud that Netra didn't want others hearing. "I don't know what you're talking about."

"Cara talks about you all the time. She thinks you're special." Adira squinted at her. "You don't look special to me."

Netra shook her head. "I'm not. Not really."

"Cara is. She's special." Adira said it like a challenge, almost daring Netra to gainsay her.

Netra looked at her old friend, steady, loyal, loving. "You're right."

That didn't seem to placate Adira at all. Her scowl never lessened. But she did step aside.

When they left the hut they found Ricarn standing there. She was staring at Shorn, who had taken a position near the wall of the hut, and was staring at her. Without looking away from Shorn she said, "Melekath created all life. On *this* world. But you are not of this world. This raises very interesting questions. How, and why, did life rise elsewhere?" Her eyes glittered. "It makes me wonder if the Shapers were sent here to do just that."

Shorn returned her stare without speaking.

"Netra, this is Ricarn," Cara said. "She is of the Arc of Insects."

Ricarn turned toward Netra. Her silver stare bore deep into Netra so that the young woman felt curiously exposed. She wanted to step back or look away, but she felt frozen to the spot. The moments ticked by while Ricarn bored deeper. Then the intensity of her stare faded. Netra sagged, feeling as if she'd been released.

"You have been touched by SeaSong," Ricarn said.

"Sea contains Song?" Cara said, frowning.

"The melody is far different from that of Life, but it is Song all the same."

"I...we were taken by the Lementh'kal," Netra said, gesturing at Shorn.

"The children of Golgath. They have not interacted with humans for a very long time. The last time did not go well for us."

Netra nodded, thinking of the destruction of Kaetria.

"They have changed you," Ricarn said. She turned her head slightly to Cara. "Netra will not be at your services today. I wish to speak with her."

"Of course," Cara said. After giving Netra a quick hug, Cara walked away, trailed closely by Adira, who had once again taken hold of the edge of her robe.

Ricarn again turned her full attention on Netra, staring at her curiously as if she were some new species she had never seen before. Netra fidgeted under that stare and finally said, "Should we sit down or…?"

"I feel no need to sit," Ricarn said. "You may, if you wish."

Netra looked to Shorn for help, saw none there. He was watching Ricarn warily.

"Yesterday you drained Song from ten soldiers and used it to save his life."

So that was what this was about. "I didn't mean—"

"The Lementh'kal saw your potential. And they saw your danger." She blinked, once. "The danger you pose to everything."

"I'm not dangerous," Netra tried to say, but the words died on her lips.

"Tell me of your time with them."

So Netra did. She told Ricarn about finding the pool underneath the buried city of Kaetria, how she'd *seen* the power there and tried to tap into it. She told about being attacked and speaking to the Council. Finally, she told of Ya'Shi taking her to see the Ancient One.

"And the Ancient One? She spoke to you?"

"Sort of," Netra replied. "It really felt more like she and Ya'Shi mocked me."

"What did they say to you?" The intensity in Ricarn's gaze suddenly increased. Netra felt the shame of everything she'd done spring to the surface and she wanted to cover herself up.

"I don't remember. Exactly."

"It is important that you do. Exactly. For the Ancient One to take notice of a human, for her to go so far as to speak to you, is extremely rare. It means that she and Ya'Shi saw something in you. Something that may yet save us all."

"I don't…" Netra felt herself beginning to tremble inside. It frightened her, where this was going. It was believing she was somehow special that had brought so much suffering on. "It was mostly nonsense."

"It was only nonsense because you were not listening. You must remember."

Netra rubbed her eyes with a shaky hand. "I don't think I can."

"Don't think. Just remember."

Netra backed up, leaning against the wall of the hut. She suddenly felt dizzy and she was starting to have a headache. She squeezed her eyes shut and rubbed her temples.

"It's all there. Inside you. Just let it out."

Ricarn's words seemed to hit her with physical force. All at once Netra could see it all again, as if she were an observer watching while it all happened.

"What are they saying?" Ricarn insisted.

"They know that I broke the prison," Netra said. She was shaking. She felt unbearably tired. "They know."

"It is not important now," Ricarn said. Netra could feel her move closer. "Tell me more."

Netra watched, once again reliving the shame and horror as they exposed what she'd done. She could hear them speaking, see herself standing with her head down.

"The Ancient One says I will have to be the doorway. She says I have to stop fighting and let go, that everything I need is within me. I just have to let it happen."

"What else?"

"Ya'Shi says I have to understand who my enemy really is." With difficulty, Netra pushed herself out of the memory and opened her eyes to the real world. The day was getting brighter. Shorn was watching her with concern on his face. "That's all. There isn't any more."

Ricarn nodded and it felt to Netra like she released her from something. The Insect Tender took a step back. "What do you think this means?"

"I don't know. I've tried to figure it out but it just doesn't make sense to me."

"The Ancient One said that you are the doorway."

"But what does that *mean*? A doorway to what?"

"Perhaps a doorway back to the Circle of Life," Ricarn said. "It makes sense. Melekath's Gift removed them from the Circle. That's why their hunger can never be sated. They are cut off from the natural flows of Song. The Gift must be undone and they must be brought back into the Circle."

"But how am I supposed to be the doorway that brings them back? That makes no sense."

Just then the bells began to toll.

The Children had resumed their attack.

Ricarn looked at Shorn. "They will need you down there," she said.

Shorn looked at Netra and she nodded. "I'm going too," she said, and started to leave, but Ricarn stopped her.

"No. He goes. You stay here. We are not done speaking of this."

TWENTY-THREE

Quyloc was in his room when the bells began to ring. He picked up the *rendspear* and headed for the door. He opened it and found T'sim standing there, looking at him.

"Lowellin is gone."

"So?" Quyloc said impatiently. "He's often gone."

"This time is different."

Quyloc frowned. He had no time for this. "Why?"

"He will not return."

"He's afraid of the Children."

"Deathly so. But that is not why he is gone. His hatred is stronger than his fear. He pursues Melekath."

"Good. Maybe they will kill each other."

T'sim frowned. "I do not know if this is true."

Quyloc started to leave, then paused. "Tell me something. Aren't you afraid of the Children?" T'sim nodded. "Then why are you still here?"

T'sim seemed to consider this. "I think it is because there is nowhere to go." With that the little man turned and walked away.

Quyloc shook his head and walked down the hall. Surprisingly, considering everything that was going on, he'd slept pretty well. He actually felt pretty good.

He turned a corner, saw Rome ahead of him—dressed in full armor, the black axe strapped to his back—and hurried to catch up to him. The big man looked awful. There were pouches under his eyes and deep lines on his forehead.

"I've been thinking, Rome."

"Yeah?"

"We need to prepare for the worst."

"Isn't that what we're already doing?"

"We got lucky yesterday. Twice. If the Tenders hadn't gotten that barrier up when they did, we'd have lost the entire city. If that Sounder hadn't been where he was, we'd have lost the city."

"Believe me, I know. I spent half the night tossing in my bed, wondering where they'd come in next."

"It's only a matter of time. We've got too much wall to defend."

"What are you thinking?"

"A lot of people left the city. By my estimates we have only about ten thousand or so citizens remaining, and just over a thousand soldiers. We could fit everyone here on the palace grounds."

"It would be tight."

"It would. But we can do it. With your okay, I want to give the order to evacuate the city."

"Right now?"

"Right now."

Rome scrubbed sleep from his eyes while he thought about it. "All right," he said at last.

"A couple other things. If the Children get past the barrier, we need to pin them in the square, at least for a few minutes. Otherwise we're going to lose most of the Tenders and quite a few of our soldiers."

"Not to mention us," Rome added. "What's your plan?"

"Be prepared to use the axe to bring down the buildings on either side of the narrow street that exits the square."

"What's to stop Heram from just smashing his way directly through one of the other buildings along the square?" The buildings bordering the square had no windows on the bottom floors and the doors were iron. The square had been designed specifically to slow down invaders in the event that the gates were breached.

"We send some men into those buildings to knock out supports so that the upper floors collapse. Heram won't find it quite so easy to break through if the inside is filled with rubble."

"They'll still be able to crawl over the two buildings I drop."

"Yes, but it will buy us some time. Every little bit will help."

"Okay. I'll do it. Anything else?"

Quyloc nodded. "One more thing." They were at the front doors of the palace by then. A servant opened the doors and they walked outside. From there they could see the main gates in the palace wall. "If we have to run, we may not have time to get a new barrier erected here before Heram destroys those gates." A soldier was waiting at the bottom of the steps with their horses and the two men hurried down the steps and mounted. As they rode for the gates, Quyloc continued, "Lord Rinley has been doing some construction on his estate."

"So?"

They trotted over to the palace gates where a squad of mounted soldiers were waiting for them. As they neared the gates the stack of cut stones that Rinley was using for construction became visible, just across the wide boulevard that ringed the palace. The stones were big, nearly chest high on a man.

"Have some of these moved inside the gates," Quyloc said. "Get rigging and teams of horses set up to move them in a hurry. Once we're back inside, have them stacked up behind the gates, filling the whole space under the wall. That should slow Heram down some, if he has to hammer his way through all that extra stone."

"We'll be trapping ourselves inside."

"You know as well as I do that there's no escaping from this."

Wearily, Rome nodded. "You're right. Have it done."

Well, Quyloc thought, either he was dreaming or the world really was about to end. Because Rome just took his advice, not once, but two times in a row. Truly it was a day for miracles.

The square was buzzing with activity. Two Tenders were manning the barrier, Song flowing from their *sulbits* to it, their bodyguards standing behind them. Off to one side were a half dozen more Tenders waiting their turn. Near them were a dozen citizens, ready to share their Songs whenever *sulbits* needed recharging.

Arranged behind the barrier were three tightly packed squads of soldiers, twenty-five men in each squad. They sported pikes, their wooden shafts nearly twenty feet long, the points sheathed in metal. They'd been Tairus' idea. If the Children got in, the pikemen might be able to hold them back long enough for the rest to flee the square. It was a job none of them were likely to survive and when Tairus told the soldiers about it he said no one would be ordered to do it. It was strictly volunteers only. Nearly two hundred men had volunteered.

It had taken Rome only a few minutes to bring down all the buildings ringing the square except for the two standing on either side of the narrow street that would be their escape route. The dust from the collapsed buildings was still settling.

Standing in the middle of the square, his thick arms folded across his chest, was the huge, copper-skinned warrior Shorn.

Rome looked at the barrier. A couple of the Children were throwing themselves at it, but they didn't look to be making any headway. He headed over to Shorn. "That was pretty impressive, what you did yesterday," Rome said. Shorn looked at him without answering.

"I'm glad you're on our side." Still no answer. Rome had known statues that were more talkative.

"I've got something for you." Shorn just stared at him steadily.

"I got to thinking about how it might be a good idea if you had a weapon." Now Shorn had a dismissive look in his eyes.

"I'm not talking about any of our normal weapons. I'm thinking something more your size.' Rome turned and gestured to a couple of soldiers standing by a wagon. "Bring it over."

While they struggled to get it out of the wagon the big warrior turned toward them. When he saw what they were carrying he actually smiled slightly. At least it looked like a smile to Rome. He might have just been baring his teeth. He preferred to think of it as a smile, but he had to admit it was somewhat chilling either way. He decided right then that he'd rather face Heram than Shorn.

The item causing Shorn to smile looked a little bit like a tree trunk. But it was actually a club. Rome guessed it weighed about as much as a full-grown man, with armor. It was made of oak, and the head was sheathed in iron.

"It's not too fancy," Rome said. "We were a little short of time."

Shorn wasn't listening to him. He was walking toward the two soldiers. He met the men halfway and took the club from them. He hefted it in one hand and held it up to look at it. The soldiers fell back away from him, their eyes wide.

Shorn took the club in both hands and gave it a couple practice swings and then Rome was sure he was smiling. It really wasn't a pleasant smile.

Shorn looked at Rome and nodded once. Then the big warrior walked to the statue in the center of the square. It was a statue of some long-dead king on horseback. Surrounding the statue was a knee-high stone wall. Shorn sat down on the wall, facing the front entry, the club balanced across his knees.

"I guess he likes it," Rome said to himself. He looked around. There was no sign of the young woman who'd accompanied Shorn the day before. Rome wondered briefly where she was.

He saw Tairus on top of the wall, saying something to the soldiers, and headed that way. He was halfway across the square when the Children suddenly changed tactics and launched a new attack.

TWENTY-FOUR

Heram and Reyna stood at a distance and watched as a handful of the Children threw themselves at the barrier over and over.

"What brilliant plan do you have for us today?" Heram asked.

Reyna turned on him. "My plan almost worked. We were inside the wall. There was no way to know they could summon those *things*," she said with a suppressed shudder. A new barrier spanned the opening under the wall. None of the Children had tried its strength. It wasn't the barrier they feared, but the creatures in the water. Being dragged out to sea and pulled deep underwater had been a singularly unpleasant experience. None of them wanted to experience that again.

"Maybe you are not as smart as you think you are," Heram said.

"You think you could do better?"

"It does not seem I would do worse."

"Prove it. Come up with something better then," she hissed.

"I will," he said simply, and started for the wall.

"It won't work!" Reyna yelled after him. Then she added, "Idiot." He ignored her. The heavy ballistae tracked his movements, but they held their fire, watching to see what he would do.

Heram walked into the gateway passage and up to the Children clustered at the barrier. He grabbed one of them at random—a bent, withered little man—by the neck and picked him up. The man yelped and squirmed, but Heram ignored him. He carried him back through the passage and outside, stopping when he was a few paces from the wall. The soldiers on the wall stared down at him curiously, wondering what he was doing.

Then Heram simply threw the man. The man squawked and flew through the air, arms and legs flailing. He cleared the wall and disappeared from sight.

The other Children stared at Heram in shock, not sure what they had just seen. The soldiers stared too. For a moment no one moved, as if frozen in time.

Then a scream came from beyond the wall and the moment broke. The Children all ran toward Heram, shouting, begging to be next. Shouts came from the soldiers as they fired arrows and ballistae bolts at Heram.

The bent little man landed on a woman, one of the group of citizens waiting to share their Songs with the *sulbits*, and knocked her down. For a moment they rolled around on the cobblestones, the woman screaming. The other people backed hurriedly away.

Then he got his mouth on her arm.

A stricken look came over her face. The color leached from her with astonishing speed and she seemed to simply collapse. A few moments later she was dead and the man leapt to his feet.

He didn't look nearly as bent and withered now. The stolen Song rippled through him and his back straightened. His body filled out, a gaping wound in his side filling in.

Of the people who had been standing there, one of them, an elderly woman, hadn't moved, but was standing there frozen, her mouth open in shock. He grabbed her and jerked her to him, wrapping her in a rough embrace.

She died without making a sound and he grew stronger.

It all happened so fast.

Owina was one of the Tenders manning the barrier that morning, along with Mery, who was also a veteran of the battle at Guardians Watch. When the first Child landed in the square behind her she started to turn, but then she remembered her duties and kept her focus the barrier. The FirstMother had drummed into all of them that, no matter what happened around them, their only concern was keeping the barrier up. If they failed at that, nothing else would matter.

A scream came from behind her and her *sulbit* chittered in alarm. The Song flowing from it stuttered. From the corner of her eye she could see that Mery was having the same problem. Owina moved instantly to soothe the creature, stroking it with her free hand, whispering softly to it, both with words and silently, through the link they shared. The creature looked up at her, the expression in its shiny black eyes unfathomable. Owina continued to stroke it and whisper to it. After a moment it calmed down, Song once again flowing from it steadily.

Then another person came flying over the wall—

And landed right beside Mery.

Mery gave a little shriek and lurched to the side, banging into Owina, both of them falling down. The *sulbits* squealed at the same time, the sound high and painful to the ears, and the Song from both of them cut off.

The *sulbits* bolted.

Somehow Owina managed to get a hold of her *sulbit* before it could get away and she clung to it grimly while it continued squealing, fighting to get away.

Beside her, Mery was trying to crawl away, her *sulbit* long gone. The woman who'd come flying over the wall got a hold of Mery's ankle, but Mery jerked her foot away and kicked the woman in the face so that she lost her hold.

Owina managed to get to her feet, still fighting to hold onto her *sulbit*. Abruptly, the creature changed tactics. It swiveled its small, blunt head around and spat Song into Owina's face.

Owina staggered backwards. Her face was burning, her eyes searing pain. Blinded, she let go of her *sulbit* and clamped her hands over her eyes.

The barrier began to flicker.

Quyloc was clear on the other side of the square when the first Child came flying over the wall. Immediately he removed the leather covering on his *rendspear* and started running. As his skin came in contact with the spear the day shifted, flows of Song suddenly visible, writhing this way and that. There was a sudden flash as the man drained his first victim.

Before he could make his way through the frightened, fleeing citizens, another one of the Children came flying over the wall and landed near the barrier. Quyloc shifted direction, shouting for one of the squads of pikemen to engage the first man.

He saw one Tender struggling with her *sulbit*, saw the burst of Song it spat in her face. Blinded, she had no idea the Child at her feet was lunging for her until the woman got her mouth on the Tender's ankle and started to drain her.

Quyloc got there a split second later. The spear flashed and he stabbed the Child in the neck, causing her to scream and let go of her victim. The Tender staggered backward and collapsed in a heap. The Child reached for Quyloc, but he stabbed her in the face.

Tender guards grabbed the Tender and dragged her away.

Quyloc stabbed the writhing Child again and again, each time eliciting screams of pain.

Nalene was almost to the square when she heard the first scream. She jumped out of the carriage she was riding in and ran. She was too late; she was sure of it. She ran down the narrow street and emerged onto a square that was in chaos. A squad of pikemen were facing off against one of the Children, who was just then dropping his second victim. Ripples were running over his body; new muscle bulged everywhere. Citizens were running in panic. Quyloc was by the barrier, stabbing someone on the ground over and over. Two Tenders were being dragged back by their bodyguards. The other Tenders were standing there, paralyzed with indecision.

The barrier was flickering wildly.

Nalene's *sulbit* chittered in fear. Before it could try to escape she grabbed hold of it, stroking it, whispering to it as she ran. The link between them opened and she felt its fear as part of her own. For a moment her steps faltered as she succumbed to her *sulbit*'s desire to flee, but then she got herself under control.

Shrieking wildly, Children were flinging themselves against the barrier, over and over. The barrier crackled and popped, weakening visibly by the moment.

Nalene dodged around Quyloc and the Child on the ground and stopped before the barrier. There were holes visible in it now. A Child got his hand through the barrier, his fingers opening and closing spastically as he reached for her.

Cradling her *sulbit* in her arms, Nalene crooned to it, urging it to release the energy it held within it. At first the thing hid its face in the crook of her elbow and she felt panic rising within her. The barrier looked like an old cobweb now, thin and tattered. Two more Children got arms through it.

"Come on," she whispered. "Come on."

Another of the Children came flying over the wall. The Child Quyloc was battling spun away from him and got a hold of one of the terrified citizens and began draining him, ignoring Quyloc's attacks. Disaster loomed.

Then all at once Nalene's *sulbit* opened its mouth. A stream of Song, small at first, but growing steadily larger, flowed from it and into the barrier.

The barrier began to solidify once again. Cries of pain came from the Children on the other side of it. Two of the arms thrust through it withdrew, but the third was not so fortunate. The holes in the barrier snapped closed all at once and the arm was severed and fell on the cobblestones.

TWENTY-FIVE

Rome started running for the wall as soon as the first Child came flying over and landed in the square. Looking up, he saw the soldiers swiveling the ballistae to take aim at Heram. The weapons twanged and the heavy iron bolts shot out. There was an angry shout from beyond the wall; at least one had flown true.

Quickly soldiers began cranking the winches to cock the ballistae as others set new bolts into place.

Then they just froze.

Rome reached the top of the wall and ran to the closest ballista, pushing the soldier manning it out of the way when he got there and taking his place. He was bringing the weapon to bear when a heavy coldness settled on his limbs. He began to tremble and he had to take hold of the ballista to keep himself upright. With a great effort he turned his head and looked over the battlements.

Reyna was standing there, less than a stone's throw away. Her arms were flung out and up and she was yelling something. The air was blurry around her. Rome realized right away what she was doing.

She was sucking the life out of every soldier on the wall. The only reason no one had collapsed yet was because her attack was spread over a large area, instead of being focused on one person.

Gritting his teeth, Rome managed to turn the ballista toward Heram, who was in the process of tossing yet another of the Children over the wall. Grunting with effort, he aimed and fired the weapon.

The massive iron bolt flew true and struck Heram hard enough that he staggered to the side. The Child he was throwing flew short, slamming into the wall about halfway up, bouncing off and falling heavily.

But there was no way Rome could possibly reload. He managed to take another bolt from the rack and set it into place, but he didn't have the strength necessary to crank the winch to cock the weapon. He slumped against the weapon, cursing impotently at the muscles which betrayed him.

The first man who had been thrown over the wall was huge now, half again as tall as a normal man, swollen with stolen Song. Gray skin was falling off him in huge chunks, revealing fresh, pink skin underneath. Muscles bulged everywhere. His proportions were wrong, one leg noticeably thicker than the other, one shoulder hugely bunched with muscle while the other looked almost normal size, and his face was weirdly puffed, proof that his control over the stolen Song was limited. He dropped his second victim, so full of power that he was nearly glowing. He threw his head back and howled with ecstasy.

Shorn hit him right at that moment. The huge club came whistling around and hit the man so hard his neck snapped with an audible crack and he was thrown backwards and down. He sat up, his head flopping to one side. His lifted his head in his hands and a second later his neck had healed. He looked up at Shorn and smiled terribly, then tried to get to his feet. Shorn pressed forward, hitting him again and again, the blows lifting him into the air with the force of their impact. They were blows that could have shattered stone, but they were having no lasting effect on him. Each time he simply healed and tried to get up once more.

But Shorn had a plan.

His next blow knocked the man back against the wall, near the base of the stairs. Against the wall was a wooden rack loaded with pikes. Shorn dropped his club, grabbed two of the pikes and held them as one. The man struggled to his feet and as he straightened, Shorn stabbed him in the chest, with such force that the two pikes were driven deep into him.

He lifted the man into the air and started up the stairs. The man cursed and fought to reach Shorn but before he could do anything, Shorn had reached the top of the wall. He threw the man, pikes and all, over the edge.

That's when he realized that something was wrong. The soldiers on top of the wall were just standing there. He turned, saw Rome clinging weakly to one of the ballistae.

"It's her," Rome whispering, managing to move one finger to point at Reyna. "She's doing this."

Shorn took a spear from the nerveless fingers of one of the soldiers, planted his feet and flung it. Reyna, focused as she was on what she was doing, didn't see it coming and it took her in the chest. She screamed and staggered backwards. The blurriness around her dissipated.

Rome straightened, flexing his hands. "Nice shot," he said. "Let's see how she likes this."

Quickly he cranked the winch, shouting orders at his men as he did so. Bolts and arrows began to fly through the air and Reyna was forced to use her efforts to protect herself.

Rome swiveled the ballista and sighted on Heram. He squeezed the trigger and felt the satisfaction as the heavy bolt slammed into Heram. A second later one hit Heram from the other side and he dropped the person he was holding and retreated into the gateway passage.

Rome turned the ballista he was manning over to some soldiers and looked around. It looked like they were going to survive a while longer. Nalene had been joined by Bronwyn and the two Tenders had the barrier solid once again. A squad of pikemen had one of the remaining Children skewered on several of their pikes. The man was clawing futilely at the weapons. Quyloc was keeping the woman busy, each stab from his spear drawing another cry of pain from her. Shorn reached the bottom of the stairs, snatched up a couple of pikes and ran to get her. He came up behind her, stabbed her in the back, then ran for the stairs, while she struggled impotently.

"Macht," one of the nearby soldiers said nervously, pointing.

Rome spun.

Reyna had jerked the spear out of her chest and flung it aside. She shouted something Rome couldn't hear and began advancing, heading straight for the ruined gates.

"Hit her with everything you have!" Rome yelled.

Reyna yanked the spear out of her chest and flung it down with a curse. "That's enough," she muttered. "This ends *now*."

She was done with being cautious. She was angry. Who were these ants to stand in her way? She was Reyna and this world was *hers*. She was taking it and she was taking it now.

She heard the shouts and saw the ballistae swivel toward her. There was nothing they could do. She'd been too sparing with her power before. It was time to change that. She was like a general who'd been holding elite troops in reserve. Now it was time to commit those troops and end the battle here and now.

Reyna drew forth her power, focusing it in her hands, and they began to glow like two small suns.

Nalene heard Rome yelling from the top of the wall and knew instantly who was coming. She pushed her *sulbit* to release yet more while to Bronwyn she said, "Give it everything you have! Hold nothing back!" and felt the tall, young Tender respond. She turned her head briefly, saw a handful of Tenders standing nearby and shouted at them to come over and help.

The barrier glowed brighter as she and Bronwyn poured everything they had into it, but she knew she wouldn't be able to keep it up much longer. Sweat was pouring down her face and she was dimly aware of the taste of blood in her mouth. She shouted again at the other Tenders and two stepped forward, but the Song they were able to coax from their *sulbits* was only a trickle.

Then Reyna arrived. Nalene could feel the power radiating off her and she quailed inside. Before that power the barrier seemed like a sheet of parchment. Her *sulbit* wailed and shrank back. The Song flowing from the other two Tenders faltered, then stopped. Bronwyn's dropped to a trickle.

When Reyna hit the barrier the first time, the shock went clear down to Nalene's bones. There was a scream of tortured energy and for a second a sizable hole appeared in the barrier, revealing Reyna's grimacing face, her teeth pulled back from her lips, eyes wild with rage and lust. Nalene's heart pounded wildly. She gripped her *sulbit* tighter, whispering reassurances she did not believe through cracked lips.

More blows fell on the barrier. New holes appeared, faster than Nalene could patch them. Her mouth was full of blood and there were ashes in her heart. Even if more Tenders arrived right now, it was too late.

She felt Quyloc's presence beside her. "Get out," she snarled at him. "Get everybody out. I can't hold it."

Quyloc only hesitated a second and then he began shouting orders to abandon the square.

A groan came from the barrier as Reyna struck it yet again. This time she got a couple of fingers into the hole she made before it could close. There was a sizzle and the smell of burned flesh as she forced her hand through the barrier. Skin and flesh burned completely away, leaving only bony fingers that reached for Nalene.

Eyes bulging in disbelief, Nalene fell back a step.

Reyna smashed a new hole and forced her other hand through it, reaching for Nalene's throat. Nalene fell back another step.

Reyna slammed her forehead into the barrier, cracking it and then forcing her head through the opening. What emerged was a death's head nightmare. Everything but the bone was burned away. Her teeth were bared in a lipless, feral snarl. Only the lidless eyes remained intact, staring, fixed on Nalene.

The lipless mouth opened. "I'm going to kill you all," Reyna said. "You're going to die."

Then she flexed—Nalene felt the building tidal wave of power—and all at once the barrier simply shattered. Nalene was thrown backwards and struck her head on the cobblestones.

Quyloc turned back just as it happened. He saw Reyna shatter the barrier and he saw Nalene go down.

Reyna yelled in triumph and jumped at Nalene. The FirstMother would have died then, but one of her guards threw himself in Reyna's way, shouting as he swung his sword. Her eyes blazed fire and she grabbed the luckless man by the throat, lifting him into the air and draining him in an instant.

Another guard grabbed Nalene and dragged her back as Quyloc moved up to face Reyna. Desperate thoughts flew through his mind. There was no way either he or the pikemen could possibly stop Reyna. She was far too powerful. But if he engaged her, angered her enough that she was distracted, he might be able to buy enough time for Rome to seal off the square.

Reyna finished draining her victim and tossed him aside like a rag doll. She glowed with new power and in an instant the flesh that had burned away from her hands and head was restored, though she remained bald. She threw her head back and howled in ecstasy—

Quyloc stepped forward and stabbed her in the chest.

Reyna screamed, her eyes blazing. She held up her hands. The flesh shifted, her fingers lengthening, razor-sharp claws emerging from the ends. At the same time she grew even taller.

She threw out one hand. A line of cancerous yellow energy snapped across the space between them, hungrily seeking Quyloc's Life-energy, but Quyloc brought the spear around and cut through it just an instant after it touched him.

Reyna screamed again and charged him.

Rome saw Reyna hit the barrier and knew it would not hold. "Fall back!" he shouted to the soldiers on top of the wall. "Fall back!" Pushing through the soldiers, he started down off the wall. Before he reached the bottom, the barrier fell and Reyna surged through. Quyloc yelled an order to the pikemen who were formed up behind him. Then he stepped up and stabbed Reyna with his spear. When Reyna charged him, he fell back and the pikemen parted to let the two of them through. As soon as Quyloc and Reyna passed through, the pikemen reformed their ranks, all three squads stepping forward to seal the entrance. The Children charged in—and met a bristling wall of pike points. They screamed in rage and pain, but they were too weak to break through.

As he reached the bottom of the stairs, Rome saw Heram appear in the gateway passage. Rome hesitated. Heram would tear through the pikemen like paper. The evacuation of the square had barely begun. Only a few people had made it to the narrow street that was the only exit. He badly wanted to charge Heram. With the axe he could hold Heram back, giving his men and the Tenders time to get out of the square.

But if he did that, he would lose his chance to drop the buildings on either side of the narrow street. He might be able to hold off Heram, but the rest of the Children would pour through that opening into the city unhindered and the slaughter would be terrible.

All this passed through his mind in an instant and then he turned and ran for the narrow street, drawing the axe as he went.

Tairus was on top of the wall when Rome gave the order to fall back. He started yelling at soldiers to get off the wall, shoving men toward the stairs.

Tairus looked down into the square just as Heram entered. A snarl of Children stood between Heram and the ranks of pikemen and he began slapping and kicking them aside. Fearfully, they fell back away from him until all that stood in his way were the pikemen. They were crouched, the butts of their weapons set on the ground, jammed in place with their feet.

Heram charged. A dozen points skewered him. Pikes flexed. A couple broke.

But the pikemen *held*. Somehow, unbelievably, they held.

Heram bellowed with rage and began slapping at the pikes, shattering a few more. He grabbed one and lifted the man holding it into the air, then threw him. He waded in deeper, snapping more of the weapons and killing two pikemen with his huge fists.

Then Shorn arrived, wielding the massive club.

"Let him through!" Shorn yelled. "Let him through!" Then he yelled something in his own language, directed at Heram. To Tairus it sounded like a challenge. Heram looked up from the pikemen, saw the foe that had humbled him the day before, and roared his response.

The pikemen opened their ranks and Heram roared through.

Immediately they closed their ranks once again, before any of the Children had a chance to make it through the gap.

Heram and Shorn closed on each other. Shorn swung first. Heram made no effort to dodge the blow, but simply let it strike him on his left side, then clamped his arm down over it, pinning the weapon to his side. Shorn let go of the club and punched Heram once, twice, in the body.

Heram smiled.

Heram swung a two-handed blow that Shorn dodged. Shorn hit him again, in the face this time, hard enough to rock Heram's head back. But as he closed to hit Heram again, the big man lunged forward and got his hands on him. Muscles flexed and Shorn was drawn into a lethal bear hug.

Shorn managed to get his arms free before they were trapped and he began hammering Heram in the face and head, savage blows that could have shattered trees.

But Heram's smile only grew wider and he pulled Shorn closer, his massive arms inexorably closing.

Shorn fought and twisted but even his great strength was no use against Heram.

Tairus hung there for a moment at the top of the stairs, watching, knowing the strange warrior was doomed. Rome swung the black axe against the building on the right side of the narrow street and a long crack ran up the side of it. If he didn't leave now, he would be trapped here.

"Gorim's balls," he snarled. He turned and ran to the nearest ballista—fortunately it was loaded—and spun the heavy weapon clear around, sighting on the struggling forms of Shorn and Heram.

Shorn had driven his thumbs into Heram's eyes, punching deep into his skull, but the huge man's hold did not release. The smile was still on his face.

147

Tairus sighted along the shaft of the bolt. The angle was bad. He'd never been any good with these things the few times he'd practiced with them. He'd be lucky not to kill Shorn.

He squeezed the trigger.

The weapon recoiled as the bolt released.

The bolt took Heram in the back, staggering him. Shorn took advantage of the opportunity and twisted free.

Tairus didn't wait to see anymore. He'd done what he could. He ran down the stairs.

The *rendspear* was like the flicking tongue of a serpent, stabbing Reyna over and over. Each wound he dealt her closed within moments, but he could see that they hurt her and where each one had been there remained a thin, purple scar, evidence that the wounds were not healing completely. As powerful as she was, the *Pente Akka* was still poison to her.

Reyna spat her rage and swung at Quyloc over and over again with claws as long as daggers, but each time he danced away, spinning, moving, striking again and again. Her speed was breathtaking. There was no way he could match it. Had he been simply responding to her actions, he would have been dead already. But he had been here before. He had fought the hunter. The way to survive was to react *before* she acted. His mind instantly registered details too small for conscious awareness, and in the same instant his body responded. Before she launched each blow, he could see how her weight shifted minutely and he was already leaving the area and counter attacking. He was only dimly aware of his body. It was almost as though it belonged to someone else. Strength and speed he didn't know was his flowed through his limbs.

Even as he fought a battle with absolutely no margin for error, he could not help but marvel at what he did. Though the ground was littered with broken stone and the bodies of the dead and dying, not once did his footing falter. He sensed the low wall surrounding the statue at his back and jumped back and up, clearing it. She swung at him again and he dodged the blow. She hit the statue instead, shattering the stone like rotten ice.

Always as he retreated he made sure to stay close to Reyna, stabbing her over and over again. He wanted her to stay focused on him. He needed her to be so angry she couldn't think. Most importantly, he needed her to be so angry that she attacked him physically, rather than with the draining attack. Just the brief touch of the first one she'd thrown at him had been enough to nearly paralyze him. He wasn't sure if he would be as lucky the next time.

Step by step he drew her in an arc away from the narrow street. He needed to give the others time to retreat. He needed to get her far enough from the narrow street so that when he made his break for it she would not be able to stop him. It had to be timed perfectly. If he broke too soon, she would escape the square. Too late, and he would be trapped here to die.

Though he did not once turn and look, because of the heightened awareness granted him by his contact with the spear, he knew Rome's exact progression. He felt Rome pause at the bottom of the stairs when he wanted to attack Heram, felt him make his decision and run for the exit. He felt the tension build in Rome's arms and shoulders as he drew the axe back to strike at the base of one of the buildings.

All at once he knew it was time—the buildings were seconds from collapsing—and he made his move. Reyna slashed at him and he slid to the side, letting her clawed hand hiss harmlessly past his shoulder. Then he stabbed her quickly in the arm pit, leaning into it, just enough to nudge her off balance so she staggered a bit.

In that brief opening, he slid behind her. Swinging with both hands, he slashed the spear blade across her hamstring, down near her ankle. The tendon split and she went down. Then he ran for the exit.

As carefully as he had planned and executed it, still it wasn't enough. Even as she hit the ground, Reyna healed and bounced back to her feet with lethal speed. He could feel her behind him, too close. The narrow street was just ahead, but it might as well have been miles away. Every detail of the scene imprinted itself on his mind. A line of soldiers was running down the narrow street. Heram was roaring. Rome was swinging the axe at the building on the left. The one on the right was already trembling, spider webbed with cracks.

But she was too close. And she'd started thinking again. He felt her raise her hand, felt her preparing the draining attack.

TWENTY-SIX

Netra ran toward the city gates. She'd put up with Ricarn's questions as long as she could, but when she felt the barrier start to waver she couldn't take it anymore and took off. If the city fell now it wouldn't matter what the Lementh'kal meant about her being the doorway. Nothing would matter anymore.

She ran down the cobblestoned streets, driven by the ever-increasing knowledge that the battle was fast swinging against them. Her heart went cold when the barrier finally fell. She wasn't going to be in time. As she got closer her passage was slowed by citizens and soldiers fleeing the square and she shoved her way through them heedlessly.

But when she got to the entrance to the narrow street a soldier grabbed her and stopped her. "You can't go in there!" he shouted. She tried to twist free of him, but then she saw Rome swinging the axe, saw the buildings on either side of the street shaking.

She was too late.

Tairus was running across the square when Quyloc made his break. He knew it was coming, knew Quyloc was leading Reyna away to give the rest time to flee. He saw Quyloc duck under Reyna's attack, hamstring her and take off running. The buildings flanking the narrow street were trembling. He cursed his short legs. He was too far away. He wasn't going to make it through there before the buildings fell.

Then he saw Reyna slow and raise her hand and knew what she was about to do.

He stopped and pulled his axe from its sheath. Could he get lucky twice in one day?

He threw it at Reyna's back as hard as he could.

There was no way this would work. The axe was completely, perfectly not designed for throwing.

It hit Reyna in the back and stuck.

With a scream of rage, she reached back and pulled it out. She turned toward him, her eyes brightly lit with her hatred, and he knew he was going to die then.

But then she threw the axe down, turned and ran after Quyloc again.

Quyloc made it into the narrow street just as the building on the right teetered and began to fall. Around him ran other soldiers. At the other end of the narrow street was Rome, waving him forward, shouting something he couldn't hear.

He felt Reyna enter the narrow street behind him. Chunks of stone fell in a rain around him. A soldier just ahead was struck on the head by one and went down. There was nothing Quyloc could do for him. Nothing he could do for any of them or for those still fighting in the square.

The wall to his right buckled suddenly and it was only his preternatural awareness that allowed him to sense it coming and leap away at just the right moment. Two soldiers near him weren't as lucky and went down with cries. Reyna was slowed as a falling stone hit her on the shoulder.

He was just reaching the end when both buildings finally surrendered completely to gravity.

They collapsed with a roar. Reyna was buried under a mountain of shattered stone.

Tairus watched the buildings fall, burying Reyna, and he pumped his fist, shouting exultantly.

About two seconds later the reality of his situation hit him and he turned around. The pikemen were still holding the Children at bay, but there were only about half of them left. He saw a few glance over their shoulders at the fallen buildings and knew what was going through their minds.

There was no point in fighting any further. They'd done what they set out to do and now it was all over except for the dying.

He turned the other way and saw Shorn. He'd recovered his club and was savagely pummeling Heram with it. Blinded as he was, Heram couldn't defend himself. His head looked misshapen from the beating and one arm was badly broken.

"Hey!" Tairus yelled. He pointed at the faltering pikemen. "It's time to go!"

Shorn took in the situation at a glance and he nodded. He took off running for the gateway passage and Tairus did as well. As he ran, he shouted to the pikemen to open a lane. They parted right as Shorn got to them, a narrow passage opening between them.

Shorn passed through their ranks and fell on the Children like an avalanche. He swung the huge club in great, scything swings, knocking the Children flying.

"Follow him!" Tairus yelled and he and the remaining pikemen charged through in the big warrior's wake, through the shattered gates and out to freedom.

TWENTY-SEVEN

Shakre looked up at the gaunt figure of Gulagh standing on top of Wreckers Gate and her heart went cold inside her. It was tall, almost twice the height of a person, but excruciatingly thin. Its skin was the black of a plague victim. Its eyes were empty holes rimmed in red; nothing human looked out from in there. Open sores covered much of its body, dripping viscous, yellow fluid. It was disease and famine brought to life.

She turned to Elihu and received a shock. There was no revulsion, no fear on his face. Instead, his eyes were shining and he was smiling. She looked at the other Takare and saw the same expressions everywhere. A few were holding their hands up, as if to embrace the figure that looked down on them. Suddenly distrustful of her own senses, Shakre looked back at the Guardian and experienced a moment of extreme disorientation. For just a second she saw a beautiful, shining figure of white and gold. Then the moment passed and again there was the black, diseased thing looking down at them. She grabbed Elihu's arm and shook him until he turned his face toward her.

"What is it?" he asked, his smile faltering. "What's wrong?"

"What do you see?" she asked him.

Elihu looked back at the figure. "What do you mean?"

"What do you *see*?"

"You're not making any sense. I see the same thing you do. He's beautiful. He's shining, all white and gold. He's here to welcome us home. We should have come sooner."

"That's not what I see at all. I see a black, diseased thing."

Elihu gave her a curious look. "Perhaps you are confused then." He turned his face upwards once again.

"No." Shakre shook her head. "Something is happening and for some reason it's not affecting me."

Without looking away from the Guardian, Elihu squeezed her hand. "You are troubled and afraid. We all are. We have been running for a long time. But it is okay now. We are home and we are safe."

"No, we're not," Shakre said fiercely. "You have to believe me. You have to trust me on this."

"I do trust you," Elihu replied, still not looking at her. "But I don't want to talk right now."

Shakre looked around, hoping for an ally. Youlin and Rehobim were standing in a group nearby and she ran over to them, shoving people aside in her desperation. There were some irritated mutters at her passing, but no one really reacted. They were too busy staring up in awe.

She made it to Youlin's side. The young Pastwalker had her hood back and was staring up with the same glassy look in her eyes as everyone else.

"Pastwalker!" Shakre hissed. "Youlin!" When Youlin didn't respond she stepped in front of her, blocking her view, and shook her by the shoulders.

It took a moment, but then Youlin's vision cleared somewhat and she focused on Shakre. "What is it, Windrider?" she snapped.

"It's a trick. Whatever you're seeing up there on top of the wall, it's not real."

"Move aside," Youlin said. "I am not so easily fooled." She tried to pull Shakre's hands off her, but Shakre held on.

"You have to listen to me," Shakre said desperately. "Something is about to happen. Our people are in terrible danger."

She was suddenly shoved hard from the side and fell to the ground. She looked up to see Rehobim standing over her, his face twisted with anger. "You will not touch the Pastwalker!" he yelled. His hands were balled into fists. Two of the Takare flanking him drew knives from their belts.

Shakre stood slowly, her hands out, placating. She could be dead in seconds. "I'm sorry, Rehobim," she said. "I was wrong."

Her words satisfied the other two Takare. They turned their gazes back to the figure on the wall. Rehobim glared at her for a moment longer, then turned his face up as well.

"Welcome home. I am the Guardian Gulagh," it said. "I have been waiting for you." It gestured and one side of the gate—obsidian laced with veins of blood red—swung open silently, the Takare moving out of its way.

Inside were hundreds of people, all dressed in white robes and holding up garlands of flowers. With welcoming smiles on their faces they beckoned the Takare in.

Shakre blinked and the white robes were replaced by dirty, gray rags. The garlands of flowers were no more than dead weeds. Everyone was emaciated; many had running sores or strange growths. Their smiles were grimaces of horror.

"Enter," Gulagh said.

When the Takare hesitated, Gulagh opened its mouth and began to sing. The song had an immediate effect on the Takare. The few frowns of suspicion there were faded and were replaced with smiles of joy. Gulagh sang a wordless melody that spoke of home and sunshine and warmth. Even Shakre was not immune to it. It was as if a hard shell around her heart cracked and she could breathe.

Shakre had another moment of disorientation. The blackness that was Gulagh shimmered and faded, replaced once again by the shining, beautiful figure. The song seemed to wrap around her heart and she felt tears in her eyes. She was so tired of running and fighting. It was all she had ever done. Here was her chance to finally set all her burdens down. Why did she always resist everything?

Slowly the Takare began to move forward. Some of them laughed. Even Pinlir, the dour man who had lived only for revenge since the outsiders killed his father, had a smile creasing his lined face. They began throwing their weapons down. Shakre found herself moving with them. It really was so much easier to give in.

Golden flakes, glittering like bits of sun, appeared then, carried on Gulagh's song, pouring out of the Guardian's mouth in a cloud. The flakes swirled around and were carried out over the Takare in a cloud that began to drift earthward.

With a tremendous effort of will, Shakre fought back. She shook her head, telling herself over and over that it wasn't real. Her people were in danger. "No," Shakre said. The song filled her with light and hope and she wanted more than anything to enter, to embrace the magic that drifted down on her from above. But she knew what she had seen and she was not so ready to give in. "No," she said, louder this time. She squeezed her eyes shut, shook her head and bit her lip until it bled.

When she opened her eyes and looked up she again saw the diseased figure on the wall. The flakes of light looked like ashes.

The first Takare had entered the gate. The people within embraced them and hung the dead garlands around their necks.

"No!" Shakre screamed.

She ran forward, fighting her way through the press of people until she was at the open gate, hitting people, pushing them, shouting at them. But it did no good. It was almost as if they couldn't even see her. They just kept blindly moving forward, huge, beatific smiles on their faces. Meanwhile, the gray flakes had begun to land on a few people.

And Shakre just lost it.

She screamed again and in that scream was a command for the *aranti*, the creature she had ridden twice before to save her people. She had not felt its presence since leaving the area of the Plateau, but she would not be denied. She was the Windrider and it *would* answer her.

At first there was nothing, and she screamed again, screamed so hard it felt like something tore inside her throat.

The *aranti* answered, swirling around her.

She seized it and twisted her will about it roughly, desperation lending her strength and even cruelty. "I command you," she grated. She forced it into a spin around her, digging into it, pressing it for speed.

The *aranti* began to race around and around her, unable to flee her clutches. Dirt and leaves and small rocks were lifted off the ground and flung into the eyes of the Takare trying to get through the open gate. They began to back away, the dirt blinding them, the rocks pelting them painfully.

Shakre pressed harder and the *aranti* responded with even more speed. It howled and in the space of the open gate a small tornado began to take shape. Shakre was lifted into the air, her arms flung out to the sides, her head thrown back. The wind whipped her hair and her clothing about her. As the speed increased, the nearest Takare were flung bodily back.

People threw their arms up to shield their faces and still the tornado grew. The gray flakes were flung skyward and disintegrated. Shakre began to drive the Takare back away from the gate, whipping them into greater speed. In moments they were all running the other direction.

She turned and saw Gulagh staring at her, hissing with rage, its red-rimmed eyes fixed on her. It raised one arm toward Shakre. Something black and toothy sprouted up from its palm and shot at her.

As fast as it moved, though, it was no match for the wind. Shakre dodged the thing easily. A glance showed her that her people were temporarily safe.

She could fight back.

"Now it's my turn," she said.

She forced her unwilling mount into even greater speed and drove it at Gulagh. Its eyes widened as it realized what she was doing and it turned to flee.

But it was far too slow.

Shakre slammed into it with all the power and speed at her disposal. With a cry it was flung off the gate and fell down to the hard ground below.

Shakre started to follow, her hatred for the thing overcoming her reason, but she had pushed too far and in so doing her grip on the *aranti* had weakened. It was slipping away from her. She was losing it. She had only seconds and if she didn't get to the ground before she lost hold she would fall. At this height the fall would surely kill her.

She tugged the *aranti* back the way she had come, racing for the ground. She was still a dozen feet up when her grip failed completely. With a victorious shriek the *aranti* bolted for freedom. Shakre fell, landing poorly, her knee buckling with the impact.

She tried to rise, but the knee wouldn't support her and she fell back down. She looked back. There was no sign of Gulagh. The mighty gate was swinging shut.

She reached out, as if somehow she could stop it—there were still Takare in there.

Then it swung closed with a hollow boom and Werthin was there, helping her to her feet.

X X X

Limping, her knee already beginning to swell, Shakre leaned on Werthin as he helped her back to where the Takare were gathered, well away from the gate.

"What just happened?" Rehobim demanded, glaring at her as if she were somehow to blame.

"Didn't you see?" Now that the adrenalin was fading, Shakre felt terribly weary. It had taken everything she had to control the *aranti* like that.

"I saw," Elihu said, coming up and putting Shakre's other arm over his shoulder to help support her. "When the figure on top of the gate attacked her it changed. It became ugly and diseased." To Shakre he whispered, "I am sorry, dear one. I should have trusted you."

"It's okay," she said. "Can I sit down now?"

"Do you think we should move further away from the gate?"

"I don't think we need to. I don't think it will try that again."

Elihu and Werthin lowered her onto a rock. Shakre began rubbing her knee. Fortunately, she didn't think anything was broken or torn.

The Takare parted and Youlin came through. She had her hood pulled up over her head once again and she stared at Shakre from within its dark recesses. "What is that thing?"

"It's one of the Guardians. They are Melekath's chief lieutenants."

"What is it doing here, in our home?" Rehobim demanded.

"I don't know. The prison is open. I would think it would be heading to join its master."

"Another plot by Kasai."

"Maybe, but I don't think so." Shakre frowned, concentrating. "Kasai doesn't appear to be going to join Melekath either. It doesn't make any sense."

"Maybe they no longer answer to him," Elihu said.

"It's possible."

"It does not matter," Youlin said. "The creature is in our home and I will not tolerate that. We will drive it forth or we will kill it."

Shakre rubbed her knee, wincing. "I don't think it *can* be killed. I think it is immortal, like Melekath."

"You would have us abandon our home?"

"I didn't say that."

"Use the wind again," Rehobim suggested. "Drive it away with that."

Shakre shook her head. "I can't hold onto the wind for that long. I don't know if I'll even be able to summon it again. I used it badly today and it will be much harder to call next time."

Rehobim scowled at her. "You speak of it as if it is alive."

Shakre sighed. She was heartily sick of Rehobim's unending hostility. "No. Not alive. But aware. Perhaps no more sentient than a deer. But a deer, frightened enough, will flee and not return."

"Then it falls to the spirit-kin to defeat this thing," Rehobim said, laying his hand on the grip of his sword.

Shakre looked at Wreckers Gate. It had to be at least two or three hundred feet tall and perfectly smooth. It spanned an opening in cliffs that were even higher, all part of a mountain range that was considered to be impassable. "Good idea," she said drily. "How do you plan on getting past the gate?"

Rehobim scowled darkly at her. "The Takare do not give up."

"Be quiet," Youlin told him. "Do not speak again until I tell you to."

Rehobim's eyes flashed and it was only with effort that he kept still. Shakre, watching, felt a chill go through her. Youlin's hold on power was not as firm as she thought. Would he challenge her? He had always deferred to her before without question, but he was different now. Not just him, but all the spirit-kin. She and Elihu had spoken of it together a number of times, how the spirit-kin were becoming increasingly hostile and irrational. Was it just the effect of having two souls inhabiting one body? Or was it something more? What if the ancient souls took control? What would happen then? She turned her attention back to Youlin as the Pastwalker spoke once again.

"There is a hidden way through the mountains. We will head for it."

"And what about Gulagh?" Rehobim said.

"I will speak with the spirits of our people. They will show us a way."

TWENTY-EIGHT

Led by Rehobim, the spirit-kin moved out a few minutes later, heading south and west. Shakre noticed that they did not confer with Youlin beforehand, and when she looked at Elihu, she saw that he noticed too. Wearily, and with many backward looks at Wreckers Gate, the rest of the Takare began to follow, the heaviness hanging over them palpable. Shakre understood their despair. They had come so far and with such high hopes—the thought of returning to their homeland was like a beautiful vision shining in the distance—and then to arrive and find it closed to them, well, part of her just wanted to sit down and give up.

As she went to haul herself to her feet, she felt a hand on her arm. It was Werthin. Ever since he had carried her down off the Plateau, he seemed to have appointed himself her personal guardian.

She took his hand gratefully and let him pull her to her feet. "Thank you," she murmured.

"We should not be moving," he said angrily, casting a dark look at the spirit-kin, already moving away at a trot. They made no effort to help the elderly or the sick or the very young, or even to moderate their pace to allow them to keep up. "Not until you are ready. Once again you save our people and your only reward is yet more disrespect."

"It's okay," she said, smiling at him. She gave him a closer look. "How are you feeling today?"

"I have recovered," he said, but she knew it wasn't true. It had not been that long since she'd cut open his *akirma* and removed the two spirits Youlin had called to him. He would have died if she hadn't done it; no *akirma* was capable of holding three selves. He had lost weight and his face had a drawn look to it that was not healthy.

"Pinlir has not ordered you to submit to the calling again, has he?" Every night after dark Rehobim sent Pinlir to gather several more Takare—usually the young, both male and female—to submit to the calling, where Youlin summoned in the lost spirits of ancient Takare warriors to take up residence inside them.

"No, he has not," Werthin said, an edge to his voice. "The spirit-kin will no longer look at me. They believe I am weak, unworthy."

"And what do you believe?" she asked, turning to look at him as they walked. He was still holding onto her arm.

Werthin turned his face away. "I no longer know what to believe. My world no longer makes any sense."

"I, too, feel that way," she said. "But I know this: You are a worthy man, a true Takare. No person could house two more spirits beyond his own and live. It is not how we are made."

"If you say so."

"I do," she said fiercely. "Look at me." Reluctantly he turned his head. "Don't let them make you doubt yourself. You are a true warrior in the old tradition of your people. I have seen your strength. You have saved me with it. You must believe this."

He held her gaze a moment longer, then nodded and looked away again. She could tell he was not convinced, but it was all she could do. The truth was that she needed him far more than he realized. So many of her adopted people had turned away from her. She was the one who was always speaking out, pointing out the dark traps of hatred and vengeance that she saw them falling into. They were views that did not make her popular among them, no matter how often she proved herself. Werthin was one of the few who seemed to truly hear what she was trying to say and she needed that. She needed it badly. The path she had chosen was too difficult to walk alone.

Shakre patted his hand. "I can manage on my own now. Thank you." She still didn't feel very strong, but she knew that Werthin needed to take care of himself first. After a moment Werthin moved away and Elihu moved up beside her. Shakre took hold of his arm.

"How is he?" Elihu asked.

"Better, but still a long way from healed," she replied. "Song still leaks from the cut I made in his *akirma*."

"How about you?"

"Weak, but mostly okay," she said. "I did not let the *aranti* inside me, so it will not take as long to recover." The times she had let the *aranti* inside her she had felt hollowed out and strange for days afterwards. She lost too much of herself when she did that. The *aranti* was like a flood roaring inside; it tore away everything that was loose as it passed through.

"I saw what you did. I don't think most of them did, they were too busy running." Shakre gave him a look. He raised his eyebrows. "It was very impressive. You rode the wind up to the top of the gate and then you threw Gulagh off. I didn't know you could do that."

Shakre shrugged. "I didn't either."

"What else can you do, I wonder?" he said playfully. "How long until we ordinary mortals must begin worshipping you?"

"Any day now," she said, squeezing his hand. "You should start practicing. You don't want to anger me."

More seriously he asked, "Do you think you will be able to do that again?"

"I don't know. It's getting harder and harder to call the *aranti*. It hates being caught like that, like a wild animal. It seems to be getting increasingly wary of me."

"After years of pushing you around, it seems the wind does not enjoy the reverse."

"That pretty much sums it up." Shakre looked at the mountains. For days the Truebane Mountains had been growing ever larger on their horizon, always a sharp, jagged mass in the distance. Now that they were up close the mountains were even more forbidding. An unbroken line of massive granite peaks, covered in a thick layer of snow even this late in the summer. She could see no break in them anywhere. No wonder the Empire had never had any success besieging the Takare. If there were any passes through those mountains, they were high up and accessible to only the hardiest of climbers. No army would ever be able to pass through them, that was for sure. All the Takare had to do was close Wreckers Gate, which controlled the only real access to the mountains, and they could wait out any siege indefinitely. There was a long valley in the heart of the Truebane Mountains, with a lake in the middle fed by the streams coming off the peaks. Anyone in there needed nothing from the outside world.

How ironic that the Takare now found themselves on the opposite side of the gate.

"What do you know about this secret way that Youlin spoke of?" she asked.

"Not much," he admitted. "Supposedly there is a hidden path through the mountains and I guess if anyone would know of it still it would be a Pastwalker. Although, I asked Rekus about it a few days ago and he said he did not know where it was." Rekus was, or had been, the Pastwalker for Bent Tree Shelter. His had been the strongest voice opposed to taking up arms against the outsiders invading the Plateau, saying they could not risk Tu Sinar's wrath on this. After the entire village was nearly executed by the outsiders—saved only by Shorn's intervention—he had never been the same. He spoke very little and kept to himself. Shakre had never liked the man; he was always arrogant in his position as Pastwalker, but she felt sorry for him all the same.

"Do you think the spirits are guiding her then?" Shakre asked.

"I don't know. I no longer know what to think. Are they even the spirits of our ancestors? I don't know that either. But I do know that I am concerned by them. Whatever they are, they are cold and even cruel."

"We may not need Kasai, or even Gulagh, to destroy us."

"Hey there," he admonished her, patting her arm with his free hand. "Do not speak this way. We are a hardy people and we are far from done."

"I know," she said. "And I'm sorry. But I'm just...I'm worried. Everywhere we turn we confront powerful enemies and our numbers are few." There were a little over a thousand Takare all told. "And the spirit-kin...I fear they have some hidden agenda we don't yet know."

"I think you are right. Perhaps tonight we should speak with Rekus together."

"Do you think he can help?"

"Rekus has been a Pastwalker for many years. I believe he knows much more than he has ever shared. We can only try."

TWENTY-NINE

The spirit-kin stopped to make camp a few hours later, as it was getting dark. The peak marking the location of Wreckers Gate was receding in the distance behind them as they circled around the edge of the mountains. It took another hour for the last of the Takare to catch up and stumble wearily into camp, Shakre and Elihu among them.

By then the cook fires were going and the smell of cooking meat was strong in the air. As usual, the spirit-kin had made their camp apart from the rest and the first food that was prepared was carried over to them. As Shakre sank gratefully onto the ground—the encounter with the *aranti* had wearied her more than she thought—she heard a commotion from the spirit-kin camp.

Birna, Pinlir's wife, was carrying a bowl of thick stew for her husband when she stumbled in her haste and dropped the bowl in his lap. With a roar, Pinlir leapt to his feet and slapped her. She fell down with a cry and he drew his axe and advanced on her.

For one heart-stopping moment Shakre thought he would kill her, but Rehobim, sitting around the same fire, made a small noise. Pinlir looked at him and Rehobim gave small shake of his head. Pinlir put his axe away, wiped the food off his clothes, and sat back down, not giving his wife a second look. Tears running down her face, Birna got up and hurried away.

"I have to go talk to her," Shakre said. Getting wearily back to her feet, she made her way over to the woman. When she got there, Birna was sitting on the ground, and two women were crouched by her soothing her. Her baby—born shortly before they fled the Plateau—was clutched in her arms.

Shakre nodded to the two women and they backed off, returning to helping with the food. She sat down beside Birna. "I am sorry," she said softly.

Birna raised her tear-stained face. "You were right," she said hoarsely. "We should have listened to you. The spirits, they are devouring us. My husband is lost to me."

Pinlir's father, Asoken, had been Firewalker for Bent Tree Shelter, and when the outsiders encircled the village, they had killed Asoken because he was too sick to leave his hut and answer the question. His murder had hit Pinlir especially hard and he'd been the first to volunteer to go with Rehobim to retaliate against them. He'd been the first Takare after Rehobim to take in one of the ancient spirits.

Birna leaned close. "I can see it when I look into his eyes. Pinlir is no longer in there. Someone else looks out through his eyes." She grabbed Shakre's arm, hard enough that it hurt. "Can you help him? You helped Jehu. You removed the black mark from him."

"I will do what I can," Shakre promised her, though she did not believe the *aranti* would be able to help in this instance, as it had helped with Jehu. *If* she could even summon it again. "If it helps, I believe that Pinlir is still in there, even if he does not hold the reins."

She stayed with Birna a few minutes longer, then stood up to go. When she did, a child she didn't know came up to her and took her hand.

"It's my mother," he said. "Something is wrong with her." Shakre followed him through the camp to where a young woman was lying on the ground. A couple of Takare were kneeling by her. "She won't get up," the child said.

Shakre knelt down beside her and touched her forehead. The woman had a fever. When she checked her eyes, she saw that they had rolled back into her head. Her pulse was erratic. Concerned, Shakre went *beyond* and what she *saw* there startled her.

There were two small gray blotches on her *akirma*. Shakre reached out and touched one of them. A sharp pain made her jerk back.

Shakre left *beyond*, alarmed. What could be causing that?

Then she knew.

It was the gray flakes. It had to be. Some of them must have touched the woman. She looked at the others gathered around. "Do you know of anyone else with these same symptoms?"

"I do," said one elderly man. He led her to another Takare, this one a girl about twelve. When Shakre went *beyond* she *saw* the same blotches. The same was true of two more of the Takare. She went back to Elihu and told him what she'd found.

"You said the people inside, on the other side of the gate, looked diseased," Elihu said.

"They were," Shakre confirmed, feeling sick at where this was leading.

"It is likely that Gulagh did the same thing to them, with the flakes."

"Which means the Takare who were touched by them are going to end up the same way."

"I'm afraid so," Elihu said grimly. Seeing the stricken look on Shakre's face he reached over and took her hands. "If it were not for you, we would all be in the same condition now. Remember that."

"I don't know if I can help them," Shakre burst out, then clamped her hand over her mouth as she struggled to get herself under control. Tears sprang to her eyes.

"You may not be able to," he said softly.

"But I—"

"No," he cut her off. "You cannot save everyone. Did you save every person on the Plateau who came to you broken or ill? Don't try to shoulder every life. If you do, you will crumble and be useless to us and we need you."

Shakre swallowed hard and rubbed her eyes. "You're right. If I lose it, I won't be able to find the cure."

Elihu regarded her sadly. "You should rest."

"I will," she promised him. "But I think we need to talk to Rekus. Tonight."

"Maybe I should talk to Youlin again first."

Shakre shook her head. "What makes you think it will do any good this time? She has refused to listen to either of us before. She can think of nothing but her obsession with returning the Takare to their place of power. When she looks at the spirit-kin she sees only weapons. Any suffering that comes of using those weapons is simply a price that has to be paid." These were all things Youlin had said to her more than once.

"You are right," Elihu said. "But at least she is only calling in one spirit each night now." Calling in the spirits took a toll on Youlin and she was now too weak to summon more than one each night.

"Besides, Rehobim and the others have been keeping a close eye on her lately," Shakre said. "I think they know we are suspicious. If we draw too much attention to ourselves, I don't know what they'll do. They may just kill us outright."

"They would never raise a weapon against a Walker or the Windrider," Elihu protested.

"I think they would. One nearly just killed his wife. Think about it. Who will stand against them? Who *could* stand against them?"

Elihu sighed and scratched his chin. "Sadly, I believe you are right."

"We need to be careful about talking to Rekus too. I think we should wait until Youlin is doing the nightly calling and talk to him then. They'll be so fixed on what she's doing I don't think they'll notice us."

Elihu thought about this for a while, then nodded. "There is wisdom in what you say. However, I believe we should wait until tomorrow night."

"But we don't know—"

Elihu put his finger to her lips. "You are worn out from today. Tomorrow will be here soon enough."

THIRTY

Shakre was walking with Elihu the next day when they came over a low ridge and saw that the spirit-kin had stopped up ahead and were gathered around Rehobim and Youlin. Wondering what was going on, they hurried to catch up. The spirit-kin moved aside to let them through when they got there, but only reluctantly and more than one gave them a hostile look.

"What is happening?" Elihu asked Youlin when they reached her.

She turned to him. "Our scout has returned. The hidden way is closed to us."

"How?" Shakre asked.

"A recent rock slide, perhaps triggered by Gulagh. A long section of the way is completely choked with rock."

Shakre and Elihu exchanged looks. Oddly, Shakre felt almost relieved. All morning she'd been wondering what they could possibly do against Gulagh. As fearsome as the spirit-kin were, they were still no match for one of the Guardians. Would they pass through this hidden way only to be destroyed by the creature? Maybe they should give up on returning to their ancestral home. Maybe it was best to leave it to Gulagh and find somewhere else to live. She'd shared her thoughts with Elihu and he'd admitted that he was considering the same thing. Now Elihu spoke again.

"It is time for a proper gathering of all the Walkers. We need to discuss what comes next."

Pinlir, standing beside Rehobim, suddenly advanced on Elihu. "The time for talking is over, old man. Go back and wait with the old women."

His outburst shocked Shakre. No one spoke to a Walker like that. Elihu frowned, something he rarely did. He stood up to Pinlir.

"Your father, Asoken, would be ashamed to hear his son speak this way to a Walker. Have you completely forgotten who you are?"

168

Pinlir opened his mouth and for just a moment Shakre saw something in his eyes that made her think he was going to apologize. Then a snarl lifted his lips and he drew his axe instead. To Shakre's surprise, Elihu still did not back down but instead, moving surprisingly quickly for a man his age, slapped the head of the weapon aside.

"Back down, Pinlir!" he barked.

Pinlir said, "Don't call me that ever again." What happened next was too fast for anyone to react to. He grabbed Elihu, spun him around and locked one arm around his throat. With his free hand he held the axe to Elihu's throat. "Don't think I am fooled. I know who you are, *Genjinn*."

Everyone froze. Every eye was locked on the two of them. Pinlir jerked Elihu backwards, back into a haldane tree with its long, hooked yellow thorns, using the tree to keep anyone from getting behind him. His eyes darted this way and that and the blade drew a small trickle of blood from Elihu's throat.

Automatically, Shakre started forward. Pinlir glared at her. "Go ahead, Tender. Try to save him. Call your wind. I need little reason to kill my old enemy Genjinn." He turned on the rest of the spirit-kin standing around. "Look at you, whining and running, taking council with Tenders. Are you truly my people? My people are strong. We would not run. We would not beg. We take what is rightfully ours."

Youlin turned on Rehobim. "He threatens Elihu, a respected Plantwalker. Why are you just standing there?" she snapped at him.

Rehobim gave her an odd, indecisive look, but made no move to intervene.

Youlin turned to the other spirit-kin. "Disarm him! Now!" None of them moved.

Fear gripped Shakre. She locked eyes with Elihu. He gave a tiny shake of his head. He looked calm and she knew he was not afraid of his death. But she was. The thought of losing him terrified her.

Pinlir's eyes landed on Rehobim. "I see you in there, Tarnin, behind the weak, frightened child who calls himself Rehobim. Can you not see me? It is Kirtet, your loyal second."

All eyes swung to Rehobim. The young warrior seemed to be fighting an internal battle. There was sweat on his face and he was trembling. His eyes rolled in his head.

"What of the rest of you?" Kirtet demanded of the other spirit-kin. "Will you stand up with me and reclaim what is ours?"

More of the spirit-kin began trembling. Two stepped forward as if to join Kirtet. One fell to his knees.

Kirtet spasmed suddenly. When it passed, the look in his eyes was different. Shakre saw and started to tell Elihu, but he must have felt it too, because he was already reacting.

Elihu closed his eyes and murmured something.

And the haldane tree answered.

Its limbs bent down, wrapping around the axe, and around Kirtet's arms and legs. Kirtet fought to bring the axe to bear, but he could not move either of his arms. Blood ran where the thorns bit deep into his flesh. He struggled futilely for a few more seconds, then subsided. Elihu freed himself and moved out of reach. Shakre ran to him and threw her arms around him.

"You win. For now," Kirtet said. He stared at Rehobim. "You know we must have the aid of the *ronhym*, whatever it takes."

Rehobim gave him a strange look, but did not reply.

Another spasm and it was Pinlir once again, looking around in confusion. "What happened...?"

Elihu made a gesture and the haldane withdrew, releasing Pinlir.

Youlin turned on Rehobim, pushing her hood back so he could see her anger. "Why did you not help him?" she demanded.

Doubt and a trace of fear showed in Rehobim's eyes. "I...could not, Pastwalker. I tried."

"That is not acceptable. You are useless to me, useless to our people, if you cannot stay in control."

Rehobim lowered his head. "Yes, Pastwalker."

"Whatever old feuds existed between our people, they cannot be allowed to erupt now. Our enemy is Gulagh. Nothing else matters. Is this clear?"

"Yes, Pastwalker."

Youlin gave Pinlir a contemptuous look. She gestured. "Strip him of his weapons. All of them." She pointed to two of the spirit-kin. "I will hold you two personally responsible for his conduct. If he does anything like that again, you will face the same consequences as he does."

Then Youlin turned and pushed her way angrily through the spirit-kin. Shakre and Elihu hurried after her. Shakre caught up to her once they were away from the others.

"What are we going to do about this?" she demanded, taking hold of the younger woman's shoulder and forcing her to face her.

Youlin's eyes blazed. "I do not have to answer to *you*. There is nothing more to be done now."

"That's it? You're just going to turn a blind eye to what just happened?"

"I warned them the consequences would be very severe if they lost control again. Nothing else needs to happen."

Her fear of almost losing Elihu pushed Shakre over the edge. "That's not enough! Pinlir, or Kirtet, almost killed Elihu!"

"What else would you have me do?" Youlin yelled back at her. "What more *can* I do? Do you really think I command them? Don't you see how thin my control really is?"

Tears started in her eyes and Shakre was suddenly reminded just how young Youlin really was. She was at most only a year older than Netra was, maybe to the end of her second decade. She wasn't even finished with her Pastwalker training and she was the leader of all their people.

"I'm sorry," Shakre said. "I was just...I thought he was going to kill Elihu." She realized her hands were trembling uncontrollably and she was starting to cry. She felt Elihu put his arm around her and then she couldn't stop the tears at all.

"We *need* them," Youlin said. "Surely you can see that."

"Do we really?"

"Look around. There are so few of us and we have powerful enemies. We need any help we can get. I know they are dangerous, believe me, I *know*. But we don't have any choice." She was staring into Shakre's eyes, imploring her to believe her. "However dangerous they are, they are still our people. They will do everything they can to defend us against our enemies. This I know in my heart. Once we are safe behind Wreckers Gate and Gulagh is driven out, then we can deal with them. Maybe the ancient spirits can be coaxed out. I don't know. We have to handle that when it comes. But for now they're all we have."

Shakre looked at Elihu, then back at Youlin. "Can you at least stop summoning in more of them?"

Youlin nodded. "It is becoming more difficult anyway. There are not so many of them left anymore." Then she pulled up her hood and walked away.

Shakre watched her walk away, then turned to Elihu. "Kirtet. Tarnin. I think we need to find out who they were."

"I agree. We will speak with Rekus tonight."

"He called you Genjinn, but I have always thought you were Dremend-reborn."

"I am. Dremend was my last life. I can name off the three before him, but not further back than that. I was never one much concerned with my past incarnations. I suppose at one time I was the man he called Genjinn."

"Kirtet hates you for something you no longer remember."

"There are lives and lives between me and Genjinn. I believe Kirtet has lingered in the darkness since that time, with no new lives to wash away his hatred."

"Kirtet. Tarnin. The rest of them. Why do you think they were never reborn to the Takare?"

Elihu's look was grim. "Either they were cast out, or they cast themselves out. My guess is that it has something to do with the dark days surrounding the slaughter at Wreckers Gate."

THIRTY-ONE

That night, after the evening meal, Shakre and Elihu sought out Rekus. As usual he was sitting by himself, staring at the ground. His long gray hair was unbound and hung down around his face. The two sat down beside him. Shakre looked around to make sure none of the spirit-kin were watching them. None of them were looking her way. She turned to Rekus.

"It is time we spoke, Pastwalker."

He gave no indication he had heard her.

"Enough of this," Elihu said sharply. "Pastwalker, your people need you."

Rekus glanced up at them briefly, surprised, as Shakre was, by the steel in Elihu's tone. But still he did not speak and his gaze turned back to the ground.

"You have taken vows," Elihu continued, leaning in close to him. "You have sworn to aid your people to the extent of your abilities, regardless of the cost to you."

Rekus shrugged. "This is true," he said listlessly. "And I did. I aided my people to the extent of my abilities." He gave them a raw look, full of self-loathing. "It nearly led to the death of everyone I know." The words hung there for a moment, then he continued. "My people are better off without my service. I lived so firmly in the past that I could not see the present had arrived. I wish the outsiders had killed me. I am of no use to my people anymore."

"That is not for you to decide."

"If you need a Pastwalker, why not speak with Youlin? She is more of a Pastwalker than I ever was."

"She is young. Too young to have completed her training. You know this to be true. You have age and wisdom that she does not."

"At least one of those is true."

"Please, Rekus," Shakre said. "We need you. I know how you feel and—"

"No," Rekus said sharply. "You don't."

"But I do," Shakre said. "On the morning the outsiders came to our shelter the wind tried to warn me but I wouldn't listen." Elihu gave her a surprised look. She had not spoken of this to him before. "If I had listened, we would have had time to escape before they arrived."

"So? That does not alter my failings."

"The point is that I didn't give up after that. I keep trying. I make mistakes, but I haven't quit."

"All we need from you is information," Elihu said. "Surely you will not begrudge your people that?"

Rekus sighed. "What is it you wish to know?"

"Who, or what, are the *ronhym*? Who are Kirtet and Tarnin?"

At the mention of the *ronhym* Rekus' face grew pained. "We do not speak of the *ronhym*," he said. "That knowledge is not to be shared."

That surprised Shakre. The Pastwalkers were the keepers of the past. Their mission was to keep it alive, to keep it pure, so that the Takare could learn and not repeat their mistakes.

"You are a Pastwalker," Elihu said, anger creeping into his voice. "It is your role to share knowledge with your people, not to withhold it."

"I did not make this decision," Rekus replied. "It was made long ago by my predecessors. Only at the end of our training does each generation of Pastwalkers learn of the *ronhym* and each of us takes a vow to keep what we know silent. It is why Youlin knows nothing of them." His voice choked off. "There are reasons."

"What reasons could be good enough to hide the past from our people?" Elihu said harshly.

"You must understand," Rekus implored him. "It is to protect the *ronhym* that we have done this."

"That is not enough. Why have you hidden the knowledge of them?"

"We betrayed them once," Rekus said, pain evident in his voice. "It must never happen again."

Shakre and Elihu exchanged shocked looks. "I accept what you have said and I apologize for my harshness. Clearly you have honorable reasons," Elihu told Rekus. "But still we must know of these *ronhym* now. We have to know more. Walk us into the past. Now."

Rekus rubbed his face, then nodded. He looked around. "We should go somewhere private, where we will not be seen."

Checking to make sure they were not being observed, the three stood and walked away from the camp into the darkness. They found a spot beside a small stream and sat down in a circle. Rekus leaned forward and placed a hand on each of their foreheads. He gave a small push, and they fell back into the past...

THIRTY-TWO

When Tarnin finished reading the parchment he crumpled it in his fist, walked over and threw it into the fire burning in the fireplace. It was nearly winter and the nights had grown cool in Kaetria, the capital of the Empire. Tarnin snatched up the goblet of wine off his desk and drank deep, the dark red liquid spilling down his chin. Then he slammed the goblet down and turned on Kirtet, his second-in-command, the one who had brought him the message and the only other person in the richly appointed room.

"Where is the one who brought this?" he snapped.

"Growing cold in a pool of his own blood, two floors down," Kirtet replied. His long hair was oiled and tied into many braids. He wore a knee-length tunic cut from rich cloth and dyed red. Moccasins of the finest leather came to his knees. His arms were bare except for a single gold band around each bicep. Swords hung on each hip, the one on the right shorter than the one on the left.

"Good," Tarnin growled. He was a tall, powerfully-built man, solidly muscled, with the deliberate moves of a serious fighter and he was dressed and armed much like Kirtet, except his tunic was dark blue. "The seal was unbroken?"

"No one else in Kaetria knows of this but you and me." Kirtet wasn't as tall as Tarnin, but he was quicker, and muscled like a cat. The two men had risen to their positions atop the Takare legions largely by virtue of being two of the best Takare fighters alive.

"Would that Genjinn stood before me right now," Tarnin said, clenching his fists. "I would tear his tongue from his head and force it down his throat."

"I share your outrage," Kirtet said.

"We have to act quickly. By now the same message will have reached a number of others," Tarnin said. According to the messenger, the same message had been sent to every ranking Takare officer across the Empire.

"My thoughts precisely," Kirtet said. "I took the liberty of ordering the Kaetrian legion to be ready to ride at first light for Ankha del'Ath."

"I want messengers to leave tonight. Immediately. They will ride to every ranking officer with a message from me, declaring Genjinn a traitor, and ordering all Takare legions to march on our homeland."

"If I am not too bold, Legate Tarnin," Kirtet said, producing another parchment, this one from his belt. He handed Tarnin the parchment. "I have scribes copying this as we speak and the messengers are saddling their horses. I knew you would want no time wasted." He gave a slight bow. "If it meets with your approval."

Tarnin scanned the parchment, then nodded. "Good," he said, handing the parchment back and taking another drink of wine. "Make sure they ride within the hour." Kirtet saluted and started to leave, but Tarnin stopped him. "Have the Ominati made any more progress with the *ronhym*?"

"No," Kirtet said. "The creature still refuses to power the crystal. It continues to claim that stone power focused through a *relif* crystal is beyond what humans can control."

Tarnin's scowl deepened. "Tell the Ominati they have permission to use whatever means necessary to force the creature's compliance." Kirtet nodded and left. Tarnin poured more wine and walked to the window to stare out at the night. The Takare needed the power contained within that *relif* crystal and they needed it soon. Let that fool Urin think they were trying to get the power to save the city of Kaetria from the encroaching sands. Tarnin cared nothing for Kaetria. In fact, it suited his purposes if Kaetria was buried forever. It would make establishing a new capital for the empire that much simpler.

No, Tarnin wanted the power within the crystal for a different reason: to dispose of the only real obstacle remaining in his way. That obstacle was not the emperor, who posed no threat. He was weak, barely more than a boy. Tarnin had him in his pocket.

He stared out at the city lights, hating the place, as he hated the weaklings he and his people were forced to serve. It was time they took control of the Empire. Under his guidance the Empire would become truly great. His gaze shifted to the massive building to his right. The Tender temple. They were the only ones with the power to thwart his plans. That was why he needed the power contained in the *relif* crystal so badly. Stone force was more powerful than LifeSong. The Ominati

177

had already made quite a lot of progress with it, as witnessed by the light source they lit their building with. But he needed so much more. With what could be focused by the crystal, he could finally move against the Tenders and bring them down once and for all.

Except that now he had to deal with Genjinn and his traitorous uprising first. The fool. Couldn't he see that what Tarnin did, he did for the good of their people? Instead he sent out his letters, filled with miserable, weak puling about external power corrupting the Takare in their quest for internal perfection. Just thinking about it made Tarnin so angry it was all he could do to keep from hurling his goblet against the wall. The worst part was that there were plenty of Takare who would be stirred by such a call. That was why it was so vital to move quickly, to crush Genjinn's rebellion before it could grow.

There was a knock at the door and Tarnin turned, surprised. Kirtet should not have returned so soon and no others would risk disturbing him in his quarters at this hour. He called out and one of the guards posted outside stepped in, a worried look on his face.

"It is the FirstMother, Legate," he said, saluting.

That was certainly odd. "Send her in." Tarnin composed himself, wiping away the anger from his face and sitting down at his desk, pulling some papers to him and making it look like she had disturbed him in the midst of work.

FirstMother Gwinen, a tall, imperious woman dressed in a white robe, her long, black hair braided and coiled on top of her head, strode up to his desk and tossed a parchment down on it. For a heart-sinking moment Tarnin thought she had obtained a copy of Genjinn's treachery. Then he looked at it and saw with relief that it was a different letter. Relief turned to surprise as he saw that it said much the same thing as the message he had received from Genjinn. The difference was that it was addressed to the Tenders and it spoke of how the Tenders had lost their way, consumed by power and wealth. It concluded by calling for all Tenders to come to Ankha del'Ath and join the rebellion. It was signed by a Tender named Aballa.

"I know you got something similar," the FirstMother said. "Don't bother trying to deny it."

In answer, Tarnin shrugged. The FirstMother had as many spies as he did. Probably he would have had word of this letter by tomorrow if she hadn't brought it to him.

"Tomorrow, when your soldiers march, I will accompany you, along with a cadre of Tenders."

"We don't need your help," Tarnin grated.

"This isn't about what you think you need," the FirstMother said, crossing her arms. "This is about eliminating a mutual threat as quickly as possible." She waited, and when he did not respond, she continued. "You don't like me and I don't like you. Someday soon we will have our reckoning. You and I both know this. But that should not stop us from meeting this threat together."

"I still maintain that we do not need you," he said.

"Spare me," she said coldly. "I know your soldiers are the greatest warriors ever, blah, blah, blah. But I have seen Wreckers Gate myself. All your vaunted martial abilities will avail you nothing against it."

Tarnin considered this. She was right, of course. His hope was that when Genjinn and the other rebels saw the massed might of the Takare fighting men and woman arrayed against them that they would back down, or that some of them could be convinced to betray the other rebels. But he was honest enough with himself to know it was a weak plan.

"We can open the Gate for you. The rest is up to you. All we ask is that you capture Aballa alive. She needs to be made an example of."

Tarnin made a sudden decision. "You and two other Tenders. No more."

The FirstMother laughed at him. "And put myself at your mercy like that? How stupid do you think I am?"

"Then you stay here."

"Oh, come now," she said, taking a seat and crossing her legs. The solid gold Reminder hanging around her neck gleamed in the lamplight. "Think about it for a minute. Are you sure you want to leave me here alone while you're gone? What kind of problems might I cause for you during that time?" Her elbows on the armrests of the chair, she steepled her fingers, pretending to be deep in thought. "Perhaps it's time to root out the Ominati. I know they have peered into forbidden powers. I am thinking I can't allow it to continue longer."

Tarnin's hands clenched in his lap as he fought the urge to attack the irritating woman right then and there. But he did not know if he was fast enough to kill her before she summoned her power and if he was not...

"Okay. We leave at first light. But one cadre and no more."

She inclined her head with a smile. "As you command, Legate," she said mockingly, then stood and left.

The bulk of Takare might had returned to their homeland. They stood there in silent ranks before the massive, gleaming blackness of Wreckers Gate. At their head stood Tarnin, with Kirtet on his right. To Tarnin's left stood FirstMother Gwinen, backed by fifty Tenders, most clad in green or blue robes, a handful in white.

On top of the gate stood Genjinn and Aballa.

Tarnin wanted to rage and threaten, but Kirtet had convinced him to try a softer approach first. There was still a chance that some among the rebels could be convinced to recant their traitorous ways. If enough of them did, he might be able to win this victory without the help of the Tenders.

"It is too late for you, Genjinn," Tarnin called. "You must pay for your treason. But for those who stand with you I say this: if you surrender now, I will spare you. You will be pardoned completely." His voice boomed powerfully, loud enough for every fighter on both sides of the gate to hear him clearly and he knew that the Tenders were using their power to amplify him.

"I do not fear for myself," Genjinn responded, his voice also unnaturally loud. "I fear for my brothers and sisters that I look out upon. I fear that it is too late for all of you. I fear that no matter what I say, you will not hear. We are sick, my brothers and sisters! Our wealth and power has sickened us. It is a sickness that grows stronger every day. What happened to the Takare of old, when the only power we sought was power over ourselves, when the battles we fought were against the inner enemy, when our wealth came from the purity of our path rather than from gold and jewels?"

Tarnin felt his anger start to rise. There would be those among his soldiers who would listen to such words. Talking was a waste of time.

"My words are not a revelation to you, my brothers and sisters," Genjinn continued. "But what I have to say next is. There is more you do not know and you should."

Tarnin and Kirtet exchanged a look. How much did Genjinn know? *How* did he know?"

"Along with our other crimes, we can now claim the crime of betraying an ally."

Tarnin felt his pulse quicken. This was bad. The Takare prided themselves on their loyalty to those who treated them with honor. To go against this was one of the worst crimes a Takare could commit. To the FirstMother he hissed, "Shut him off! Do not let them hear him!"

But she ignored him and it was already too late. Genjinn continued to speak.

"Some months ago representatives of Legate Tarnin met with our ancient allies the *ronhym*, those friends responsible for the creation of this gate you see before you. Afterwards one of the *ronhym* accompanied them back to Kaetria, for what purpose we do not know. What we do know is that the *ronhym* was taken captive there and he is even now being tortured to reveal secrets of power."

There was an uneasy shifting amongst the gathered soldiers and looks were exchanged. The *ronhym* were their oldest allies, going back beyond memory. These were serious charges. Tarnin knew he had to act.

"These are lies!" he yelled. "The *ronhym* is our guest. No harm has come to him. Genjinn is only saying this to sway you."

"Then explain why the deep ways are sealed," Genjinn responded.

Disturbed murmuring arose from the Takare soldiers. Such a thing was unheard of. The deep ways—the massive complex of tunnels and caverns underneath the Truebane Mountains that was home to the *ronhym*—had always stood open to the Takare.

"We have tried other means to contact them and we have been rejected. When we asked why, they told us of the torture of one of their own. When we heard that, we knew we must act," Genjinn said.

"Enough of this," Tarnin growled. He gave the signal and archers released a wave of arrows. But Genjinn and Aballa were ready for that and they jumped down out of sight.

Only minutes later a messenger galloped up and slid from his horse. He saluted and went to one knee. "Legate Tarnin, I bring dire news from the capital. The Ominati have been destroyed. They are all dead."

Tarnin drew a sharp breath, his hand going to the hilt of his weapon. Beside him, Kirtet did the same. They both looked at the FirstMother, standing with her Tenders a short distance away, both wondering the same thing. Had she chosen this opportunity to strike at them?

"What killed them?" he asked.

"No one knows. Some monstrous creature. It raged unchecked through the entire building complex and killed everyone. Then it disappeared. I was dispatched to inform you before an investigation could be completed."

Tarnin motioned to his personal guard to follow and he and Kirtet walked over to the FirstMother. The FirstMother saw them coming and turned toward them. The other Tenders spread out in a row to face them. Tarnin felt the buzz in his bones and saw the faint glow around their hands that told him they had summoned Song.

The eyes of every Takare there were on him by the time he reached the FirstMother. Before he could speak, she did.

"I assure you, we had nothing to do with the death of the Ominati. I heard about it some days ago."

"You knew about this, yet you said nothing," he seethed.

"Because I knew you would react this way. It was my hope that we would have this settled already and be on our way before you learned of it. Yet we are still here, because you wanted to handle this your way instead of listening to me."

"You expect me to believe this?" Tarnin itched to make the gesture that would unleash thousands of Takare warriors on these hated women.

"No. I don't. But think about it. If I was going to move against you, would I be here? Look around you, man," she said sharply, becoming irritated. "You are backed by thousands of your soldiers. We are only fifty. If it comes to open conflict a great many of your people will die, but we will lose. You know this. I know this. I would be a fool to attack you now. This attack on the Ominati is as much a surprise to me as it is to you." She gestured at the gate. "Let us open the gate for you. Let us finish what we came here to do. Then we will return to Kaetria and we will learn the culprit behind this attack."

"Your words make sense," he said, his eyes narrowing. "But if you did not do this, then who did? There is no other party with the power."

"Are you sure?" she asked him. "I know that the Ominati—with your backing—toy with powers far beyond anything you can imagine. They tamper with forces within the Spheres of Stone, Sea, and Sky. Is it not possible they angered something?"

Tarnin pondered this. He could see no flaw in her reasoning. He shot a look at Kirtet, who shook his head slightly. Slowly Tarnin took his hand from the hilt of his weapon. Following his example, the gathered warriors did the same.

"Good," the FirstMother said. "Now, can we open this gate and finish this?"

Tarnin nodded. The assembled warriors made a path and he and Kirtet walked with the Tenders up to Wreckers Gate.

"This won't take long," the FirstMother said. "Have your soldiers ready. You may want to stand back."

The Tenders in green, of the Arc of Plants, arrayed themselves in a line in front of the gate. Behind them the blue-clad Tenders, of the Arc of Birds, lined up. Each of the green Tenders pulled something from a pouch she was carrying. The sun had set and it was hard to see in the uncertain light, but it looked to Tarnin as if they were seeds, though far larger than ordinary seeds. Each was about the size of a melon.

Power spilled from the blue-clad Tenders, coalescing above them, swirling around. There was a blur of movement within the power and glowing birds materialized out of it. The birds flew up and hovered there, wings flapping. The green-clad Tenders threw the seeds into the air. The birds snatched the seeds out of the air and carried them up into the sky. They flew over the gate and released the seeds, winking out of existence a few seconds later.

Then Tarnin and Kirtet could do nothing but wait, wondering what was going to happen.

The handful of Takare rebels guarding the gate looked up as they heard the seeds fall, several jumping aside to avoid being struck. The seeds hit the ground and burrowed into it. Within seconds they sprouted. Shoots tipped with sharp thorns shot out in every direction. The rebel guards never had a chance. The shoots pierced them, stilling their cries before they could be uttered. Every guard slumped to the ground, dead.

A moment later the shoots attached to them pulsed and the bodies stirred. One by one they stood upright, faces slack, eyes vacant. They stumbled to the gate and began to open it.

Tarnin stared at the mighty gate, willing it to open. He was vaguely aware of the white-clad Tenders, of the Arc of Humans, standing off to one side, a low hum of power coming from them. Part of him wondered what they were doing, thought it might be important, but most of him simply wanted to make the traitors pay. His rage was increasing by the second. He wanted to see every one of the traitors die and die painfully. He realized that he was making a growling sound but he couldn't seem to stop himself. He didn't want to stop. He wanted to tear them limb from limb. If he could have he would have climbed the gate and flung himself down into their midst, sword flying.

The gate swung open and Tarnin sprinted toward it, an inarticulate roar of rage coming from his throat. Like a single-minded, enraged beast, the rest of the Takare surged forward as well, howls of bloodlust coming from thousands of throats.

They poured into Ankha del'Ath in a flood and found the rebel Takare waiting for them, standing in a group, every man, woman and child who lived in the homeland. There were only a few thousand of them, and most were either very young or very old. None of them held weapons.

Genjinn stood at their head. As Tarnin and the rest charged at him, he stood calmly, his hands at his sides. "We will not fight you!" he yelled. "We are your kin!"

Tarnin's first blow nearly cut him in half. There was a madness on him, on all of them. He swung his weapon wildly, hacking children, old women, everyone he came across without holding back or slowing down. He hated them. Hated them more than he had ever hated anything in his life. All that mattered was killing them, chopping them into pieces.

In only a few minutes it was done.

The dead and dying covered the ground. The Takare warriors stood there uncertainly, staring at each other's blood-spattered faces, eyes dull with shock.

Outside the gate, the FirstMother gestured and the white-clad Tenders released their power. It flickered and subsided.

"It is done," the FirstMother said, her face lit with fierce, savage joy. The Tenders' only real threat had been destroyed this day. Now the Empire would belong to them. The Takare had turned on their own. All they'd needed had been a little nudge to push them over the edge and her Tenders had provided that, turning anger to rage, and rage to homicidal fury. It had been a risk. Had the Legate suspected at all he would have attacked and she and her women would have been slaughtered.

But it had worked.

"Time to leave," she said.

The horses were already saddled. Bolstered by Song fed to them by their riders, they could run faster and further than any horse ridden by the Takare, should the Takare decide to pursue them. But she didn't think they would. She had broken them this day. They would never recover from this.

She had only just mounted when a vision came to her, hitting her so hard she almost fell off the horse and had to cling to the saddle like a child. It was a collection of images sent by Vetla, the Tender she had left in charge in Kaetria, and she knew the woman had sent it with her dying breath.

She watched through Vetla's eyes as the barrier of pure Song protecting the city of Kaetria, the barrier the Tenders had erected, collapsed suddenly. With the barrier gone, the Guardians charged into the city, slaying people in the hundreds and thousands. She watched, helplessly, as Tharn charged into the Emperor's elite troops, scattering them like match sticks. The Emperor died screaming, smashed by Tharn's huge fists.

Kasai and Gulagh attacked the Tender temple together. The huge brass doors fell and they entered. Tenders died by the score, their Song attacks bouncing off the Guardians harmlessly.

Refugees fled screaming from the city. The streets ran red with blood.

Kaetria had fallen. The capital of the Empire was destroyed and with it most of the Tenders. The last image she received was of a huge sandstorm, bigger than anything she'd ever imagined, roaring in from the sandy wastes, dunes forming in the streets, already swallowing the city.

Kirtet made his way through the carnage to Tarnin. "What happened?" he asked hoarsely.

Tarnin had no words. He realized his hands were shaking and he sought to control them, to hide them from the others.

"What have we done?" someone cried out.

"They had no weapons," another said.

That was when Taka-slin spoke up. The legendary warrior had climbed up onto stairs cut into the mountainside, stairs that led up onto Wreckers Gate. "We have destroyed ourselves," he said, his voice cracking. "On this day we have betrayed everything we stood for, everything we held dear. We have killed defenseless people. We have killed our own people."

There were anguished cries from the warriors. Tarnin heard Kirtet yell, "They were traitors. They deserved what they got." A few voices answered him, but most of the gathered Takare said nothing. Their eyes were on Taka-slin.

Taka-slin threw his sword down. It clattered on the cobblestones with a loud noise. "Never again," he said. "From this moment forth, I will never raise a weapon against another person."

A hush greeted his words. Then came the sound of another sword hitting the ground. More followed in rapid succession, until most of the warriors had followed him.

"You're all fools!" Kirtet yelled, climbing up beside Taka-slin. "We are the Takare. We are the true rulers of the Empire. This isn't our fault. It was the Tenders. We were tricked."

"No," Taka-slin said, crossing his arms. "Never again."

Kirtet drew his sword and held it to Taka-slin's throat, but the man did not move. "Kill me," Taka-slin said simply. "It will make no difference."

Others who had thrown their weapons down also crossed their arms and stood resolute. Kirtet looked them over, then at Tarnin. He saw no help there. Tarnin's face was white.

As if Kirtet wasn't there, Taka-slin climbed down off the stairs. "This is no longer my home," he said. "I will go into exile." He walked into the crowd, which parted before him, and passed through the gate. Most of the Takare followed him silently.

In a few minutes only Tarnin, Kirtet and a few score Takare remained. Tarnin yelled after them. "It is you who have failed our people! We are the true Takare! Heed my words. No one who stands here will again be born to your people. We defy you until you are once again true Takare!"

THIRTY-THREE

Rekus pulled his hands away and the vision ended. Shakre was bent over, her arms over her stomach, trying not to cry. She felt absolutely sick to her stomach.

"The Tenders caused the massacre," she whispered. Though she'd been exiled by the Tenders and had lived away from other Tenders for almost twenty years, she still had always thought of herself as one. "I knew that we did terrible things during the Empire, but I never dreamed of anything like this. How could we have done this?"

Elihu put his arm around her. "Your order only amplified the rage that those warriors already felt. Had we not lost ourselves as well, the massacre would never have happened."

Shakre sat there for a long minute, shaking, then she got a hold of herself and wiped the tears away. "What's done is done. It was a long time ago. We have enough to worry about now."

"You see now why the knowledge of our betrayal of the *ronhym* was kept hidden," Rekus said. "It was to protect them from us. If we could do it once, we could do it again."

"Yet it did no good, because the spirit-kin remember," Elihu replied.

"Do you think the *ronhym* will help us?" Shakre asked.

"Would you?" Elihu responded. "If armed soldiers came to your door, representatives of a people who had already shown themselves to be without honor, would you help them?"

"I would keep my door locked and run."

"The question we should be asking is how will the spirit-kin react when the *ronhym* refuse to help?" Elihu asked.

Shakre winced. "It's going to happen again. Only this time it will be worse. We have to warn the *ronhym*."

"How?" Elihu asked. "We don't know where the entrance to their domain lies."

"Rekus, do you know?" Shakre asked.

"It will take some time, but I may be able to walk the past and find the memory we need."

"How much time?"

"I don't know. Much of the night probably."

"That's not going to work, then. The spirit-kin aren't wasting any time. Even if we get ahead of them by a few hours, they'll catch up to us tomorrow," Shakre said.

"Then we will just have to make sure we are near when they enter the deep ways," Elihu said. "We may still find a chance to warn the *ronhym*."

"Maybe they will agree to help us. Maybe we can convince them that Gulagh poses a threat to them."

"But does the Guardian really? It may not even be aware of them. Helping us may only expose them to it."

"We should get back to camp," Shakre said, "before any of the spirit-kin notice we are gone."

THIRTY-FOUR

Quyloc stood there, panting, as the echoes of falling rock died away and the dust began to settle.

"I thought you weren't going to make it," Rome said, putting his hand on Quyloc's shoulder.

Quyloc wiped sweat from his forehead. "Yeah. Me too."

"If we're lucky, she's trapped forever."

"I don't think we're that lucky. She's too strong. She'll get out." As if in response to Quyloc's words, the pile of rubble settled somewhat and a handful of small stones slid down the side.

Rome, looking at it, just shook his head. He slid the black axe back into its sheath. "Tairus is still back there," he said. Quyloc shot him a questioning look. "He threw his axe, hit her right in the back. Right when she was about to do that web thing she does."

Quyloc went still. Holding the spear in both hands, he closed his eyes and seemed to be listening. A moment later he opened them. "He's still alive. So is the big guy. We better send someone around to the north gate to let them in."

"That's great," Rome said, feeling a small smile on his face. Suddenly the day didn't seem quite as bleak. "I should have known the little runt is too tough to die."

"This isn't going to hold them for long," Quyloc said.

"No. I don't guess it will." The grayness closed back in. He scrubbed his face with his hand. He wanted to ask Quyloc how long he thought they could hold out behind the palace wall, but he kept it to himself. He knew he wouldn't like the answer. "I guess we better help with the evacuation." Some soldiers nearby were holding horses for them and he and Quyloc walked over and mounted.

Once on his horse, Rome looked down at his men. There were a couple hundred of them in the street, most of them men who'd been in the square. Their officers had them lined up, awaiting orders. Every one of them was looking at Rome and it seemed to him that every one of them had the same sick expression on his face. Rome suddenly wondered if any of the surviving pikemen would follow Tairus back into the city. Why should they? If he was in their place, he'd run. Better to die in the open than trapped like rats behind the palace wall.

"Spread out!" Rome yelled. "Hit every street and sweep back toward the palace. Get everyone you can. Carry them if you have to. I want sentries posted all around the edge of the square with horns. When the first of the Children shows his face, blow the horns. When you hear the horns, head for the palace at once."

Then Rome clapped his heels to his horse and rode off down a side street. He could feel their eyes on him as he rode and it hurt. They'd stayed to fight because of him. He'd led them to believe that there was hope. He'd led them to believe they could put up the good fight. Yet here they were, less than a day since the Children arrived, already falling back to their last line of defense. What good would it do any of them? Would the palace wall hold any longer than the city wall did? Maybe he should have ordered them all to flee, to run as fast and as far as they could.

He rode along, lost in self-recriminations for a while, and when he looked up, he realized he was outside the Grinning Pig tavern. He got down off his horse, tied it, and went inside. He was not surprised to see Gelbert inside, standing behind the bar, wiping glasses with a rag. An open, half-empty bottle stood beside him. A half dozen of the regulars were there as well, all of them drinking hard.

"Bereth's tail, man," Rome growled, walking up to the bar. "Are you deaf *and* stupid? Didn't you hear the order to retreat to the palace? What are you still doing here?"

"Aye, I heard," Gelbert replied. He poured some liquor out of the bottle into a glass and set it before Rome. "On the house."

Rome tossed back the drink and set the glass down. "They're coming. If you don't get out now, you're dead." He turned to the rest of the room. "You're all dead."

"We all die someday," Gelbert said, taking a drink directly from the bottle.

"But it doesn't have to be today."

"This is my tavern. I'm not leaving."

"You're a damn fool."

Gelbert looked up for the first time. He had watery eyes that were pale blue, something Rome had never noticed before. "I'm staying."

He didn't sound afraid. He didn't sound desperate. He sounded like man who had reached a decision and Rome knew nothing he said or did would dissuade him.

"When they get here, they'll drain you. Every person they drain makes them stronger. If we're going to hold them off…"

Gelbert reached under the bar and took out a small, stoppered bottle, filled with a yellow fluid. "Once you leave, I'm barring the door. No one gets in or out." He paused and looked over the men in the room. They met his eye, but none said anything. "When they get here, one drop of this in each cup and one last drink for each man."

Rome looked at him, then at the rest of the men. He saw the same look on every face. "Okay," he said simply. He held up his glass. "One more?"

Gelbert poured and Rome drank. From habit, Rome reached for his coin purse, but Gelbert waved him off. "Won't need them where I'm going."

"Gelbert giving away free drinks?" Rome said, attempting a smile. "Now I know it's the end of the world."

"Get out of here before I change my mind."

Rome strode to the door and left without looking back.

THIRTY-FIVE

When the pikemen, led by Shorn, broke through to freedom, Karrl chased them for only a little way before realizing that a far greater prize lay behind him, at which point he broke off and headed back for the square. Linde, his wife, turned back when he did and followed him. Once in the square, he looked around. The stone buildings ringing the square looked solid, formidable. He didn't need to try the iron doors sealing them to know he wasn't strong enough to break through. His gaze swung to the two collapsed buildings and the huge pile of rubble they had formed. That was the way through.

He walked to the bottom of the pile of rubble and began to climb up it, ignoring Linde, who begged him to help her. The rock was loose and twice he slid back down, but he didn't give up. The third time he made it, while Linde cursed him and threw small stones at him. By then other Children had begun to climb the rubble as well.

Karrl got to the top and saw the sentry waiting down at the bottom on the far side. The sentry bolted, blowing his horn as he went, and Karrl chased after him heedlessly. He lost his balance almost immediately and slid down the pile, triggering a small landslide as he did so. He ended up at the bottom with a fairly large piece of stone lying partially across him. He pushed it off and stood up. The sentry was too far away for him to catch, but he could smell other people nearby.

Following the scent, he ran into an alley, rounded several corners, then emerged onto a narrow street. A couple blocks away was a group of a dozen people. They were carrying bundles of possessions on their backs and one man was pulling a small cart with an old woman sitting in it. With a cry of hunger, Karrl gave chase.

They looked over their shoulders, saw Karrl, dropped their bundles and took off running. The man pulling the cart called for help, but none turned back to help him. He pulled as fast as he could, but Karrl caught up to the cart easily. As he drew near the old woman spat at him, then

192

took her shoe off and threw it at him. It hit him in the forehead. When he grabbed her ankle she stabbed him in the neck with a long knife she had hidden in her dress. Karrl screamed. It hurt, but his hunger was stronger than the pain and he didn't let go of her ankle.

Moments later she was dead and he was chasing new prey.

Behind him, more and more Children made it over the pile of rubble and into the city. Every street leading up to the palace had people in it. Some were burdened by possessions they refused to leave behind. Others were old or infirm and simply couldn't move fast enough. The soldiers did what they could, but it wasn't enough. Soon screams echoed down every street and what had been a fairly orderly evacuation became a stampede.

There were also those people still in their homes. Some were too sick or too old to flee. Some hid in fear, praying that the scourge would pass them by.

And, with each person they drained, the Children grew stronger, faster.

Quyloc stood on top of the palace wall, watching. The gates were open, citizens streaming through them onto the palace grounds. Three squads of pikemen were arranged outside the gates, ordered to hold the way open as long as possible. Soldiers waited by the gates, ready to slam them closed at his order. Stone masons stood with teams of horses by the large stack of cut stones recently piled just inside the gates. Pulleys had been set up, anchored to the wall. As soon as the gates were closed, they would go into action.

By Quyloc's estimate roughly two-thirds of the remaining population of Qarath had made it in. Thousands more still choked the streets. Screams echoed up from below. None of the Children had yet made it to the palace, but he could see two of them a half dozen blocks away down one of the main streets.

There was still no sign of Rome.

A shout came from one of the soldiers on the wall to Quyloc's right. Quyloc hurried over there. From the northwest came Tairus, leading the remaining pikemen. Shorn was close behind them, still carrying the massive club.

While Quyloc was looking down at them, he caught movement from the corner of his eye and turned just in time to see one of the Children come running out of an alley and fall on a small group of citizens. They cried out and scattered as he fed on one of them. Quyloc shouted an order and one of the squads of pikemen moved to engage the man. Quyloc scanned the area. There was still only the one, but down several other streets he could now see more Children rapidly converging on the palace. Soldiers on the wall also saw the Children coming and they cast nervous glances at Quyloc, wondering when the order to close the gates would come.

"Where are you, Rome?" Quyloc whispered.

He feared for his old friend, but also he feared the order that he would have to give if Rome didn't show up in time. At some point he would have to close the gates, dooming those still left in the city. He would have to stand there, watching, listening, as those poor people died. More than anything he didn't want to be the one to give that order.

Tairus entered the palace grounds and climbed up on the wall to stand with Quyloc. He looked down over the stricken city, his face grim under the sweat and the blood.

"Rome's still out there?"

Quyloc nodded, his eyes fixed on the distance.

"We're going to have to close the gates soon," Tairus said. "They're getting too strong. Even the pikes aren't really working anymore."

The lone Child in the street below had already killed two of the pikemen facing him. One body lay at his feet, the other hung limply in his hands. Finishing that one off, he dropped the body. His eyes closed and he shuddered as the stolen Song coursed through him. Seconds later he opened his eyes and charged at the remaining pikemen. Another one went down.

"You think I don't know that?" Quyloc snarled.

Tairus did not reply. The minutes dragged by. Two more Children made it onto the broad boulevard encircling the palace. The remaining squads of pikemen moved to intercept them. More of them died.

"We will need time to set the stones in place," Tairus said.

Quyloc sagged against the battlements. "I know."

"Now?" Tairus asked.

"Now," he whispered.

Tairus yelled an order and the pikemen began to withdraw, Shorn bringing up the rear. They made it through just before the gates swung shut. A moment later the first of the Children following them hit the gates, which shuddered under the force of the impact. From the sound of it, had he continued beating on the gates, they would have collapsed pretty quickly. But he gave up on them after a couple more blows and turned on the easier prey that was still streaming toward the palace, unaware that escape was now closed to them.

The teams of horses pulled, the ropes tightened and the first of the huge stones lifted into the air and was swung into place.

"Get those rope ladders over the edge! We may still be able to save a few of them!" Tairus called. Rope ladders were dropped over the edge of the wall.

More people entered the wide boulevard. A small group, two men and three women, bolted for the palace gates. One of the Children, an elderly man with a strange, limping gait, caught wind of them and gave chase. They reached the gates and began pounding on them, screaming for them to be opened. Quyloc winced at their cries, each one a poisoned blade digging deep into his heart. Soldiers on the wall yelled down to them, telling them to run to the rope ladders, but in their panic they didn't hear.

The elderly man reached them and fell on one of the women. She went down and was dead in moments. The other four people went crazy, tearing and scratching at the gates until their fingers bled. The elderly man got up off the woman's lifeless body. Ripples ran over him and for a few seconds he just stood there, shaking, as his limbs filled out with new flesh. His abdomen swelled so much that the skin split and gray, withered intestines spilled out. He screamed once, then jumped on one of the men.

Finally, the soldiers' yells got through to the surviving woman. She turned, saw one of the rope ladders and ran for it, the other two men following her. She had just started up the rope ladder when one of the men grabbed her around the waist. She screamed and swung back at him with her elbow, catching him hard in the jaw. He lost his hold and she scurried up the ladder. The other man climbed up after her, but the one she had hit wasn't fast enough and was grabbed by one of the Children.

Similar scenes were happening all over the boulevard. A few people stayed clearheaded enough to realize the gates were closed and run for the rope ladders. But many panicked. They ran this way and that, screaming, pursued by wild-eyed Children. The carnage was awful and Quyloc wanted nothing more than to run away from it. He knew this was a memory he would never escape. But he forced himself to stand there, showing nothing, watching.

All at once a shout went up from the soldiers on the wall. Men pointed off to the left. Quyloc turned his head and saw Rome, on horseback, galloping toward the gates. He had two small children on the saddle in front of him and the black axe in his free hand.

One of the Children, a short woman with odd tufts of hair sprouting irregularly from her head, sprang at him. He swung the axe, nearly severing her head. She went down with a yelp, but as she fell she grabbed onto one of the horse's hindquarters.

The horse whinnied and lurched to the side as the strength left that leg. Another one of the Children closed in and got a hand on the animal's flank. With a cry of terror, the horse collapsed. As it went down, Rome wrapped the two children in his left arm and rolled, shielding them from the ground with his body. He came back to his feet in an instant, the crying children pressed to him, the axe already swinging at a leaping attacker. The axe bit deep into the man and he screamed. Rome struck him again and then ran past him.

Quyloc's fists were clenched so tightly that his nails had bitten into his palms. Over and over he whispered, "Come on, Rome. Come on."

Two more Children closed on Rome. Rome chopped off a hand that was thrust at him, spun and hacked the other one in the chest. In a heartbeat he was off and running again.

He ran for the nearest rope ladder. The two Children he had just attacked recovered and came after him. He reached the ladder several seconds ahead of his pursuers. He put the children he was carrying on the ladder, waited until they took hold of it, then tilted his head back and yelled at the soldiers on top of the wall to pull the ladder up. Then he turned to face his attackers.

They charged him mindlessly, their hunger overwhelming all reason. His face contorted, Rome waded into them, swinging the axe two-handed.

He cut the head clean off the first one and the body toppled over. He caught the next one on the shoulder and cleaved him down into the chest cavity.

By then the soldiers had pulled up the ladder, retrieved the children, then lowered it again. Men shouted for Rome to grab the ladder, but instead he stepped away from the wall, screaming something at the rampaging Children, waving the axe around his head.

Four of them moved toward him. All had clearly fed several times already. They were taller than Rome, their bodies weirdly distorted by new muscle. They came on cautiously, clearly not as maddened by the need to feed as the others had been. They spread out in a half circle.

For an awful moment Quyloc was sure Rome was going to charge them. He saw it in the way the big man leaned forward on the balls of his feet, the axe held up before his chest.

"No, Rome!" he yelled.

Rome settled back on his heels, glanced quickly around the boulevard, then leapt for the ladder. Soldiers were drawing it up the instant he caught hold of it and though the four Children ran for the wall and jumped at him, they got nothing but air.

A minute later Rome was standing beside Quyloc and Tairus, his face ashen as he looked down on the carnage below.

"How many didn't make it?"

Quyloc swallowed. More than anything he didn't want to say the words. "Maybe two or three thousand."

Rome let out a long, shuddering sigh. He slumped against the battlements. "I failed them. I got those people killed."

"I don't see what else you could have done," Tairus said sharply. "Gods, you nearly got yourself killed just now!"

Rome whirled on him. "I could have evacuated them yesterday! I had a feeling the barrier was going to fail. I should have acted on it."

Tairus stared back at him without flinching. "Worrying about what you could have done is just tormenting yourself. What matters is now. You don't have time for this."

Rome looked down at the masons, setting the huge blocks of stone into place. The horses were skittish and hard to control. One tried to bolt and the stone it was attached to, already in the air, swung dangerously.

"I shouldn't have tried to defend Qarath. We should have run away. I've killed everyone here." He looked back at Tairus. "You were a fool to come back. You should have run while you had the chance."

"I came back for the same reason all these people stayed. This is my home. I'll die to defend it," Tairus said, his eyes blazing. "They knew the risks, just like I did. You didn't lie to them. They wanted to defend their homes. Don't take that away from them. Don't you dare. It's their sacrifice, their choice, and you won't take it away."

Rome stared at him for a long moment, his face twitching with suppressed emotion, then he scrubbed his face with his hands. "All right," he said. "I hear you." He straightened himself, then turned to some soldiers standing nearby. "You men go down and help them control those horses. Get those stones in place and do it fast." The soldiers saluted and ran down the stairs.

"Come on," he said to Quyloc and Tairus. "Let's go find Ricarn and the FirstMother and plan our next step."

THIRTY-SIX

They had just gotten down off the wall and Rome was still gripping the black axe in his left hand when suddenly it began to vibrate. It surprised him so much he almost dropped it.

"What is it?" Quyloc asked.

"It just moved." He looked it over closely. The eyes carved into the sides looked...*wet*. He turned the axe slightly, looking at it from different angles and, as he did so, he saw that the eyes moved, tracking him.

Quyloc saw it too. "It's nearly awake."

Rome swore. "Not now," he growled. Then, in his mind, he heard: *Free me.*

"It just spoke to me," Rome said, and relayed the words to the other two men.

"This is bad," Tairus said. "I hate to say it, but we need that thing."

"Hold it up where I can see it," Quyloc said. He slipped back the leather covering on his spear and gripped the haft in his hand. His eyes took on an unfocused look. A moment later he shook his head, his eyes coming back to normal. "There's nothing I can tell that way."

"Something I hate to say," Tairus put in, "but has anyone considered what that thing might do once it's awake? What if it's pissed off?"

The three men looked at each other. Then Rome said, "One problem at a time. Let's worry about the Children first."

They found the FirstMother sitting on the steps of the palace. Bronwyn was crouched beside her, holding a cup of water to her lips. The FirstMother looked up, saw the three of them approaching and pushed the cup away. She struggled to get to her feet, refusing the young Tender's offered hand. She faced the three men defiantly.

"How long until you can get a new barrier up?" Rome asked her. The *sulbit* on her shoulder looked to be unconscious and she was weaving slightly.

"Can't you see she needs to rest?" Bronwyn snapped.

Rome ignored her, staring at the FirstMother.

Nalene made as if to speak, closed her mouth, then looked away. In a low voice she said, "I can't do it. Not yet. I'm too weak. I wouldn't be able to control it."

"When?"

She gave him a dark look. "What difference does it make? They broke the barrier before. They're stronger now and we're weaker."

Opus walked out of the front doors then and came down the steps to them. He bowed slightly to Rome, then turned to Nalene. "FirstMother," Opus said, his manner every bit as decorous and proper as ever. "I have a room ready for you. If you will follow me?" She seemed about to refuse him, then her shoulders sagged and she followed him up the steps and inside.

To Bronwyn, Rome said, "Can you do it, make a barrier?"

"I could try. But I'm not nearly as strong as the FirstMother. My control isn't nearly as good. If I make a mistake, people will die."

"We'll all die without the barrier."

"I'll need to prepare."

"Do it." She walked away and he turned to Quyloc and Tairus. "Better hope the wall holds."

THIRTY-SEVEN

At sunset, Rome, Quyloc and Tairus stood on top of the wall and looked out over the city.

"It's awful quiet," Tairus said. The screams of dying people had gradually subsided over the past few hours and finally disappeared entirely. The last of Children who'd been in the boulevard below had wandered away a few minutes ago, weaving drunkenly, gorged on stolen Song.

"They're resting," Quyloc said. "Digesting their food."

Tairus made a disgusted noise. Below them, Bronwyn was standing near the gates with a dozen Tenders, waiting for Rome's orders. "Want me to tell them to start on the barrier?" Tairus asked.

Rome looked at Quyloc, who shook his head. "As long as it's this quiet, there's no need to risk it. I have a feeling we're not going to face another attack again until morning."

"I wonder where Heram is," Rome said. "As strong as he was before, I can't imagine what he's like now. He may be able to just punch right through the wall."

"If he does that, we're finished," Tairus replied.

"We're finished anyway," Rome said gloomily. "It's only a matter of time."

Tairus and Quyloc exchanged looks. Neither tried to argue with him. There was nothing to say.

✗ ✗ ✗

"There's one. Gods, look at that thing." Ralf elbowed Lery and pointed and both men squinted in the uneven light from the torches.

From a side street a lone figure approached, a man, though twice the size of any ordinary man. He was naked and completely hairless, his skin a dull yellow color. As he came closer, they could see that there was what looked like a vestigial arm growing out of his side, underneath his left arm. His face was misshapen, his skull bulging out on one side.

It was the first time Lery had seen one of the Children and he paled at the sight. "He's huge," he finally managed to say. "Are they all that big?"

Ralf had been on the outer wall and he shrugged. "There was a red-skinned one who was that big, but the rest were no bigger than you or me, and most of them skinny, pathetic-looking things." He leaned on the battlements to get a better look. "They're growing. All those people left in the city, they've been feeding on them, getting stronger, getting bigger."

They both stared, entranced, as the man shambled closer. He staggered more than walked, like a man who's been out drinking late. He walked up to the gates and pounded on them a few times. Even from on top of the wall they could feel the vibrations, the blows were so strong.

"There's no way we can hold them off with pikes now," Ralf said. "They'll snap them like twigs."

Though Ralf spoke in a low voice, the man must have heard him because he looked up suddenly, backing up a few steps until he could see them, standing there frozen at the battlements. His eyes were bright and fever-intense and as he stared at them Lery felt sweat start to run down his spine, though the night was cold.

A whine started in the Child's throat, an eager, wordless sound, like a dog makes when it sees something it badly wants to eat.

Then he jumped at them.

They both jerked back in alarm. He only made it about halfway up the wall, but then for one long, hideous second, he clung there, scrabbling for a purchase on the stone and they feared he would make it up.

Then he lost his precarious hold and slid back down the wall, thumping heavily to the ground.

Ralf slapped Lery on the shoulder. "Run get the sergeant!" he said in a harsh whisper. "Hurry!"

Lery ran for the sergeant as another one of the Children emerged from the shadows of a street and approached the palace wall. Then another.

THIRTY-EIGHT

Netra and Cara were sitting on the low stone wall behind the palace, looking out over the sea. The cliff stretched hundreds of feet below them to the crashing surf far below. Shorn was a silhouette a short distance away, standing motionless with his arms crossed.

"Ricarn thinks that the Children have to be brought back into the Circle. She thinks the only way to stop them is to undo Melekath's Gift."

Cara turned her head to look at her. "That makes sense," she said. "The Gift makes them immortal. Undoing the Gift would make them mortal again. Then they could die. Did she say anything about how she thinks that could be done?"

Netra rubbed her face and continued in a smaller voice. "She thinks I have to do it."

"She does?"

"She says that's why the Ancient One of the Lementh'kal spoke to me. I'm supposed to be the doorway back, whatever that means."

"Does she know how you're to be this doorway?"

"I don't think so. She just kept asking me questions. She acted like I should know."

Cara put her hand on Netra's arm. "Maybe you do."

"What? Not you too."

"Think about it. Think about what you've been able to do. Think about the things you've done."

"That's pretty much all I do," Netra said gloomily.

"That's not what I mean. I know you don't like to hear it, but there *is* something special about you. You've been places, seen things, encountered creatures, that no one else has. Maybe the Mother's hand is guiding you in this."

Netra put her head in her hands. "I can't think like that. It's too much. It's too big. I'll only ruin everything again."

Cara pulled her hand away. "So, just like that?" Netra glanced at her, wondering. "You're scared of making another mistake so you're just going to give up? You're not even going to try?"

Netra was stunned. There was a harshness in Cara's voice that she'd never heard before. "It's not like that," she said weakly.

"It's not? Because that's sure what it sounds like."

Netra flared briefly. "You can't put that much responsibility on me."

"I haven't put anything on you. *You're* the one who went looking for it. No one made you go. But you did and now you found it and it's not what you thought it would be. So what? The question is, what are you going to do now? Are you going to give up, and doom the rest of us with you, or are you going to fight?"

The words were sharp and they cut deep. Netra flinched away from them. "You don't understand what you're saying. I tried. I really did. And all I did was make things worse."

"You didn't answer me. Are you going to give up, or are you going to keep fighting?"

Netra shot a sidelong glance at her old friend. She had changed so much she hardly recognized her. "Okay," she said with resignation. "I'll keep fighting."

"Good. Now let's look at this logically," Cara said. "The Children can't die because they've been set outside the Circle of Life."

"And that's also what's driving their insatiable hunger," Netra added.

"The only way to stop them is to undo the Gift and return them to the Circle."

"But how?"

"That's the question, isn't it? But I'm thinking that if you want to undo the Gift, it makes sense that you talk to the one who created the Gift in the first place."

Netra suddenly saw where Cara was going with this. "Melekath."

Cara nodded. "Exactly."

Netra stared out over the ocean. "Do you think he'd help?"

"You told me that the Children turned on him. What do you think?"

"He just might. But he disappeared. Where do I find him?"

"When the prison was created, there were thousands of his Children trapped inside it, right? All of them had the Gift, which means they're all still…alive. But there's only a hundred or so here. Where are the rest of them?"

204

"Probably still in the prison," Netra said. "You think he went back there when the others turned on him."

"It makes sense."

"So, assuming he's there and that he's willing to help, that still doesn't tell me what to do. How am I supposed to be the doorway?"

"That I don't know. I guess we have to just hope it will come to you. Maybe it will make sense once you talk to him."

"But how am I supposed to get there?"

Cara got up off the wall. "That I *do* know. Quyloc is the answer. He goes into the borderland and comes out somewhere else. It's how he and the macht were able to attack Melekath. Let's go find him."

They entered the palace through a side door, Shorn following them, and found themselves in a long hallway. There didn't seem to be anyone about. They opened a couple of doors, found the rooms beyond filled with sleeping figures, and backed out quietly. The hallway led to another hallway, this one larger, with more doors opening onto it.

"Where do we go?" Netra asked.

"I have no idea," Cara replied. "I've never been in the palace before."

"There must be a servant around here somewhere."

Then, striding toward them, dressed in a robe, came a short man with a neat, black mustache. "Are you lost?" he asked.

"Chief Steward Opus," Cara said. "We're Tenders and—"

"I am aware of who you are. What do you need?"

"We need to talk to Quyloc. It's very important."

Opus gave a brief nod. "Follow me." He led them down more halls and up several sets of stairs until finally they reached a set of ornate double doors. He rapped sharply on the doors.

"Come in," a voice said from beyond the doors.

They entered and found Quyloc sitting at his desk. Books were piled all around him and a lamp was burning on the desk beside him. He looked at them questioningly.

"Tenders to see you, Advisor," Opus said, then backed out of the room and closed the doors behind him.

"What do you want?" Quyloc asked without setting down his book. "I'm very busy."

"She needs to go to the prison at once, to Durag'otal," Cara blurted out.

Quyloc lowered the book and turned his penetrating gaze on Netra. "Why?"

"It's something the Lementh'kal said," Netra replied. To his blank look she added quickly, "They are these yellow-skinned...fish-people, I guess. They rescued us from Kaetria and—"

"Yellow-skinned?" Quyloc frowned. "Was one of them very old? And they spoke in riddles?"

"That's the Ancient One and Ya'Shi, I think," Netra said.

Quyloc's manner changed then. He set the book down and stood up. "What did they say to you?"

Netra explained about the Children and how the Lementh'kal thought she was the doorway to return them to the Circle. Then she explained Cara's reasoning about Melekath and finished by saying, "We think he could be in Durag'otal."

Quyloc pondered this for a moment. "It makes sense."

"That's why she needs to go there," Cara put in. "Right away."

"It seems unlikely that he will help you. He may just kill you out of hand."

"I'm willing to take that chance," Netra said.

"What other choices do we have?" Cara said.

Quyloc gave her a look, but did not reply.

"Can you take me there?"

"I don't know. I can at least get you closer, to the edge of the desert probably. I don't know if I can travel across the desert itself. It is already claimed by the *Pente Akka*."

"I think that would be good enough."

"I should talk to Macht Rome about this first."

"Why?" Cara challenged him. Netra gave her a surprised look. Did she even know this woman? "That wall isn't going to hold the Children out for very long. Every minute counts."

"He is the macht."

"What harm can it do to take her there? At the worst there is nothing there."

Quyloc looked down at the books on his desk. Then he slammed shut the one he'd been reading. "I have found nothing here, nothing that helps in the slightest." He came around the desk. "Okay. Let's go." He looked at Shorn. "Is he going too?"

"Yes."

"Good."

THIRTY-NINE

Nalene opened her eyes, wondering what had awakened her. For a moment she couldn't recall where she was, then it came to her. She was in the small room Opus had taken her to. She vaguely remembered him apologizing for how small it was, how the palace was somewhat crowded at this time and this was the best he could do, but she'd paid him little attention, heading straight for the bed in the corner.

Now she lay there, faint starlight coming in through the window illuminating the room. Her *sulbit* lay curled up on her stomach, its awareness distant and sleepy. She was terribly thirsty. Maybe there was water on the table. She tried to get up, but gave it up as too difficult. The exhaustion she felt seemed to go clear to the bone.

What was the point anyway? The Children had shredded the first barrier. Now they would be even stronger. Lowellin was gone. There was nothing she, or anyone, could do. It would be better if she had died at Guardians Watch.

"Where are you, Xochitl?" she whispered to the darkness. "Have we angered you so much that you will abandon all life in our time of need?"

There was no answer. There was never any answer. Faith in Xochitl, in any god, was foolish. Maybe Quyloc was right, when he said there were no gods, only Shapers like T'sim and Lowellin. Maybe everything she thought she knew was a lie.

"Your problem is that you stand with too much weight on your beliefs. Shatter one of them and your entire foundation crumbles."

The voice, coming from the darkness, startled Nalene so much that she gave a little cry and jerked upright in bed. Her *sulbit* squeaked and jumped onto her shoulder. "Who is it? Who said that?"

From out of the shadows a familiar figure stepped into the rectangle of starlight and looked down on her. Her red robe looked black in the dim light. Her porcelain skin almost seemed to glow.

"It's you," Nalene said. Her heart was still pounding fiercely. "Don't do that."

"Why do you do that?" Ricarn asked. "Why does it matter so much if what you believe is true?" She sounded genuinely perplexed, as if she was so completely different from the rest of the human race that this was a concept she could not grasp.

"I have to believe in something. I have to have something to hold onto."

Ricarn considered this. "Why does it matter that you have something to hold onto?"

"I don't know. So it all makes sense somehow?"

"That's not it." Ricarn's eyes were piercing. Nalene wondered how she could see them so clearly in this darkness. "There's more. Tell me the real reason."

"I don't—"

"*Tell me.*"

And just like that Nalene's self-control cracked. "Because I'm too small!" she burst out. "The world is too big. Everything…it's too much. I can't stand alone before it. I have to have something to hold onto or it will all sweep me away."

"Ah," Ricarn said. "I see." She was silent for a minute.

"Can you just…go away?" Nalene asked. What was it about this woman that so unbalanced her? "I need to rest."

"You think that holding onto something larger than you will keep you safe," Ricarn said, as if she hadn't heard Nalene.

"I guess. I don't know. Why are you here anyway? Did you just come to torture me?"

"I came because we must have something better. The new barrier will hold no better than the old. We require something else."

"I thought you didn't care." Ricarn turned an inquiring look on her and Nalene continued, "When you first arrived here, we talked and you told me you and your kind don't care if you live or die. Why do you care now?"

Ricarn bent closer. The way she did it looked unnatural. She seemed like she should be overbalanced, but she did not put out a hand to steady herself, did not sway at all. She seemed to be studying Nalene's face.

"The simplest form of life still fights to survive. It is the way of life. It is true that I said we didn't care if we died or not. I did not say we would not do anything."

Nalene rubbed her eyes. It was uncomfortable having Ricarn stare at her like this. "You keep saying 'we,' but I don't see the other two, the ones in yellow, anywhere. What are their names? Yelvin? I haven't seen them in days. What happened to them?"

"Yelvin is not a name. It is what they are."

"Don't tell me. They're not human, right? What are they, giant bugs or something?"

The faintest smile from Ricarn. "Human, and yet more. Something else. They are here, when they are needed. When they are not, they are somewhere else. I do not think you would understand."

Now Nalene felt like she was getting a headache. "So what can we do that would work better?"

Ricarn straightened. "In the morning. I will tell you then what I think." She turned to leave.

"That's it? You woke me up for that?"

But it made no difference. Ricarn glided to the door and was gone silently.

FORTY

The area was deserted when something moved underneath the pile of rubble choking the narrow street. Pebbles and small stones cascaded down the pile. One of the larger stones shifted, then slid down as well, raising a small cloud of dust. Two more stones were pushed aside and a hand emerged from underneath them. Then another hand. They gripped the stones on either side and pulled.

Slowly, Reyna emerged.

Her dress was in tatters. Both legs were broken badly. Her rib cage had been crushed and several rib bones jutted out from her flesh. She lay there for a moment, panting and cursing softly. She closed her eyes, concentrating.

She grimaced. Slowly her rib cage shifted. Ribs cracked as they moved back into place. Her legs straightened. Torn flesh knitted together.

She tried to stand and slid down to the bottom of the pile. With a groan, she stood, wobbly at first. She hurt everywhere. Worse than the pain were the traumatic memories triggered by being trapped under the stone. How long had she screamed under there, as centuries of lightless imprisonment collapsed down around her all over again?

The men who did this to her were the same ones who attacked them a few days ago and crippled Melekath. Her hatred for them was a growing flame within her. She hoped they were still alive so she could kill them herself. As slowly and as painfully as she could.

But right now she needed to feed. She was badly weakened from the energy she'd burned to shift all that stone, to reknit her shattered body.

She lifted her face, sniffing the air. Off in that direction. It wasn't much, and it was weakening, but it was all she could find nearby.

She headed down a street at a broken run. Her right leg didn't work right. It buckled on her and she fell hard, hearing a bone crack in her wrist as she landed. Gritting her teeth, she forced herself up once again. The city was completely dark. How long had she been trapped under there? Had the others already devoured everyone in the city?

The last thought terrified her. If they had fed on thousands, they would all be stronger than she. She would be at their mercy.

She lurched into a run once again, following the faint trickle of Song she smelled. As she ran, her worst fears began to come true. She found a number of bodies on the street, saw a man's corpse lying half out a window two stories overhead, but nothing living. In the distance she could sense the other Children, burning brightly.

They were strong, and she was weak.

She kept following the one, faint trickle of Song, though every step closer to it brought her closer to two of the other Children. She came around a corner and there they were.

There was a man, lying on his face in the street, barely alive. He was trying to crawl away, his progress painfully slow. Crouched over him were two figures. They turned and looked up as she approached. It was Karrl and Linde. Both were grossly swollen. Karrl had a split down his back, his spine showing in the wound. Linde's head was huge. Linde frowned at her.

"Go away. This one's ours."

"You'll share with me," Reyna snapped.

They stood as she got to them. Karrl had a dark smile on his face. "Get out of my way," Reyna said, and shoved him, putting much of her dwindling power into it.

Karrl's smile got larger. The shove didn't even move him.

Then Linde hit her from the side.

The power of her attack was astonishing. Reyna was thrown across the street and slammed into the wall of a home. She tumbled to the ground. Sharp pain in her left shoulder told her more bones had broken.

She hissed with rage and started to stand.

Karrl kicked her legs out from under her. He grabbed her by her ankle, swung her and threw her down the street.

This time she couldn't stand. She could only lie there, trying not to scream as they kicked her and slammed her into walls, over and over for what seemed like an eternity.

At last they tired of their sport and wandered away. Reyna lay there, battered and broken, engulfed in a new horror, one she had never experienced in her three thousand-plus years of existence.

She was helpless.

Sometime later she heard someone approaching and she felt fear. Whoever it was, there was nothing she could do against them. Whining with pain and desperation, she began dragging herself toward a nearby doorway using only her left arm, the only limb that was still unbroken.

She made it through the doorway and into the shadowy recesses just as whoever it was passed. Slowly the footsteps receded.

She lay there on her back, fighting to keep from giving in to despair. She was Reyna. She had broken countless people who stood against her. She'd fought back through every desperate battle and always come out on top. She would do it this time too.

A glimmer of an idea.

Slowly, carefully, she gathered her remaining strength, pouring it into her inner senses, staring fixedly into the darkness above her.

There. Barely visible. A ghost thread of Song, a tiny flow of power. She reached for it.

FORTY-ONE

It was shortly after dawn when the Children began showing up in earnest outside the palace wall, drawn by the Song gathered inside. Working all night, the masons had gotten all the stones into place and it was a good thing because the gates only lasted a few minutes before they were pounded into toothpicks mixed with twisted strips of metal.

The Children were utterly transformed. They were grossly swollen, two and three times as big as the day before. Most had grown erratically, sprouting extra limbs, with weird, bulging musculature. Some now moved on four legs and there was one whose skin was scaled like a lizard's.

"Here comes Heram," Tairus observed, pointing. He, Rome and Quyloc were on top of the wall. Heram came walking up the main street that led to the gates. "Looks like his eyes grew back."

Heram's face was massively scarred, especially around his eyes, but he did have eyes once again. Flanked by his two followers, he strode up to the wall. He looked up at the men standing there and he smiled.

"Nowhere else to go!" he yelled. "Jump into the sea now, while you still can!" The two flanking him laughed.

"I'm starting to not like that guy," Tairus said sourly.

"I don't see Reyna anywhere," Quyloc said. It looked like most of the Children were there. Several were pounding on the stones stacked behind the gates. A few others were pounding on the wall itself. Some were leaping, trying to climb the wall, though so far without success.

"Maybe she didn't make it out of the rubble," Rome said.

"None of them seem to be able to seize a man at a distance like she could," Quyloc observed. "At least not yet."

"Yay, we're winning," Tairus said.

Down below them the Tenders, led by Bronwyn, with Nalene watching, were finishing a new barrier. Ricarn stood off to one side.

When the barrier was up, Ricarn called up to the men. "We need to talk."

Ricarn led them to a pair of benches sitting in the shade of the palace. The palace grounds were busy with soldiers and civilians. Babies cried and children chased each other in games of tag. Long tables had been set up and servants were carrying tray after tray of food from the palace to them. Quite a few people had already eaten. The line of those waiting was still long.

"I have been thinking," Ricarn said, "and what we need is a shield like Melekath erected around Durag'otal."

"What are you talking about?" Rome asked.

Nalene answered him. "When Xochitl and the Eight besieged Durag'otal, Melekath raised a shield that covered the entire city. It was so strong even the Eight could not break through it." She looked at Ricarn. "But we have no idea how he did it. Even if we did, we couldn't possibly—"

"You give the impossible power it need not have," Ricarn interjected. "It is why our order is so lost." Nalene closed her mouth, blinking rapidly. "Melekath created the shield by drawing on the power at the Heart of the Stone."

"I still don't know what you're talking about," Rome said. "How does this help us?"

"There's power within the Stone," Quyloc told him. "Like LifeSong, but deeper, slower. And far, far stronger." To Ricarn he said, "But how do we do this?"

"Melekath wasn't strong enough to build the shield alone," Ricarn said.

"Then what good is talking about this?" Tairus snapped. "You're wasting our time."

Ricarn didn't even glance at Tairus. Calmly, she said, "Melekath had help. From one of the *ronhym*."

"He had help from *what*? How do you know this?" Nalene asked.

"My Arc never destroyed or suppressed knowledge," Ricarn replied. "We saw what was happening, soon after Xochitl left, how the FirstMother began to hide or destroy information she did not trust the rest of us to handle. We began copying what we could, things like eyewitness accounts from Tenders who were at the siege." She pointed at the axe Rome had strapped to his back. "I believe that is one of the *ronhym*."

"Does someone want to tell me what a *ronhym* is?" Rome asked, irritation in his voice.

"I do not know much," Ricarn admitted. "Only that they are a very old race, maybe even older than the Shapers. They dwell deep within the Stone."

"If it is a *ronhym*," Quyloc said, "that would explain a lot. Why it can cut through stone like it does."

"So this is some kind of creature called a *ronhym*?" Rome said, drawing the axe. He handled it gingerly, as if it might bite him.

"I believe so," Ricarn replied.

"What was it doing in the wall of the prison?" Rome asked.

"Think about it," Quyloc said, a measure of excitement creeping into his voice. "The thing helped Melekath erect the shield around Durag'otal. If it did that, we can assume it was friendly with Melekath, at least allied with him, right?" Rome nodded. "Somehow it ends up stuck in the prison wall. You come along, pull it out, and that provides the crack that lets Melekath break the prison and free himself and his Children."

"You're saying that thing put itself into the wall on purpose?" Tairus asked, frowning.

"It makes sense," Quyloc replied, looking at Ricarn. She nodded, ever so slightly. To Rome he said, "You told me it's been communicating with you, asking you to free it."

"It happened again yesterday," Rome said.

"So you think if we free it maybe it will help us too, put up one of those shields here?" Tairus asked.

"It's worth a try," Quyloc said.

Everyone looked at Rome. "That's a lot of guessing," he said. "It may not be one of those creatures. It may be mad at us. It may just attack us." He pulled at his beard, thinking. "But we're out of options." To Ricarn he said, "How do we wake it up?"

"It already is waking up. Just keep doing what you've been doing. Keep using it."

Rome looked around. If they still had access to the city, this would be easy. There were lots of stone buildings everywhere. There were stone buildings in here also, as well as the palace itself, but all of them were either housing refugees or packed with food and other supplies. Then it occurred to him.

In front of the palace was a wide, circular drive, where the nobles would pull up in their carriages, back during King Rix's reign. In the center of the drive was a huge statue of King Rix, one hand holding up a sword, the other shading his eyes as he looked off to the horizon. Rome started for it.

"I've always hated that statue," he said. "Been meaning to get rid of it."

The first time he hit the statue the axe vibrated so hard in his hands he almost dropped it. The scales on the haft grew more pronounced. The head of the axe seemed more rounded. He swung again and again, the vibration growing stronger with each blow. The statue went down and he chopped it into pieces, cutting off the head first, then the arms and legs and finally cleaving the torso in two. By then the axe was buzzing so hard it hurt his hands. He dropped it on the ground and stepped back. The weapon began to writhe. Legs, spindly at first, but then growing thicker, separated from the haft. The thing's back arched and its neck grew longer.

Tairus started to draw his weapon, but Rome stopped him.

"Let's not have it thinking we're the enemy," he said. Tairus slid his axe back into its sheath.

A couple of minutes later the transformation was complete. The *ronhym* lay on the cobblestones, four-legged, sleek and black, with what looked like fine scales covering its body and a tapered head similar to a dog's. It squirmed, then got up onto its feet, the head turning and pointing up at them. The eyes it turned on Rome were very liquid and deep. It opened its mouth—it seemed to have no teeth—and strange sounds came from it.

"What?" Rome said.

The *ronhym* shook itself. A strange shudder passed over it and it seemed almost to be melting. Its front legs became shorter, thinner, and its rear legs grew longer, thicker. The spine straightened, the neck shortened. Its muzzle retreated into its face.

When next it faced Rome it stood on two legs, in shape very similar to a human, though very slim and lithe. There were faint suggestions of ears on the sides of its head and its thin-lipped mouth was very wide. It was a head shorter than they were.

"This form should be easier for you to relate to," it said. Its voice sounded rusty, the words odd, but recognizable. It sounded female. "I forgot that I cannot speak your language in my true form." She bowed to him. "You have my gratitude for freeing me."

Rome stared at her, wondering what to say. "Do you know who we are?" he finally managed.

The *ronhym* nodded. "I have been listening to you for some time." She looked to the pile of stones in place behind the gates. "I know something of your situation."

"What's your name?" Quyloc asked.

"I am..." The creature paused. "You would not be able to pronounce my name. You may call me Ketora, as the Children did." As she spoke of the Children her mouth drooped and she lowered her head. "They were not like this...back then."

"So you *did* enter the prison wall willingly," Quyloc said.

"Your kind is not meant for living underground, cut off from all that sustains you. I felt pity for them and acted."

"You are no living creature," Nalene said. Her *sulbit* was acting strangely, pacing back and forth across her shoulders, making chittering noises. She put her hand on it to try and calm it.

"No. The *ronhym* were old long before Life. We are creatures of the Stone. We have been here since the beginning. We watched the Nipashanti fall from the sky."

"You helped Melekath build the shield," Ricarn said.

Ketora nodded. "I was there when Melekath created the Gift. I saw what it cost him to give of himself like that. You might say we were friends. He was the only one of the Nipashanti to visit my people and learn about us. Most were too arrogant to see beyond themselves."

"Can you help us put up a shield here?" Nalene asked.

Ketora looked at the front gates again. "Even if I do, and the Children go away, their hunger will not abate. You still have no way to stop them."

"We have to start somewhere," Rome said. "Hard to find a solution if we're all dead."

"I will help you. The Children do not know what it is they do. I say again: they were not always this way."

There came the sound of heavy blows against the stones blocking the entrance and it seemed like they moved fractionally.

"I will need a *relif* and the help of one of the Nipashanti. Otherwise the power is too much even for me to control. How big we can make it will depend on how strong the Nipashanti is. I am only a conduit." More heavy thudding against the stones. "There is, however, one thing I can help you with right now."

Ketora walked over to the cut stones filling the passage under the wall. The masons still working there all scattered at her approach. She ignored them and placed her hands on the stones. Ketora spoke to the

217

stones in her language. The stones began to melt, though there was no heat. When she pulled her hands away, the gaps between the stones were gone and they were fused to the wall. It looked like no gate had ever been there at all.

"Well, that's one problem solved," Tairus said. "It's going to be hell to clean that out, though."

Ketora returned to them. "What is a *relif*?" Nalene asked.

"A kind of crystal. A focus point for Stone power."

"How do we get one?" Rome asked.

Ketora's eyes closed. She held her arms out, palms down, and turned slowly in a circle. Then she lowered her arms and looked at Rome. "There is one in the stone, underneath there." She pointed at the tower.

FORTY-TWO

They walked over closer to the tower. It was completely shrouded in the strange vine from the *Pente Akka*. Hardly any of the structure was still visible underneath the huge, bright green leaves with their crimson borders. Bright orange flowers the size of shields were dotted here and there. The dune it emerged from was engulfed in the vine as well.

"The vine is of the *Pente Akka*," Ketora said, and a shiver passed over her. "It whines with chaos power." She shook her head emphatically. "I will not allow that thing to touch me. Do not ask me to do this. My willingness only extends so far."

"Then we have to get you in there without it touching you," Quyloc said.

"You said you live in stone," Rome said. "Can't you just, I don't know, cut through the ground to get to the crystal? Then you don't have to worry about the vine at all."

"Normally, I could do so, but I am still weak from my long captivity. If I go in that way it is possible I would not then have the strength to help you, not for some time. I sense that under the tower there are tunnels and in one of them there is an opening into a deep chasm that leads nearly to the *relif*. It would be much easier to go that way."

Quyloc thought of the chasm he crossed when he went to his room under the tower, the tiny flicker of red light he'd seen in its depths one time when his lantern went out.

Rome looked at Quyloc. "You think your *rendspear* can cut those vines?"

"It did so when I was in the *Pente Akka*. It should do so here. But that's only part of our problem. Ketora said she needs one of the Nipashanti to help her control it." Turning to Nalene, Quyloc said, "Have you had any word from Lowellin?"

Her face twisted harshly. "There has been no sign of the Pro— of Lowellin since the Children arrived. He has abandoned us."

"It does not matter," Ketora said. "Lowellin is not First Ring. He is not Nipashanti. He is Lesser."

"What about T'sim?" Rome asked. "Is he one?"

Ketora nodded. "He will do."

Rome looked around. "Where is he when I need him?"

A sudden puff of wind, and there was T'sim standing behind Rome, looking as if he'd been there all along. "You require my assistance?" T'sim said mildly.

"Can you help this…help Ketora make us a shield?"

T'sim looked the *ronhym* over carefully. Then a curious look came over his face and he took a step back. "You *knew*," T'sim said.

Ketora nodded.

"What are you talking about?" Rome asked.

T'sim looked at Rome. "She knew what would happen to the Children in there. It is why she sacrificed herself, so that someday the prison would be broken."

"It is true," Ketora said.

"Was it worth it, enduring what you did for the sake of mere humans?" T'sim waited expectantly for her answer.

Ketora hesitated. "I do not know. It was uniquely painful, the touch of the abyss. I do not think I will ever completely be free of it."

"Yet still you stand ready to help them once again."

"I do."

"They tortured and killed one of your kind in Kaetria, in the days before the sand swallowed the city."

"I did not know of this."

"They were afraid. They thought the *ronhym* could save them."

Ketora gave the people gathered around her an unreadable look.

"It was a long time ago," Quyloc said. "Centuries before any of us were born."

"Is it true what the Nipashanti says?" Ketora asked.

Quyloc wanted to deny it, but he sensed Ketora pulling back, rethinking her decision. If she thought he was lying to her, they'd lose any chance they had of getting her help on this. "I don't know," he admitted. "We don't have any records from that time. But I think it is probably true. When we're afraid we don't always act wisely." He winced as he said the words, afraid he'd chosen wrongly.

"Remember also that the one who calls himself Rome has used you as a weapon and was prepared to continue to do so," T'sim added.

"Really, T'sim?" Rome asked. "This is your idea of helping?"

"This is my idea of truth. I only wish to be sure she knows and does not go into this blindly," T'sim replied.

"Look, Ketora," Rome said. "I'm sorry for what I did, using you as a weapon and all. At first I didn't realize you were a living thing and then…" Quyloc caught his eye and shook his head ever so slightly. Rome's eyes widened and his words died away. He scratched his neck. "Oh, hell. No excuses. Even once I knew there was something living in the axe I didn't do anything about it. We're in a war here, a war that could mean the death of every person on this world. I'll do anything to keep that from happening."

She thought about this for some time. The thudding at the gate sounded very loud in the silence as they all waited for her to decide. At length she said, "I respect your honesty." To T'sim she said, "I will still do this."

T'sim turned to Rome. "The *ronhym* make no more sense to me than you humans do." He looked over the rest of them. "It is not the way of my kind to become involved."

"When the Children have devoured all that there is of Life, they will turn to the Spheres," Ricarn said.

T'sim waved her words away as if they were flies. "I am aware of this. It has no weight with me."

No one said anything then. There was nothing to say, no arguments that would sway this *aranti*, this creature of the Sky. No threats that would turn him. No rewards to offer him. He would agree or he would not. They could only wait.

"Find the crystal," T'sim said at last. "I will consider this."

Rome turned to Quyloc. "Are you ready?"

In answer, Quyloc unwrapped his spear, took a firm grip on it and looked up at the tower. Now that he was touching the spear directly there was a high-pitched whine in his ears, like mosquitos trying to get past a screen and drink his blood. There was a sense of something hungry waiting, watching. It was not just the vine that would threaten them. There were things living in it and they were perhaps even more dangerous.

But it was only what he had expected and he had already warned the others. There was nothing to do now but go forward. "I'm ready."

Nicandro and two other soldiers were standing there with them, each of them carrying a large, rectangular, metal-sheathed shield. Rome had a similar shield. "Are you ready?" Rome asked them. The three men nodded. Quyloc could feel the fear that they held tightly in check. He was afraid too, but it was a familiar feeling and somehow more bearable than it had always been before.

"Are you ready?" Rome asked Ketora.

"Yes."

"Then I guess there's no sense in putting it off any longer." He clamped his helmet down on his head and lifted the shield. "Let's go chop some weeds."

The six of them approached the Tower cautiously, Quyloc in the lead, Rome flanking him on the right and Nicandro flanking him on the left, both with shields held out in front of them, leaving only a narrow gap for Quyloc to see through. Behind them came the other two soldiers, shields held over their heads to protect them from above. Ketora was pressed close behind Quyloc.

Partway there, Quyloc realized Ricarn was following them.

"I don't know if we can protect you too," he told her.

"I just want to get a closer look at the vine. I do not need protecting," she replied calmly. "The vine does not see me."

Quyloc wondered briefly what she meant by that, but this was not the time to ask. He could afford no distractions. In his heightened state the leaves were so bright they almost glowed. He felt itchy everywhere, as if a rash had broken out all over his body.

As they drew near the Tower the vine seemed to grow larger. It was much thicker and denser than it had been even that morning. Insects buzzed in its depths and there were hints of movement in the deep shadows within the leaves. A rustling sound came from the right and the leaves there shook.

There were half a dozen flowers in the foliage covering the door and they all swung to face the approaching party. An intoxicating mix of reds and yellows swirled in their depths, drawing the eye in, beckoning, promising. Nicandro increased his pace slightly, moving ahead of the group.

"Don't stare at the flowers," Quyloc said sharply, grabbing him by the shoulder and hauling him back. Nicandro shook his head and shifted his eyes away.

"So, when you made your spear, you passed through a whole jungle of this stuff? Alone?" Rome said. He spoke in a whisper, as if the vine would hear. "I don't know if you're stupidly brave or just stupid." A hint of a chuckle came from one of the soldiers behind them and Quyloc realized Rome was doing what he always did, finding a way to defuse the tension.

"Open up a little," Quyloc said as they reached the outer edges of the vine. "I need room to move." Rome and Nicandro moved their shields to the sides and Quyloc stepped into the gap.

He slashed at the first runners of vine on the ground in front of them, the spear slicing through them easily and scoring the stone underneath. When he did the whole vine trembled. The wounded runners slithered back, while the pieces that had been cut off writhed on the ground like dying snakes. Quyloc kicked them out of the way and pressed forward.

"Ready to close up on my mark," Quyloc warned Rome and Nicandro.

He stepped forward and slashed down into the heart of the vine, cutting through leaves and thicker stems. The whole vine trembled. From the two closest flowers clouds of pollen suddenly puffed outward.

But Quyloc was already calling a warning and jumping back and they closed up the shields in front of him, blocking the pollen cloud, which landed on the shields with the sizzling sound of water thrown into a hot frying pan.

"Once more," Quyloc said.

They opened the gap between the shields and Quyloc leapt through. Two quick slashes and the flowers tumbled to the ground. The spear blurred in his hands and bit deep into the vine. Then he jumped backward.

Rome and Nicandro slammed their shields together, crouching as the soldiers bringing up the rear brought their shields down to rest on the front shields. There came a sudden barrage against the shields as tendrils of vine shot out and struck them in numerous places.

"Push forward now, before it can recover!" Quyloc said.

They pressed forward, pushing the vine back with the shields.

"Open it up!" Quyloc snapped.

They shifted, once again opening a space between the shields. Quyloc hacked off pieces faster than the eye could follow, carving an opening and driving forward. The little party followed, packed tightly together, and then all of them were within the vine's depths.

It was dark in there, far darker than it should have been, the little light there was was gray and filled with shadows. Things whispered and scurried through the leaves. All at once Quyloc felt something larger making its way toward them, coming down the wall of the tower above them. They didn't have long.

Quyloc hacked and slashed in a frenzy, the cut pieces piling up around his legs. He felt the sting of something on his ankle. One of the soldiers behind him cried out in pain and stumbled against Rome's back.

"It's got my leg!" the man cried.

Quyloc turned, saw a vine wrapped around the man's leg. He slashed and the vine fell away. Blood ran down the soldier's leg.

Quyloc spun back around just as a vine shot through the gap between the two shields. Before he could react it had wrapped around the haft of the spear. It tightened and pulled. He fought back, but it was too strong for him.

Then Rome had his axe out, wielding it in one hand. He chopped down and the vine fell away. Quyloc tore off the remaining piece. Two more vines shot in and he barely had time to cut through them.

It was hard to move; everyone was pressed so tightly together. The soldiers were grunting with the effort as the vine pressed ever harder against the shields. Quyloc began to think they had made a terrible mistake.

Then the spear hit metal.

The door.

Quyloc hacked some more, leaves and stems fell and then the door became visible. He grabbed the handle and pulled.

The door didn't budge.

FORTY-THREE

"It's cutting us off!" one of the soldiers in the rear said.

Quyloc shot a look over his shoulder. The opening he'd cut through the vine was rapidly closing up, new vines slithering in from the sides and dropping down from above, weaving together to form an ever more impenetrable mass.

"Time to open the door, Quyloc," Rome said. His voice was still calm. He might have been telling Quyloc to close a window against the chill.

"I'm trying!" Quyloc snapped, jerking on the door harder. It still didn't budge. In his mind's eye he saw the inside of the tower packed with growth. He'd get the door open only to find that what waited on the other side was worse.

"I can't hold it much longer," the soldier behind Rome rasped, fear evident in his voice. "It's pushing down too hard. It's getting too heavy."

"I got you," Rome said, using the axe to push up on the man's shield and help steady it.

All at once Quyloc saw what was blocking the door. Growing across the base of it was a thick piece of vine as big around as his arm. He hadn't been able to see it because it was obscured in the darkness.

The first couple times he slashed it had no effect.

A vine snaked around the shield held by the soldier behind Nicandro and tightened. The shield buckled and then it was ripped away, lifting the soldier into the air before he got his arm out of the straps and dropped back to the ground. He jerked his sword free and hacked at another vine as it wrapped around his ankle.

"The door, Quyloc," Rome said. Now his voice was rising.

"Just hold on!" Quyloc yelled. It was hard to get a clear shot at the vine. Finally, he stabbed down into it and threw his weight against the end of the spear, levering the blade down through the woody mass.

"Got it," Quyloc gasped. He jerked the door open and they all jumped through. Two more vines shot in after them. One almost got a hold of Ketora, but Nicandro pushed her out of the way just in time. Rome dropped his shield and hacked at the vines with his axe until they withdrew. He pulled the door closed and dropped the bar across it.

They stood in the tower, breathing hard. It was very dark.

"That was close," Nicandro said.

"Are we going to be able to get back out?" one of the soldiers asked.

"Of course we will," Rome replied confidently.

Quyloc felt around in the darkness and found the lamp hanging on the wall by the door. A few seconds later he got it lit and held it up.

"Oh, gods," one of the soldiers moaned.

The vine had grown down the stairway that led to the upper floors of the tower. It spilled out of the stairway in a thick mass of green that filled the far side of the room. The leaves shivered.

"In here," Quyloc said, leading them across the room and into a storage room. Crates and barrels were stacked against the walls inside the room. He slammed the door shut behind them and immediately the soldiers started grabbing crates and stacking them in front of the door. Quyloc hurried to the back wall of the storage room and moved a barrel, revealing the trap door that led to the tunnels underneath the tower.

"You men wait here," Quyloc said to the soldiers. He started down into the shaft, taking the lantern with him.

Rome looked at Nicandro. The stocky, dark-skinned man looked calm enough, but the faces of the other two soldiers were pale, their eyes wide. "That's a strong door," Rome said. "You'll be all right. If you can't hold it, though, follow us down. I think Quyloc said there's another way out at the base of the cliffs." He neglected to mention that the tunnel leading down there might have collapsed or that if the tide was in the exit would be underwater. No sense in upsetting them.

"You going to leave us here without a light, Macht?" Nicandro asked him.

"Quyloc, hold on a second."

Only Quyloc's head was still sticking out of the trap door. "What?"

"A light?"

"Over there on that crate is another lantern." He ducked down out of sight. Nicandro hurried to grab the other lantern.

Rome climbed down the ladder. Once down at the bottom of the ladder, Ketora took the lead, heading off down the tunnel. Quyloc followed her, Rome close behind.

Rome remembered the last time he came down here—when he convinced Quyloc to help him attack Melekath—and how poorly that turned out. He also thought of the first time he followed Quyloc underground, when they found the black axe. That didn't work out so well either. He decided that he could develop a serious dislike for tunnels of any kind.

Ketora led them to the place where the wide crack cut across the floor of the tunnel. She stood at the edge of the crack staring down. "One of the Shapers has been here recently," she said.

"Probably Lowellin," Quyloc replied. "He's come down here before to find me."

"I know this name. Melekath spoke of him. There is no friendship between the two of them."

"Was Lowellin after the crystal?"

"He must have known it was here, but I do not believe he sought to take it. Without the help of a *ronhym* it is dangerous to touch such a thing, even for a Shaper. At the very least it would cause him great pain."

"But you can touch it?"

Ketora nodded. "And I can open it. But I do not have the strength to connect it to the Heart of Stone power by myself. If more of my kind were here…" Ketora trailed off. "I would that we are done with this quickly, so I may return to my people. It has been far too long."

"What do you want us to do?" Rome asked.

"Wait here." And with that Ketora slipped over the edge. Quyloc held the lantern over the crack and the two men leaned forward to watch her descend. It looked as though the *ronhym* just kind of slid down the face of the rock, hands and feet seeming to stick to it with no trouble.

"Are you thinking what I'm thinking?" Rome asked when she was out of sight.

"What's that?" Quyloc replied.

"How are we going to get back out of here?"

Quyloc nodded. "I've been thinking about it."

"Any thoughts on that?"

Quyloc glanced at Rome. The lantern light left most of his face in shadows. "You mean something besides the usual Wulf Rome fare? Charge straight at them and ram it down their throats?"

"I was hoping you'd have something a little more creative." Rome didn't add that he thought they'd gotten lucky on the way in. They might not be so lucky on the way out. Did that plant *think*? Would it try new tactics? What if they opened the storage room door and found the area beyond completely full of the plant?

"While I'm honored that you're finally actually interested in my advice, I don't really have anything here other than charge the thing and chop as fast as you can."

"I was afraid of that. Some adviser you are." Rome tried to add a chuckle to the end of that, but it didn't really come out right. Would the weirdness ever end? Wasn't it enough that they had to contend with the Children? Did they have to be attacked by bloodthirsty plants as well?

They stood in silence for a minute. Rome didn't like the silence. There were too many thoughts in it. "How's your leg?" Rome asked.

"Why do you ask?"

"You were limping on the way in here."

"Something stung me. I'll look at it when we get out of here."

"Something in the vine?"

Quyloc nodded.

"Aren't you a little worried about *what* stung you?"

Quyloc gave him a quick look before averting his eyes. His voice, when he spoke, sounded tired. "Yeah, Rome. I am. I'm actually terrified. Everything about the *Pente Akka* scares me. But somehow I keep having to go there so I guess I just have to deal with it. Maybe if we actually survive this I'll just lock myself in a room and scream for a couple of days straight."

"That sounds reasonable to me." And it did. Ever since he started going into the shadow world Quyloc had been telling Rome about the place. He'd seen the effect it had on his friend, how it haunted him. He'd seen him trapped by the place, on the way to Guardians Watch. But somehow it never seemed real to him. Somehow he'd always thought of it as something in Quyloc's mind. Now here he was, his second encounter with the place, and it was all too real. Frankly, it *was* terrifying, like Quyloc said.

"I've had enough of the *Pente Akka*," Rome said.

"Yeah. Me too."

Ketora was back a few minutes later, carrying a yellow crystal about the size of Quyloc's forearm. As she neared them, the crystal changed colors, first turning orange, then deepening into red. Rome and Quyloc

228

backed away. The thing's presence was making Quyloc nauseated. A strange, sickly heat seemed to radiate from it and he rubbed his arms, feeling like he was going to break out in a rash.

"Do you feel that?" he asked Rome.

"I don't know. All I know is there's no way I'm touching that thing."

"It would be deadly to you," Ketora said.

"Thanks for the warning. But a person would have to be an idiot to touch that," Rome said.

"Let's go," Quyloc said. "Every minute we waste down here is another minute that vine has to prepare some new surprise for us."

They started back towards the surface, Quyloc leading, Rome behind him and Ketora in the rear.

"You really think that plant *thinks*?" Rome asked.

"I don't know. But I do know this: it's not actually a plant. At least, not like we think of plants. Nothing from that place is what it appears to be. Personally, I think the things in that world are trying to copy us. The whole *Pente Akka* is a copy of our world, a terribly poisonous copy."

"But I've never seen any forest like what was growing around that volcano."

"Neither have I. But that doesn't mean there isn't forest like that somewhere on our world, somewhere we haven't been. Or maybe there isn't. Maybe the things in there are simply that place's rendition of plants and animals and so on."

"I guess there's no point in asking you why they want into our world so bad."

"No. There isn't."

"Wonderful."

They climbed back up into the storage room. The three soldiers looked tremendously relieved to see them even as they recoiled from the *relif* crystal. "There's things moving around out there," Nicandro said. "Scratching at the door." His voice was strained and his normal cockiness seemed to have deserted him.

"Well, let's give them something to chew on then," Rome said, picking up his shield. He paused and looked at the soldiers. "That might have been a bad choice of words. I meant chew on steel, not on us."

No one answered him. They were all looking at the door. Something was tapping on it.

"What's the plan, Macht?" Nicandro asked.

"Stay close together. Chop anything that moves. Go like hell for the door."

They moved to the door. Moving as quietly as they could, the soldiers moved the crates aside that were blocking it. The tapping noise had stopped. Quyloc put his hand on the latch. The spear in his other hand seemed almost to pulse. "Is everybody ready?" The men nodded. Ketora had the *relif* cradled to her chest. She nodded as well. Quyloc took a deep breath and opened the door.

The vine now completely choked the stairwell and blanketed one whole wall of the entrance room of the tower. It had begun to spread across the floor as well and one tendril reached clear to the door. One of the soldiers swore. Gripping the spear tightly, Quyloc stared into the leafy depths. He could sense things in there, watching them, but nothing more than that.

"Move!" he hissed. "Protect Ketora at all costs."

He slashed the tendril at his feet. The cut piece writhed on the floor while the rest recoiled. A chittering noise came from the depths of the vine. In a tightly bunched group they ran to the outer door of the tower. With every step he could feel the menace at his back growing stronger and he felt terribly exposed. He reached the door and flipped the bar out of the way. As he was reaching for the handle, there were sudden shrieks behind him and he spun.

Four hairy, clawed creatures were charging across the room. They were the size of men and they ran hunched over, using their arms nearly as much as their legs. Each had a row of bulging, yellow eyes. They shrieked again, showing canines as long as daggers.

One of the soldiers in the rear was slowed by his shield and by the time he turned the first of the creatures fell on him, tearing his throat out with a single swipe of its clawed hand. He gurgled and went down in a spray of blood that seemed to go everywhere.

The instant he died, for Quyloc, it was as if the whole scene froze for just a second: the creatures in mid-leap; Rome and the two remaining soldiers fighting to bring weapons and shields around, their mouths and eyes wide; Ketora ducking away, the crystal tucked in tight to her chest.

In that frozen second, Quyloc saw a strange, sulfurous light bathe the room. An opening appeared in the air. Through the opening he saw the volcano, the *gromdin* perched on top of it. Then a burst of light he knew to be the man's Selfsong shot through the opening. The frozen moment ended.

The dead man had barely struck the floor when Quyloc stabbed the creature that killed him in the chest.

Another of the creatures slammed into Rome's shield just as he got it into place. Rome fell back a half step, then got his feet under him, and swung the war axe with his right hand.

The third creature rammed into Nicandro, knocking him down and clawing wildly at the shield.

The other soldier, his shield lost on the way in, screamed in fear and desperate defiance and chopped at the last creature with a wild, two-handed blow.

The creatures had no chance.

Rome cut the head of the one attacking him almost completely off with one fierce swing of his axe.

The one attacking Nicandro was on top of him, the shield blocking its attacks, while Nicandro hacked at it with his short sword. Spinning away from the one he had just killed, Quyloc slashed Nicandro's attacker across the throat. The spear made a sizzling sound as it cut into the creature's flesh and it sprawled in a heap on Nicandro's shield.

The final soldier's swing, powered as it was by fear and adrenaline, cut clear through the creature's arm, the blade then biting into its shoulder. It shrieked and Rome hit it from the side and finished it off.

Silence then, except for their breathing. Nicandro pushed up on his shield, the creature slid off, and he picked himself up off the floor.

The other soldier jerked his weapon free. "Wow," he said.

From the stairs came the sound of ponderous footsteps. A gray, humped back appeared for a second above the mass of leaves.

"Time to leave," Rome said. He got no arguments.

Quyloc turned back to the exit. The others prepared their shields, the last soldier picking up the one dropped by his dead comrade. When they were ready, Quyloc jerked open the door, tensing, expecting to see a solid mass of vine covering their escape.

To his surprise, the way was clear. Kneeling on the path just beyond the outer edge of the vine was Ricarn, her hands placed flat on the ground before her.

There was a harsh, throaty growl from the depths of the vine behind them and the men ran for daylight. As they passed Ricarn, she stood up and stepped back. Once they were safely past the vine, they stopped. Quyloc turned to Ricarn.

"What did you do?"

"Let us just say that plant discovered that not all Life in this world is palatable," she said, smoothing her red robe calmly. "Some things are poisonous."

"That would have been nice to have on the way in."

Ricarn only looked at him without answering.

"What's *that*?" Nicandro asked, pointing at the tower door. Something lurked just inside its shadows, something large and hunched over, with a row of baleful red eyes.

"I don't know," Quyloc replied. "I'm just glad it doesn't seem to want to follow us out in the open."

Tairus hurried up then. "Increase the guard on the tower," Rome told him. "Triple it." To Quyloc he said, "We have to kill that vine."

"Sure. Any good ideas?"

"Can we burn it?"

Quyloc shrugged. "Maybe." He gestured toward the front gate, where the sound of pounding had gotten louder. "Maybe we have bigger problems to deal with first. Besides, even if we kill it, we'll just get something else. There's a hole between our worlds. One we made when we escaped."

Rome winced. The hole was there because of him. Neither of them needed to say it. "No good way to close it?"

"The Kaetrians, with the full might of the Tenders behind them, never figured out how to close the hole by the prison."

Tairus swore. "Don't you two ever have any good news?"

FORTY-FOUR

"We got the crystal, didn't we?" Rome said to Tairus.

"I noticed," Tairus replied, rubbing his arms. "I don't like that thing. You're sure it's not just going to kill us all?"

"Of course not. Ketora said as long as we don't touch it we'll be okay." But he looked at the creature as he spoke and he wondered. She had no expressions that he could read. They knew nothing about her other than one of her people had been tortured and killed by humans and other humans had used her as a weapon. Could this be her opportunity to get revenge on them? He looked at Quyloc. As usual, Quyloc seemed to know what he was thinking without words. He met Rome's gaze and turned his hands palm up as if to say, *Your guess is as good as mine.*

"It's not like we have a lot of choices," Rome said. "Sooner or later those things are going to break in here." He heard a sound he could have sworn was stone cracking.

Ketora was looking at him, her face betraying nothing.

"Let's get started," Rome told her.

"You have forgotten that I require the assistance of the Nipashanti."

Of course he did. What with almost being killed by a crazed plant and all, it had just slipped his mind. He must be getting old. "T'sim!" he yelled.

"I am right here," T'sim said from right behind him.

Rome spun on him. "How do you do that?"

"Do what?"

"Never mind. Are you going to help or not?"

"I have been giving it a great deal of thought. I—"

"No offense, T'sim, but I don't want to hear it right now." This time he definitely heard the sound of stone cracking. There were yells from the vicinity of the gates. "We're a little short on time. Are you in or not?"

233

"Yes. You, in particular, have—"

"Great," Rome said, cutting him off. To Ketora he said, "What do you need to do this?"

"I need to be as close as possible to the center of the area you wish shielded."

"Okay." Rome looked around, then led the *ronhym* to a spot off one corner of the palace. The ground was paved with flagstones. The whole area was covered with tents being used to house the refugees. "This should be pretty close."

Tairus gestured to some soldiers and they began moving people back and taking down the tents. Within a few minutes the area was clear.

"This will not be pleasant for you," Ketora said to Rome. "You will want to stand back."

"What shall I do?" T'sim asked.

"You will need to lend me your power."

"Oh," T'sim said. "Like this?" He raised his hand and the wind began to blow. In seconds it was howling, but it was no ordinary wind. It was focused around his hand. Rome, standing only a short distance away, couldn't feel it at all.

"No. That is only control of something outside you. I require the power that makes you what you are."

For the first time T'sim seemed disturbed. "Melekath shared this with you?" he asked. Ketora nodded. "Truly there is no length he will not go to for his Children."

"This is so."

"I have been so long in this form that I may not be able to reach it."

"I require the power that is your essence, Nipashanti. Nothing less will do."

"I will be uniquely vulnerable."

"This is also so."

T'sim looked at Rome, then back at Ketora. There was another loud crack from the direction of the gates. Rome realized he was holding his breath.

T'sim nodded.

Ketora raised the *relif* crystal high, then slammed it down, end first, into the ground. There was a loud cracking noise as the crystal pierced the flagstone and sudden cracks radiated in all directions. A gasp came from the people watching and they all moved back further.

"I am thinking this will not be pleasant for me," T'sim said.

"No. It will not."

"Then let us proceed quickly before I change my mind."

Ketora took T'sim's hands in hers and clamped them both down on the crystal. T'sim's eyes went very wide and he began to shake all over. It looked to Rome as if he tried to pull away, but Ketora did not let go.

His shaking grew more violent. It became hard to focus on him because he was vibrating so fast that his outlines had become blurry. His mouth opened and a painful, high-pitched wailing came from him. People put their fingers in their ears and moved further back. The ground underfoot was quivering madly. Rome's teeth had begun to hurt and he felt a headache starting.

Still Ketora held his hands to the crystal. T'sim's feet appeared to no longer be on the ground. He was beginning to change shape. It was as if he was dissolving in water. His arms and legs were no more than amorphous blobs. His head was nearly gone. The wailing coming from him had become the scream of the wind.

Fed by T'sim's power, the crystal was glowing orange, so fiercely that Rome couldn't look at it. Ketora was just visible as a black shadow in its midst.

Now Rome was sure T'sim was trying to get away. The shrieking coming from him seemed almost like a bizarre language and he was whipping about, jerking this way and that. But Ketora's grip was implacable and he could not get free.

Flashes of light began to come from inside T'sim, like lightning seen in the depths of clouds. The flashing grew faster until it was nearly continuous. People were crying out and covering their eyes. Rome had his hand up to shield his face and caught only glimpses of what happened next.

All at once T'sim seemed to split in half. A ball of blue-white lightning burst from inside him, beginning to expand…

Then it was sucked back into the crystal.

Ketora let go. There was nothing left of T'sim but something like tattered bits of cloud that shredded in a sudden wind and was gone.

The crystal was pulsing madly, the light coming from it turning redder and redder by the second. The heat coming off it was incredible, worse than any furnace ever built. Rome heard yelling and wasn't sure if it was him or not.

Then Ketora rapped on top of the crystal. The crystal cracked and wild energy began to spew upwards in a geyser. For a moment, Rome was sure they were all dead. That power would incinerate them all within seconds. Ketora had betrayed them.

Ketora stuck her hands into the geyser of Stone power. He could see how difficult it was for her, how close the power was to knocking her flying. Somehow she held on, forcing her hands down through the geyser until she reached the hole in the crystal, which she clamped her hands over.

The power still geysered upwards, but now it was changing. Fierce red cooled to orange. After a moment, Ketora removed her hands. She reached into the light and somehow took hold of part of it, which she bent away and down.

Again and again she did this and the geyser grew smaller as its power was diverted. Rome turned and saw that the air was shimmering with this orange light, that it was curving back down in an arc toward the perimeter of the palace grounds.

A few minutes later it was done. Ketora stepped back and sat down heavily on the ground, putting her head in her hands.

A thin stream of orange-tinged power still flowed upward from the crystal, much smaller than the geyser of before. It was feeding a translucent orange dome that covered the palace grounds. It looked seamless.

It looked impregnable.

Rome approached Ketora, Quyloc accompanying him. She looked up when they reached her.

"It is done," she said. Her voice sounded very weak. "Goodbye."

Her body began to lose shape, as if she were melting. In seconds she had seeped into the ground and was gone.

The Children stared up at the shimmering orange shield and all of them—even through the haze of three thousand years, even through the haze of insanity—knew instantly what it was.

A cry of despair went up from every throat.

FORTY-FIVE

After Qarath's wall fell, Josef entered the city along with the rest of the Children. The hunger drove him and he was helpless to resist. Nor did he want to resist. The plants he loved so much were lost to him. They crumbled and died under his touch. Existence was agony and the only thing which offered the least respite was Song, even if it was only temporary.

The next hours were a blur of running through the streets, chasing fleeing people, tearing through homes, sniffing out those who were hiding, and the sweet taste of Song, cold water to a throat that had been parched for thousands of years. How many people he fed on he couldn't say, but at some point he began to feel sick and he dropped the woman he was holding and stumbled out of the house and into the street. For a moment he stood there, surprised at the darkness. What happened to the light? When did it become night? Then he fell over on his side, holding his stomach, wondering if he was going to split open like an overripe watermelon.

Some hours later he opened his eyes and saw that day was coming. He had always enjoyed mornings the most. It was then that the plants he tended were at their freshest. They seemed to strain toward the morning sun, every leaf, every flower petal, brand new and beautiful.

He stood and looked around. He was on a narrow, cobblestone street. Stone buildings enclosed him on all sides, reaching upwards to block out most of the sky. It was a sterile place, not a single plant visible anywhere. He began stumbling down the street, hoping to find something to ease the ache inside him.

The street led to a larger one, then one even larger than that, one wide and clean and bordered by high walls, behind which could be seen opulent homes.

He walked along the wall of one estate until he came to the wrought iron gates. What he saw through the gates staggered him. It wasn't the soaring towers of the mansion that weakened him. It wasn't the verdant gardens wound with tiled footpaths, or the vast, green lawns. It was the trees. In the center of the estate, spaced around a small pool, were four huge, stately silver oaks. They were magnificent trees, taller than the mansion, trunks so broad it would have taken a half dozen men to put their arms around one.

Josef made a small sound of pleasure. Something ancient and rusty creaked to life within him as he looked at them. He had a passion for all growing things, a passion that even three millennia in the prison had not been able to quench, but trees were what he loved most and of all trees, silver oaks were his favorite.

With hardly an effort he ripped the iron gates from their hinges and threw them aside. With his hands outstretched before him he shambled forward, a smile on his craggy face.

Halfway there he came to a halt, the smile fading. He remembered what happened in the town of Ferien, when he touched the tree growing in the center of town, how it died under his hands.

He sank to his knees on the grass, afraid to go closer, but unable to make himself leave.

Their leaves fluttered in the morning breeze off the ocean. The leaves had just begun to turn, their silver edged in crimson and orange. They were brilliant, magical. They promised him life and hope when his world had been only bleakness and horror for so long. A smile stretched his cracked lips. This was what had kept him going during the long millennia of his imprisonment. Even the hunger pangs, already growing within him once again, didn't seem so bad here, where he could stare up at his beloved trees.

How long he knelt there he didn't know, but at some point he became aware of a nagging sense of wrongness. It was like a small rash in the corner of his mind. His brow furrowing, he looked around.

And gave a wounded gasp.

The grass all around him was gray and dead. Like a stain, the gray had spread across the lawn and had already reached the two closest silver oak trees. Josef scrambled to his feet and backed up a few steps. But it was too late. Before his eyes the gray blight began to rise up the trunks of the trees. Where the blight spread the bark turned black. Within seconds the blackened bark split open and black ichor dripped from the raw wood underneath.

Heedlessly, Josef ran to one of the trees. He was flush with power; it seethed beneath his skin, and he summoned a small amount of it to his fingertips, thinking that with it he could wash away the infection and heal the tree.

But the Song that poured from his fingers was tarnished with gray and where it touched the blight it was like pouring oil onto a fire. The blight spread with frightening speed, across the trunk and deeper into the heart of the tree. It seemed he could hear the tree itself cry out in his mind.

Alarmed, Josef shut off the flow of Song and backed away from the tree. But it was too late. The blight was spreading like wildfire. Josef's face twisted in horror. He tore at the wisps of hair that had grown in on his scalp overnight. *What had he done?*

The gray at his feet was still spreading, reaching out across the estate lawn with probing fingers. Before his horrified, disbelieving eyes it reached the other two trees and began to spread up them as well. Trembling, Josef backed away, watching helplessly as all four of the oak trees were consumed, the blight racing up their trunks and spreading out to cover the limbs, which began to thrash as if caught in a windstorm. The leaves turned black and fell to the ground. Smaller limbs cracked and broke off.

There were anguished cries in the depths of his mind as the trees died.

Josef wept, but there were no tears. There would never be tears again. As the last of the trees died, something within Josef finally, irrevocably snapped. His cherished memories of green things growing disappeared and with their passing the final, slender strand of sanity he'd clung to broke.

With an anguished cry, Josef fell to his knees and jammed his fists into the earth. "No!" he screamed. "You will *not* die!" With that he released a massive burst of stolen Song. It surged outwards from him, crackling across the dead grass and racing up through the mighty trees. Bands of gray-tinged light wrapped around the trees in a flash. More small limbs cracked and rained down on the ground.

Exhausted, the stolen energy spent, Josef stood. He saw no light, only blackness. He had only one thought in his mind.

Song.

He needed more. If he could not nurture the living things he remembered, he would create his own life.

He turned and walked toward the gates of the estate and, one by one, the massive oak trees tore themselves free of the earth and followed him.

FORTY-SIX

Reyna prepared to try again. Trembling with pain and weakness, she summoned the last wisps of stolen Song she still possessed, wrapping it around her hand. Nearby was a faint, twisting flow of raw LifeSong. She forced herself to be patient, watching it, waiting for her opportunity, knowing she only had one left.

The flow drifted closer.

She lunged and just managed to catch hold of it.

It burned. Raw LifeSong was never meant to be touched directly. It flows into a body through the *akirma*, which acts as a sort of filter, refining it, turning it into Selfsong, the energy which sustains Life.

Like electricity it sparked through her, arching her back, eliciting involuntary cries of pain. It felt as though she had taken hold of lightning. The raw energy sparked and snapped within her. She fell on her back, heels drumming on the stone floor of the building she lay in, limbs jerking convulsively, the back of her head slamming into the stone floor.

But she did not let go.

Biting her lip to hold back the screaming, she pulled herself off the floor, wrapped her other hand in stolen Song—it was the stolen Song that allowed her to touch the flow; without it her hand would merely pass through it—and grabbed the flow. The pain doubled. She staggered but somehow kept her feet, somehow kept pulling herself along the flow as if it were a lifeline and she was caught in a flood.

Now she *saw* her true goal: A feeder line.

Where the flow she held onto was little more than a spider web, the feeder line it was attached to was as big around as her forearm. When she took hold of it she was slammed backwards against the wall, as if she'd been hit by a tidal wave. It poured over her, energy too raw and powerful to be touched by a living body.

But Reyna was no longer living.

She screamed again and again, but she did not let go. It was tearing her apart, one piece at a time. She was splitting open. She was already in pieces.

But still she did not let go.

She held on and she fought back.

Gradually, the pain began to ease. Gradually, she began to find how to hold onto the line, to make it serve her.

And she began to remake herself.

FORTY-SEVEN

"That was wild," Tairus said. "When that light turned red and started pulsing, I thought we were all dead. I thought what's-her-name had turned on us."

"I did too," Rome replied.

Quyloc was standing nearby, the spear—its haft bare—in his hand. He was staring at the crystal, an unfocused look in his eyes.

"Then she just melted away," Tairus said, looking at where Ketora had disappeared. "Nothing left. Not even a stain." He scratched his stomach. "What happened to T'sim, do you think? Is he dead?" He looked around as if expecting the little man to show up once his name was spoken.

"I don't know," Rome said. Quyloc broke off his stare and walked over to them. "Do you know what happened to T'sim?" Quyloc shook his head. "That's too bad. I kind of liked the little guy." It was true. He'd gotten used to having him around. As servants went, he wasn't half bad. Mentally he thanked T'sim for his sacrifice. He certainly hadn't had to do it.

"Well, if it keeps the Children out, it's worth it." Tairus looked up at the shimmering orange dome overhead. "You think it'll hold them out?"

"You heard them yelling," Rome said, breaking out of his thoughts about T'sim. "They didn't sound too happy about it. Let's go take a look."

The three men climbed the wall and looked down. The Children were still visible through the shield, though they were hazy and tinged orange. The shield came down directly on the outside of the wall. All the soldiers on the wall were silent, all wondering what would happen next. On the palace grounds, people stared upwards, waiting, watching.

Heram was the first to approach the shield. He wound up and struck it a mighty, two-handed blow.

There was a concussion, felt more than heard, and Heram was thrown backward. The shield showed no signs of weakening.

The soldiers burst into cheers. The cheers were picked up by the people down below. They hugged and cried and slapped each other on the back.

"It's about time some chips fell our way," Tairus said, a huge smile on his face.

Rome nodded, so overcome with relief that at first he didn't trust his voice. He turned to Quyloc and saw an uncharacteristic smile there.

"We did it," he said.

Quyloc nodded and his smile faded. "We bought some time. There's no way to know how much."

"Oh, would you just leave off!" Tairus cried. "Don't be such a dead dog. We finally won a victory. Just enjoy it already."

"I'm only pointing out that we have only—"

"Leave off, Quyloc," Rome said, cutting him off. "Everyone needs this. I know *I* need it. I bet you need it too."

Quyloc gave him an unreadable look, then nodded. Suddenly, surprisingly, he admitted, "I'm tired. No, I'm exhausted. A break will be good. Maybe we will yet find a way." A thought occurred to him then and he added, "Maybe the young Tender will succeed."

"What young Tender? What are you talking about?"

"The one who arrived with the big warrior. Netra."

Rome looked around. "Now that you mention it, I haven't seen them all day. Where are they?"

"They're gone."

"Gone? Where would they go?"

"To the prison."

At first Rome thought he heard him wrong. It was loud, what with all the cheering going on. "They're *where*? How did they get there?"

"I took them. Last night. We went along the border of the *Pente Akka*, the same way you and I went to attack Melekath."

"And you didn't think this was important enough to tell me?"

"I thought it was important enough to make the decision and make it fast. Besides, my advice to you would have been to let them go and I've noticed that you started listening to my advice lately so why wake you up and bother you when you probably needed the sleep?"

"Okay," Rome grumbled. "If you thought it was that important. Am I allowed to at least ask *why* they wanted to go to the prison?"

"To find Melekath."

"Of course. It makes perfect sense now. Who wouldn't want to go to the prison and find Melekath? Were they just planning on joining him for a picnic?"

"Do you want real answers from me or do you want to act like a child?"

Rome started as if he'd been slapped. He looked around, but no one else seemed to have heard. All of them, including Tairus, were too busy celebrating. "I am your macht, you know," he growled.

Quyloc opened his mouth to say something, then closed it abruptly. He rubbed his eyes. "I apologize, Rome. As I said before, I'm exhausted."

Rome took a deep breath. "It's nothing. Now, would you mind telling me why they went there?"

"She had the idea that maybe Melekath could be talked into undoing the Gift." To Rome's blank look he added, "The Gift is what makes them immortal. But if Melekath can undo the Gift, if she can somehow convince him to do so, then they'd be mortal again."

"But why would he do that? They're his Children, right?"

"They turned on him after we attacked him. He's seen what they've become. Maybe it's enough. Maybe it isn't. But it's something and we have precious little of that."

"You're right," Rome said. "For what it's worth, I think you did the right thing. There's not much they can do here—though it would have been nice to have the big guy when we went into the Tower—and out there they just might be able to save us all."

"It is still highly unlikely."

Rome smiled. It felt good to smile again. He slapped Quyloc on the shoulder and smiled even broader when Quyloc's face tightened as he did so. He knew how much Quyloc hated when he did that. "Highly unlikely looks pretty good from where I'm standing right now, old friend. It's a far sight better than no chance at all."

"You better get up here, Rome!" Tairus called from the top of the wall.

Rome cursed as he ran for the stairs. Somehow he'd just known their respite was too good to be true.

Even expecting the worst as he was, he wasn't prepared for the sight that greeted him when he got to the top of the wall.

"Just when you think you've seen everything," Tairus said.

"Are those really trees?"

"They used to be. I don't know what to call them now."

Rome turned to Nicandro, who'd followed him up onto the wall. "Get Quyloc up here. Fast." Nicandro took off at a run. Before Nicandro even got off the wall one of the front doors of the palace opened and Quyloc came out. He ran to the wall and climbed it.

"What do you think?" Rome asked him when he got there.

Four huge trees, their trunks and limbs blackened and twisted, their leaves gone, were making their way across the boulevard toward the wall. Thick roots splayed in all directions around the trees. The ones nearest the wall skittered across the cobblestones, reaching as far as they could. Then they dug in, wooden fingers that pushed easily through the gaps between the cobblestones and dug into the soil underneath. The roots contracted, drawing the trees closer.

"They are following *him*," Quyloc said, pointing.

In front of the trees was a man. He had not grown huge like the other Children. The Song he'd stolen had not gone into bizarre growth. He was skeletally lean, his skin still completely gray. He walked hunched over, his spine bent by some long-ago injury. Bad as he looked, he was clearly not weak. There was on his face a look of savage determination that was truly chilling. His was a focused madness that the other Children lacked.

"I don't like the looks of this," Tairus said. "If only we could set those things on fire." Which they couldn't. The shield wasn't just impervious to the Children's attacks; it was impervious from their side as well. Soon after it was erected, a soldier had thrust his spear into it. The concussion shattered his spear and nearly knocked him off the wall. No one had made any attempts since.

"They're just trees, whatever he did to make them move like that," Rome said. "They won't have any more luck getting through the shield than anything else." He turned to Quyloc. "Right, Quyloc?"

Quyloc was holding the *rendspear*, staring at the trees with that distant look he got.

"Right, Quyloc?" Rome repeated. There was something really unnerving about those trees. He needed Quyloc to tell him he was overreacting. "They're still just trees, aren't they?"

Quyloc shook his head a moment later and glanced at Rome. "They're not still just trees. He's done something to them, something truly unbelievable." He almost sounded impressed by it.

"You're not helping," Rome said.

"But no, I don't think they will be able to get through the shield. It is powered by Stone force. I don't know what power there is that could smash through it, but I don't believe those trees possess it."

Rome breathed a deep sigh of relief. "Did you hear that, Tairus? Nothing to worry about."

"Sure, Rome. Whatever you say." Tairus' gaze was fixed on the trees.

"You worry too much, you know that?"

Then Tairus did look at him. "Strange monster trees are dragging themselves across the street to attack us. You see that, don't you?"

"Yeah."

"I think I don't worry enough," Tairus grumbled, and turned back to watch the trees again. "I should have taken up farming," he said under his breath. "Somewhere far away from cities and kings and monster-damned-trees."

The hunched man reached the shield directly below where Rome stood and tilted his head back, staring up at it. Even from here, Rome could see the man's eyes glittering as he surveyed the shield. His unease returned in full force.

The trees reached the shield and stopped, the four of them making a semicircle around the hunched man. He gestured and one of them reached a limb toward the shield. The limb touched the shield, there was a loud pop and the limb jerked back, smoke rising from it. Scattered cheers came from the watching soldiers.

The hunched man gestured again and a thick limb reached down to him. It encircled his waist and lifted him into the air. As he rose up, the soldiers nearby all stepped back. Rome had to resist the urge to do the same. There was no need to be afraid, he told himself. No way the man could get through the shield.

When the man was at eye level, Rome said to him, "It's not going to work, whatever you think you're doing. So why don't you take your new friends and go away? Why not go throw yourself off the cliff into the sea?"

The man's eyes flicked to Rome for the briefest instant and then away. He didn't look at any of the soldiers. He was looking past them. Rome turned, wondering what he was looking at. Quyloc and Tairus turned as well.

It was Quyloc who realized it first.

"He's looking at the *relif* crystal."

He was right. The hunched man stared steadily at it, his head cocked slightly to one side. Tairus muttered under his breath. Rome clenched his fists, a growing sickness inside him.

"Still," he said to Quyloc, "there's nothing he can do, right? So he knows about the crystal. He can't get through the shield."

Quyloc didn't answer at first. He was looking at the crystal, his expression one of deep concentration.

Rome knew that look. His old friend was on the verge of figuring something out, something everyone else was missing. "What is it?" he hissed.

"The shield," Quyloc replied. "Does it extend underground?"

FORTY-EIGHT

There was an odd crunching sound behind Rome and he spun. It was coming from the base of the wall. He looked down. The roots of the tree that was holding the hunched man were boring into the ground like thick, gnarled worms.

"No," Tairus moaned. "It can't be. It just can't."

"Down off the wall!" Rome yelled. "Now!"

The soldiers began running for the stairs. Rome stayed, watching. He could have sworn he felt the roots digging through the ground underneath him, though that was surely impossible. What was the man doing? Even if the roots made it all the way to the crystal, touching it would burn them just as touching the shield had. There was nothing to worry about.

A minute later dozens of roots broke from the ground in a circle around the *relif* crystal, tilting slabs of flagstone up and back. They converged on the crystal from all sides, then swarmed up over it. There was a series of sizzles and sharp pops. Most of the roots burst into flames. But they did not pull back.

The roots flexed and the crystal tilted.

The beam of light shooting upwards from the crystal stuttered.

With a convulsive heave the roots pulled the crystal underground.

The beam of light disappeared.

Rome spun. Now the hunched man was looking at him. There was something truly terrifying in those dead, empty eyes.

The shield died.

From the Children came a shout of glee.

The limbs of the four trees snaked forward and fanned out across the face of the wall, moving with frightening speed. They pushed into the stone like it was so much butter.

Rome turned and ran.

Rome was halfway down the stairs when a limb suddenly poked through the stone at his feet. He caught his foot on it, stumbled and had to grab the wall to catch himself. He jerked his hand away from the wall as more limbs came snaking through. He had to jump down the last couple of steps as they split apart underneath him.

He hit the ground, rolled, and came to his feet. He turned and looked up at the wall.

Myriad roots and limbs seethed across its surface.

Huge chunks of stone began to fall from the top. The wall groaned and cracks appeared everywhere. More chunks of stone fell.

Rome drew his axe and stepped back. It seemed horribly inadequate after using the black axe for so long.

"Soldiers! To me!" he yelled. It was hopeless. There was no way they could hold once the wall fell, but he was not going down without a fight. Bonnie and their unborn child flashed through his mind and he whispered a silent goodbye to them.

Soldiers ran and began forming up on either side of him, weapons drawn.

The wall came down.

Dust filled the air, killing visibility and making breathing difficult. From out of the dust cloud loomed one of the trees, holding the hunched man up high, his features stretched in a savage grimace. He looked down on the soldiers gathered before him and gestured. Tree limbs shot out. Two soldiers were snatched up and lifted high into the air. The limbs tightened and the soldiers were crushed. Their lifeless bodies were flung into the midst of the defenders.

Another gesture and the limbs came at them again. One struck at Rome, but he was ready for it. He swung his axe, timed it just right, and cut through the limb, then ducked as the stump swung at his head. The soldier to his right wasn't fast enough and he grunted as the limb caught him in the ribs and sent him flying.

The dust began to settle and through the gloom Rome saw Heram leap to the top of the pile of shattered stone. His eyes gleamed fever bright. Immediately after him appeared a half dozen more of the Children, all of them huge, all of them wild-eyed with excitement. They knew that at last Qarath was theirs. There was nowhere left for the defenders to run. No more walls to hide behind.

Screaming with excitement, they poured down through the wreckage toward the meager line of defenders.

FORTY-NINE

When the wall fell, Quyloc almost felt as if he had been freed. All his life he had feared the worst. Now it was finally here. No more running. No more pretending. They were all going to die.

It was strangely liberating.

Quyloc looked at Rome, who was about twenty-five paces to his right. Usually right before battle—sometimes even in the midst of it—he and Rome exchanged looks across the battlefield. It wasn't something they planned; it just happened, triggered by the deep connection between them.

Rome didn't look back at him.

Even from here he could see the despair wrapped around the big man, the slight lowering of the shoulders, the minute change in his stance. Probably no one else would be able to see it, but to Quyloc it was as plain as day.

Rome had already given up.

Quyloc raised his spear and silently saluted Rome. He wished he had a moment to say one last thing to his old friend. He wanted to say that he was…sorry.

Quyloc blinked, as surprised as if the thought had come from someone else.

All this happened in a few heartbeats. Then the monstrous tree forced its way through the shattered remains of the wall and there was no more time for thought or regret. There was only time for action.

And time for dying.

Quyloc spun the spear slowly in his hands, the weapon he had obtained at such great personal cost, and flung himself into the battle.

Rome gripped his axe and watched them come. Usually when the battle began he was filled with overwhelming raw energy. Despite the horror of battle—and he'd seen enough to know there was no other accurate way to describe it—there was something weirdly exciting about it as well. The rush of adrenaline. The knowledge that any mistake could be his last. The challenge of besting his foe. And, above all, the thrill of survival.

But this time all he felt was sick. He'd failed. Ever since the day Lowellin first appeared in Qarath his every effort had been bent toward defeating this one enemy and he'd failed completely. This was it. The end. Everyone would die and there was nothing he could do about it.

This knowledge wrapped around him in a suffocating fog, weighing down his limbs and clouding his mind. Part of him wondered if he would be able to react at all when the battle was joined. Would he just stand here and let them cut him down?

Did it even matter?

One of the Children rushed at him, greedy hands reaching out for him. He was half again as tall as Rome, with a weirdly lopsided head and a torso that was oddly long for his height.

At the last second, Rome's martial instincts took over with no thought or command from him. His attacker had no skill as a warrior. It was an easy matter to duck under his awkward grasp and slice across his stomach. The man howled and his intestines spilled out into the harsh light of day. His feet tangled in them and he tripped. As he fell forward, Rome sidestepped and hit him on the side of the neck. The force of the blow cut the man's head nearly off.

The man fell to his knees, raising one arm to fend off further blows. Rome chopped deep into his forearm.

But already the wound in his neck had sealed, though his head was left tilted at an unnatural angle. He lurched to his feet, swinging wildly at Rome as he did so, his strength so great that Rome was thrown back. With one hand he grabbed the gray ropes of his intestines, tore them away and threw them down. The wound in his stomach closed right afterwards.

He fixed his eyes on Rome and charged him again. The soldier to Rome's right stepped forward and intercepted him, his sword flashing.

The man didn't try to duck or block the blow. He just threw himself at the soldier, his arms spread wide. The sword struck him in the shoulder and stuck. In the next heartbeat his arms wrapped around the soldier, who gave one scream and then shriveled to nothing.

He threw the withered corpse at Rome, who batted it aside with his free hand. The corpse was oddly weightless, more a scarecrow than a man.

Once again he rushed at Rome. Rome chopped off one hand. The other grazed him and he felt most of his strength leave him in a rush. He staggered sideways. A tree root snaked around his ankle and he chopped at it feebly, was surprised when the axe cut most of the way through it.

Around him the battlefield was oddly silent, the usual screams of the dying and horribly wounded mostly replaced by choked off cries and moans. Those the Children got hold of simply died. They didn't lie on the ground thrashing as their lives bled away.

Off to Rome's left Heram rampaged like a mad bull, grabbing up soldiers three and four at a time, draining them and tossing them aside like twigs. Their swords barely scratched his hide.

Surprisingly, only a few soldiers had fled the carnage. Maybe they stayed and fought because their loved ones were only a few paces away. Maybe it was because there was nowhere left to run to. Whatever the reason, they continued to throw themselves at the Children, at the massive tree with its hunched cargo. And they continued to die.

Rome's attacker had paused when he lost his hand. He stared at his stump as if in surprise. Then his eyes narrowed as he focused his attention. The hand grew back. It didn't look right. It only had three fingers and they were oddly swollen, but they opened and closed when he flexed. He looked at Rome again.

"It's pointless, you know," he said. His tone was strangely conversational. He might have been remarking on the weather. "I think you could chop off my head and it wouldn't matter."

Rome fell back a step, bringing the axe up and holding it in both hands. Some strength had returned to him but it wasn't enough. "Why don't I try?" he replied.

The man shook his head. It was still tilted to one side. "No. I'm too hungry."

He came at Rome again. Rome took a step back, put his foot down on one of the withered corpses and felt his leg buckle.

He fought to bring the axe around as the man reached for him, but he was too slow, too weak.

This was it. The one battle he would not win.

FIFTY

Just before the man's hand closed on Rome, something unexpected happened.

Something flashed in from the side—something long and thin and orange—and struck the man on the wrist. It hit him with just enough force that his hand missed Rome.

Rome turned his head and saw that the weapon was wielded by a tall, slim creature with yellowish skin. Though the creature had no hair and had unusual bulbous eyes and a lipless mouth, it was somehow feminine looking. She was wearing only a thin shift, belted at the waist, no shoes, and her weapon seemed to be some kind of long staff.

Rome's attacker lunged at her, arms spread wide in a bear hug, but she was already moving, sliding sideways with eerie grace and speed. As she did so, she jabbed him in the ribs with the end of her staff, again not very hard, but just in the right spot so that he was knocked sideways and staggered and fell.

She stepped closer and swung again, but now the staff was flexible, like a whip. It struck Rome's attacker across the back. Upon impact, a piece of the weapon broke off, becoming fluid, changing, elongating. As the man was getting his arms under himself, pushing himself up off the ground, the piece that had broken off wrapped eel-like around him several times. It tightened and his arms were pulled to his sides. The man collapsed back onto the ground.

Another one of the Children, a woman with a bizarre mane of thick, yellow hair that stuck out in wild directions, lumbered up and tried to grab the yellow-skinned creature, but she was once again moving. As she twisted away, she jabbed the woman with her weapon, which was once again rigid like a staff. She did not strike very hard, but the woman lost her balance and fell.

Another blow from the weapon—once again flexible like a whip—and another eel-like piece separated, wrapping itself around the woman's torso, pinning her arms to her sides.

Around them dozens of the yellow-skinned creatures had entered the battle. Some carried the same orange weapons, but others had only odd bracelets, a dozen or more on each wrist. All wore the same simple shifts and were barefoot. As Rome watched, one who looked to be male, with faint brown spots running up his torso, pulled free two of the bracelets and threw them at one of the Children. The things struck the man in the chest, changing as they did so, becoming creatures with multiple, segmented legs and hard, chitinous exoskeletons. The things scurried up over the man's shoulders, one continuing up onto the top of his head, the other racing around to the base of his spine. From the mouth of each a thin spike pierced the man, anchoring them in place, while their legs suddenly grew longer, wrapping around and around him. He was soon encased from head to toe and fell over on his side.

The female who had saved him turned to Rome and gave him a quick bow. "Respectfully, Macht," she said, "but these will not hold them for long. We need to leave quickly."

Rome looked in the direction she pointed and his eyes widened. The top of what looked like small mountain was visible over the top of the palace, though it didn't look like any mountain he'd ever seen. It was faintly yellow with what looked like seaweed growing all over it.

He squinted. It looked like there was a solitary figure standing on top of it. The figure seemed to be waving at him.

"It is our home, ki'Loren," she said. "There is room for everyone, but we must hurry."

There was a roar from behind Rome and he spun. Heram had four of the yellow-skinned creatures around him. Two had just struck him with their weapons and pieces were twining themselves around his torso. Heram roared again, flexed, and the eel things were torn apart. A half dozen of the multi-legged creatures were perched on him in various places. He slapped at one, knocked it off, then swatted and crushed one of the others.

Two more of the yellow-skinned creatures joined the fight. Each carried what looked like a huge pearl. These they rolled under Heram's legs, where they popped open with a flash of light. From each a bizarre, leafy plant sprouted, growing up and enshrouding him in moments. With one more muffled roar, Heram toppled over.

"Now, please," she said.

Rome turned back to her, a hundred questions on his lips, but he knew when it was time to act and when it was time to talk. He heard the horns blowing retreat just a moment before he began yelling for his men to break off and fall back.

"Form a rear guard!" he yelled. "Protect the citizens!"

But there really was no need. Every one of the Children was down on the ground. Even the strange trees that had broken through the wall were just standing there motionless.

FIFTY-ONE

The evacuation went surprisingly quickly. The people of Qarath didn't even blink at the sight of a floating island suddenly appearing on the ocean behind the palace. Nor did they hesitate at the idea of crossing the drawbridge that led to a large opening in the side of the island and going inside. They'd seen the nightmare that lay behind them; whatever was inside the floating island couldn't be worse.

They gathered up their children and those who couldn't walk on their own and they *ran*.

As the last of the Qarathians made their way across the drawbridge, Quyloc saw Rome and went over to intercept him.

"What in Gorim's name is this thing?" Rome asked. "Who are these creatures?"

"They're the Lementh'kal."

"The who?"

"They helped us escape from the *Pente Akka*. Well, two of them did."

Rome shook his head as if it would help him think. "I didn't see anyone helping."

"It was…it's complicated. I'll tell you later. But I think we can trust them."

"Not like we have a lot of choices," Rome replied.

Tairus came running up. "Well, now I really have seen everything. Seriously, nothing will ever surprise me again."

Opus came running out of one of the rear doors of the palace. "The palace is empty, Macht," he said. His black livery looked as neat as ever. "I regret that I was unable to collect any of your clothes from your quarters, but time would not permit."

"Is Bonnie…?"

Opus nodded. "One of the first."

"Thank you, Opus. Now get on and let's get out of here."

They walked across the drawbridge, which was made of some reddish, porous material, followed by the rest of the Lamenth'kal.

Once through the opening, Quyloc found himself on the side of a wide valley, lit by a soft, yellow light. People were streaming down the side of the valley and spilling out across the bottom.

A few moments later Ki'Loren began to move. Quyloc turned back. The drawbridge slid back, disappearing into the side of ki'Loren. The opening began to close. Heram was rounding the corner of the palace at a run, yelling. Other Children were right behind him. Tairus waved at him and made a rude gesture with his hand. Then the opening closed and he was staring at a low, blank cliff face.

None of them saw the hunched figure who clung to the side of ki'Loren as it floated away from Qarath.

"Welcome to ki'Loren. I am Jenett of the Lementh'kal."

Rome turned at the sound of the voice and standing there was a Lementh'kal who looked familiar. "You're the one who saved me," he said.

She nodded.

"Well I owe you my thanks. I won't forget that."

"We would have been here sooner," a new voice said, "but it took Golgath some time to die. Gods can be like that." The Lementh'kal who came walking up had skin the color of yellowed ivory. There were lines around his mouth and eyes that spoke of great age, but his eyes shone like a child's.

"It's you," Quyloc said. "You're Ya'Shi." He turned to Rome. "He's one of the ones who helped us when we were trapped in the *Pente Akka*."

"And it worked!" Ya'Shi clapped delightedly. "You listened and here you are! What a great reunion!" He began dancing, moving his legs to some melody only he could hear. He looked at Tairus, who was staring at him with disgust. "Won't you join me? It's really lots of fun." Tairus scowled and shook his head.

"Where, exactly, is here?" Rome asked. "What is this place? Some kind of floating island?"

"This is ki'Loren," Jenett said, as if that explained it all. "It is our mother. It is our home."

"So...it's alive?"

"Of course."

"And we're inside it." Rome wasn't sure he liked the thought of that.

"I assure you that you are safe," Jenett said.

"For now," Ya'Shi said ominously, ceasing his capering. When he saw the looks they gave him, he laughed. "What? You didn't really think you were going to win this war, did you?" He shook his head at their foolishness, smiling broadly. The smile looked unusual on his lipless mouth, as if he had suddenly donned a mask. "Let me tell you something," he said, beckoning them closer and lowering his voice. "The Children are immortal." He nodded very seriously. "Immortal means they can't die."

"Are you some kind of idiot?" Tairus blurted out.

Ya'Shi considered this, then nodded. "Yes. Yes, I am."

"This is serious. It's no time to be clowning around."

"That is where you are wrong, young man," Ya'Shi said, holding one finger up like a teacher lecturing a slow student. "This is *exactly* the time for clowning around. Watch." He bent backwards and placed his hands on the ground behind him. It was done perfectly smoothly and fluidly. Then he raised his feet into the air so that he was standing on his hands. He began to bounce about on his hands.

"What do you think?" he called to them.

Rome looked at Quyloc, who shrugged. Tairus crossed his arms, his frown deepening.

"Look what else I can do," Ya'Shi said. He began to execute an unbelievable series of flips and contortions that looked impossible, doing them all with a speed that was simply breathtaking.

"Are they impressed yet, Jenett?" he called. "I can't tell. I'm starting to get dizzy." Suddenly he fell, ending up in a tangle of limbs on the ground. For a moment he just lay there, groaning.

"Serves you right," Tairus said.

Ya'Shi sat up, then climbed to his feet. His movements were the slow and creaky ones of an old man. He held his back. "I shouldn't have tried that so soon after a heavy meal," he moaned.

"Where are you taking us?" Tairus demanded.

"I'm not taking you anywhere. Ki'Loren is. You're much too heavy for me to carry around." He held up his arms to show them how thin they were.

Tairus turned away from him to Jenett. "Can you give us some real answers?"

"I will try. But I do not know where we are going either. We do not control ki'Loren."

Nalene and Ricarn came up then. Ya'Shi waved happily at Nalene, then gave Ricarn a deep bow. Ricarn inclined her head.

"What is this place?" Nalene demanded. "Who's in charge here?"

Ya'Shi's look grew pained. "Do we have to go through this again? I'm tired. I want to talk about something else."

"It's some kind of floating island," Rome said. "And it's alive. But that's not important. Right now we need to figure out what we're going to do next. I don't think he is going to be any help at all."

Ya'Shi's eyes grew very wide at his words. "It was *my* idea for Netra to go to Durag'otal," he said in a hurt voice. "That seems pretty helpful to me."

"What are you talking about?" Rome asked.

"I took Netra to the edge of the desert because of what he told her," Quyloc said.

"What's he talking about? What did you tell her?" Nalene demanded of Ya'Shi.

Ya'Shi scratched his jaw thoughtfully. "I remember telling her to get on a giant turtle."

"What?" Rome turned to Quyloc. "Does he make any sense to you?"

Quyloc shook his head. Ricarn had a small, faint smile on her face. Nalene looked outraged.

"Why don't you just tell us straight?" Tairus growled. "This is serious."

"Yes, yes," Ya'Shi agreed. "Deadly serious." His face grew very grave.

"So?"

"She wanted to go back to land. The turtle took her."

"Unbelievable," Tairus said.

Cara approached tentatively then. "I may have something to add." Quyloc beckoned her closer. She then proceeded to tell Rome what Ya'Shi and the Ancient One had told Netra about being the doorway to returning the Children to the Circle.

As she told the story, Ya'Shi brightened. "I *remember* that now! I *did* say something like that! What do you think it means?"

Tairus shook his head with disgust. The look on Nalene's face was murderous.

"It means that Netra is our only chance now," Ricarn said. "There is nothing we can do about it. She will either succeed or she will fail."

"Can't we go help her?" Rome asked Quyloc.

Just then ki'Loren shuddered, hard enough that people staggered.

"What is it? What happened?" Nalene asked.

Ya'Shi held up one hand, his head cocked to the side as if listening to something. Then, very seriously, he told them, "It could be gas. She ate something recently that didn't agree with her." He turned to look at all the people streaming through the valley below. "A whole lot of something."

"I'm going to kill him," Tairus said.

There was another shudder. Every Lementh'kal within sight was standing stock still, looking upwards.

"Or it could be this," Ya'Shi said. He walked over to the place where they had entered ki'Loren. As he did, a new opening appeared, much smaller this time. The rest followed him out into the sunlight.

Ya'Shi looked up the slope of ki'Loren and pointed. "There it is. Definitely indigestion."

The hunched, gray-skinned man was a stone's throw up the slope. He was on his knees, his hands plunged into ki'Loren's side up to his elbows. He seemed completely unaware of them.

"It's the one who brought the trees," Tairus said.

"What's he doing?" Rome asked.

"I do not know," Jenett said, "but it is troubling to ki'Loren."

A handful of Lementh'kal had followed them outside and now two of them detached from the rest and walked up the slope. Each was carrying one of the odd staves. When they were close, they stopped and spread out. Taking their staves in both hands, they slammed them down on the ground.

Immediately a handful of strange, multi-legged creatures burst from the ground around the man and swarmed over him.

Every one of them shriveled up and died, rolling harmlessly to the ground.

"Look!" Cara cried. "There's something around him!"

"What?" Rome asked. "I don't see anything."

Quyloc had slid back the leather wrapping on his spear and was staring at the man. "Look closer," he said. "Unfocus your eyes."

"That doesn't—"

"Just try."

Rome did as he said and a minute later he started. "I see it. It's like a blurriness around him, stained with gray. It's on the ground too. It's spreading. The plants where he's touching…they're changing. What's happening?"

Ki'Loren shuddered again.

FIFTY-TWO

Josef smelled the approach of ki'Loren long before any of the other Children did. He looked up and saw it float up behind the palace. This was something he had never encountered before. It brimmed with Song, but not ordinary Song like he was used to. It smelled of the Sea. It was so rich, so vibrant, that it almost hurt.

He released his hold on the oak trees and jumped down to the ground, then made his way around the palace, drawn by the promise of that unusual Song.

As he came around the side of the palace, he saw a group of Lementh'kal emerge from ki'Loren and run around the opposite side of the palace. There didn't seem to be anyone else around. It was simple to jump over to the thing.

Josef climbed up the side, shaking with anticipation. An idea began to form in his mind.

He knelt down and put his hands on the ground.

As ki'Loren moved away from Qarath, Josef knew what he was going to do.

Normal life was lost to him forever. He couldn't ever again touch the plants he loved so much. But what he had done with the trees had showed him something, showed him that he could make something new.

Josef sank his hands and forearms into ki'Loren's side and then he began to pour himself into her, to merge with her.

To alter her.

If he could not have the life he knew and loved, he would make new life in his image.

FIFTY-THREE

Shorn and Netra stood on the sands of the Gur al Krin, looking down into the gaping mouth of the tunnel that led to the prison. It was still dark, dawn more than an hour away, but the hole showed as a patch of deeper darkness. Just standing there was almost too much for Netra. Her hands were shaking and there was desolation in her heart as she remembered the last time she'd been on this spot: euphoric, confident, sure. Filled with stolen Song.

And it all went terribly wrong.

All at once she felt as if she couldn't breathe. The sands were rising up around her to swallow her. There was no way she could go down into that hole. There had to be another way.

"What if we're wrong?" she asked, turning to Shorn, imploring him for an answer. "What if he's not down there at all?"

"Then we look somewhere else" was his implacable reply.

Netra clenched her hands into fists, trying to quell the shaking. It did no good.

"Time is short," Shorn said.

"I can't do this," she replied.

"You can," he said, his voice surprisingly gentle. "You are the strongest person I know."

"You don't know what you're saying."

He turned to her and took her arm. His almond eyes glowed faintly in the darkness. "No one but you can do this."

She pulled her arm away. "It's too much."

Shorn did not reply. He simply walked down the sandy slope into the mouth of the tunnel. In seconds he was gone from sight.

Netra stared after him for a long moment. Then she rolled her shoulders and forced her hands to unclench, took a deep breath, like a diver before leaping into the water, and followed him.

It was icy cold in the tunnel or perhaps the coldness was inside her. Netra stood in the blackness utterly blinded. The darkness was absolute. It had been so easy the last time she passed this way. She remembered running confidently through the darkness as if she carried the sun with her. Now it seemed to almost physically repel her.

"Please," she said. "I can't see."

"You don't need to see," Shorn said. "You can *feel*."

Netra started to deny him, but then she paused. He was right. Her eyes were useless, but she didn't need them.

"What have I become?" she asked the darkness.

"I don't know," he replied, "but I believe in you. You can do this. *Only* you can do this."

"Promise you will stay with me. No matter what."

He took her hand between his two huge hands. "I promise."

Netra took a deep breath. When she exhaled, some of the tension left her. She thought of Cara, waiting for her in Qarath. She thought of Siena, dead by Tharn's hand. She thought of the mother she had never known. She thought of her silent god, Xochitl.

"Okay."

Tentatively at first, then more confidently, she led them down into the earth.

They walked for hours. How long it was Netra couldn't have said. The darkness removed all time. It removed everything. The only thing remaining was that sense of cold emptiness that she came to realize was the prison. With every step it grew stronger.

And it grew more frightening.

As bad as Thrikyl had been, the prison would be immeasurably worse. She felt it sapping the strength from her limbs, stealing the courage from her heart.

But, strangely, at the same time it gave her renewed determination. The horror of what the Children had endured in there was heartbreaking. Every step she drew closer gave her a stronger sense of it and with every step she realized more and more how necessary it was what she did. Because, even though the physical prison was broken, what it had done to the Children was still very much intact. Nothing the Children did, no amount of Song consumed, could ever change that.

Only she could.

Finally, out of the darkness loomed a pale glow which gradually grew stronger. The tunnel opened up and they walked down a long slope and into a huge cavern, its far reaches lost in the dimness. The light came from a massive wall that bisected the cavern. The wall was the color of rotten ice and the light coming from it pulsed slowly. Netra understood instinctively that touching the wall would be painful, perhaps even deadly. It looked like stone, but it wasn't. It was chaos power bound into a permanent shape. No Song could pass through it. No Song could touch it without being absorbed.

In the center of the wall was a jagged opening, the area around it littered with large blocks of stone. There was something unusual about the blocks of stone. Netra paused by one, feeling around with her inner senses. There was an awareness within it, dim and faint. She reached deeper and suddenly realized that it was the Shaper known as Sententu, who had once held the door to the prison. Now shattered because of her.

From the jagged opening itself a wave of bitter cold spilled out. It was not the cold of a winter night. It was different, not something felt on the skin at all. It was the cold of emptiness, of a complete absence of Song.

Netra shivered. She put her hand on Shorn's arm and looked into the prison. Cautiously, she extended her inner senses inside. Immediately she was assaulted by a cacophony, a prolonged silent wail of pain and terror that pierced her so strongly she whimpered and put her hands over her ears, though that did nothing to stop it.

"I can hear them. Inside my head. There's so many of them." She turned her gaze up to Shorn, tears standing in her eyes. "Why are they still in there? Why don't they leave?"

Shorn looked into the opening. "When I was young, we captured a Sedrian-controlled moon. There was a prison there, filled with our people. They had been held captive for many years. When we opened the prison, only a few emerged. The rest had to be dragged out and some tried to run back inside."

Netra's eyes widened as she suddenly understood. She turned to look back into the opening. "This is all they know now."

Shorn looked impatient. "Is he in there?"

"I'm not sure. For a moment I felt something…different. A presence not like the others. I will have to go inside to be sure."

Once again, Shorn led the way.

"Wait!" Netra cried. She glanced around the cavern one last time, then gritted her teeth and plunged after him.

The cold was an ache that immediately penetrated to the core of her being. She felt as if she had fallen into a vast, deep well with no bottom. She would fall and fall forever. She would never find anything to hold onto, would never stop falling…

Shorn grabbed her arms and lifted her upright. "Fight back," he told her harshly. "You can do this. You *must* do this."

Netra clung to him like a stone in the midst of a flood. She clung to him as if she had nothing else in the world. She poured every ounce of trust that she felt toward him into that hold.

And the falling stopped.

Netra opened her eyes. Shorn was looking down at her. "Can you do it now?" he asked her.

Netra nodded. She still felt like she was suffocating. It was similar to how it felt to enter Thrikyl, only much, much worse. There was no Song in here other than the flows which supported the two of them, and those thinned as they passed into the prison. There was a weakness in her limbs that she knew would only get worse. If she stayed in here too long the thread of Song supporting her would dissolve and she would just lie down and die.

"I'm okay," she said faintly. Still holding onto his arm, she looked around. What she saw made her gasp.

The wall of the prison curved overhead like a huge bowl inverted over the city. It glowed like the full moon, lighting up Durag'otal.

They were standing on the edge of a large plaza that had once been the entrance to the city. For just the briefest moment she was able to picture the city as it had once been. A place of soaring spires, of broad, open streets. A place designed to bring people together, with parks and benches and fountains everywhere. A city made of different colors of stone and every bit of it lovingly shaped by Melekath.

But the moment passed and in its wake was the overpowering destruction of the place. The statue that had stood in the center of the plaza lay on its side, smashed into hundreds of pieces. The graceful spires were broken. Buildings had fallen—or been torn—down. There were blackened outlines of ancient fires.

"Now can you tell if he is here?" Shorn asked.

Netra listened inside, then pointed to the heart of the city. "He is that way."

They started down the broad boulevard that led from the entrance plaza into the center of the city. The light from the prison wall cast an eerie glow over everything. Here and there buildings alongside the boulevard had been toppled, shattered pieces of stone spilling into the street, partially blocking it.

They had gone only a short way when Netra became aware of a woman, within the ruined building ahead on the right. Netra wanted more than anything to avoid her. She didn't want the woman's pain to touch her. But she also knew she couldn't do that. The woman deserved better and so Netra reached out and brushed up against her mind.

Her name was Randa and she was trapped underneath the rubble of a fallen wall. Crushed, but still alive. Once upon a time she had been a mother, had nurtured and loved her twin boys fiercely. But both of the boys drowned in the sea, and the grief nearly drove her mad. She became obsessed with protecting her surviving child, a girl. The girl was only five when Melekath appeared and Randa took her to him to receive the Gift, desperate to keep her safe.

Now the girl lurked in the darkness nearby, her hands shredded from trying to move the blocks of stone that pinned her mother.

"We're not going in there," Shorn said, grabbing her shoulder.

Netra broke out of her spell, realizing that she had started walking toward the ruined building. "She's trapped under the stone," she said softly. "She's so frightened. We have to help her."

"We are trying to." Shorn tilted his head, then looked off into a narrow street between two buildings. "One approaches," he said, pointing.

Netra looked where he pointed. Shuffling, dragging sounds in the dark. After a moment she could just see a dim shape. It was a child, a boy, his lower body crushed beyond recognition. He was pulling himself with his arms. He raised his head. Their eyes made contact and she felt his hunger as almost a physical jolt.

He growled at her and began dragging himself faster.

A new sound came from within the ruined building. The little girl had come to the doorway. Her eyes were wild. She snarled and rushed at Netra.

Netra shrank back as Shorn stepped between them. He slapped the girl open-handed and she flew to strike against the wall. Almost immediately she was on her feet again.

"We cannot stay here," Shorn said. "More are coming."

From all around them came shuffling, dragging sounds. Dozens, maybe hundreds of them, drawn by the siren call of Song. Three appeared on the other side of the street. Eager yips came from them as they broke into a stumbling run, hands outstretched.

Shorn took Netra's arm and nearly dragged her down the street. Netra stumbled, but his grip kept her from falling. Her legs did not seem to work right. Too much was assailing her from every direction. The Children's pain was her pain, a ceaseless litany of it pounding on her. Was this what Melekath had gone through, for all those centuries? Feeling the pain of those he loved and unable to do anything about it?

They moved deeper into the city and in a few minutes had left their pursuers behind. Around them were more fallen buildings. In places the ground had buckled, split apart by some great upheaval. One large round building had been completely flattened by a taller one that had fallen on it. Trapped under the tons of stone were hundreds of people. They'd been gathering there, using the place for shelter. Others had toppled the taller building on purpose, crushing most of them instantly. Their collective wail of pain—a silent wail, from shattered bodies— was so strong it staggered Netra.

"How could you do this to them, Xochitl?" she whispered. "How could you trap them in this place?" How many of the Children had asked the same question, over and over in the dark?

Slowly they drew closer to the center of the city, where a huge spire stood. It alone seemed to have escaped most of the ravages of three millennia. Made of some kind of greenish stone, it soared almost to the arc of the prison wall overhead. Balconies encircled each level, numerous windows and doors cut into its outer walls.

They came to the foot of the building and Netra stared up at it in awe. "He built this to be the heart of Durag'otal," she said. "A place for his Children to create and show their art. A place for dancing and music. Even after he stopped trying to solve the endless conflicts between them, he kept this place free from the violence."

"Is he inside?"

Netra nodded. She took two more steps toward the building, then froze. "How did I miss that?"

"Miss what?"

She looked up at Shorn. "Melekath. He's not alone."

FIFTY-FOUR

"Who is it? Who is with him?"

"I don't know. But he's not human." Her eyes widened as the realization hit her. "Lowellin. It must be him." To Shorn's inquisitive look she said, "Cara told me that Lowellin always seemed to have a special hatred for Melekath. She said Ricarn told her Lowellin was never really there to help the Tenders, but that he was using us to take his revenge on Melekath. It all makes sense now. Somehow he learned about Melekath fleeing from his Children and he guessed, like we did, that Melekath would come here."

"Is he aware of us?"

Netra listened for a moment, then shook her head. "I don't think so. He is too focused on Melekath." She started for the doorway. "We have to hurry. Melekath is very weak. We don't have much time."

Shorn stopped her. "Do you have a plan?"

"Not really. I guess we'll have to make it up as we go." She pulled away and went through the door. Shorn made an exasperated sound and followed her.

Inside the doorway they found themselves in a short, broad hallway, which led to a large, arched opening. Curved corridors branched off either side of the hallway. Netra stopped at the arch and peered through. Beyond was a massive amphitheater with a stone tiled floor. On every side tiered rows of seats circled the amphitheater, stretching upwards at least fifty rows high.

Each of the levels above the amphitheater had broad balconies. Each level was smaller so that a person on any level could stand at the edge of the balcony and look down on the central amphitheater.

In the center of the amphitheater, lying spread-eagled on a waist-high block of stone, was Melekath. Lowellin stood over him. In his right hand he held a long, thin stone spike. Several more were in his left hand. There were spikes through Melekath's wrists and his feet, holding him in place.

As they watched, Lowellin held up the spike in his right hand, concentrating on it. Netra sensed, rather than saw, the Stone power building within the spike. Lowellin pushed it through Melekath's stomach, then into the stone beneath him. Melekath moaned and struggled weakly as he did so.

Lowellin stepped back, surveying his work. His face was lit by a fierce inner light.

"How does it feel, Melekath? Does this mean as much to you as it does to me?"

Melekath rolled his head to face him. "It hurts. Is that what you want me to say?"

"It is a start."

"But it does not hurt as much as the pain of knowing I have failed my Children. This is nothing compared to that."

With a snarl, Lowellin clenched another one of the stone spikes until it pulsed with power, then stabbed it through his chest. A moan came from Melekath, bitten off halfway through.

"Is it what you thought it would be?" Melekath said when he had gotten himself under control once again. His voice was faint. "Are the years you waited worth it?"

"Not yet," Lowellin replied. "But this is only the beginning." He drove another spike through Melekath's chest. "It is strange how much this hurts you," he mused. "You gave too much of yourself when you made the Gift. And for what? You sacrificed so much for them and in return they hate you."

"They are right to hate me," Melekath said. "The Gift I gave them turned out to be a curse. In their place I would feel the same."

"How can you be so old, so powerful, and still be so foolish?"

"A worthy question. One I have asked myself many times. There was much time for it, trapped in here."

"You'll have plenty more time when I am done with you. You'll have forever. I am going to destroy you like you destroyed Tu Sinar and Golgath."

"You can lay many crimes on me," Melekath said weakly, "but not those. Their destruction was not my doing."

Lowellin looked down on him, clearly surprised. "Truly?"

"It must have been Kasai. His hatred of the Eight was greater than anyone's and he was ever impetuous in his wrath."

"So the Guardians have also turned against you."

"It is true."

"It is almost redundant for me to torture you, cursed as you are by all those who were closest to you."

"Your hatred must have an outlet. You must have someone to blame."

"What are you saying? What is this talk of blame?"

"You are weak. You always have been."

Lowellin hissed with rage at his words and stabbed him with another stone spike. "You forget where you are and who has control over you," he snapped.

"Your hatred of me, I understand," Melekath said. He coughed. Something dribbled out the corner of his mouth. "Always you were jealous because I am First Ring and you are not."

"I have *never* been jealous of you."

"Jealous of the time I spent with *her* then."

"You understand nothing. Ultimately, she cared no more for you than for me. Believe me, my full hatred is not for you."

"Then who? Who do you hate so much?"

"You really don't know, do you? Can the great Melekath really be so blind? Did you never figure it out in all your years down here?"

"Tell me."

"*I* was Xochitl's favorite. *Me.*" Lowellin's face twisted from some powerful emotion. "She spent her time with *me*. Until you created *them*. Then I was no longer enough. From the beginning she was fascinated by them. It was all she could speak of. Nothing I said made any difference."

"You're jealous of *them*," Melekath said wonderingly.

"And why shouldn't I be? From the time you created them, she was ever enthralled by them. I thought it only a passing thing. I went along and I hid my true feelings because I was certain she would tire of them." Lowellin's voice was hoarse agony. "The centuries passed and still she could see only them. And you. You were their creator and that drew her in some way I could not understand. Don't you see? Between them and you, there was nothing left for me. She gave me only crumbs and I was supposed to be happy with them."

Melekath was staring at him. "I had no idea."

"No one did. I hid it well. I knew if I acted openly against her precious children that I would lose her forever. When you went away to create the Gift I saw my chance. I poisoned your creation against you. I poisoned her against you. I even managed to cause a gap between her and them, a gap that only I could cross over." He was pacing now, caught in his own tormented memories. "I was ready for your return. Once you saw how much they hated and feared you, once you saw how even Xochitl had come to distrust you, you would go into a rage and perhaps even destroy them yourself. Even if you didn't, surely there would be opportunities for ridding the world of them and you both."

He bent over suddenly and seized Melekath around the throat, squeezing, banging his head on the stone. "I never dreamed you would actually succeed in making them immortal. But when I saw that you had, I discovered a new opportunity. As I knew they would—weak, stupid creatures that they are—some took you up on your offer of immortality and I knew that you had made your fatal mistake. I knew that the other Nipashanti would not stand by as you subverted the ancient agreement that allowed Life to exist. Do you remember that agreement?"

Melekath nodded. "When Life dies, what it has taken from the Spheres is then returned."

"You were a fool to forget that. It was easy to rouse the rest of them against you. Xochitl was the only one who was difficult to convince. She thought you could be reasoned with in time. She thought she could make you see what you had done and undo it. But I stayed after her and I roused her followers against you as well, showing them how you were the destruction of all they held dear. In the end I think it was her pets that convinced her to move against you. That and the fact that the other Nipashanti were prepared to act with or without her.

"I was surprised by the shield you erected around your city. I had no idea such a thing was possible. That was the most difficult point. Several of the Nipashanti wanted to quit right then and return to their own lands. But I stayed on them, telling them over and over what would happen if they let this pass.

"And it was I who suggested using chaos power. The prison was *my* idea. I knew they would not listen to me, but I knew that, given time, Xochitl would. She trusted me. I showed her how the prison was the only humane way to go. You and your followers would be safely sealed away, but still alive. She could never have borne any solution that led to your destruction."

He let go of Melekath and stood upright, staring off into the darkness, remembering, lost in his own world.

Then he recovered himself and looked once again at Melekath. "It almost worked perfectly. You would have been sealed away forever. But she weakened in her resolve at the wrong moment. She lost her hold on the chaos power and an imperfection was introduced. A hole that Sententu—noble fool that he was—volunteered to seal with his own body. Even that would have been enough, except that you had one more hidden chip. The *ronhym* that helped you erect the shield."

"I never dreamed she would do that," Melekath said. "I had no idea Ketora cared enough to sacrifice herself to save my Children. She is the one true hero in this tragedy."

Lowellin continued as if he hadn't heard him. "I have to admit, you freed yourself from the prison faster than I expected. It surprised me. I thought then that my plans might come to naught. How happy I was to discover you so badly weakened. And I cannot tell you how perfect it was that your own Children turned on you, injuring you so badly that this would all be so simple."

Lowellin rubbed his hands together. "And that is how we came to be here. Now there is only one step remaining and I will be done with you forever."

"What is it?" Melekath's voice was utterly weary. It was clear he had no fight left in him and had abandoned himself to his fate.

Lowellin turned half away and stuck his hand out. "Come, Ilsith, my Other!"

The shadows coalesced around his hand and when they lifted, he was holding the black staff Ilsith.

"One last surprise," Lowellin said, taking Ilsith in both hands and holding it horizontally over Melekath. "Show him, Ilsith."

The staff shivered and seemed to split open. From its depths came a bulge, a transparent sac seemingly filled with some kind of purplish liquid. Within the liquid swam two creatures, like living slashes of darkness. Things of endless hunger.

Netra fell back a step, recognizing them instantly. They were the things that devoured Tu Sinar. They would devour Melekath and all hope of undoing the Gift would be lost forever. She turned to Shorn.

He was gone.

"Shorn!" she whispered, as loudly as she dared. Where had he gone? She looked down the two curved corridors that ran off the hallway but saw nothing. Her heart beating fast, she turned back toward the two Shapers.

"*Ingerlings*!" Melekath gasped. "What are you doing?"

"Why, I'm destroying you, that's what I'm doing," Lowellin said, giving an odd laugh. "I'm glad to see you know what they are. Ilsith discovered how Kasai obtained them. I have been waiting only for the right moment."

"But you can't control them. They are creatures of the abyss. What will they do once they have finished feeding on me?"

"I suppose they will devour your beloved Children next," Lowellin answered, gesturing toward the city around them.

"And after that?"

"The rest of the pathetic Circle of Life," Lowellin said with a shrug.

"And that really means nothing to you?"

"You clearly haven't been listening. Your creation was a mistake from the very beginning."

"Then you're a fool. Eventually they'll come after you too."

"I can handle them," Lowellin said confidently. "I have given it much thought." He held Ilsith close and stared into the watery sac.

"Once I touch this to you…"

Then, from the far side of the block of stone, Shorn leapt up. Lowellin was just starting to turn when Shorn wrapped his arms around him from behind, his huge hands closing over Lowellin's, around the staff.

His mighty arms flexed and he began pulling Ilsith toward Lowellin.

Lowellin's eyes bulged. Tendons stood out in his neck as he fought to keep Ilsith and its deadly cargo away from him.

But his strength was no match for Shorn's. Gradually, inexorably, the staff came closer. Lowellin's eyes fixed on the *ingerlings*, which had stopped swimming around and were pressed against the side of the sac, facing him. Their mouths opened and closed.

"No, please," Lowellin gasped.

With a final jerk, Shorn overcame the last of his resistance. The staff struck him, the bubble burst—

And the *ingerlings* were free.

Shorn pushed Lowellin away from him. Lowellin staggered across the stage, slapping wildly at the creatures. They tore through his clothes and latched onto him. In seconds they were gone, burrowed inside him.

Lowellin stared at Shorn, his eyes bulging.

"What you've done…" he gasped.

There was movement under his skin. He began to scream. The movement became more frenzied. Lowellin tore futilely at his skin. He seemed smaller already, as if he was collapsing in on himself.

Netra ran up to the stage. "Grab Melekath!" she yelled at Shorn. "We have to get out of here! I don't know how long it will take them to finish him."

Shorn turned to the block of stone and began yanking the spikes out of Melekath. In moments he had him free and slung him over his shoulder. He glanced at Lowellin. Lowellin had fallen to his knees. Something was coming out of his mouth. He reached one shaking hand out for Ilsith, lying nearby on the floor. Ilsith slithered away out of reach.

Lowellin raised one hand to Shorn as if in supplication.

Shorn turned away and jumped off the stone. Then he and Netra ran for the exit.

275

FIFTY-FIVE

Reyna made it to the palace just as ki'Loren was receding into the distance. She kicked the fallen stones of the wall out of her way as if they were mere pebbles. The trees Josef had animated were standing there, bereft of motion now that he was gone and she knocked them aside with hardly a thought as she made her way around the palace. The Children were packed at the back wall, staring out at the ocean, cursing and moaning the loss of their prey.

Heram was the first to feel Reyna's presence and he turned. His mouth dropped open and his normally stolid face stretched in a grimace of disbelief at what he saw. Then awareness of her filtered down to the rest of the Children and they began to turn as well.

Reyna was at least thirty feet tall and so filled with power that she glowed like a forge. It was raw, exhilarating, beyond anything imaginable. Nothing and no one could stand against her now. There was a tall stone tower nearby, wreathed in vines, and she knew she could knock it down with only the slightest of efforts. She didn't even need to touch it. She needed only a slight exertion of will, a release of a tiny portion of her power, and it would be done.

But right now she had more important things to do with her power. It was time for a final reckoning.

Heram shut his mouth and set his jaw. A look Reyna had not expected appeared on his face—resignation and something that might have been scorn—instead of the fear and awe she had planned for. He strode towards her until he was standing only a few paces away, then he crossed his thick arms over his chest and looked up at her. His two followers, Dubron and Leckl, cowered by the wall, their faces turned away.

"What did you do?" he asked.

"What I had to," she replied. "You ate them all." She wagged a finger at him. "That wasn't nice, you know. You didn't leave any of them for me."

Heram grunted. "It is no more than what you would have done."

She nodded. "So true. But then, I've never been a very nice person."

Karrl and Linde had been edging off to the side as she spoke and now they bolted like frightened rabbits, their stolen Song giving them the power to flee in huge leaps and bounds. In seconds they would be off the palace grounds and lost in the city.

Reyna didn't even look at them.

She raised one finger as if to make a point and both of them were seized in midair. They hung there, squirming and squealing. The other Children looked from them to Reyna and most of them froze, their expressions fearful. "I have a bad habit of holding grudges," she said. "I'm really not a very good person to cross."

"That's not true," Heram said.

Reyna cocked her head to one side. "You don't say?"

"Call it what it is. You're a bitch, Reyna. It's what you've always been."

Reyna laughed. "You're *right*. I couldn't have said it better myself."

"Stop playing with them and be done with it."

"It's not really that much fun," she replied. "There's no challenge to it."

Heram just stared at her.

"Okay," Reyna said. She snapped her fingers and Karrl and Linde simply *exploded*. Pieces of flesh rained down around them. The rest of the Children began to edge away. Only Heram stayed put, looking up at her calmly.

Reyna tossed her hair, which was an impressive mane of red and gold that hung down past her shoulders in lustrous waves and curls. She was completely nude. Her curves were perfect, her skin a flawless white. Her beauty was awesome, but it was frightening as well.

"What now?" Heram asked.

"It won't come as a surprise that I've never liked you, will it?"

Heram shrugged.

"I could keep you alive. You're no threat to me at all."

"But you won't."

"No. Again, not a nice person. And there's always the chance you'd figure out what I've done and do the same."

"I'd sure try."

"You're as thick as they come, but even an idiot can be right now and then."

"I'd crush you instantly if I could."

"You're taking all the fun out of this, you know. Right now you should be begging me to spare you."

Heram said nothing, only glared up at her.

"Won't you play?" she asked.

"What do you think?"

Reyna sighed. "I imagined this would be more entertaining."

Heram turned his head to the side and spat. It was a symbolic gesture. Nothing came out.

"You could run," Reyna suggested.

Heram tapped his chest. "Get it over with. I'm sick of listening to you."

Reyna scowled and flicked her finger toward him.

Heram exploded in a spray of dried flesh. Shrieks came from the other Children and they broke and sprinted for cover.

"Stop!" Reyna shouted, flinging out her will.

They froze in place, trapped by her power.

Reyna surveyed them. "I could destroy you all right now."

Whimpers and renewed struggling greeted her words.

Reyna frowned. This was not at all what she had imagined. For three thousand years she had conspired with and against these very same people. She had exerted all her will and cunning playing the only game that gave life in the prison any meaning at all. It was what had kept her sharp. Not just that. It was the one thing that kept her going when the despair tried to drag her down into madness and surrender.

"Is that all you have?" she implored them. "Don't you have anything else?"

None of them would even look at her. They kept struggling, but it was utterly futile. She was too strong.

"Fight me!" she screamed.

Nothing.

Reyna looked around wildly. On the ground to one side was one of Heram's forearms, the hand still attached. She bent and seized it, then looked around for more. He wasn't dead. He couldn't die. If she could find enough pieces, maybe she could put him back together. She saw a foot over near the wall and she hurried and grabbed it up.

Forgetting about the rest of the Children, she released them. They stampeded, trying to get as far away from her as they could.

Reyna saw what looked like a shoulder and snatched it up, looking desperately around for more.

But the rest of the pieces were too small. When she tried to pick them up they fell from her fingers back into the dirt.

She went to her knees and screamed her despair at the sky.

FIFTY-SIX

Cara was helping an elderly woman when a new tremor, harder than the rest, shook ki'Loren. The elderly woman stumbled and Cara barely caught her before she fell.

"What was that?" the woman asked.

Cara thought of the hunched man clinging to the side of ki'Loren. What could she tell the woman? "It's probably nothing," Cara replied. But then people around her started looking up and pointing and when she did what she saw made her grow cold inside.

Ki'Loren didn't have a sky in the normal sense. Instead, the area where the sky would be had a diffuse, uniform, yellow glow. Now though, there was a gray blotch on one section, and it was visibly growing larger. Ki'Loren had an abundance of wildlife, including creatures that were similar to birds, though they seemed to float through the air—propelling themselves by flapping unusual flexible wings—rather than fly. While Cara was looking, a bright orange bird flapped across the front of the gray blotch.

The bird immediately plummeted to the ground. It stumbled around on the ground, clearly dazed, its movements stiff and uncoordinated. Most disturbing was the fact that all the color had leached from it.

"Oh dear, that can't be good," the elderly woman said. "Look, it's coming down the hillside now."

Like oil sliding across the surface of the water, the gray blotch was spreading onto the land. As plants were engulfed in it, they changed. Their leaves and flowers shriveled and fell off. They lost all color and turned gray.

A four-legged, furry creature, kind of like a large rabbit, emerged from a clump of bushes that had been touched by the blotch. Large clumps of its fur had fallen out and its movements were erratic and unsteady. It spooked and bolted down the hill. People cried out and hurried to move out of its path.

As it approached Cara and the elderly woman, they could see that its eyes had turned white. It ran headlong into a tree, fell over, then struggled back up and continued running.

"We haven't gotten away after all, have we?" the elderly woman said.

Cara squeezed her arm. Inside she said, *Come on, Netra. You're our last hope.* "The gray area is getting closer. Let's keep moving, shall we?"

"Maybe a little further," the elderly lady agreed. "But I am mostly done. This doesn't seem to be something you can run away from."

Ya'Shi and the Ancient One were outside ki'Loren, sitting on its highest peak, looking down at Josef. Josef had sunk halfway into ki'Loren's side. Periodically, it was as if a wave came off him, radiating outward. With each wave, a shudder passed over ki'Loren and the gray area around him grew larger.

"If he cannot have the world he remembers, he will remake it in a new image," the Ancient One observed.

Ya'Shi snorted. "Now, when we're both about to die, you want to waste our last moments stating the obvious?"

"It is what I'm good at," the Ancient One agreed.

"Well, I want in." Ya'Shi sprang to his feet. "We're all about to die!" he yelled. "Help, help!" He stopped and looked around. Josef didn't respond. There were sea gulls in the distance. They didn't respond either. He sat back down. "That actually felt pretty good."

"It's too bad, really," the Ancient One said. "Many people will miss this world."

"Not once they're dead," Ya'Shi corrected. The Ancient One nodded. "So you don't think that Netra will figure it out in time?" he asked her.

"Who's Netra?" the Ancient One asked.

"The young Tender with the giant bodyguard."

The Ancient One looked at him quizzically.

"The one that visited here awhile back. Haven't you been paying attention?" Ya'Shi's voice had risen.

The Ancient One shrugged. "I am very busy."

"Doing what? All you do is sit here!"

"Jealousy is an ugly trait, old friend."

"You're right." Ya'Shi sat down abruptly. "Getting excited is very tiring."

"See? You're learning."

"She may still figure it out," Ya'Shi said. "Nothing we can do now but wait."

"And sit," the Ancient One added. Ya'Shi nodded and they both sat there looking at the sky.

FIFTY-SEVEN

"I can walk on my own," Melekath said when they were outside the building. "Put me down."

Shorn paused and looked at Netra, who nodded.

Back on his feet, Melekath looked shaky, but he stayed upright. He turned to look back inside. "I never thought he was so far gone." He looked at the two of them. "If you are waiting for my gratitude, you will be disappointed. It was only what I deserve."

"We're not here for gratitude," Netra said. She was finding it increasingly hard to concentrate. The edges of her vision were starting to go black.

"Why are you here then?" Melekath asked. He peered more closely at her. "I remember you. You broke Sententu and opened the prison." Netra winced at his words. "I suppose I do owe you some gratitude after all."

"This isn't the place to talk," she said. "I have to get out of here. This place is killing me."

"I would remain here with my Children."

"Too bad," Shorn said, taking hold of his arm.

Netra was already starting down the broken street. Shorn propelled Melekath after her. Melekath offered no resistance.

Netra was running by the time she reached the edge of the city. She burst through the shattered opening in the prison wall, made it a half dozen steps into the cavern beyond, then sank to her knees, gasping, her heart hammering. It still wasn't pleasant, but she no longer felt like she was drowning. She could feel the wall of the prison at her back, a cold deadness that made her skin itch, and she crawled further away from it.

She stood up when Shorn and Melekath emerged. It struck her then, how small and frail Melekath looked. She had been raised to believe unquestioningly that he was the embodiment of evil, but he didn't look evil. Mostly he looked sad and old. He was bent over, his face lined with deep wrinkles. His clothes were little more than rags. There was a huge wound from his shoulder down into his chest that had only partially sealed closed. In his torso were half a dozen puncture wounds from which something clear seeped.

She was surprised to discover that she felt sorry for him.

Shorn let go of Melekath's arm and the old Shaper straightened himself and faced Netra. "I figured it out. I know why you're here. You have come to ask me to undo the Gift."

Netra nodded. "You don't know what they've become. There's nothing we can do to stop them. They just keep getting stronger and stronger."

Melekath shook his head.

"Why not?" Netra snapped, suddenly angry. She gestured toward the prison. Lurking in the shadows of the doorway was a woman, her hair and teeth gone, her face a ruined mess. Both her legs were missing. She whined and held up a hand to Melekath. "Look at her! How can you not see that your Gift is a curse! You claim to love them; why won't you free them?"

"You misunderstand me," Melekath replied, giving the woman a pained look. "I would undo the Gift if I could. Don't you think they begged me for death, over and over during the centuries we were lost in there? Don't you think I tried to give it to them? If I could undo the Gift, even if it cost me my own existence, I would do so. But I can't. It's hopeless."

"It's not hopeless," Netra said stubbornly. "It can't be. There has to be a way."

"There isn't. There's nothing you or anyone can do. Leave here. Go to your loved ones, if they still live. Spend what time you can with them. That's all you can do."

Netra sagged, the faint hope she'd felt on the way here evaporating. Everything she'd been through, all the running, all the suffering. All of it for nothing.

"No," Shorn said abruptly. "You will *not* quit now. So long as you draw breath you will not quit."

"You heard him," she said bleakly, not meeting his gaze, not wanting him to see her failure. "There's nothing we can do."

"I heard the words of one who has already given up, who is already dead. I will not hear those words from you." He sounded angry.

"Then what do you want me to do?" Her voice rose. She wanted to scream. "Because I can't see anything at all."

"The yellow-skinned fool, Ya'Shi. He said you were the key, the doorway for them to return."

"I thought you said his words were nonsense," she retorted.

Shorn came closer and put his hand on her shoulder. With his other hand he lifted her chin so she would look into his eyes. "They are. Most of them. But I believe in this he was saying something important."

"Then why didn't he just tell me what to do? Why cloak it in a riddle? 'Be the doorway for them to return.' What does that mean?"

"I don't know why he did it," Shorn responded. "But I think he does not much care for the world either way."

"The doorway for them to return?" Melekath said, looking thoughtfully at Netra. "Did he know you were the one who opened the prison?" Netra nodded. "You tapped the power of a trunk line to do that. Not since the earliest days has any human done so and lived." He rubbed his chin, thinking. "Is it possible?" he murmured.

"Is what possible?"

He looked back up at them. "With every living thing, even if it avoids all injury and disease, eventually the *akirma* grows brittle with advancing age. Sooner or later the *akirma* fails, Selfsong flees the body and that which was alive is no longer so. When I sought to create the Gift it was my thought that if I could find a way to make the *akirma* stronger, impervious even, I could end death.

"It took many years, but eventually I learned how to do this. I discovered that I could dissolve part of myself—not this body you see standing here, but my fundamental self—and then share that. I could make others more like me. It made me weaker to do so, but I counted that as no real cost."

"Is there a point to this?" Shorn rumbled.

"I'm getting to it," Melekath replied. "My Children don't die because each carries within them some small part of my essence, woven into their *akirmas*. The problem has always been how to remove that part, to return them to what they once were. That was the part I could never figure out. But I think I know now how to do so."

"How?" Netra asked.

"They must be washed clean."

"What is that supposed to mean?"

"The Gift must be washed from them. But there is only one thing I think would be able to do this: the River."

"The River?" Shorn asked. "The place where Song comes from?"

"Yes," Melekath said.

"And the Children must be put there?"

"In a manner of speaking, yes."

"It is not possible. They are too strong now," Shorn said.

"You must understand that the River is not an actual thing set in an actual place," Melekath said. "It exists everywhere and nowhere."

"This makes no sense."

"It's okay, Shorn. You don't need to understand it," Netra said. To Melekath she said, "I still don't see how we can possibly get each one of them to the River."

"You also misunderstand me. I am not saying you bring them to the River." Melekath looked from one to the other. "I am saying you bring the River to them."

Netra stared at him openmouthed. "That's even more impossible," she said at last. "No one can control the River like that. No one can even touch it. Anyone who tried would be torn apart instantly."

"You're right. No one can *control* the River." Melekath gave an odd little half smile as he said it. "And anyone who tries to *touch* it will be torn apart."

"You begin to sound like Ya'Shi," Shorn growled.

Netra was starting to have a terrible feeling. "What are you saying?"

"I'm saying that someone will have to throw herself *into* the River."

"You mean me." He nodded. "Why don't you do it? You're basically a god."

"You know I cannot do that. I am not a living creature. It would tear me apart instantly."

"But you think I can."

"Ya'Shi thinks you can."

"What do you think?"

"I think that as a living thing, you are part of the River and it is part of you."

"There's no way I have the strength to do that. I took hold of a trunk line but the only reason I could do that is I…" Her voice caught. "I killed all those people. I would have to kill thousands more to do what you say and I will never do that. Not even to save the world. I will not make that mistake again."

"You are still thinking of control. Even if you held the Selfsongs of every person in the world within you, you would not have the power to take hold of the River."

"Then what am I supposed to do?"

"Surrender. Enter the River knowing there is nothing you can do. Enter knowing that if you try to fight it you will be destroyed. Enter knowing that you belong there, that you are of it and it is of you."

"That sounds crazy."

Then Melekath did smile. It was painful to see. "It *is* crazy," he whispered.

"And then what? Say I enter and am not instantly killed. Then what do I do?"

Melekath shrugged. "Be the doorway."

"What does that mean?"

"I don't know. But somehow you will have to immerse my Children within the River's currents."

"And that will wash them clean."

He shrugged again. "Maybe."

Netra looked at Shorn. "What do you think?"

"I have never fought my enemies in such a way," he replied.

"You think it's crazy too."

"I did not say that. The way I have always fought will not work here. Anyone can see that. A new way always seems crazy the first time."

"But I can't..." Netra said, thinking of the immense power of the trunk line, how close it had come to shredding her. And the power of the River was far vaster than that. As well compare a drop of water to the ocean's vastness. "I don't see how I can possibly do it," she said softly.

"Then my Children will destroy everything," Melekath said sadly. "And still they will live on. They will never be free of the prison I made for them."

Netra turned away. Her eyes fell on the broken woman lying inside the doorway. She thought of the Children, perhaps even then loose on the palace grounds, devouring everyone. "I have to try."

"No," Melekath said. "You cannot try. You have to surrender. It is your only chance."

Netra thought about how long she had been running and fighting. How everything she had tried had only made things worse. There was only one exception, she realized. When the blinded man held her captive, about to burn her alive, her spirit guide had appeared to her and looked at her with its glowing eyes. It had assured her she knew what to do.

If she would simply let go and do it.

It had been simple to burn her bonds away then. Effortless. The one time she let go was the one time her bonds disappeared.

"Okay," she said, turning back to them. "I surrender."

FIFTY-EIGHT

Reyna stood and threw down the tattered pieces of Heram's body. She knew with utter certainty that no one and nothing on this world could challenge her. She could crush all who stood in her way. She was a god.

And it was all utterly pointless.

With no one to scheme against, no one to test herself against, there was nothing left for her.

She looked to the south. Somewhere down there was the Gur al Krin and underneath that the prison. Melekath would be there. There was nowhere else he could have gone. His guilt would demand nothing else.

One thing left, then.

She could make him pay.

She threw up one hand and summoned Song to her. She could feel it there, all around her, flowing ceaselessly. It could not resist her call.

The sky split open, revealing a glowing lattice work of feeder lines, humming with power. But she wanted more. She pushed deeper and the feeder lines parted, revealing the massive, intertwining trunk lines beyond them.

She curled her fingers and one of the trunk lines bent toward her. She grabbed hold of it with both hands and tore it in half. Power sprayed from the broken ends and surged through her, so much of it that sparks danced across her skin and she began to glow.

All around her in a wide area every animal, every bird and every insect suddenly fell to the ground, dying. Plants wilted and turned gray.

She dropped the trunk line. The ends dangled limp and blackened.

Her first leap carried her completely outside the city. The second took her even further.

She tore open another trunk line and absorbed its power, used it to jump even further.

So much power and yet not enough to fill the void inside her.

FIFTY-NINE

Netra threw her arms around Shorn and gave him a long hug. Then she pulled back and looked into his eyes, her small hands lost in his huge ones. "Thank you for everything you've done," she whispered to him. "You saved me so many times."

"It is you who saved me. You showed me that what I thought was weakness was actually strength. I am always in your debt."

"If I don't return…" Netra swallowed and had to start again. "If you can, find Cara. Tell her I love her."

Shorn nodded and Netra moved away from him. She seated herself cross legged on the ground, well back away from the prison wall, and closed her eyes. She slowed her breathing, let her breath wash all thoughts from her mind. When she had grown calm inside, she caught hold of an outgoing breath and let go of her body, letting her breath pull her out of herself and into *beyond*.

In that ethereal place she took one last look back. She could see Shorn standing protectively over her; she saw Melekath go back into the prison and kneel down beside the broken woman.

I can't do this, she thought.

She let that thought slide away from her, reminding herself that there was nothing she *could* do, that she was here only to surrender. The one thing that nothing in her life, nothing in her entire make up, had ever prepared her for. She was a doer and a fighter. Giving in was not something she understood.

And it was the only thing with any chance of saving them all.

She turned her focus on the tiny flow of Song that connected to her *akirma*. The cavern and everything in it faded from sight as she followed the flow deeper and deeper into *beyond*. The flow joined with other flows and eventually became a feeder line that glowed brightly in the darkness.

Still deeper she went and after a while the feeder line led to a trunk line, as big around as a tree trunk and pulsing brightly.

Deeper still she went, following the trunk line, and at last she beheld it.

The River.

It was a vast, golden artery floating in the darkness. It had no end; it had no beginning. Its surface was calm and smooth, but there was the sense of powerful currents moving within it. The power radiating from it was unbelievable. Next to it Netra felt as weak as a butterfly caught in a hurricane. Her *akirma* was no more than the faintest puff of smoke, sure to be torn apart in seconds. How had she lived within it for so long, weak thing that it was?

Trunk lines branched off the River at intervals, twisting and arcing out into the darkness, fat, golden tributaries carrying the melody of Life to every living thing.

She willed herself closer. There was no way this was going to work. It would be easier to throw herself into an active volcano. The power of the River was beyond comprehension. It was foolish to even think of such an action. There must be another way. She started to pull back from it, then *saw* something that stopped her.

There was a strange turbulence in the River, something roiling its surface. A purple-black stain that marred the golden perfection. A shock went through her. What could be causing this?

She followed the stain around and back to its source. What she saw then made her feel sick. One of the trunk lines was completely black. Poison spewed from it into the River.

It shocked Netra so much that she didn't think, she simply reacted, and that was what allowed her to do it.

She threw herself into the River.

The River took her and tore her into a million pieces. Then every piece was smashed over and over on invisible rocks. The pain was all-encompassing, unlike anything she had ever experienced. Nothing could have prepared her for this. It was utterly terrifying and disorienting, as if she were caught in a massive, raging flood. Her perception spun crazily about her until all sense of who or where she was was lost.

She had made a terrible mistake. The River was too vast and she was too insignificant. If she didn't get out of it soon there would be nothing left of her.

Yet no matter how hard she tried, she could find nothing to hold onto. She couldn't slow herself down, couldn't stop the wild tumbling.

She was almost gone now. The pieces of who she was were slipping through her torn fingers.

And would it be so bad, really? So much running, so much uncertainty and fear. What a relief it would be to quit fighting, to simply give up.

In her mind's eye there appeared a figure then, a rock lion with glowing eyes.

Do not give up.

I have nothing left.

You can still surrender.

It won't work. I don't know how.

Let go of yourself. Trust in that which is larger than you.

It made no sense. Fighting and clinging were all she knew.

Then you will fail and everything you love will die.

There was no judgment there, no threat. Only a simple statement of fact. There were no other choices.

Give yourself to the River. Let it carry you.

Netra quit trying to hold on. She quit trying to fight her way to the surface. She gave herself over to the River.

Almost immediately something changed. The River's turbulence eased. She no longer felt like she was being pounded on unseen rocks. She felt weightless.

Free.

She floated to the surface. The River was now utterly calm. It held her gently in its grasp, bathing her wounds and easing her suffering. She was finally home.

The beauty and wonder of it were so great that she began to weep for the sheer joy of it. She wept for herself, for all those years she had run away from her true home. She wept for everyone she knew and everyone she didn't know, for all their fears and despair. Above anything else, she longed for each of them to experience this, to know at least one moment of true safety and peace.

Then she looked outward.

Out in the darkness that surrounded the River were millions of tiny points of light, each connected through the flows of Song to the River. She knew that she looked on every living thing and she wondered at the beauty of it all.

But then she saw that there were other points of light that were cloudy and diseased, with sharp, painful edges to them. They were not connected to the River. From them came unending screams, a wail of torment that pierced her to her core.

Without being aware of what she was doing, she reached out to one of the sharp lights, driven by a desire to bring it back to the comfort and safety of the River, to share with it the oneness and beauty that she felt.

SIXTY

Shorn watched helplessly as Netra twitched and cried out. Her face contorted with pain so strong it seemed he could feel it as well.

"It's killing her," he said.

Melekath looked up from the woman he was holding and his expression was grim. "It is. Because she's fighting it."

"How do I help her?"

"There's nothing you can do. Nothing anyone can do."

Shorn shook her. "Come back," he implored her. "Don't die."

But it did no good. She began spasming, so that Shorn was worried she would injure herself and he laid her down.

Just when he thought that she would surely die, the spasms suddenly ceased. The pain lines on her face went away. A look of peace took their place.

"It's working," Melekath said, awe in his voice. "She's doing it."

Shorn looked over to where Melekath sat with the broken woman in his lap, just in time to see the woman suddenly sit bolt upright. A smile lit up her ruined face as she stared off at something only she could see and she gave a small cry of utter joy.

She held up her hands. A bright light shone out from her. Shorn had to close his eyes.

The light grew stronger and stronger, so bright that Shorn could see it clearly even with his eyes shut.

All at once it flared, just for a second, and when the moment passed, she was gone.

Melekath came to his feet, age and weariness sloughing off him like dried mud. His face shone with a new smile. "My Children!" he cried, running off into the prison. "It's time for you to go home!" There was another bright flash of light in the darkness, then another and another.

In the city of Thrikyl, Orenthe stirred slightly and one eye opened.

"Mother?" she whispered.

The glow filled her, washing away the pain and thousands of years of despair. She sat up, laughing joyously as she flared brightly and returned home.

χ χ χ

In Qarath, shortly after Reyna took off to the south, Dubron attacked Leckl, slamming him into a stone wall so hard that he went completely through it. Dubron leapt through the hole after him, but Leckl had already recovered from the impact and he slammed a big rock down on Dubron's head, cracking his skull. Dubron fell to the floor and Leckl rose up over him, the stone poised for another blow.

But all at once Leckl froze and looked up. A smile appeared on his face and he began to glow brightly.

Dubron, his skull already knitted back together, seized his opportunity and snatched up another stone. But as he swung it at his enemy, Leckl flared with the brightness of the sun and disappeared.

Dubron stood staring at the spot where Leckl had been, confusion on his face. Then he began to glow as well and confusion was replaced with joy.

χ χ χ

Ki'Loren was suffering. The gray blotch had spread completely down one side of the island. Shudders passed over ki'Loren every few seconds. A crack started from beside Josef and radiated outwards, rapidly growing wider.

Inside, pieces of the roof were peeling away and falling on the humans and the Lementh'kal. Many of the refugees from Qarath were running down the length of the valley, trying to stay ahead of the growing gray blotch, but a large number were just standing and staring.

The elderly woman she was helping looked up at Cara and said, "No more. I'm done running. It does no good." Then she simply sat down.

Then suddenly Josef sat upright. He pulled his hands from ki'Loren's side and raised them into the air. He began to glow.

"Well, look at that," Ya'Shi said, still on his perch at the top of ki'Loren's peak.

Josef leapt to his feet with a shout of joy. The light grew blinding. There was a flash and Josef was gone.

"It worked. She did it."

"I never doubted her," the Ancient One said, stroking the scraggly strands of her gray hair.

"Yes, you did. You were already planning your next life."

"That's ridiculous. I was completely confident the entire time."

"Being old does not give you a free pass to lie," he said.

"Being *ancient* gives me a free pass to do whatever I like."

"You're right," Ya'Shi said. "I hadn't thought about it like that."

The Ancient One patted ki'Loren's side. "She is not well."

"Not at all. Josef was not gentle. No doubt she could use our help with healing."

The Ancient One nodded her agreement, but remained sitting.

"Aren't you going to get up and do something?" Ya'Shi asked.

"Oh. You were talking to *me*?"

"Who else would I be talking to?"

The Ancient One shrugged. "You do spend a lot of time talking to yourself. That's what everyone says."

"How would you know what everyone says? You haven't gone anywhere or done anything in a hundred years."

She nodded. "That's true."

"Then let us do this. May I?"

Ya'Shi held out his hand to her. She took it and he helped her to her feet. Together they walked down the slope toward the spot where Josef had been.

𝗫 𝗫 𝗫

One moment ki'Loren was shaking badly and wave after wave of wrongness was passing over the place and the next it was just…gone.

Rome looked around, disbelieving. "What just happened?"

Quyloc stared upwards, toward where Josef had been. "He's gone," Quyloc said.

"What do you mean, gone? Where would he go? Did he jump into the ocean and swim away?"

"No. He's *gone*. There is no trace of him."

"How can that be?" Tairus asked.

"Give me a minute," Quyloc said. "Both of you. Just don't say anything for a minute." He took hold of the spear in both hands and the faraway look came into his eyes.

Rome motioned to Tairus and they walked a short way away. "You don't think…" Tairus began.

"I hope so. But I'm not going to start thinking. Not yet."

The people of Qarath were looking around in confusion. For the most part they were still afraid, still waiting for the next blow to come. How long had it been since they'd had truly good news?

Quyloc came out of his trance and walked over to them. "I think…they're *all* gone," Quyloc said doubtfully. He looked to Ricarn for confirmation and she nodded.

"I can't sense them anywhere," Nalene said. "Before their presence was like a background buzz, like angry bees. But now it's just…silent."

"She returned them to the Circle," Ricarn said.

"You mean the young Tender?" Rome asked.

Ricarn nodded. "She went into the River and she opened the way for them to return."

"But that's not…it's impossible," Nalene said.

"Tell that to Netra."

"But how?"

"We all come from the River. Why can we not return to it?"

"It's too much. It will destroy anyone who—"

"Nevertheless."

"Who cares if it's possible or not? Who cares how she did it? What matters is she did it," Rome said. The words felt strange in his mouth. It seemed impossible, but it was true. Just like that he felt the weight of the world slip off his shoulders. He wanted to laugh and cry and scream with joy all at the same time. A huge smile split his bearded face and his eyes landed on Quyloc. He took a big step toward Quyloc, who put his hands up and took a step back. But Rome was not going to be denied.

He grabbed Quyloc in a bear hug, lifting him completely off the ground and spinning him around. Quyloc started to push away, then, awkwardly, hugged him back. Rome set him down and hugged Tairus, also picking him off the ground. Tairus cheered and pounded him on the back. Rome set him down and turned to his people, some of whom were moving closer, questioning looks on their faces. Laughing, he shouted, "The Children are defeated! They're gone!"

People stared at him in stunned silence and then a few of them cheered. Word spread quickly and the cheering spread, growing steadily stronger.

Rome turned to Ricarn, his arms spread wide, but then he remembered who she was and he resisted the urge to hug her. She'd probably turn him into a bug or something.

To Nalene he said, "We did it. We beat them." He stuck out his hand and she shook it.

Rome saw Jenett waiting nearby. "Turn this thing around," he told her, clapping her on the shoulder. "Let's go home!"

Then he ran off down the slope, whooping as he went. He had to find Bonnie. He was going to grab her tight and never let her go.

SIXTY-ONE

Netra was lying there peacefully, a small smile on her face. Shorn felt a tremendous sense of relief. She was going to be okay. Curious, he walked away from her to peer into the prison. The intense flashes of light, which had been appearing nearly continuously, seemed to have faded away.

Suddenly Shorn felt a new presence behind him, powerful and malevolent. He spun just as a mighty concussion struck the cavern, as if a star had fallen from the sky and struck the ground. He was knocked to his knees and before he could get up, the roof of the cavern cracked open. Sunlight flooded in and Reyna jumped down into the cavern.

She was huge and blazing with awesome power. Her eyes spun with madness. She roared, her fury so powerful it knocked Shorn backward.

He made it back to his feet, knowing with awful certainty that he was too late to stop her, too late to do anything.

"You will not take this from me!" Reyna screamed, her eyes fixed on the small, still form of Netra.

She raised one foot and stomped on Netra. The force of the impact rent the earth and her foot drove down into the cavern floor.

Shorn yelled and ran toward her.

All at once light began to shine from Reyna's eyes and mouth. The rage vanished from her face, replaced by wonder and awe. She uttered a cry of joy—

She flared and disappeared into nothing.

Shorn ran to the hole. With Reyna's dissolution the sides had fallen in.

For a moment he stared in stunned disbelief, then he jumped into the hole and began furiously grabbing rocks and throwing them out of the hole. It was hopeless. He knew it was hopeless. There was no way she could have survived that. But still he had to try.

SIXTY-TWO

Ki'Loren floated up behind the palace and came to a stop. An opening appeared in the side and a drawbridge extended and came to rest on the low wall behind the palace. Tairus was the first one across the drawbridge, followed closely by Rome.

"I'm going to do it," Tairus said. "Just like I said."

"You don't have to," Rome replied, trying to catch hold of his arm. "I believe you."

But Tairus pulled away and as soon as he was on the palace grounds he went to his knees and kissed the ground. Still kneeling on the ground, he tore at the straps and got his breastplate off, tossing it aside. The emblem of his rank was sewn to his tunic and he put his hand on it. "I don't know what the proper way is to do this, but I do hereby resign, or something." Then he tore off the emblem.

Or tried to.

It wouldn't come off. He couldn't get a good grip on it. Giving up, he peered up at Rome. "In case that wasn't clear, I quit. I'm done with all this crazy shit. I'm going to buy a farm and get old and fat."

Rome just shook his head and laughed. "Okay, okay," he said, pulling Tairus to his feet. "But stand up at least. Do you want everyone to think you've gone simple?"

"I don't care what they think," Tairus said with mock gruffness. "I don't care what anyone thinks or says or does ever again. You hear? I'm a civilian now!"

"I hear you. You don't need to shout. But could you at least wait a few days? The city is a wreck and I could use your help."

Tairus sighed. "If I don't say yes, you're just going to try and appeal to my better nature, aren't you?"

"If I have to."

"Okay, I'll do it. But as soon as things get square, I'm gone. And you won't try to talk me out of it, you understand?"

"I promise," Rome said with a smile.

"Don't give me that look. I mean it this time."

"I know." And Rome thought that probably Tairus really meant it this time. He certainly wasn't a young man anymore. Rome stretched and felt the stiffness in his neck. None of them were young anymore. He saw Jenett walk across the drawbridge and he walked over to her.

"I want to thank you, to thank all your people," he told her. "If you hadn't come along when you did, well…I don't have to tell you what would have happened."

"On behalf of my people, I accept your gratitude," she said, lowering her head slightly.

"You can consider Qarath your eternal ally," Rome continued. "If there's ever anything we can do to help you, and I mean anything, all you have to do is ask."

"We will remember."

Rome scratched his neck. "This feels kind of odd. Maybe I should be talking to your leader. You have a king or something?"

"There is no such thing among my people."

"What about the crazy guy, Ya'Shi?"

"Following Ya'Shi would be more than any of us could manage."

"Well…" Rome hesitated, unsure what to say. Where was Quyloc when he needed him? "Just remember, if you ever need anything."

"Look, there is Ya'Shi now," Jenett said, pointing.

Ya'Shi was back on ki'Loren's highest point. There was someone seated beside him. Ya'Shi waved vigorously and yelled something, but Rome couldn't hear.

"What?" he yelled back.

Ya'Shi kept waving and shouting, becoming very animated. Then, all at once he lost his balance and fell. It was an impressive fall. He did a complete flip, landed on his back, then bounced and continued falling and rolling. Rome watched him with alarm, sure that he was injuring himself, but when he glanced at Jenett he saw no sign of concern on her face. If anything, she seemed almost to be smiling.

Ya'Shi kept bouncing and rolling until finally, with one last tumble, he flopped onto the drawbridge. Groaning, he stood up unsteadily. Rome started to go to him, but Jenett put her hand on his arm, stopping him.

Ya'Shi staggered over to Rome. "Oh my," he said. "That didn't work out so well."

"Are you okay?" Rome asked him.

Ya'Shi looked himself over, then shook his head doubtfully. "I don't think so. But at my age, it's hard to tell."

"What were you yelling?"

Ya'Shi gave him a blank look.

"Before you fell, you were yelling something."

Ya'Shi's face lit up. "Oh. Yes. I was saying goodbye."

"That's it?"

"Yes. That's it." Without another word, Ya'Shi turned and walked back into ki'Loren.

"What a strange man," Tairus said. "Or whatever he is."

"It seems your people have all made it off ki'Loren," Jenett said. "So I will say goodbye as well." They watched her walk across the drawbridge, which then pulled back. The opening in ki'Loren's side closed and the island began to move away.

Rome saw Perganon standing to one side, watching ki'Loren leave, and he walked over to him. "I'm glad to see you made it all right," Rome told him.

Perganon adjusted his spectacles and turned to look at Rome. "I am as well."

"How's that history coming along?" Before leaving for Guardians Watch, Rome had told Perganon he wanted a history of these events written.

"I haven't gotten much of a start," Perganon replied. "There's been a lot going on."

"I guess you'll have time now."

"I hope so."

"Just make sure you don't leave them out." Rome gestured at ki'Loren, which was already sinking under the sea.

"I assure you I won't."

Quyloc was standing there, staring at the vine-wreathed tower. Several hours had passed since their return. There was no one else nearby. Everyone else had moved on, some to the tents set up for them on the palace grounds, others back into the city itself. Relief and excitement mixed equally with grief and resolution. There was a great deal of rebuilding to do and so much had been lost. Rome walked up to stand beside Quyloc.

"I was kind of hoping that would be gone too," Rome said.

For a time Quyloc said nothing. Then he pointed at the sand dune in front of the tower, just barely visible underneath the vine, and said, "It has grown larger."

Rome winced. "So it's not just my imagination then? What are we going to do about it?"

"I don't know."

"Maybe we could just build a wall around it?"

"You remember the Gur al Krin, don't you?"

Rome winced again. "Yeah."

"There's a hole here, a rift in the Veil. Just like there is by the prison."

"Are you saying that's going to keep growing and we're going to have another desert like the Krin right here?"

Quyloc sighed. "I think so."

"Isn't there any way we can seal the hole?"

"The Kaetrians never figured out how. The Shapers never figured out how."

"We're going to have to abandon Qarath, aren't we?"

"Not right away. But eventually."

Rome looked over his shoulder. Night was falling and someone had started a fire. People were gathering around and throwing wood on it. There was scattered laughter. "I can't do that to them. They've been through too much."

Quyloc looked down at the spear in his hands, then at the dune again. "It's my fault," he said in a low voice.

"What is?" Rome asked, turning back to him.

"The hole. It was caused by me."

"Wait a minute. The hole was caused by that *gromdin* thing, when it had us tied to the top of that volcano. If anything, it's my fault."

Quyloc shook his head. "The *gromdin* merely focused the energy it stole from us on a weak spot in the Veil. That weak spot was caused by me, going back and forth into the *Pente Akka*. If I hadn't done that, it wouldn't have been able to break through here."

"That's not fair," Rome said. "You were searching for the spear. You were doing what Lowellin told you had to be done. There was no way you could have known."

"No. That was only an excuse. I went into the *Pente Akka* because I wanted *power*. Lowellin just gave me the excuse. I would have gone anyway."

"We wouldn't have survived without that spear. Kasai would have beaten us at Guardians Watch. Reyna would have overrun us before we could fall back to the palace grounds."

"That doesn't change the fact that the hole wouldn't be there if I hadn't been so obsessed with my own desire for power."

"I'm too tired for this, Quyloc. *You're* too tired for this. Let it go for now, okay? We'll figure this out. For now, let's just go join the party."

"You go. I'm staying here."

Rome stared at him for a while, then walked away and left Quyloc standing there alone.

"Now that the Children are gone," Ricarn said, looking at Nalene's *sulbit*, "what will you do with those?" They were sitting on the steps of the palace. It was dark, the only light coming from the bonfire that had been built out in the middle of the circular drive. Jugs and flasks were being passed around the fire. There was a great deal of laughter, most of it too loud, too raucous. It was the laughter of people who have survived when they thought they were dead, relief and horror all mashed into one. Someone was playing a violin. A few people were dancing unsteadily.

Nalene's *sulbit* was pacing back and forth across her shoulders. She put one hand on it, trying to calm it. It did no good. "I hadn't gotten around to that yet," she admitted.

Ricarn just looked at her.

"There's no rush," Nalene said defensively. "We can do a lot of good with them still. There's a lot of rebuilding to do."

"And how, exactly, will you use them to rebuild?"

"I don't know," Nalene said irritably. "I'm tired. I haven't had time to think about it yet."

"You are afraid to lose what the creature has brought you."

Nalene meant to deny it, but for some reason the truth spilled from her. Maybe she was just too tired to hold back any longer.

"You can't imagine what it was like before," she said. "They scorned me. They treated me like dirt. And I had to just take it. I was too weak. There was nothing I could do."

"Do you really think, after all that has happened, that things will go back to the way they were?" Ricarn asked.

Nalene glanced at her. The firelight flickered off her porcelain skin. She looked away. "I don't know what to think anymore. I'm just...I'm afraid to be alone again. I have gotten used to having the comfort of Song around me."

"You do not need that creature to know your connection to LifeSong. You know that."

"No, I don't know that."

"I can teach you."

"Can't we just wait?" Nalene asked. All of a sudden she felt panicky. "We've all been through so much. Can't we just wait a few days to make any big decisions?"

"The *sulbits* have grown a great deal in the last few days," Ricarn observed.

Nalene looked at her *sulbit*. She remembered when it had been the size of her thumb, so small and helpless.

"How did this happen?" Ricarn asked. "How did they grow so much, so fast?"

Nalene answered slowly, knowing where this was going. "We fed them. We had no choice. We had to do it, if we were to have any chance against the Children." Her heart was speeding up.

"What will you feed them now?"

"They won't need as much now," Nalene said, trying to find some way to slow this down. "Now that the danger has passed."

"Do you really believe this?"

An angry retort came to Nalene's lips, but then she hesitated. She could feel her *sulbit*'s hunger. She could feel the hunger of *all* the *sulbits*. It was steadily growing stronger. She remembered what happened on the return from Guardians Watch, the guards who died during the night.

"You think we need to return them to the River," Nalene said numbly.

"What do *you* think?"

Nalene put her hands over her face, hating Ricarn, hating how ruthless, how *right* she was. Why couldn't the woman just leave her alone?

Ricarn merely waited.

"Okay, you're right," Nalene said finally. "But I don't know if we can. Lowellin is gone."

"After all this, still you make excuses."

"I'm not making excuses!" Nalene snapped. "I don't know how to do it!"

"And I had hopes you would relinquish at least some of your belief in your own weakness. One of our order saved us all by entering the River and still you bleat to me about your helplessness." Ricarn's voice was even colder than it normally was. "Do you not yet see that your limitations are self-imposed?"

"That's outrageous!" Nalene yelled, leaping to her feet. Her *sulbit* hissed at Ricarn. Several nearby revelers heard and turned to look, openmouthed. "You dare to speak to me like this? I should…" Her words trailed off. Ricarn was simply staring her, expressionless, remote. Nalene sagged back down on the steps.

"You don't understand. It's the way I've always…I don't know what to do." She rubbed at the sudden tears that sprang up when she saw what she was going to have to say. She looked up at the sky for help. The next words were unbelievably hard. "Can you help me?"

To her great surprise, from the corner of her eye she saw the faintest hint of a smile on Ricarn's face. "Are you laughing at me?" she demanded.

"Not at all," Ricarn said. "I just heard you say perhaps the first intelligent words I've ever heard from you, that's all."

"*What?*"

"Yes, I will help you. I am your sister, after all."

Nalene sighed and put her head in her hands. "You make me tired."

"You make yourself tired. Don't blame that on me."

Nalene sighed again. She badly wanted to go to sleep.

"Do you know why Tender power waned?" Ricarn asked. "It's not what you think. It's not because we angered Xochitl and she took our power away from us. She couldn't do that to us because our power doesn't come from her. Our power comes from Song. No, we lost our power because we turned away from our true selves and put our faith in external things. We forgot that our strength lies *within* us, in our connection to the flows of Life. The first step toward real power lies in recognizing this. If you want to keep your connection to Song, if you want to make it strong, so it never leaves you, you must give up all the false beliefs you have learned. You must become like a child again and start over. Only then can you learn properly."

"What…?" Nalene said, trying to process what Ricarn was saying. "I don't know if I can do that."

"If you try, if you are willing, you must succeed."

"Why would you do this for me?"

"Do not confuse yourself. I am not doing this for you. I do this for *all*."

"I don't know if that makes me feel better."

"And still you have not learned that *I do not care*."

Nalene thought about that. The words seemed cold, but were they really? "When do you want to do this, return the *sulbits*?"

"Now."

"Should we not let the women rest first? Everyone is exhausted."

"No. Stop delaying. The danger will only grow greater."

"How will we summon the River without Lowellin's help?"

Ricarn lifted one eyebrow slightly. "You are going to take a long time to learn. Did you not listen? *Any* of us could do it. I could even teach you, though we would no doubt be dead of old age by the time that happened."

Nalene lowered her head and gritted her teeth. "Okay. Tell me what to do."

Together the Tenders walked in the moonlight down the street toward the estate house. A few people marked their path, but none spoke to them or followed them. Already the power of the *sulbits'* hunger was such that all could feel it and none wanted to be close to it.

Cara walked near the back of the group. Not having a *sulbit*, she knew she didn't need to go with them, but somehow it felt important to her to do so. Why? To show her support? To see for herself that the creatures were actually gone? She couldn't have said.

Partway there one of the Tenders fell back from the main group and began walking beside her. It was Owina. The older woman took hold of Cara's hand and squeezed it tightly.

"I don't know how I feel about this," Owina whispered to Cara.

Cara, having no idea what to say, simply squeezed Owina's hand back. It was still strange to her how often Tenders came to talk to her these days. Usually they came in the evenings, when she was sitting alone in her tiny hut in the trees. She didn't know why they came. It was just something that started sometime after she began leading the morning services. The fact that she never knew what to say to them, that for the most part she just sat and listened, didn't seem to bother any of them.

"I'm afraid to lose my *sulbit*," Owina continued. "It seems like it's always been a part of me. I can't imagine life without it." She gripped Cara's hand even more tightly. "At the same time, I *want* to be rid of it. It frightens me. You can't imagine how hungry it is. I'm glad we're doing this tonight. I'm so tired, but I think if I fell asleep it would get away from me and…" She didn't have to finish the sentence. Both of them knew what the *sulbits* were capable of.

"What if it doesn't want to go?" Owina asked.

Cara gave her a startled look. She hadn't considered that. "Why wouldn't it? It already tried once."

"You're right, of course. But it was frightened then, they all were. I think it wants to go home, but what if it doesn't? I'm worn out, Cara. I can't fight with it anymore. I'm afraid…" She paused, then lowered her voice even more. "You remember what happened to Lendl, right?"

"She came back with two *sulbits*."

"And they took control of her. They made her do things and she couldn't stop them. She hasn't gotten over that. She might never get over it. You've seen how she is."

All of the Tenders had seen Lendl, wandering around the estate like she didn't know where she was, sitting alone crying for hours on end. She rarely responded when anyone spoke to her, seemed to be in another world completely.

"What if I end up like her?"

"You won't," Cara told her firmly. "The FirstMother and Ricarn are both here. They'll make sure of it. You're going to be fine." She hoped she sounded more positive than she felt. She looked over her shoulder. Trailing them, just a shape in the dimness, was a figure walking by herself. It was Lendl.

They entered the estate and stopped in the carriage way.

"All Tenders with *sulbits* stand in a circle with me," the FirstMother said. "The rest of you stand back."

The FirstMother took her *sulbit* from her shoulder and cradled it in her arms. She stroked its head and whispered to it. Other Tenders were saying goodbye to their *sulbits* as well. A few shed tears.

After a minute, Ricarn said, "It's time."

"Meld with your *sulbits*," the FirstMother said. "Go *beyond*. Once there we will follow Ricarn. She will lead us to the River."

The Tenders closed their eyes. Ricarn turned and looked at Cara. "Come with us. You need to see this."

Cara didn't argue, but closed her eyes as well and stilled her thoughts. Using the technique Ricarn had taught her, she went *beyond*. The mists rose up around her and she pushed on through them, guided by the glowing forms of the other Tenders' *akirmas*. The *sulbits* had no *akirmas* and appeared as dim, unhealthy-looking smudges. Ricarn's *akirma* was very bright and clear.

She followed them as they went deeper still. The mists faded away. Feeder lines and then trunk lines appeared at intervals and then, finally, there was the vast glow of the River.

As they drew close the *sulbits* began to vibrate. They grew brighter. They leapt away from their Tenders and dove into the River. As each one struck there was a bright flash.

Cara's last impression was of the creatures racing around and around, reveling in their return home.

SIXTY-THREE

"It's been weeks," Cara said. "She should be back by now." She and Owina were sitting on one of the stone benches on the estate grounds. It was the end of the day and the women had just returned from their labors in the city. All the Tenders spent their days helping the Qarathians rebuild their lives. The FirstMother didn't exactly order them to do so—she'd been strangely subdued—but she rose early each morning, ate quickly and went to work. Any Tender who didn't do the same got the uncomfortable feeling their FirstMother was distinctly displeased with them, though the only thing the FirstMother ever said about it was "We've lost our power, but we still have hands."

"I went to the palace and spoke with Quyloc," Cara continued. "He traveled to the edge of the desert, but he said there was no sign of her or Shorn."

"Then they must still be on their way here."

"I don't know. What you're saying sounds so reasonable, but something just doesn't feel right. I can't help being afraid."

"I wouldn't be," Owina said. "From what you've told me, Netra has survived more things than either of us could imagine. I'm sure she survived this as well."

"I want to tell you something I haven't told anyone else yet."

Owina gave her a quizzical look. "What is it?"

"I followed you that night when the *sulbits* were returned to the River and when we got there I had a strange feeling. It felt like Netra was there."

"What do you mean by there?" Owina's eyes widened. "You mean it felt like she was *in* the River?"

"I don't know. Kind of."

"You know that's not possible."

"I know. That's what I keep telling myself. But I can't shake that feeling." She gave Owina a miserable look. "That's part of why I'm so worried. What if she *was* in the River?"

The realization of what she was saying came to Owina then. "Oh. You think she might have gone into the River to undo the Gift."

Cara nodded. Owina put her arm around her shoulders and pulled her close. Neither could bring herself to speak the words. If Netra went into the River, she would never return.

There was a commotion at the front gates and both women turned to look.

"It's Shorn!" Cara cried, jumping up. Then she sagged back. "Where's Netra?" she cried, all her worst fears returning at once. "Netra's not with him."

She took off at a run for the gates. Shorn saw her coming and moved to meet her. Before he even spoke she started crying. She could tell instantly that he carried bad news.

"She is…gone," he said. His normally stolid face twisted and real pain leaked out before he could once again get himself under control.

Cara started shaking. "What happened?"

"It was Reyna," he told her.

Cara sagged against Owina, sobbing uncontrollably. Her best friend, gone forever. After a minute she realized Shorn was speaking to her and she struggled to control herself enough to listen to him.

"I would talk with you," he said. "There is more you should know."

Owina hugged her. "Go with him."

Numbly, Cara followed Shorn away from the others. He sat down and she sat down as well. "Did she…did she suffer?" she asked him before he could speak.

He shook his head. "It happened fast."

Cara wiped her eyes. "That is something I guess."

"It is strange," he said.

"What is?"

"I could not find her body."

Cara stared at him. "What do you mean?"

"She was…gone. I could not find her."

Cara felt hope glow inside her. "Do you mean she might have escaped somehow? Why did you leave? Maybe she's still there somewhere!" In her excitement she got to her feet, as if to run to the Gur al Krin right then.

"No," Shorn said. "There was nowhere she could have gone. And I looked. I waited."

Cara sagged back down. "I don't understand what you are saying."

"She went to the River. But she left her body behind. While she was there, Reyna returned and…" He stomped on the ground once. Cara winced. "But when I looked in the hole, there was nothing."

"So she could still be alive," Cara breathed.

"Melekath said it could not be so. He said that she must have brought her body to the River in the instant before Reyna went for her, but there is no way it could have survived. Her consciousness may still survive in the River, but that is all."

Cara put her hand over her mouth. So it *was* true. Netra went into the River. "Is that it?" she asked finally.

Shorn nodded. "I waited, but there was nothing. I came to tell you."

Cara felt fresh tears start. "Thank you," she said, "for telling me." She lowered her head.

"Her last words were of you. She wanted you to know that she loved you."

Cara began weeping again, shaking with the sobs. Cautiously, Shorn put one hand on her shoulder. Then he wrapped her in a hug while she cried.

SIXTY-FOUR

Early in the morning Rehobim and Pinlir called the Takare to gather around. The spirit-kin formed up in ranks behind the two men while the rest of the Takare stood in a loose group facing them. Shakre noticed right away that Pinlir was once again carrying his weapons, despite Youlin's order from the day before. She looked at Youlin to see if she also noticed, but the young woman was hidden in the depths of her hood and it was impossible to tell.

"Today we enter the deep ways," Rehobim said. "Where the *ronhym* live."

Shakre realized right away that his voice sounded different. It sounded deeper, older. She and Elihu exchanged looks. She looked at Pinlir and saw that he was glaring at Elihu. Amongst the spirit-kin were a number who had come from Bent Tree Shelter, men and women she had known for years, but when she met their eyes she saw no one she recognized there.

"It seems the old spirits are no longer hiding," Elihu murmured.

"You are surprised by this," Rehobim-Tarnin continued. "You know nothing of the *ronhym*, or the deep ways. There is much you do not know, much that has been hidden from you by those with their own purposes."

His gaze landed on Elihu and Shakre felt a shiver go through her. Did he know about their meeting with Rekus?

"Today, that changes. Today, you learn the truth. I am Tarnin, your last, true leader, and this is Kirtet, my second. Since the tragedy at Wreckers Gate those you see standing up here before you have waited for our people to return to us. We have waited for the day when we could reclaim our homeland and claim our rightful place as rulers of Atria."

Shocked silence met his words. Many looks were cast at the Pastwalkers among them, but none of them spoke up.

314

"The *ronhym* are our oldest allies," Tarnin continued. "A race of creatures who live underground in a vast warren of tunnels and caverns that we call the deep ways. It was they who built Wreckers Gate for us. It is our plan to contact them, to seek their help in defeating Gulagh."

"Why?" someone called out. "Why was all this hidden from us?"

"They sought to divide us," Pinlir-Kirtet burst out suddenly, his face dark. "They spread lies so that they could seize power for themselves." Tarnin gave him a look and he subsided, though he muttered to himself.

"It was during the last days of the Empire," Tarnin said. "We faced a great threat from the Tenders and we sought help from the *ronhym* in dealing with it. While helping us, one of them was killed in an accident."

Shakre felt Elihu move when Tarnin said this and she grabbed his arm fiercely, afraid that he would say something and Kirtet would kill him.

"The traitor Genjinn took the creature's death as an opportunity to try to usurp my power. He spread lies that we tortured and killed our ally. Unfortunately, there were those among us who believed him and they joined him in his rebellion. They seized our homeland and closed Wreckers Gate against us. In the battle that followed, many of the rebels were killed. Afterwards, guilt over those deaths led most of our people to go into exile and renounce our ways." He swept his arm, encompassing the ranks of spirit-kin who stood behind him. "Those you see here are the Takare who refused to leave. We swore to remain true to our brethren and remain behind to keep the flame pure. We vowed to reject the forgetfulness that comes with reincarnation so that when the time came, when our lost brethren finally returned, we could lead them back to the truth."

Shakre looked around to see how the other Takare were taking this. Most seemed spellbound. A few looked skeptical, but the great majority looked like they were accepting his words as the truth.

"There will be more time to speak of this after we defeat Gulagh," Tarnin said. "I bring this up now because the time has come to end the lies. Only the truth can reunite us and only if we are united can we defeat the enemies who stand against us."

"What about those whose lives you've stolen?" a woman said. It was Birna. She stepped forward, her tearful eyes fixed on Kirtet. "After this is over, will you give my mate back to me?" Other voices, mostly the close kin of those who were possessed by the old spirits, also spoke up.

"I assure you they are alive and well, residing within us," Tarnin said smoothly. "When our homeland is once again returned to us, we will leave those we inhabit and allow ourselves to once again be born to you."

The rest mostly subsided then, but Birna remained standing out front of them, still staring at Kirtet. "If you can hear me, Pinlir," she said, "know that I will not rest until you return to me."

Tarnin and Kirtet exchanged looks, then Tarnin spoke again. "Only the spirit-kin will enter the deep ways. The rest will stay behind to protect our people. You will retrace our path and wait near the Gate for us to open it from within."

"I am coming too," Youlin said. After a moment Tarnin nodded.

Shakre stepped forward. "You may have need of a healer."

She expected an argument or at least scorn, but to her surprise Tarnin nodded. "I have seen your healing skills. Only a fool leads warriors into battle without a healer. And we may again need your power over the wind." Shakre's face must have registered her shock because he smiled then. "I see that surprises you, but it should not. I do not harbor the ill will towards you that Rehobim does. Where he sees an enemy, I see one who will fight with all she has to help the Takare rise again." He walked up to her and she was made forcefully aware of his raw power and strength. He could kill her before she could move. "Know this, though. I have also seen your weakness in your compassion for our enemies. I will not tolerate this. If you try to stand between us and our enemies, we will cut you down without a thought. Do you understand?"

Shakre, looking up at him, could only swallow hard and nod.

"When we meet the *ronhym*," he added in a low voice that others could not hear, "do not interfere. One way or another, they *will* help us."

Shakre nodded again, her mouth dry.

They set out a few minutes later, moving fast. They headed straight back into the mountains, going up the bottom of a steep, narrow canyon with a small stream rushing down it. Pine trees and aspens began to dominate the landscape, with carved pinnacles and rocky buttes overlooking from the tops of the ridges. The air grew colder.

After an hour, Tarnin led them up a side canyon which soon grew so narrow that Shakre could reach out and touch both sides at once. It grew steeper as well until the sides were sheer cliffs that soared higher and higher overhead. The bottom of the slot canyon was ankle deep in icy water. There were areas where floods had wedged dead logs in the canyon overhead, testament to how deep the water could get. In other areas boulders choked the bottom of the canyon so that they had to crawl underneath them or climb up over them. The sun disappeared completely and the sky was a narrow ribbon of blue high overhead.

It was all Shakre could do to match their pace and she eventually developed a stitch in her side that made breathing difficult. Without the help of one of the spirit-kin, a young woman who had probably been ordered by Tarnin to do so, she wouldn't have been able to keep up. The woman stayed right behind her the whole way, helping her through the more difficult spots.

The narrow canyon grew very dark and filled with icy, chest-deep water. After wading through it for long minutes, Shakre began to shiver violently. She could see nothing beyond the person right in front of her. She began to wonder how much longer she could survive in there. Already she had lost feeling in her feet. Hypothermia could not be far away.

So focused was she on the cold that she didn't realize the person in front of her was gone until she found herself staring at a tangled mass of boulders. She stared at them, her cold-fogged mind unable to grasp what had happened to the person she was following.

"Windrider, you must duck under the stone. See, there is room," the woman behind her said.

Shakre saw then that there was a gap between stone and water about a foot high. She ducked down and went under the boulders. It was harder going now, since she could no longer stand upright completely and more than once she tripped over stones hidden in the water and plunged completely under water. She was still shivering, but she realized she no longer really felt cold and part of her mind told her this was a very bad thing, that she didn't have much longer.

She had never liked enclosed places and she began to feel a little panicky. What if this were a dead end? It had been almost a thousand years since anyone passed this way. The stones might have collapsed into the canyon. The *ronhym* could have even done it deliberately. There was no way she could make it back the way she had come; she simply didn't have the strength.

But at last the water grew shallower and the stone overhead rose so that she could stand upright. A few minutes later she emerged from the water completely. She stood there, shivering uncontrollably, while Takare continued to file past her. The young woman took her arm.

"Remember what you have learned in your time among our people. The cold cannot take you if your mind is strong."

Shaking, Shakre nodded. All Takare children on the Plateau learned a technique for mastering the cold that involved breath and mental control. She had learned it somewhat, though never as well as the Takare. Now she fought to bring her shivering under control.

In a couple of minutes, she had recovered somewhat. She was still freezing, but she did not think she was still in danger of dying. She and the young woman were the only ones left. The rest had gone on ahead. She looked up. The sky was gone. There was only stone. In the stone were veins of some kind of crystal that glowed with a faint blue light.

"Can you continue?" the young woman asked her. "We should not get too far behind."

"I can manage," she replied. "Thank you for staying with me."

They walked down what appeared to be a natural tunnel that most of the time was only wide enough for them to walk single file. Shakre's uneasiness began to grow stronger. Being underground, with stone pressing in from all sides, was difficult. She kept imagining that the passage was closing in on her, though her logical side told her it wasn't true. She realized she was breathing harder than necessary too and she struggled to get her breath under control.

Finally, the tunnel opened up and Shakre stopped. What she saw made her forget her discomfort temporarily.

They were in a huge cavern. The thin veins of blue, glowing crystals turned huge here, crisscrossing the walls, floor and ceiling of the cavern. Huge piles of glowing crystals littered the ground. It was a fantastic sight and utterly beautiful. The light they gave off was so bright she could see clearly.

They had caught up to the rest and up ahead she could see Tarnin and Kirtet conferring with a half dozen of the spirit-kin. Youlin was standing nearby, though clearly she was not part of the conversation. The six spirit-kin were carrying spears that looked different to Shakre. As she drew closer she saw that the spears had no metal points. Instead, the points were carved from wood and were barbed near the tips.

Tarnin looked up at her approach and gave her a hard smile. "I thought maybe we had lost you," he said.

"I thought so too."

"Stay close. It is very easy to get lost down here." He turned and gestured and the six spirit-kin with the wooden spears raced on ahead and disappeared.

They continued on, going deeper into the earth. The cavern ended after a time. They passed side passages, some with streams gushing out of them. There were places where the ceiling overhead pressed low and others where it soared out of sight. Gradually the crystals thinned and stalactites and stalagmites began to appear. Water dripped unceasingly from the stalactites. Many of the formations were clear, like huge icicles, but others were a translucent yellow or pink. When Shakre accidentally banged into one it gave off a clear chime, like crystal.

The formations became increasingly varied and bizarre. Some were huge, broad things, where the slow deposits formed arched openings and fantastic pinnacles. Some were large enough, the openings in them deep enough, that she wondered if *ronhym* lived within them. But she saw no sign of movement so if there were *ronhym* there they were staying out of sight. Maybe the *ronhym* would just stay hidden and let them pass through unhindered. It was something to hope for.

That hope was dashed an hour or two later when Shakre saw some Takare pointing overhead. They were in an area where the ceiling wasn't too high up, maybe twenty feet or so. Most of the stalactites had grown down to the point where they joined with the stalagmites, forming columns. The columns varied from the diameter of her little finger to huge things that it would take several people to put their arms around. They seemed almost deliberately placed there to support the ceiling.

A black shape could be seen moving across the ceiling toward them, running on all four legs, alternately appearing and disappearing between the columns. Tarnin and Kirtet stopped and stood side by side, watching the creature. Youlin moved up beside them. Shakre moved through the ranks of Takare and got closer to the front, where she could see and hear what was happening.

When it got close, the creature scurried down a column to the floor. It had a long tail and broad, clawed feet. Its head was tapered, its eyes very large. Its skin seemed to be covered in very fine scales.

The *ronhym* stopped a short distance from the Takare and looked up at them. It began to shudder and as it did so it changed shape. Its tail receded, its hind legs grew longer, its front legs shorter. Its head rounded, the snout withdrawing. Seconds later what stood before the

Takare was man-like in shape, though slightly built and only about chest high on the Takare.

"You may not pass this way, Takare. The deep ways are closed to you." Though its voice was very strange, to Shakre it sounded male.

Youlin started to reply, but Kirtet put his hand on her arm and shook his head. Tarnin spoke instead.

"We have been looking for you. We require your help against a mutual enemy."

The *ronhym* looked him over. "You speak of Gulagh. The Guardian has not proven itself an enemy of the *ronhym*."

Tarnin crossed his arms. "It is a foul creature and not to be trusted. In time it will turn on you. Ally with us and we will defeat it together."

The *ronhym* did not hesitate with his reply. "Never again. The Takare have proven themselves to be faithless allies."

"It was a long time ago," Tarnin replied. "It is possible a mistake was made."

The creature stared unblinking at him. "We would call it other than a mistake. We would call it betrayal. You tortured and killed one of us after we trusted you, after we agreed to help you against one of your enemies. An enemy who did not threaten us."

"He refused to help," Tarnin said through gritted teeth. Shakre could feel his anger starting to rise. "Was I supposed to simply stand by and watch my people die?"

"He tried to save you. The power within a *relif* crystal cannot be controlled by a living creature. Stone power is too great for your kind."

"He could have used the crystal himself," Tarnin hissed.

"The *ronhym* do not war on others. We have been on this world even before the Shapers. We have seen the consequences of conflict and so we choose to remain outside. We observe, nothing more."

"I will give you one more chance. Help us to destroy that thing and you will never hear from us again."

"Our answer remains unchanged. We will not help you, nor will we allow you to pass through our lands. You would be wise to reconsider your decision to attack the Guardian. It is an ancient, powerful creature. Your weapons cannot hurt it, therefore, you cannot defeat it. Accept that it has stolen your home and move on."

"Never," Kirtet said fiercely. "We will *never* abandon Ankha del'Ath to that thing."

"That is your choice," the *ronhym* said, inclining his head slightly. "But you will attack it by another route."

Shakre saw Tarnin make a gesture behind his back. A spirit-kin to her right looked off to the side and repeated the gesture. She felt sick suddenly. Here it came. Tarnin had said the *ronhym* would help, one way or another.

Her first thought was to call out, warn the *ronhym* of his danger, but she remembered Tarnin's threat and was suddenly very aware of the spirit-kin that flanked her. They would kill her without hesitation.

There was nothing she could do but watch.

"Is this your final decision?" Tarnin asked mildly. The anger he'd shown a minute ago seemed to have subsided.

"It is."

"Then there is nothing we can do but leave," Tarnin said. He and Kirtet turned as if to leave. The rest of the Takare began to turn around also. The *ronhym* shuddered and began flowing back into his normal shape.

When he was about halfway through the transition, the spirit-kin wielding the wooden spears burst out from where they had been hiding and charged forward on cat feet.

The *ronhym* started to turn, one arm coming up.

The lead spirit-kin stabbed with his spear. The point entered the *ronhym*'s back, where a human's shoulder blade would be. The force was great enough that the spear went completely through the *ronhym* emissary, emerging from his chest.

The *ronhym* cried out, a high, mournful keening. He stumbled forward, hands coming up to grab clumsily at the barbed spear head.

The spirit-kin jerked the spear back so the barbs dug into the *ronhym*'s chest. With a sweep of one foot he kicked the *ronhym*'s legs out from under him.

It all happened in the space of heartbeats. The *ronhym* was on the ground moaning. Instinctively, Shakre started to step forward, but the spirit-kin on either side of her clamped onto her arms and restrained her.

Tarnin and Kirtet walked back to the *ronhym*. "The Ominati, useless idiots that they were, did learn some useful things. They learned that you are weakest when changing shape. They also learned that you have a curious vulnerability to wood," Tarnin said, crouching beside the *ronhym*. "It seems that you cannot be hurt by metal or stone weapons of any kind, but wood pierces you easily. They also learned that it causes you great pain." He tapped the haft of the spear, bringing forth a fresh moan of pain from the creature. "It seems they were correct."

Shakre tried to shake off the hands holding her. Tarnin looked up at her. "Do not interfere, Windrider."

"Surely there is a better way," she said.

"And I tried to find it. You were here. You heard. I would have preferred they aid us willingly, but when they did not…" He shrugged. "If you will remember, I said that they would aid us one way or another."

Shakre looked at Youlin, but the young Pastwalker refused to meet her eye. "At least let me tend to him," she said. When Tarnin did not respond she added, "He will be no use to you as a hostage if he's dead."

Tarnin considered this, then nodded. Shakre hurried forward. In truth, she had no idea if she could do anything to help or not. But she had to try.

At a gesture from Tarnin, the spirit-kin holding the spear used it to turn the *ronhym* on his side, which brought another moan. Shakre knelt down beside him. He looked at her with large, liquid eyes.

"I'm sorry," she whispered. The *ronhym* did not reply.

Shakre looked at the wound. There was no blood or anything at all leaking from it, but the flesh around the wound had turned gray. She held out her hands, stilled her thoughts and went *beyond*. Around her the flows of LifeSong sustaining herself and the Takare came into view, pulsing gently, along with the gentle glows of their *akirmas*. There were no flows connected to the *ronhym*. Nor did he have an *akirma*. In fact, he looked exactly the same except that his eyes glowed.

There is nothing you can do.

Shakre sat back, surprised. She looked around. No one else had responded. No one else had heard.

She left *beyond* and stood up. "I don't think he's in immediate danger," she told Tarnin.

"Good. Now get out of the way." To the man holding the spear Tarnin said, "Get him on his feet."

The man jerked on the spear and Shakre said, "Wait! You don't have to do it like that. Just ask him to stand up."

The *ronhym* gave her an unreadable look, then climbed to his feet gingerly.

"It is true what I said," Tarnin said to him when he was standing. "I would have preferred that you helped us of your own will. A willing ally is always better."

The *ronhym* straightened as much as he could. It was clearly difficult for him to stand upright, halfway between forms as he was. "What do you want?"

"Guidance through your lands, for one thing."

The *ronhym* nodded almost imperceptibly. "I will do so. But that is not all, is it?"

"No. It's not. I also require a *relif* crystal."

"Which you cannot use."

"No, but you can."

The *ronhym* stared at him unblinking. "And if I refuse, you will torture and kill me."

Tarnin nodded. "Something like that."

"You want us to unleash the power of the crystal on the Guardian."

"I do. It will work, won't it?"

"I do not know. It has never been done. But at least it will weaken the creature considerably."

Tarnin looked at Kirtet. "What do you think?"

"I think if we get an opening we can chop that thing into pieces."

The *ronhym* spoke again. "Once the Guardian is defeated, you will leave us be."

"You have my word on that," Tarnin said.

"This is not worth so much as you seem to think."

Tarnin gave him a cold smile. "Nevertheless, it is all you have."

The *ronhym* looked down as if thinking. Then he looked back at Tarnin. "It will be as you say."

"I am sure you have more of your kind hidden nearby," Tarnin said. "Call and tell them to fetch the crystal."

"The crystal is buried deep. It will take some time to acquire," the *ronhym* replied.

"You have until we make it out of here."

"This will not be enough time."

"Unfortunately for you, I don't believe you. I know that your kind can move through stone as if it were water. Have the crystal for us by the time we emerge on the other side of the mountains or we will begin torturing you."

The *ronhym* stared at him for a long moment. Then he turned his head to the side and called out loudly in a series of clicks and whistles. There was an answering call, then silence.

Tarnin looked at Shakre. "Harsh times call for harsh measures. It has ever been thus. Had Genjinn accepted this truth, all those years ago, we would not be in these straits. The world would be a very different place under our rule."

Shakre stared at him. "Okay," she said at last. There was nothing else she could say.

SIXTY-FIVE

"Legate, we have arrived," one of the spirit-kin scouts said, saluting. Shakre peered past the scout, hoping to see some glimmer of light, but saw nothing. She couldn't wait to get back above ground. By her estimate they had been in the deep ways for more than a day, though it was hard to tell for sure. After capturing the *ronhym* they'd walked for long hours through terrain that was often very difficult. When they finally stopped to sleep, she'd basically collapsed on the spot and slept like the dead until she was roused to continue on.

There'd been no sign of other *ronhym* the whole way, no evidence they were trying to hinder the Takare in any way. But now, as the Takare started eagerly toward the exit, a *ronhym* appeared in their path. It didn't approach as the first one had. Rather, it seemed to simply flow up out of the ground right in front of them, like a cork bobbing to the surface of the water.

Tarnin held up his hand and the Takare halted. Weapons appeared in every hand. The spirit-kin around Shakre looked uneasily at the ground. How would they fight an enemy that came up from underground?

"What is it?" Tarnin asked. "Do you have the crystal?"

"We do," the *ronhym* replied. This one sounded female. She didn't look at the captive, sagging limply on the spear that skewered him. The captive *ronhym* was not doing well, that much Shakre could tell. She'd checked on him when they stopped to rest and discovered that the gray area around the wound had grown larger and the flesh closest to the wound had turned completely white and was starting to crumble away.

"Where is it?"

"It is in our possession, but it will be some time yet before we can deliver it to you."

"You were told to have the crystal for us by the time we left your lands."

"Yes, I know. But transporting a *relif* crystal is a dangerous task. Even we are not immune to them and if the object is not handled carefully there will be catastrophic consequences."

"How long?"

"No more than an hour, as you measure time."

Tarnin and Kirtet exchanged looks, then Tarnin nodded. "You have one hour."

The *ronhym* did not reply, but simply slid back down into the ground and disappeared.

"I believe they are up to something," Kirtet said. "They mean to betray us."

"It is what I would do," Tarnin agreed.

They continued on, every warrior extra vigilant. A few minutes later, to Shakre's great relief, a dim glow appeared up ahead. Fortunately, this entrance was much easier than the one they'd used to enter the deep ways. They only had to pass through a small waterfall and wade across a shallow pool. Shakre walked gratefully out into the sunshine, thinking she had never seen anything so beautiful before.

They were on a thickly-wooded slope. Behind them loomed the mass of the Truebane Mountains. Before and below them a long, wide valley could be glimpsed through the trees.

As the last of the Takare crossed the shallow pool, a grinding noise came from behind the waterfall. The warriors spun toward the sound, wondering if this was a surprise attack.

The opening behind the waterfall collapsed with a crash, buried in tons of stone. This entrance to the deep ways would never be used again. Whatever happened from here forward, the Takare would not be leaving that way.

Tarnin led them down the slope. As they passed through a meadow, Shakre could see that they were near one end of the long valley. Wreckers Gate was visible to her right less than a mile away. There was a sizable lake in the distance to the left, near the center of the valley. Most of the valley floor was thickly forested, with only a few grassy clearings here and there. Most of the buildings the Takare had erected were gone, wooden structures that rotted away centuries before. Jutting up from the forest here and there were a few stone buildings, trees growing up through them, blankets of moss and vines covering them. Cities had never been the Takare way. Spending most of their time outdoors, they built primarily simple wooden homes.

They headed to the right and continued descending. A few minutes later they came to a spot where they could see clearly. Over near Wreckers Gate a fairly large area had been recently cleared of trees. Dozens of tents and several crude wooden buildings had been erected on one side of the clearing.

In the center of the clearing stood Gulagh. The Guardian wasn't moving. It appeared to just be standing there, its back to them, looking at Wreckers Gate.

All around it, lying scattered on the ground, were its followers. None of them were moving.

"I think they're dead," Kirtet said wonderingly. He looked at Tarnin. "Why?"

Tarnin shrugged. "Who knows what is in the mind of that creature? All that matters is that we destroy it."

Shakre stared down at the bodies, a sense of unease growing inside her. She saw a few dressed in the clothing of the Takare, those that had made it inside the Gate before she knocked Gulagh down with the wind.

She found herself listening for the wind, but the air was utterly still. She couldn't even hear any birds or insects. It was like the whole valley was holding its breath, waiting for something. Was it a trap? But if so, why would the Guardian kill all of its own followers?

The *ronhym* flowed up from underground in front of Tarnin a few minutes later. In her hands, the *ronhym* held a dark yellow crystal, which quickly began to turn orange as she held it out to Tarnin.

Shakre instinctively took a step back, as did most of the spirit-kin. There was something profoundly unsettling about the thing, a sense of being too close to power that was unbelievably vast.

Tarnin held his ground, though it clearly took effort to do so and he did not reach out to touch the thing. His expression grew suspicious. "It is cracked," he said. It was true. The surface of the crystal was spider webbed with cracks.

"It was the only one nearby. If you wish another, it will take several days to retrieve it." The *ronhym* stood motionlessly, the crystal lying across her hands.

"I don't believe you," Kirtet said.

"Your belief does not change what is," she replied. "You may believe this though: this crystal contains enough power to weaken and perhaps destroy the Guardian." She paused. "If it does not suit you, we can deliver another, but it will take several days."

Tarnin and Kirtet turned away and spoke together in whispers. Then they turned back and Tarnin spoke to her again. "We will take your word on this. How close do you have to get to attack Gulagh with it?"

"I must be right next to the Guardian," she said. "The quantity of Stone power that I must release is too great for me to have much control over it. If I am too far away, I may miss completely and afterwards the crystal will be too depleted to try again for many days."

"And you can come up right beside it with no problem?" Kirtet asked.

The *ronhym* looked at the ground where she had emerged. The ground showed no sign of being disturbed. Whatever the creature's powers were, she clearly did not move through the ground by digging. "This is not a problem."

The two men looked at each other. Shakre could see that they were suspicious, but she also realized they had little choice. At some point they had to gamble that the *ronhym* would do what she said she would do.

"Give us ten minutes to get our men into position," Tarnin told her. "Then attack."

"It shall be as you say." She turned to the captive and said something in her language. He replied, then pointed at Shakre and Youlin, who were standing together, and added something else.

"What was that?" Kirtet demanded. "What did you say?"

"I merely reassured him that his ordeal is nearly over."

"Don't betray us," he snarled. "Or he will die."

"The *ronhym* want only to have our brother back and to be left alone as you promised."

"Just make sure you do what we told you."

The *ronhym* did not reply. She simply slid back down into the earth and disappeared.

Tarnin gave an order and the spirit-kin began to move down the slope. Three stayed behind to guard the hostage. The plan was to get as close to the Guardian as possible while still staying hidden. Once the *ronhym* appeared and attacked Gulagh, they were all to charge the Guardian. Meanwhile, a half dozen spirit-kin were given orders to head for the Gate and open it. If they could not destroy the creature, they wanted to give it an escape route that led it out of their homeland.

"You two wait here," Tarnin told Youlin and Shakre. "You'll only get in the way."

Then he turned and followed the others, who were already disappearing into the trees.

Several nerve-wracking minutes followed. Shakre paced as she waited. Something about this wasn't right. It still made no sense that the Guardian had killed its followers. Nor did she think they could trust the *ronhym*. If she were in their place, she would seize the first opportunity to turn on the spirit-kin. They had no reason to believe the human intruders would stick to their word once Gulagh was defeated. *If* the Guardian was defeated. This all seemed far too easy.

She wondered if she would be able to summon the wind again. She wanted to try, but was afraid to make any noise that might betray their presence to Gulagh. She looked at Youlin, but she was no help. She was lost in the depths of her hood once again.

Then it began.

SIXTY-SIX

The *ronhym* rose up out of the ground beside Gulagh. She raised the crystal over her head and slammed it point first into the ground as Gulagh turned and looked down at her. Before the Guardian could react, she wrapped both hands around the top of the crystal. There was a sudden, high-pitched whining, and the crystal turned a deep, burnt orange.

A beam of orange light shot out of the crystal and struck Gulagh in the chest.

Gulagh staggered backwards with a thin cry.

Instantly, the spirit-kin burst from the cover of the trees around the clearing and raced forward. In seconds they were amongst the bodies of the dead followers. The bodies were clustered so thickly that it was impossible to avoid stepping on them, which slowed their advance considerably.

Then what Shakre feared worst happened.

The *ronhym* removed her hands from the crystal. The beam of light went out.

Gulagh straightened and stepped over to her. The Guardian did not look wounded in any way. The *ronhym* pulled the crystal from the ground and held it out to Gulagh, who took it from her hand.

She slid down into the ground and disappeared.

Gulagh looked at the oncoming spirit-kin and on its face appeared a ghastly parody of a smile.

Shakre heard a noise nearby and turned just in time to see black hands rise up from the ground beneath the spirit-kin guarding the hostage and grab onto their ankles. As they looked down, disbelieving, they were pulled swiftly down into the ground, until only their heads were still showing.

They began screaming, blood pouring from their eyes and mouths as the ground pressed in on them and crushed them to a pulp. In seconds they were dead.

Two *ronhym* rose up from the ground. Shakre and Youlin fell back a few steps, but the *ronhym* paid no attention to them. One held the hostage upright while the other snapped the spear in half and pulled it out of his chest.

The one who had been held hostage looked at Shakre and nodded once. Then all three slid down into the ground and were gone.

Gripping the crystal in both hands, Gulagh held it up. It began to glow brightly once again. Most of the spirit-kin slowed their charge, unsure.

Gulagh yelled something in its fell language. The crystal pulsed, and from it an orange gas began to spew.

Shakre realized she was yelling at the spirit-kin, screaming at them to run away before it was too late.

The orange gas spread outward quickly, engulfing all of the spirit-kin and the dead followers.

Shakre knew then, without a doubt, that it was too late. The spirit-kin were as good as dead. She raised her face to the sky, screaming for the wind. If only she could summon it, just once more, maybe she could blow away the gas. Maybe there was still time.

But there was nothing. Though she screamed until something tore in her throat, there was no response.

Gasping, her throat burning, Shakre watched as the gas began to quickly dissipate. As it faded, she could once again see the spirit-kin, looking about themselves in confusion. They seemed all right. She felt hope. Maybe the Guardian had made a mistake.

Then she saw something that filled her with horror.

The dead were rising.

Gulagh's followers were climbing to their feet. Each one glowed with an unearthly orange light.

The spirit-kin responded quickly, hacking at them as they rose. One swung his sword, hitting what had once been an elderly woman solidly in the neck as she struggled to her feet.

The blade touched her and he began to scream.

Like flames following a line of oil, the orange glow raced over the weapon, onto the man's hand and up his arm. As it touched him, his skin turned instantly black. He dropped the sword, his eyes bulging as he stared down at his blackened arm.

Two more heartbeats and the glow had spread up his neck, engulfing his head. He spasmed, then fell dead.

Other spirit-kin struck with their weapons and suffered the same fate. But those who did not attack fared no better. The bodies were too thickly strewn about them. The dead grabbed onto them, the orange light spread over them, and they fell dead. Panic swept over the spirit-kin. They forgot about attacking, they forgot about Gulagh. They forgot everything except getting away.

But there was nowhere to go. They had gone too deeply into the trap. The dead were too thick to avoid. Screams filled the air as more and more of the spirit-kin were infected with the rot.

Gulagh's trap had worked perfectly.

In the midst of the chaos Shakre suddenly saw something. Not all the spirit-kin were trying to flee. Two figures were still moving toward Gulagh.

It was Tarnin and Kirtet. They alone had not paused when the orange gas appeared. As a result, they were far closer to Gulagh than any of the others were, each approaching from a different angle. Only a small number of dead separated them from their target.

"Come on, come on," Shakre heard Youlin whisper.

Even as close as they were, it still took nearly superhuman ability to avoid the dead, who threw themselves at the two men from every direction. But somehow, miraculously, both men managed to avoid their deadly touch.

Tarnin broke free first. He darted between the last two undead standing between him and his target and attacked. Gulagh looked down in disbelief as Tarnin charged across the last few paces of open ground and swung his sword, burying the blade deep in Gulagh's side.

Gulagh roared and shifted the crystal to one hand so that it could swing with the other at Tarnin. But Tarnin had already jerked his weapon free and was once again moving. Gulagh's swing, slow and clumsy in comparison to Tarnin's lethal grace, missed the spirit-kin completely.

Tarnin ducked under the swing and got behind the Guardian. As Gulagh tried to turn, he hacked at its hamstring, the blade biting deeply enough that Gulagh's leg buckled and it pitched forward.

As it threw out its arms, fighting to regain its balance, it brought the crystal down to about the level of its waist and Shakre all at once realized what it was Tarnin was doing.

Tarnin was distracting the thing, opening it up for Kirtet.

Just at that moment, as Gulagh's full attention was focused on Tarnin, Kirtet burst out of the press and charged. He leapt in the air, swinging the heavy axe—

And struck the *relif* crystal squarely.

The crystal exploded.

The shockwave burst outward, throwing up a huge cloud of dust as it came.

A heartbeat later the shockwave reached Shakre and Youlin and they were thrown down onto their backs.

SIXTY-SEVEN

Shakre lay there feeling like she'd been hit by a wall. Her ears were ringing and she could feel blood coming from her nose. The wind had been knocked out of her and it was a few moments before she could recover enough to draw a breath. Then she sat up, trying to blink away the dust in her eyes.

As the dust began to settle, she could see Youlin lying off to the side, moaning softly. Shakre got up onto her hands and knees and crawled over to her.

"Can you hear me? Are you okay?" she asked her. It hurt to speak, her throat still raw from trying to call the wind.

Youlin rubbed her eyes and nodded. Shakre helped her sit up.

"I think my arm is broken," Youlin said, cradling her right arm.

"Let me look at it."

"No," Youlin said, pushing her away. "Later." She hauled herself to her feet and Shakre did as well.

The devastation down below was complete. The crude shelters had been completely swept away. No sign of them remained. Whole ranks of trees had been turned into splinters and many more were standing crookedly. Bodies had been flung everywhere. Some were wedged in amongst the shattered trees and others were stuck up in the limbs of trees that were still standing.

Then Youlin, her mouth open, pointed.

The blast had torn a huge hole in Wreckers Gate. One side of the gate hung at a sharp angle. The other side looked close to falling completely down.

Movement drew Shakre's eye.

Gulagh was lying at the base of the shattered gate. One of the Guardian's arms flopped around, then found something to grab onto and the creature pulled itself up to a sitting position.

Its other arm had been torn completely off. One side of its skull had been caved in and there was a deep gash in its chest.

It tried to stand, but one leg was missing below the knee and it fell back down. On the next try, by holding onto the gate, it made it upright. It turned slowly, surveying the wreckage of the battlefield. Shakre realized she was holding her breath, wondering what would happen next.

Gulagh grabbed onto the edge of the hole in the gate with its remaining arm, pulled itself up into the opening, squirmed there for a moment, then fell through and disappeared from sight.

SIXTY-EIGHT

Later that day the rest of the Takare returned. The remaining pieces of Wreckers Gate had collapsed by then and they made their way through the rubble of that once-impregnable barrier in silent awe.

Shakre stood up from where she had been sitting on a piece of stone. "Welcome home," she said simply. Her voice was hoarse.

One of the first to enter was Elihu and Shakre hurried to him and put her arms around him. For some time they stood thus, she grateful for his simple, warm presence, he content to hold her until she was ready to speak.

At length Shakre let him go. "What happened here?" he asked her.

"There was an explosion. Kirtet broke the crystal."

Elihu raised an eyebrow. "That leaves far more questions than it answers," he said.

"I know. But it's all I have right now. Later I'll tell you the rest."

He nodded, accepting.

Shakre saw Birna then. She'd just entered and was looking around. She was holding her baby. Shakre knew who she was looking for. She went to her and put her hand on her shoulder. "I'm sorry, Birna. I tried to find his body but the explosion…"

Birna stared into her eyes, then nodded. She brushed away a tear.

"His was the blow that defeated Gulagh," Shakre said. "If that is any consolation."

"Not really. He was a good man. I will miss him, but I have been missing him since the day the outsiders attacked our village." Birna walked away.

Shakre walked back to Elihu. "Did you feel that, what happened earlier?" she asked him. While waiting with Youlin, Shakre had a sudden feeling as if a vast door opened. For a short while the world seemed bathed in light, though it was not light she could see with her eyes. Youlin had felt it too. Then the feeling shut off suddenly.

"I did," he replied. "Do you know what it was?"

"I don't know for sure," she admitted. "But something is different now. The distant feeling of unquenchable hunger is gone. I think things are all right now."

"I do not see Gulagh's body."

"The Guardian was badly injured. It went through the Gate after the explosion. I don't think it will come back."

"And none of the spirit-kin survived?"

Shakre shook her head. "All but three were killed here. Those three, the ones who held the *ronhym* captive, were killed by the *ronhym*."

"So we betrayed our ancient allies once again."

Shakre nodded. "I've been thinking about it and I think they planned for this to happen." She indicated the destruction from the blast. Elihu gave her a quizzical look. "The *ronhym* knew they couldn't trust the spirit-kin. It's likely they did not trust the Guardian either. I think they deliberately handed over an unstable crystal. They gambled that either it would break apart under the strain of Gulagh's using it, or that the spirit-kin would destroy it themselves. Either way, they'd be rid of two enemies at once."

Elihu's gaze swept over the destruction once again. "Was it part of their plan that Wreckers Gate be destroyed too, or was that just random?"

"I don't know. Maybe they think we won't stay here without the Gate to protect us."

"I think the destruction of the Gate is a good thing," he said, surprising her.

"Why?"

"I think our people have hidden from the world for too long. It is time we were part of it once again. Look at us. Our numbers are few. If we are to survive, we will have to mix with other people. I think it is time we do this."

Shakre just looked at him. She hadn't considered this. "I think you're right," she said finally.

SIXTY-NINE

She drifted, alone and lost.

She was fading away. It was becoming harder and harder to remember who she was, *why* she was.

It wouldn't be long now until there was nothing left.

Was that really so bad?

Her most vivid memory was of being in the River. *Being* the River. Encompassing all life and looking outward, seeing the lost glows that were Melekath's Children. Feeling compassion for them, for their isolation and loss.

It was easy to reach out to them and embrace them, to draw them back to the River where they belonged.

She remembered sensing the approach of one far vaster and emptier than the others. Fast. She turned the focus of her attention, realizing all at once who it was.

A sudden shock as she realized what was about to happen.

Jolted by the oncoming violence, she reacted, though she already knew it was too late. There wasn't possibly time to travel all the way back to her body, reenter it, and then move it from the path of danger.

She remembered jerking on the thin silver line that connected her to her body, even as she reached out with the River to embrace Reyna, to bring her back home.

Surprisingly, the line didn't snap. She was whole once again, body and spirit united. But she was nothing and nowhere. It took her some time before she realized what had happened.

She was lost *beyond*.

Beyond has no landmarks. It is not a place. Those who travel there know the only thing that keeps them from drifting away, from being irrevocably lost, is that slender, shining connection to the body they left behind. Break that connection and there is no way home. No way to move. Nowhere to go.

She knew real fear.

How long she'd been drifting she had no idea. Time has no meaning *beyond*.

If she could have flung herself back into the River, even though her physical form would be instantly shredded, she would have. She longed for the sense of completion, of utter safety, that she'd felt while immersed there. Besides, anything was preferable to this non-existence.

As she drifted there, slowly fading away, strange fantasies came to her. Or they were real, and she was the strange fantasy. She had no idea.

She saw Cara sobbing and knew she wept for her. She longed to comfort her old friend, but she had no way to reach her and when she tried Cara bobbed further away.

She saw Shorn staring down, his shoulders shaking with suppressed emotion. How much they had been through together. If only she could speak with him one last time.

He, too, eluded her touch.

Both of them she saw as if they were *beyond* too, their normal surroundings stripped away. She had the feeling that if she could see either one of them in their world, she could use them as a beacon and draw herself back, but she had no idea if that was right either or just part of her bizarre imaginings.

There was Ya'Shi, seemingly standing on light. He was more solid than she was. *You're doing it again*, he said. *Haven't you learned anything?*

But when she tried to ask him for help he faded away and she might have only imagined him.

At least she had stopped the Children, saved lives, brought them home, redeemed her own crimes. That must count for something.

But that didn't seem real either and she could no longer be sure it had really happened.

I am…?

She realized she could no longer remember who she was. Was it important? She saw other figures drifting around her. An older woman with a kindly face who seemed familiar. A stern woman with her white hair pulled back into a tight bun. A prim woman with perfect bearing.

Who were they?

She drifted. Alone. Lost. Nameless.

✗ ✗ ✗

There was something different in the darkness. A pulsating glow, flickering red and yellow. It was so bright it was almost painful.

She reached out for it and somehow managed to draw closer to it. She didn't know what it was, only that she had wanted to find this particular glow for a very long time. Her need was almost painful.

Closer yet, but there was something in the way, some sort of gauzy barrier. She reached out to tear it out of the way and knew sudden, sharp pain.

She drew back with a soundless cry.

What was it? Some kind of web or veil. She was afraid to touch it again.

But she longed for the bright glow. She had to get to it, though she was not sure why.

Hey.

Floating near her was some kind of strange man with yellow skin and no hair. Was he part fish?

You have to leave your body behind to go there, he told her.

I'm afraid. It is all I have left, all that remains of me.

He shook his head. *Still you do not learn. Your body is not you. It is a construct, a thing that houses the idea of you for a short while. You can lose it, but you cannot lose yourself.*

I don't understand.

Your body is not real. It is only a projection of your thoughts. Change the thought that you must hold onto it and you will be free of it.

But what will I come back to?

He shook his head. *You don't have to come back to it. But if it is important to you, then you can come back to it.*

How?

He tapped his temple. *Use this. Use your mind.*

She thought about it. *I can't do it.*

Then you can't go in there.

She looked from him to the glow and back. *There is no other way?*

You could leave.

But I want to go in there. There is something in there I want very badly to see, though I cannot remember what it is.

It is your choice. It has always been your choice.

340

She considered this, then turned back to the barrier. *I have waited too long. I have to know.*

Then go. The only thing standing in your way is your fear. It was ever your only real obstacle.

She let go. A weight seemed to fall away from her. Her body sank away into the darkness. She was less and more at the same time. She passed through the barrier easily.

She broke through into light. Not daylight. It was too leaden and sulfur yellow. She was flying. Far below was thick, twisted jungle that stretched in every direction. A vast, turgid river. Beside the river on one side was a barren stone plateau. A black creature of blades and hard angles looked up at her, but it could not trouble her.

She could no longer see the scarlet and yellow glow which had drawn her, but she could feel it. With no body to encumber her it was simple to drift that way.

Off to the side, on the opposite side of the river from the barren plateau, was a rocky peak, smoke drifting from the hole in the top. Something huge and rubbery crawled from the hole and bellowed at her, but she was too far away to care.

She did not notice as it began to pursue. Nothing mattered but the lodestone that drew her onwards, a sense that she was approaching something vital.

No, not something. *Someone.*

An anxiety that was not her own gripped her and she willed herself to move faster. The terrain below raced by.

She came to a place where the strange world ended, just dropped away into nothing. Down below was only a writhing, purple darkness. There were things in that darkness, things that hungered and clawed their way toward the light. Now the fear she felt was her own.

The river was not turgid here. It poured up out of the purple darkness, foaming and crashing as if chewing away at unseen rocks. The presence which drew her was there, under the surface of the river.

Her fear increased. Looking back the way she had come, she saw the huge, rubbery creature pursuing, rapidly drawing closer. She did not have long.

A voice in her mind: *Help me.*

She went lower. There, submerged in the river, was a long, rectangular thing, a coffin made of stone. The river was gnawing at it, had been for a very long time. It was worn thin and brittle. How it had survived for so long was a mystery.

She had to get it out of there before it collapsed completely, but it was impossible for her to move it. It was too big. She was too insubstantial. She could feel the huge, rubbery creature getting closer. Like the rabbit tensing as the predator approaches, she prepared to flee.

In her head was the yellow-skinned man again. *Have you really forgotten already?*

What did he mean?

The huge creature was almost on her. It reached for her with its bloated hands.

You were *the River. Your only limits are those you have given yourself.*

Oh. Suddenly it made sense. What he said was true. She remembered the vastness of the River. She remembered it *now*.

Casually, almost negligently, she pushed outward. The rubbery creature fell back from her, roaring at the indignity.

She turned her attention back to the stone coffin. It was simple to wrap her will around it and pull it up out of the current. She turned and thought the gauzy barrier she had passed through to enter this place. It appeared instantly. The huge creature foamed and snarled at her. She ignored it.

A nudge with her will and the gauzy barrier parted. She took the coffin and passed through while the huge creature bellowed in impotent rage.

Back in the depths of *beyond*, around her the darkness, tiny, faint pinpoints of light gleaming in the vastness.

She tapped on the stone coffin. Once more and it cracked open. A figure spilled out from within it.

The figure stood up and looked at her. Then it took hold of her and pulled.

SEVENTY

She was choking. She couldn't get any air. She'd forgotten how to breathe. Someone patted her on the back and all at once she remembered. She gasped and rolled over onto her back.

Bright sunlight hurt her eyes. She put up her hand to block it. Her hand shook. She was so weak that she couldn't hold it there.

Someone was helping her sit up.

"What is your name?"

She considered this. She started to say she didn't know, but then she realized she did. "Netra."

"Thank you, Netra. You saved me."

It was a woman's voice. Netra turned her head to look at her. She looked like no woman Netra had ever seen. There was something inhuman about her, though she was composed of all the features recognizable as human. But her skin was too hard, like glazed stone rather than flesh. Her features were too symmetrical. Her eyes were too blue, like the sky on an impossible summer day. They hurt to stare into.

"Who are you?" Netra asked her, although she knew already.

"Once I was known as Xochitl, but that was long ago and that name may not mean anything to you."

Netra felt her heart begin to race. Once again she had difficulty breathing. "Are you real?" she asked. "Am I real?"

The not-woman smiled. "Yes to both of those."

"How did you get here?"

"You saved me. You came into the *Pente Akka* and pulled me free."

"I did?" Netra pondered this. "Yes, I remember. A little." Other things began to come back to her then and she remembered the Children, the danger that they posed. She looked around, alarmed. "The Children?"

Xochitl frowned. "Are you speaking of Melekath's Children?"

Netra nodded.

There was sorrow in Xochitl's eyes. "They are sealed away in an eternal prison."

"No. They escaped. They were about to destroy everything." Netra paused. Like images seen at the bottom of a body of water, fragments of memory began to filter back. "I brought them home," she said, awe in her voice.

Xochitl went still and closed her eyes. For a minute she remained thus, then she opened her eyes and smiled once again. "It is true. You have restored them." There was wonder in her voice. "How did you do this?"

"I don't know." Then Netra remembered Shorn, his immovable loyalty, his unbreakable strength. She remembered Cara, her gentle, yet fierce, love. "I had lots of help."

"It is a remarkable story, I am sure," Xochitl said. "I would like to hear it."

Netra opened her mouth, then frowned. Her past was shattered pieces. "I can't tell you. Not yet. It's like a dream. I only remember pieces and I don't know where they fit."

"You went into the River," Xochitl said suddenly, her eyes widening.

At her words a whole series of pieces clicked into place all at once. "I remember now," Netra said breathlessly. "I remember being there."

"Tell me what it was like." Xochitl was looking at her oddly. Was that hope in her eyes? Was it awe?

"I don't know if I can. The words won't fit."

"Try."

"It was eternity and yet…it was only an instant. I was no longer me. Well, I still was, but I was everyone at the same time. I realized then that we had forgotten who we are. We thought we were many instead of one and we were all afraid and our fear was making us do crazy things."

Xochitl was staring at her raptly.

"Among us were those whose fear and isolation were magnified beyond the rest. So much pain." Her voice wavered.

"The Children," Xochitl said.

"When I felt their pain…" Netra frowned. "*Our* pain. When I felt our pain I reached out to them and drew them to me. I drew them back where they belonged."

"You accomplished what I thought was impossible. I thought the Children would never be returned to the Circle. I had some idea that if

344

they could be brought to the River it might be done, but I thought that was impossible as well. The power there is too great to be controlled. It would have destroyed even me if I had tried. Yet somehow you managed to do it. This is what I want to know. How did you do it?"

"I don't..." Netra struggled to find the words. How could she explain what had happened? It was something beyond her comprehension and already it was slipping away from her. An inspiration came to her. "I didn't *do* anything. It was *doing* that had caused all my problems. Instead, for the first time in my life, I let go. I abandoned myself." She made a frustrated sound. "There's no way to explain it, but once I did that I realized that I belonged there. It was only my thinking that I didn't which made it difficult. Does that make any sense?"

Xochitl pondered this for a time, then shrugged. "I don't know if it does. I don't know if it ever will."

"I wish there was a better way to explain it." Netra rubbed her temples. "It's already fading."

"You've been through a lot. For now, you should rest and there is something I must do." Xochitl stood up.

Netra tried to get up too, but she felt weak and she quickly gave up. "Where are you going?"

"To finish what I started. The rift we made into the abyss when we created the prison is getting bigger. It has to be sealed. That's what I was trying to do when I became trapped."

Netra stared at her, perplexed. "I don't know what you're talking about. What abyss? A rift?"

"Later. Stay here. I will return for you." Xochitl laid a cool hand on Netra's forehead. Netra felt Song pouring into her, restoring her. All at once she felt wonderfully sleepy. "Rest," Xochitl said.

As Netra lay down she heard Xochitl calling out familiar names: Tu Sinar, Gorim, Golgath, Sententu, Protaxes, Khanewal, Bereth.

"Some of them are dead," Netra said sleepily, wondering where that knowledge came from. "Maybe all of them."

Xochitl gave her a look and then continued calling.

The last thing Netra saw before falling asleep were three figures rising up out of the ground. One appeared as a beautiful woman with feline eyes. Another was on all four and bestial in form, with a long tail. The last was tall and regal, with gold skin.

When Netra awakened Xochitl was back, sitting on the ground beside her. She looked tired. Netra sat up. They were in a small meadow bordered by pine trees. Birds called in the distance and there was the sound of a stream.

"Did it work?" Netra asked.

"I believe so. At least for now it will hold."

Netra reached out tentatively and touched Xochitl's arm. So much was still foggy, but the memory of longing to meet Xochitl was strong. "You were gone for so long," Netra said. "We thought you were angry and had turned your back on us."

"I went to try and fix the problem that I created. I saw that the abyss was leaking into our world and I knew if it was not stopped we would eventually be overrun."

"What happened? How did you become trapped there?"

"Here, let me show you." She touched Netra on the temple.

Netra saw her, kneeling at the edge of purple darkness. There was a black rip, sparks coming from it intermittently. Nearby was the gauzy boundary that marked the edge of the *Pente Akka*. Xochitl's hands were glowing as she wielded a flow of Stone power, directing it at the rip, sealing it shut.

There was a tremor, like an earthquake. The *Pente Akka* rippled and suddenly, without warning, it swelled, spilling over Xochitl.

As it closed around her, just before the flow of Stone power was sliced through, Xochitl used the Stone power to seal herself in raw stone.

The vision ended.

"If I hadn't been already wielding Stone force, I would have been destroyed nearly instantly. As it was, there was nothing I could do but stay there and wait."

"But...that was thousands of years ago. You've been there this whole time?"

Xochitl nodded. "As I imprisoned Melekath and his Children, so I was myself imprisoned. The irony of my predicament did not escape me. Perhaps there is justice in this world."

"You couldn't have known what would happen when you created the prison," Netra protested. "You had to do something. The Children were dangerous."

Xochitl's expression was stark. "Do not make it something it was not. I buried them alive, knowing they could not die. I should never have listened to Lowellin. I should have found another way. There was still time."

Netra shuddered, suddenly remembering what it had felt like to be in the prison. "At least they are free now."

"They are free." Xochitl regarded her, sadness on her face. "When I shared my memory with you just now I saw some of your memories. I did not mean to intrude."

"It's okay."

"You have been through a great deal."

Netra's brow creased as she tried to recall. She felt the truth in Xochitl's words, but so much of it was still missing or disconnected.

"You broke the prison because you thought I was trapped in there," Xochitl said.

Netra shuddered as the memory returned to her. "I did. I was lost and desperate. I thought it was the only way." She remembered running across the desert, filled with power and rage, but it seemed almost like something that had happened to someone else. The emotions had lost their impact.

"It needed to happen," Xochitl said. "Everything. Just as it did. It was the only way."

Netra was silent, remembering the destruction of Thrikyl, the siege of Qarath. So many lives lost. But no, not lost. Returned to the River where they belonged. "I think I can see that now. Only pure desperation could have driven me to risk the River as I did."

"So you will lay down your burden of guilt?"

"I think I already have. I can still feel it there, but it doesn't hurt to touch it."

"Good." Xochitl laid her hand on Netra's shoulder. "There are those I wish to find now, Melekath and Lowellin. We have much to speak of. Is there somewhere you would like me to take you first?"

"Qarath. But there is something you should know. Lowellin was...the *ingerlings* devoured him."

Xochitl shook her head. "I wish I could say I was surprised. I assume he went after Melekath?"

Netra nodded.

Xochitl stood, helping Netra up. "He always hated Melekath. It was something I never understood."

"Hatred doesn't always need a reason."

"You are correct in this. Are you ready? It is best if you close your eyes. Traveling through the Stone can be very disorienting."

347

Netra did as she said. Xochitl wrapped her arms around her. There was a brief, frightening feeling of tremendous weight pressing on her from all sides, and then she felt the sun on her skin once again.

"Here we are," Xochitl said.

Netra opened her eyes and saw Qarath in the distance, about a mile away. Xochitl started to sink into the ground.

"One more thing." Xochitl paused. "The *ingerlings*. Lowellin said they would devour the Circle once they were done feeding on Melekath. Are those things still out there? Should we do something about them?"

"I am not sure what these things are," Xochitl replied. "But you have my assurance that I will look into them." She started to sink again.

"You will come back, won't you?" Netra asked. "Your Tenders need to see you. We have been on our own for a very long time."

Xochitl nodded, then was gone.

Netra started walking toward the city.

SEVENTY-ONE

"Something has changed," Ricarn said.

She, Rome, Quyloc and Nalene were standing looking at the tower, which was completely invisible under its thick layer of the unnatural vine.

"It looks the same to me," Rome said.

"No, she's right," Quyloc said. He was holding the *rendspear* and he looked down at it. "My spear feels different too."

"The vine is no longer growing," Ricarn said.

"Well, that's good," Rome said. "What does it mean?"

"You might not have to abandon Qarath, for one," Ricarn said.

"I like the sound of that."

"And maybe it means our world isn't going to be swallowed by the abyss," Quyloc added.

"This is just getting better and better," Rome said.

"But I don't think we're going to get the tower back anytime soon," Quyloc said. "Just because it's stopped growing doesn't mean it's going to just die."

"Who needs a tower anyway?" Rome said. "I think we'll just build a wall around it, just to prevent any surprises." He looked at Nalene. The FirstMother had not been herself ever since she gave up her *sulbit*. He couldn't say he was sad to see the last of those things. They'd always seemed creepy to him. "How is the hospital doing?" The Tenders had set up a hospital on their estate to help those who'd been injured in the siege.

"No one died yesterday," she said. "A few more were well enough to go home."

"Is the one Tender—what's-her-name, Cara?—still running the morning services?"

"She is. The people love her."

"Good. I think we all need whatever help we can get for a while."

Nalene and Ricarn left then, heading back down into the city. Rome and Quyloc stood there looking at the tower. It was a chilly morning, a sharp wind blowing in off the ocean. Quyloc's green cloak fluttered in the wind.

"I wonder what happened," Quyloc said.

"What are you talking about?"

Quyloc gestured toward the tower. "Why did it stop growing?"

Rome shrugged. "Who cares? As long as it did. That's all I care about. I've had enough of that supernatural stuff. I'd like to just face ordinary problems from here on out."

"I agree," Quyloc said. Suddenly, unexpectedly, he threw the *rendspear* into the vine. It disappeared without a trace.

Rome looked at him, his eyebrows raised. Quyloc shrugged. Rome patted him on the shoulder. "Probably for the best," Rome said.

SEVENTY-TWO

As Netra approached Qarath she fell into the rear of a group of people who were clearly just returning to the city. They pulled carts laden with belongings and elderly relatives. Men were working on the front gates that Heram had destroyed. One of the gates had already been fitted back into place and the other was being repaired. There were several soldiers standing guard, but they did not hinder the returning citizens or give Netra a second look.

Inside, in the large square, she saw that the rubble from the buildings that Rome had collapsed had already been cleared away. The buildings themselves were already partially rebuilt. Scaffolding ran around the buildings. Teams of horses pulled on ropes, lifting stones into the air to be set back into place. It looked like Macht Rome himself was up on the scaffolding, the axe he usually carried replaced by a workman's hammer.

Everywhere the city was a hive of activity. Carts laden with debris rolled toward the gates. Groups of people were rebuilding stone walls, cutting timbers, replacing roofs and doors. It looked like Qarath would thrive once again.

Netra was passing a row of buildings that were a blackened wreck when she heard a familiar voice yell her name. She turned to see Shorn sprinting toward her.

"It's you! You're alive! I can't believe it!" he yelled, a huge smile on his face.

Then he swept her into a massive bear hug. She tried to hug him back, but she couldn't really move and it was like hugging an actual bear he was so large. He was saying something in his own language, over and over. She didn't know what it was.

"Shorn," she said finally. "I can't breathe."

He released her and when she looked up at his face she saw something she'd never seen before.

He was crying.

Tears rolled in broad tracks down his face. When Netra saw that she burst into tears as well. Then there was nothing she could do but hug him again. Fortunately, this time he was a bit gentler and she didn't have to worry about any cracked ribs.

When that hug ended he took her hands in his giant ones and said, "Where did you go? I searched, but I could not find you."

"It's kind of hard to explain. I don't really understand it all myself. I guess somehow I pulled my body *beyond*."

He frowned, thinking. "But you said it is not a place, that nothing from this world can go there."

"I know I did. Like I said, I don't really understand it. But I was in the River when I did it. Maybe that gave me the strength to bend the rules."

Shorn shrugged. "You are safe. That is all that matters."

"I'm glad to find you here. Do you know where I can find Cara?"

"She will be at the estate. The sick and the wounded are there. I will go with you." Shorn turned and yelled to a burly man who was carrying a load of rubble out of the building.

The man waved in response and then yelled to Netra as they were walking away. "Don't keep him too long. He does the work of ten men."

They walked up the broad street. Netra thought about how many roads they had walked together, how much they had faced together.

"We've walked a long way together, haven't we, Shorn?" Shorn rumbled his agreement. "I bet you never dreamed what you were getting yourself into when you decided to follow me."

"I do not dream," Shorn said, very seriously.

Netra laughed. It felt good to laugh. It felt even better to have things to laugh about.

There were no guards at the gates of the Tender estate, though people were coming and going, bringing in food and supplies and carrying away waste. Here and there across the grounds were people convalescing, some sitting on benches taking in the sunlight, others walking slowly. A few Tenders moved among them, though none that Netra recognized. She noticed right away that the *sulbits* were gone and wondered at that.

Then Cara came out of one of the long, low buildings that the Tenders bunked in. She was carrying a stack of folded cloths and she turned toward the estate house.

She saw Shorn first, as she was turning, and turned back, a question forming on her lips. Then her eyes fell on Netra.

She uttered a cry and dropped the cloths, which spilled across the ground. "Netra!" she yelled, and ran toward her.

SEVENTY-THREE

"I'm going to go back to Rane Haven for a while," Netra said to Cara. They had just finished dinner and were sitting outside, though the night was rapidly getting cold. Netra had been back in Qarath for a few months.

"I'll come with you," Cara said.

"And who will conduct the morning services then?" Netra asked her gently.

Cara frowned. "Maybe I can ask Velma."

"I thought you said Velma hated doing the morning services." Lowering her voice, Netra said, "I even remember you saying something about how awful she is at it. You said it nicely, of course."

"I'm sure I didn't say anything like that," Cara said in mock seriousness.

"Of course not. I probably just imagined it."

"Maybe Bronwyn would do it," Cara mused.

"Really? During her free time?" Bronwyn had become the FirstMother's second-in-command and she was practically the FirstMother herself these days. Nalene turned more and more duties over to her all the time and it was whispered among the Tenders that soon Nalene would anoint Bronwyn as her successor. The FirstMother had changed greatly since the end of the troubles. She hardly spoke anymore. She spent a lot of time in silent prayer.

"I can't go, can I?" Cara said miserably.

"Do you really want to? Or is your place here now?"

Cara sighed. "It's here. I feel strange saying this, but I feel like I'm right where I'm supposed to be. It used to terrify me, but now I really love doing the morning services."

"I'll come back," Netra said. "I promise."

"Is Shorn going with you?"

"I haven't asked him yet, but I think he probably will."

"Why are you going?"

Netra took a moment to answer. "I'm not exactly sure. Part of the reason is I want to visit Siena's and Brelisha's graves. I want to sit there with them. I miss them."

"I do too," Cara said sadly.

"But it's more than that. I need to get out, away from the city. I need some quiet to think. So much happened and I...I think I need to spend some time with it, figure out what it all means." She looked at Cara. "Does that make any sense?" Cara nodded.

"Promise me you'll be careful, no more crazy adventures?"

"I promise."

Cara filed into the huge dining room along with the rest of the Tenders. The Tenders murmured amongst themselves, wondering to each other why the FirstMother had called them here, hours before dinner would be served. The FirstMother was sitting at the head of the table, her eyes closed, her hands folded. Behind her stood Ricarn. Ricarn met Cara's eye and nodded slightly.

They all took their seats and the whispers ceased. Every eye went to the FirstMother. For several minutes she sat there without moving, then she looked up.

"I officially resign my position as FirstMother," she said in a low voice. From the gathered Tenders there was a collective intake of breath. "As is customary, for my last act as FirstMother, I name my successor."

Everyone, including Cara, looked at Bronwyn, who was sitting to the FirstMother's immediate right. Bronwyn lowered her eyes. Then Cara looked to the FirstMother and saw something unusual.

The FirstMother was looking at her.

The FirstMother stood and took the heavy gold Reminder from around her neck. She walked around the table, past Bronwyn, past Velma, finally stopping behind Cara.

Cara couldn't breathe. She wondered if this was really happening.

The FirstMother placed the Reminder around Cara's neck and said, "Welcome your new FirstMother."

SEVENTY-FOUR

Several months had passed since Gulagh was defeated and winter was coming. More snow fell on the peaks nearly every day. The cold air blowing down out of the mountains seemed to sweep the pains of the past away from the Takare. There was laughter again from the children and smiles on the faces of the adults as they worked together to build shelters against the coming winter.

They built their shelters around the shores of the lake, which was several miles from where Wreckers Gate had stood. Up there the valley was a large bowl, grassy and open in the bottom, with thick forests on the sides. It was a good place in which to rebuild.

Somehow, over the course of those weeks, Elihu had become their leader. He did not ask for it. The people just naturally turned to him. There was a calming steadiness and wisdom to him that naturally drew them.

Freed of the demands of leadership, Youlin slowly emerged from within herself. The first few days she sat alone, withdrawn inside her hood, but one morning she got up and began helping to build a shelter. Now she hardly ever wore her hood up at all and Shakre had even heard her laugh once.

For the most part the Takare abandoned their martial arts training. The swords and battle axes were stored away in a small hut and their time went into hunting and building. The gentle, happy people Shakre had come to love returned. There were far fewer of them, it was true, but this land was much kinder than the land on the Plateau and they would thrive here.

One morning Shakre got up and knew it was time. There were no injured Takare for her to tend. Those who had been infected by the ash flakes had all healed on their own once Gulagh was gone. Besides, there were two other healers to look after the Takare if necessary.

She was putting food in her old pack when Elihu returned to the simple hut they had built together. He looked at her gear, then at her. "Is it the wind again, pushing you off to begin a new adventure?" He said it with a smile and she knew he was joking.

"No, not the wind this time. But there is something pushing me. I'm thinking that the Takare are not the only ones who have been hiding from the world for too long."

Elihu understood, as he always did. "You are going to find your daughter."

"I am. Rane Haven is not too many days from here."

"I would not like to see you go alone."

"Oh, I'm not. I have someone coming to keep an eye on me."

Elihu looked around and saw Werthin approaching, carrying a pack. He nodded. "Good. He will make sure you return safely." He gave her a look. "You *are* returning, I take it?"

She embraced him. "I am going to see my daughter, but this is my home. I will return."

SEVENTY-FIVE

Netra and Shorn took their time and traveled slowly. They stopped early most days and spent a lot of time sitting around the fire, not speaking much. They passed through small towns and villages and everywhere saw signs of people getting back to their lives.

At some point the road led them to a small city that Netra remembered all too well. Nelton. The place was deserted. They did not enter. Netra wondered what had become of the Guardians.

When finally they came over the last ridge and saw the ruined Haven down below, Netra was surprised to see that there was someone there, a woman.

"I wonder who that could be," she said to Shorn. He did not respond.

They made their way down the ridge. Long before they got there the woman saw them coming and stood waiting for them.

As they drew close, Netra suddenly felt her heart drop.

"Can it be?" she asked.

All at once Shorn said, "Shakre?"

"What did you just call her?"

"It is Shakre, the one who found me after I crashed here on your world."

Netra stared at him, realizing that she had never once told him her mother's name.

He hurried forward and Netra followed. She was suddenly terrified. She had dreamed of this moment her whole life and now that it was here it wasn't happening right at all. What would she say? Why did she come?

Shakre greeted Shorn, but her eyes were fixed on Netra. Netra tried to speak but her mouth wouldn't work. She realized she was shaking.

"Is it really you?" Shakre asked, walking forward with her hands out. "Is it my little girl after all these years?"

"Mother?" Netra asked.

"Oh, Netra," Shakre said and ran the last few steps and threw her arms around her. "It's so good to see you. I thought of you every day." Her words were filled with tears. "I'm so sorry. I should have come back sooner but I thought...I was afraid you'd hate me for leaving you."

"I don't hate you. How could I? You're my mother." Netra said the words without thinking. They felt right. Everything felt so right.

SEVENTY-SIX

It was late and almost everyone in the palace was asleep, but in the library a lantern burned. Perganon sat at his desk. Before him was a large, leather-bound book.

Technically, it wasn't a book. Not yet, anyway. Every page was blank, waiting for the words that Perganon would write on them. He meant to start in the morning, writing the complete story of recent events, as Rome had charged him to do.

Tonight he just wanted to do the cover. He had a fine brush and a small pot of gold paint. He took a sip from the glass sitting beside him and picked up the brush.

Dipping it in the paint, he started to apply it to the cover, then paused. He had meant to write *Macht Wulf Rome*. It was, after all, at his macht's behest that he wrote this tome.

He shook his head. That wasn't right. It wasn't what Rome would want. Rome had ordered this book be written, not to immortalize or glorify himself, but so that future generations might learn from what they had gone through. As he had learned from the books of history left over from the days of Empire.

Perganon started again. In large, bold letters he painted:
Immortality and Chaos

The End

Return to Atria in the epic fantasy series
Chaos and Retribution
Free sample chapters on the next page

Free sample chapters of *Stone Bound*, book 1 of *Chaos and Retribution*

PROLOGUE: FEN

The man stumbled unseeing down the cobblestone street. The pains were worse today, the worst they'd ever been. Every step was agony. His bones were on fire. His joints felt like they were full of glass. His greatest fear was not that he would die—he'd long since accepted the inevitability of that—but that he would not be able to make it home. If he was going to die today, he wanted only to see his wife and son one last time.

The buildings on this street were built of stone, four or more stories tall and jammed tightly together. This late in the day the street was completely in the shade. Horse-drawn carts moved down the middle of the street. Along the edges hurried people on foot, none of them paying any attention to the man. To the casual observer he was merely another drunk, and drunks were not uncommon in this part of the city.

A new wave of pain hit the man and he staggered, bumping into a woman who was carrying a large basket filled with loaves of bread. "Watch where you're going!" she snapped at him.

Falling, the man instinctively put out his hand to catch himself. When his hand made contact with the wall of one of the buildings there was a cracking sound and the stone split suddenly. The concussion knocked the man back and he fell down.

The woman looked from the crack in the wall to the man and her eyes widened. She gripped the basket tighter and hurried away. Other passersby noticed him for the first time, and began veering around the man, careful to stay out of his reach. It had been years since the red plague last struck the city of Samkara, but people remembered it readily enough. The sweating, wild-eyed man lying on the ground could be infected with it.

The man crawled to the side of the street. He looked at his hand, where he'd touched the wall. The skin was slate-gray and when he tried to flex his fingers they were stiff and he could barely curl them.

The changes were accelerating.

He had to get home.

Careful to avoid touching the wall with his bare skin, he climbed to his feet. Heedless of those around him, he began half-running, half-staggering down the street. People cursed at him as he bumped into them and when he cut across the street to turn down a smaller one he was almost hit by a wagon drawn by a team of horses, the driver snapping his whip near his face.

The smaller street had less traffic and the man made it all the way to his building without running into anyone else. This street was poorer than the one he'd left, narrow and lined with wooden tenements. Gone were the cobblestones, replaced by rutted dirt and garbage.

The man tried to opened the door of the building he lived in with his right hand, the one he'd touched the stone wall with, but he couldn't get his fingers to move at all now and he had to give up and use the other hand. He stumbled through the door, not bothering to close it behind him. He dragged himself up two flights of stairs, every step fresh agony.

He reached the door of his home, made it through, and collapsed on the floor.

His wife gave a little cry, dropped her sewing, and hurried to him. Taking his arm, she helped him to his feet and over to the room's sole bed.

Sitting on the floor by the iron cook stove was a small boy, only a few years old, playing with some broken pieces of colored tile. He stared up at his parents with wide eyes, old enough to know something was wrong, but too young to understand what it was.

Not that his parents understood it either. In the months since the strange pains started, they'd gone to every healer and priest they could afford, trying to find out what was wrong, and none of them had any answers.

"I knew you shouldn't have tried to go to work," she told him, gently stroking his forehead.

"It's...it's happening faster," he gasped and held up his right hand.

Her breath caught in her throat as she stared at his hand. She touched it gingerly. "How did it happen?"

"I touched a stone wall. The stone split." A spasm of pain hit him and he winced. When it had passed he looked up at her and what she saw in his eyes made her gasp.

"Your eyes," she said. "They're red, like a fire burns in them."

"What's happening to me?" he moaned, closing his eyes.

She hesitated only a moment before wrapping him in her arms and holding him close.

"I'm losing the feeling in my arm," he said. He pushed his sleeve up and she saw that his forearm was streaked with gray. Even more unusual—she bent closer to get a better look—there seemed to be chips of stone embedded in his flesh.

He went rigid suddenly and his head arched back. His mouth stretched open, so wide that his jaw popped. For a long moment he froze like this, more a statue than a man, then he began spasming. Shivers ran up and down his limbs. His eyes rolled back in his head and spittle drained from his mouth.

He began thrashing violently. She tried to hold him still but the seizure was too strong for her. He bucked and she was thrown off the bed onto the floor. She got back up and went to him, but there was nothing she could do.

Then the building began to shudder, as if it were caught in an earthquake. She pitched sideways and almost fell down. A small crack appeared in the ceiling and plaster dust sifted down. The little boy wailed and crawled over to his mother, wrapping his little arms around her leg.

After a minute, his seizure ended and a few seconds later the earthquake stopped as well. She looked at her husband and what she saw made her scream.

He was lying on his back, unmoving, his eyes wide and staring. His eyes glowed like lava. His skin had turned completely gray. All of his hair had fallen out.

At first she was sure he was dead and she stood there, one hand over her mouth, frozen by fear and grief. Then, slowly, his head turned. Gray flakes chipped and broke off his neck as he did so. The molten eyes fixed on her.

"*Please...*" His voice grated like stone sliding over stone. More flakes broke off around his mouth and fell to the blanket he lay on.

Her paralysis broke and she hurried to him. Her hands hovered over him for a moment as she wrestled with her fear, but love won out and she placed them on his cheeks. His face was cold and lifeless.

"Oh, my love," she moaned.

"Hold Fen up," he said in his broken voice. "I want to see him...one more time."

363

Tears pouring down her cheeks, she lifted the small boy and set him next to his father on the bed. Fen showed no fear, only curiosity as he leaned forward and touched his father's face.

His father tried to touch him but his arm froze in place halfway. A last tremor shook him.

The fire in his eyes faded and went out.

PROLOGUE: AISLIN

Netra was in her cottage, bundling herbs for drying, when she heard the cries of alarm. At first she thought someone had been injured, perhaps one of the workers in the quarry in the hills outside the village where she lived. If that was the case, they would be coming to her, carrying the wounded man to the village's healer. In her mind she was already preparing, mentally reviewing her inventory of bandages, needles, catgut and so on.

But a minute later she realized she was wrong. This was no injury. There would be no bleeding patient hustled into her cottage by concerned friends. The cries of alarm were not drawing closer, but they were spreading.

Perplexed, she put down the herbs, crossed the room, and opened the door. It was only an hour or so after dawn and the sun had not yet broken through the thick clouds that had rolled in from the sea overnight. A brisk wind whipped her simple, cotton dress about her ankles and tugged at her long braid. In the air she could feel the rain that would likely come later in the day.

Her cottage stood on the outskirts of a small village. It was a quiet place, far removed from the excitement and activity of Qarath, the nearest city. A place where the most that ever happened was an occasional injury and the usual ailments that people suffered from. Which made it perfect for Netra. After all that she'd already been through in her life, the last thing she wanted was more excitement.

Her cottage was on the landward side of a small hill, where it got partial protection from the winds that blew in off the sea, so when she looked down into the village, all she saw at first was people milling around, talking and exclaiming loudly to each other. Then she realized that all of them were turned toward the sea, and a number were pointing.

She hesitated, wondering if she should bring her bag filled with healing herbs, ointments and salves with her, then decided not to. It didn't sound like anyone was hurt, and she could always send someone running to fetch it if she needed it.

She headed down the path toward the village and as it wound around the hillside, she saw for the first time what had everyone so excited.

Just offshore was an island.

An island where there had never been one before.

Besides the impossibility of an island simply appearing out of nowhere, there was something clearly unusual about this island. It had a yellowish hue to it and the plants that grew from its surface were of a variety and vibrancy of colors not seen anywhere on land.

Netra stopped, struck by the appearance of this thing she'd thought never to see again.

For this thing that appeared to be an island wasn't. It was a living creature, though not in any normal sense.

She began hurrying down the hill. Her heart was filled with foreboding as she went. The appearance of ki'Loren, and the Lementh'kal who lived within it, could not but bode ill. Something bad was happening or was about to happen and they were here to seek her out.

She didn't want to know why the Lementh'kal had come. She wanted to go back into her cottage, close the door, and bury herself in her work. She'd been through enough in her life. She'd earned the right to peace and tranquility.

But at the same time she knew that she could not avoid this. Whatever it was, it would have to be faced head on.

By the time she got down the hill, every villager was standing on the beach, staring up in awe at the island, which towered several hundred feet in the air. For the adults, it was not the first time they had seen the floating island. The other time they had seen it was during the war, when it had saved their lives. Which did not mean they were happy to see it now. Questions were asked and more than one accusing look was thrown Netra's way as she passed through their midst. They did not know what, exactly, their healer's role had been during the war, and Netra never talked about it, but they knew she had played an instrumental part in it. If ki'Loren was showing up again, it must have something to do with her.

Netra did not reply to their questions. She made her way to the edge of the surf and stood there waiting.

The island was only a dozen yards offshore when an opening appeared in its side about halfway up. A figure appeared in the opening.

It appeared to be male, though it was difficult to be sure. He was about the height of a human, but built much more slightly. He was hairless, his skin yellow. His eyes were very large and set somewhat on the sides of his head. He carried no weapons and wore only a thin shift made of some kind of shimmery, almost translucent material.

The villagers went very quiet and took several steps back. Some still carried the implements of their trade—spades, pitchforks, hammers, brooms—and they held these up as if to fend off this strange invader.

The figure saw Netra and his wide, lipless mouth stretched in something approximating a smile. But it wasn't really a smile, more like something he'd seen humans do and was trying to copy. The nervous villagers took another step back.

He waved. "Hi, Netra!" He started down the side of the island but didn't make it very far before he tripped. He bounced and rolled clear down the side and then plopped into the water.

Netra sighed. She'd seen all this before.

He thrashed around in the water for a minute before emerging, spluttering and dripping.

"Hello, Ya'Shi," she said.

"You remember me!" he exclaimed. Up close she could see the white spots and streaks mixed in with the natural yellow coloring of his skin, signs of his advanced age. She didn't know exactly how old he was, only that his age was counted in centuries. Even amongst a people who lived very long lives, Ya'Shi was unusual.

"As if I could forget you," she said. She saw movement in the opening as a new figure emerged and made its way down the side of ki'Loren and she smiled. She remembered Jenett fondly. Jenett was carrying a bundle wrapped in cloth and unlike Ya'Shi she didn't stumble. Rather, she moved with the same eerie, almost supernatural fluidity and grace that marked her people.

Ya'Shi turned, following her gaze. "Oh, that's Jenett," he said offhandedly. "You probably don't remember her. She wasn't nearly as important as me in our last adventure."

"That's what it was to you?" Netra asked. "An adventure? Because it felt like the end of the world to me."

"When you're young, like you are, *everything* seems like the end of the world, I suppose," he said. His voice was strange, missing normal human inflections that lend words so much of their meaning, yet somehow he managed to convey an exaggerated condescension.

"Especially the actual end of the world," she replied.

Ya'Shi flicked a grain of sand off his arm. "There was never any actual danger."

Netra gave up trying to argue with him and crossed her arms. "What brings you here, Ya'Shi? Is there a purpose or is this just more of your old foolishness?"

"What's that you say?" he asked, cupping his hand around where his ear would have been, had he actually had one. He peered at her, blinking in confusion. "Who are you again? You seem familiar, but I can't quite place you." The transformation was astonishing. Almost instantly he'd become old and bent, with barely the strength to stand, his mind nearly gone.

Netra sighed again. Being around Ya'Shi was tiring. He flitted through moods rapidly, went from clowning to serious in the blink of an eye, constantly blending profundities with sheer foolishness. Being around him meant being always off-balance, never quite knowing where things were going next.

"I really don't feel like playing your games today. Can you tell me why you're here? I have things to do."

Ya'Shi began nodding as she spoke. "Oh, yes. Things. *Very important* things, I'm sure." He rubbed his hands together briskly and all his feigned age and weariness disappeared. "We must get to business. Vital events are afoot. Huge, cataclysmic, earth-shaking events. We mustn't waste a moment. If ever there was a time that called for great haste—"

"Just tell me already!" Netra snapped. She thought of Shorn then, how angry Ya'Shi had always made him, and wished her old friend were there with her.

Ya'Shi blinked at her, his eyelids sliding up from underneath his eyes, then back down. Quite slowly. "Why, it's the end of the world, of course. I wouldn't waste your time otherwise."

Netra waited for him to continue, to give her more details, but he stood there staring at her, his head cocked slightly to one side. "Well? Aren't you going to tell me any more?"

He frowned. "About what?"

Netra bit off the angry words she wanted to shout at him. "This is why Shorn always wanted to choke you," she said.

He shook his head. "No. Shorn and I understood each other. We were very close. Anyway, here's Jenett. She has something for you."

Jenett was emerging from the water. She looked much like Ya'Shi but was more slightly built and her yellow skin was tinged with green streaks here and there, a sign of her youth. She smiled when she approached Netra—showing the bristles that lined the inside of her mouth instead of teeth—and on her the smile looked more natural, more inviting than Ya'Shi's.

"It is very much my pleasure to see you again, Netra." Her voice was soft, whispering past the ear like a gentle breeze. "Though I wish it were under happier circumstances."

The bundle she was carrying moved, drawing Netra's eye.

"Hurry, hurry! Give it to her!" Ya'Shi was bouncing from one foot to another like an excited child. He clapped his hands together. "I can't wait to see what she thinks of our gift!"

"He hasn't changed," Netra said to Jenett.

"He is Ya'Shi," Jenett replied. "The currents that move him are inscrutable to the rest of us."

"Or maybe he's just crazy."

Jenett frowned. "I understand what you mean by the word, but it has no real meaning among my people. The Lementh'kal are the People of the Way, and it is not for us to judge where someone's way takes them."

She stepped closer to Netra and pulled back the cloth from one end of the bundle.

Netra thought she wouldn't be surprised at anything the Lementh'kal gave her, but she was wrong.

"A *baby*?"

Tiny hands, pink cheeks, and wide, green eyes that stared up at her.

Neta swallowed and tried again. "A baby? You brought me a baby?"

Ya'Shi held up one finger. "Not just any baby. A *special* baby."

"Why…why…?" Netra couldn't seem to get the words out.

"There's no need to thank us."

"It's a human baby," Netra said.

"Yes and no," Ya'Shi said. "There is more to her. Listen."

Netra stilled the question she'd been about to ask and listened. Not with her ears, but with her inner senses, inside where LifeSong could be heard.

"You're right," she breathed. "Mixed in with LifeSong, I can hear the Sea as well." She looked at the two of them, then back at the baby. "How is this possible?"

"When a mommy and a daddy love each other very much..." Ya'Shi trailed off. "Sorry. It wasn't like that at all. But how it happened isn't what's important."

All his silliness disappeared and his tone grew serious. "A storm is coming. A terrible storm. Nothing you or I, or any of us, can do will stop it." He set his fingers on the baby's forehead.

"But she might. She and two others."

Jenett held out the baby and Netra took her. The green eyes had stayed fixed on her the entire time. They were the green of the deep sea and there were flecks of white in there like whitecaps on a windy day.

"One from each of the spheres, Stone, Sea and Sky," Ya'Shi continued. "Only the three of them, working together, have any chance in what is to come."

"I'm sorry," Jenett said. "Truly I am. You of all people know what a burden it can be, saving the world."

"But that's why you're the right person to raise her," Ya'Shi said. "Well, enough idle chat. We must be going so you can get back to your important things." He took hold of Jenett's arm and began to guide her back into the surf.

"Wait!" Netra called after them. "What's going to happen? Where are these other children?"

"One is to the north," Ya'Shi said over his shoulder. "Another is across the sea. Don't look for them. When the time is right they will be drawn together."

"You have to tell me more than that," Netra pleaded.

"Goodbye!" Ya'Shi called, still holding onto Jenett and propelling her firmly in front of him. "Good luck!"

They walked through the surf, then up the side of ki'Loren. They passed through the opening, it closed behind them, and the floating island began to move away.

Leaving Netra with a baby.

PROLOGUE: KARLISS

The wind was crazy the day the baby was born. It shrieked around the hide yurt where the expectant mother lay, attended by Spotted Elk Clan's midwife and two other women. It scratched and clawed like a wild thing trying to get in, tearing at the flap, trying to get under the edge of the yurt and send it flying across the high steppes where the Sertithian people lived their nomadic lives.

But the Sertithians were familiar with the ways of the wind and the yurt was strongly constructed and tightly staked down so it stayed intact and in place, though the hide it was made of thrummed and vibrated steadily.

"It will be over soon," the midwife said, as one of the other women bathed the expectant mother's forehead with a damp cloth. "One more long push should do it." The yurt was lit by a pair of oil-burning clay lamps. There were two small wicker baskets containing clothes and another filled with tools and sewing implements. A sheathed sword leaned against the wall of the yurt, along with an unstrung bow and a quiver of arrows.

"For months this child has fought and kicked, as though he could not bear his captivity another moment. Now the time comes and he won't budge. Will he always be this difficult?" The expectant mother spoke in a light tone, but her face was pale with pain. The furs she lay on were wet with her sweat. She was a young woman and this was her second child but she had been half a day trying to deliver the child already.

"Just breathe, Munkhe," the midwife said. "It will all be over soon."

"The *tlacti* told me it would be a son," Munkhe said. The *tlacti* was the clan's shaman. "He said the wind told him so." The other women already knew this. Such things became common knowledge quickly in such a tightly-knit community. They also knew she spoke to take her mind off the pain.

"If Ihbarha said it will be a boy, then it will be a boy," the midwife replied calmly.

Munkhe grimaced as another contraction came on. She gritted her teeth and pushed.

"I can see the top of his head," the midwife said. As if to punctuate her words a fresh gust of wind shook the yurt.

"The wind is also anxious for your child to be born," the fourth woman in the yurt said. Henta was elderly, with a severe expression and a downturned mouth that said she rarely smiled. "Perhaps this means he will be touched by it."

"Pray to the four winds it is so," Munkhe said through gritted teeth. She wasn't sure she wanted her son to be the next *tlacti*, but Ihbarha was old. It was past time for a wind-touched child to be born to the Spotted Elk Clan.

"One more push and it will all be over," the midwife said.

Munkhe's back arched as she gave another, mighty push. A cry came from her as the pain increased but she did not let up and a few moments later the baby slid forth into the world.

At that same instant a new shriek arose from the wind as it buffeted the yurt. The wooden pins holding the door flap of the yurt closed snapped under the strain and the flap blew open.

The wind raced into the yurt like a wild animal, whining in its eagerness. It seemed to focus on the child, whirling around it with such strength that for a moment the midwife feared it would be snatched from her and she clutched it tightly to her breast. The other women cried out and Henta made a sign against evil.

Then, as fast as it appeared, the wind was gone. The women stared at each other, shaken and confused.

"Never have I seen such a thing," Henta said.

"My baby!" Munkhe cried, struggling to sit up and see. "How is my baby?"

The midwife brushed the baby's mouth and nose clear. "He is healthy."

"It's a boy?" Munkhe asked.

But the midwife didn't answer right away. She was looking at the baby, a strange expression on her face.

The other women bent close. "Most peculiar," Henta said.

"What's wrong with him?" Munkhe said, fighting against the furs which seemed determined to wrap around her. "Is something wrong with him?"

"It's nothing," the midwife said soothingly. "Help her sit up," she told the others, and when they had done so she handed Munkhe her child.

"Oh," Munkhe said. "I see."

The baby's eyes were wide open, which was unusual by itself. But even more startling was the color of those eyes. They were the blue of a summer sky and blue eyes were extremely rare amongst the Sertithians.

Not only were the baby boy's eyes wide open, but he had a huge smile on his face. He looked like he was laughing at some secret jest.

"I think it is time to fetch the *tlacti*," the midwife said, and the younger of the two women bustled out of the yurt to summon him.

"So long as he is healthy. That is all that matters," Munkhe said stoutly. The midwife and Henta nodded their agreement, but neither of them spoke. Munkhe looked from them to her baby and clutched him close, murmuring to him.

When the *tlacti* arrived he swept into the yurt without a word or look for any of them. The furs Ihbarha was dressed in were old and ratty. He had a piece of felt wrapped around his head like a turban. On each cheek was tattooed an arcane symbol. His white hair was long and twisted into twin braids, into which were tied a number of small bones, colorful stones, and clay discs. Around his neck, on a leather thong, hung his *krysala*, the relic he used to summon and control the spirits in the wind.

He went straight to the baby and took him from Munkhe's arms, who gave him up without complaint. He held the baby up and closed his eyes. He stayed that way for a minute, then lowered the child and pressed his ear to the baby's chest. He listened for another minute, then raised his head.

"He's touched by the wind, isn't he?" Henta said. She tried to keep the unhappiness out of her voice but didn't quite succeed.

The old shaman shook his head. He looked down at the tiny infant, his creased and weathered face betraying his awe and surprise.

"The wind has not marked him. The wind has made its home *inside* him."

Glossary

abyss – place deep in the earth that is filled with unknown entities. It is the home of chaos power.

akirma – the luminous glow that surrounds every living thing. Contained within it is Selfsong. When it is torn, Selfsong escapes. It also acts as a sort of transformative filter, changing raw LifeSong, which is actually unusable by living things, into Selfsong.

Ankha del'Ath – ancestral home of the Takare. Empty since the slaughter at Wreckers Gate.

aranti – Shapers of the Sphere of Sky that dwell within the wind. They are the only Shapers never to war against the others.

Atria – (AY-tree-uh) name commonly used to refer to the landmass where the story takes place. It is a derivation of the name Kaetria, which was the name of the old Empire.

Banishment – when the Eight created Melekath's prison and sank the city of Durag'otal underground.

Bereth – a Shaper of the Sphere of Stone, one of the Eight, who together with Xochitl laid siege to the city of Durag'otal. Along with the Shaper Larkind, he discovered the abyss and tried to enter it. Larkin was destroyed and Bereth was permanently damaged. He is the primary god in Thrikyl.

beyond – also known as "in the mists," the inner place where Tenders can *see* Song.

Bonnie – Rome's girlfriend, pregnant with his child.

Book of Xochitl – the Tenders' sacred book.

Brelisha – old Tender at Rane Haven who taught the young Tenders.

chaos power – The power that comes from the abyss. It is completely inimical to all power in the normal world, including LifeSong, Stone force, Sky force, and Sea force. Chaos power was drawn from the abyss by the Eight to form Melekath's prison. When they did so, they did not seal the opening completely and chaos power has been leaking into the world ever since, forming the shadow world of the *Pente Akka*. The sand dunes of the Gur al Krin are a physical manifestation of chaos power that has contacted the normal world.

Children – people who received Melekath's Gift of immortality.

Dreamwalker – the Dreamwalkers are those who are responsible for guiding the Takare in spiritual and supernatural matters.

Dubron – one of Heram's minions.

Durag'otal – (DER-awg OH-tal) city founded by Melekath as a haven for his Children. It was sunk underground in the Banishment.

Eight — eight Shapers of the First Ring who besieged the city of Durag'otal, formed a prison of chaos power around it, and sank it underground.

Elihu – (eh-LIE-who) the Plantwalker for Bent Tree Shelter and Shakre's closest friend.

feeder lines – the intermediate sized current of LifeSong, between the trunk lines, which come off the River directly, and the flows, which sustain individual creatures.

FirstMother – title of the leader of the Tenders.

First Ring – the oldest and most powerful of the Shapers, the first to arrive on the world. They refer to themselves as the Nipashanti

flows – the smallest currents of LifeSong. One of these is attached to each living thing and acts as a conduit to constantly replenish the energy that radiates outward from the *akirma* and dissipates. If the flow attached to a living thing is severed, it will only live for at most a few hours longer.

Genjinn – leader of the rebel Takare at the time of the slaughter at Wreckers Gate.

Gift – immortality. Melekath, seeing that the *akirmas* of living creatures eventually grow brittle and crack open, thus leading to death, came up with a way to make *akirmas* unbreakable. Essentially, he siphoned off from his immortal essence and infused it into the *akirmas* of those who chose to accept the Gift, permanently altering them.

Golgath – one of the Shapers that stood with Xochitl at the siege of Durag'otal. He was the only one of the Eight who was a Sea Shaper.

Gorim – one of the Shapers that stood with Xochitl at the siege of Durag'otal. Worshipped in Veragin, the dead city Rome found at the end of the summer campaign, where T'sim was found.

gromdin – the leader of the *Pente Akka*. It seeks to steal enough Song to shred the Veil, thus allowing the *Pente Akka* to spill freely into the world.

Gulagh – one of the three Guardians of the Children, also known as the Voice.

Gur al Krin – desert that formed over the spot where Durag'otal was sunk underground. The dunes are formed by power leaking from the *Pente Akka* and contacting the normal world.

Gwinen – FirstMother who temporarily allied with Legate Tarnin to crush the rebels at Wreckers Gate.

Heartglow – the brighter glow in the center of a person's *akirma*. Like concentrated Selfsong. When it goes out, the person is dead.

Heram – one of the two leaders of the Children, a blocky, muscular man who was a blacksmith in his former life.

Ilsith – Lowellin's staff. Nothing is known of this creature or why it obeys Lowellin.

ingerlings – ravenous creatures Kasai took from the abyss.

Jenett – young Lementh'kal who helped Shorn and Netra.

Kaetria – (KAY-tree-uh) capital city of the Old Empire.

Karthije – (CAR-thidge) kingdom neighboring Qarath to the northwest.

Karrl & Linde – husband and wife of the Children.

Karyn – (CARE-in) Tender from Rane Haven.

Kasai — one of the three Guardians of Melekath, also known as the Eye.

Ketora – *ronhym* who helped Melekath erect the barrier which protected Durag'otal during the siege by the Eight. She placed herself into Sententu when the Stone Shaper closed the hole in the prison wall with his body, so that there would be a chance of the prison being broken someday. Her time trapped within the wall, and her proximity to the power of the abyss, left her vulnerable. When she was drawn from the prison wall by Rome, she had no true shape and only became the black axe because in the moment he pulled her free he wished for a weapon that would allow him vengeance against King Arminal Rix and his primary weapon in battle is an axe. As time passed and he used her to cut stone repeatedly, she began to awaken.

Khanewal – one of the Eight, the hooded figure Quyloc sometimes encountered at the entrance to the *Pente Akka*.

ki'Loren – sentient, floating island that is home to some of the Lementh'kal.

Kirtet – second-in-command of the Takare at the time of the slaughter at Wreckers Gate. He inhabited Pinlir.

Leckl – one of Heram's minions.

Lementh'kal – beings who live on the ocean. Created by Golgath.

Lenda – simpleminded Tender who accidentally received two *sulbits* and lost control of them.

LifeSong – energy that flows from the River and to all living things. It turns into Selfsong after it passes through the *akirma*, which acts as a sort of filter to turn the raw energy of LifeSong into something usable by the living thing.

li-shlikti – a lesser Shaper of the Sphere of Sea.

Lowellin – (low-EL-in) Shaper of the Second Ring who turned the humans against Melekath while he was away creating the Gift. He also created a rift between humans and Xochitl.

macht – title from the old Empire meaning supreme military leader of all the phalanxes. Adopted by Rome for himself instead of king.

Melekath – powerful Shaper of the Sphere of Stone, one of the First Ring. After eons of existence, he became bored with Shaping and created Life by taking energy from the three Spheres of Stone, Sea, and Sky. Still this was not enough. He desired living things who were free-willed, that he could talk to, and so created people. However, then he could not bear to see them die, so went away for hundreds of years and created the Gift of immortality. It was during this absence that Lowellin turned people against him and caused them to forget he was their creator.

Nalene – FirstMother of the Tenders.

Nelton – small city where Netra and Siena encountered the Guardian Gulagh.

Netra – a young Tender of Rane Haven.

Nicandro – aide to Wulf Rome.

Nipashanti – what the Shapers of the First Ring call themselves.

Ominati – secret organization in Kaetria that was studying the power within the Spheres in an attempt to harness that power to defend Kaetria against the encroaching sands of the Gur al Krin. It was their headquarters where Netra and Shorn took refuge in *Hunger's Reach*. They were all killed when they began to meddle with Sea force, the power within the Sphere of Sea. Golgath sent the *zhoulin* to slaughter them all.

Orenthe – Tender who received the Gift. Filled with horror over those she has killed, she tries not to join in the slaughter at Thrikyl. When she does anyway, she takes hold of a trunk line so that she is torn to pieces and can never hurt another person again.

Owina – one of the Tenders from Rane Haven.

Pastwalker – the Pastwalkers are entrusted with remembering the past. They can take others to actually relive past events from the history of the Takare.

pelti – Shapers from the Sphere of Stone.

Pente Akka – the shadow world that Lowellin showed Quyloc how to access. It is formed of chaos energy leaking from the abyss.

Perganon – palace historian/librarian.

Pinlir – Takare man who was opposed to the use of violence until his father was killed by the outsiders. He is Rehobim's right-hand man and is later inhabited by the spirit of Kirtet.

Plantwalker – the Plantwalkers are Takare who are sensitive to plants and can even communicate with them in a fashion.

Protaxes – one of the Eight, who together with Xochitl laid siege to the city of Durag'otal. Worshipped in Qarath by the nobility.

Qarath – (kuh-RATH) city ruled by Rome.

Quyloc – (KWY-lock) Rome's chief adviser and oldest friend.

Rane Haven – where Netra grew up.

Rehobim – (reh-HOE-bim) Takare who is first to receive one of the old spirits, that of Tarnin, former leader of the Takare.

Rekus – (REE-kus) Pastwalker for Bent Tree Shelter.

relif crystal – type of crystal that can serve as a focal point for Stone power. In *Hunger's Reach*, Netra encountered one in the dead city of Kaetria and realized that no person could touch one without being destroyed.

Reyna – one of two leaders of the Children, she was a powerful noblewoman in old Qarath.

Reminder – a many-pointed star enclosed in a circle, the holy symbol of the Tenders.

rendspear — weapon Quyloc made in the *Pente Akka* from a tooth of the *rend*, lashed to a tree limb from the jungle, then doused in the River. It is capable of slicing through the flows of the three Spheres, as well as those of Life.

Ricarn – Tender of the Arc of Insects.

River – the fundamental source of all LifeSong, deep in the mists of *beyond*.

ronhym – race of ancient shapeshifting beings that are able to merge with the stone, manipulate it and move around in it at will. They are the ones who created Wreckers Gate. Think of them as elementals.

see – the act of perceiving with inner, extrasensory perception. It has nothing to do with the eyes yet what the mind perceives while *seeing* is interpreted by the brain as visual imagery.

Selfsong – when LifeSong passes through a person's *akirma* it becomes Selfsong, which is the energy of Life in a form that can be utilized by the body. It dissipates at death. It is continually replenished, yet retains a pattern that is unique to each individual.

Sententu – a *pelti*, Shaper of the Sphere of Stone, one of the Eight who joined with Xochitl to besiege Durag'otal. He sacrificed himself to be the door of the prison.

Shakre – Netra's mother. She lives with the Takare, having been driven to the Plateau by the wind after being exiled from the Tenders.

Shapers – powerful beings inhabiting the world long before life. Each belongs to one of the three Spheres, Stone, Sea or Sky, though some left to be part of the Circle of Life.

shlikti – Shapers of the Sphere of Sea.

Shorn – powerful humanoid from Themor who was exiled and crashed to earth near the Godstooth.

sonkrill – talismans that the Tenders receive/discover at the end of their Songquest. The use of *sonkrill* came about after the fall of the Empire, as the Tenders sought to recover their lost power.

Sounder – one who worships the Sea and its denizens. Due to the ancient wars between the Shapers of the Sea and those of the Stone, in which many people died and the seas and coastal areas abandoned, the people of Atria have a long history of fearing the Sea. As a result Sounders risk injury and death if they are found out.

Spheres – Stone, Sea and Sky. The three elements.

spirit-kin – Takare who have received the spirit of a Takare ancestor. The spirits are those who did not follow the Takare into exile, believing it to be a mistake.

spirit-walking — an ability that the Tenders of old had, a way of separating the spirit from the body, the spirit then leaving the body behind to travel on without it. A thin silver thread connects the spirit to the body. If the thread is broken, there is no way for the spirit to find its way back to the body.

sulbit – creatures that dwell in the River, living on pure LifeSong. In an effort to gain allies in the fight against Melekath, Lowellin gives them to the Tenders. When a Tender melds with her *sulbit*, she gains the creature's natural affinity for Song. As the *sulbit* becomes larger and stronger, the Tender can use its ability to touch and manipulate Song.

T'sim – (TUH-sim) *aranti* Rome meets in the dead city of Veragin.

Tairus – (TEAR-us) General of the army.

Takare – (tuh-KAR-ee) the greatest warriors of the old Empire. After the slaughter at Wreckers Gate they renounced violence and migrated to the Landsend Plateau.

Tarnin – leader of the Takare at the time of Wreckers Gate.

Tharn – the Guardian known as the Fist.

Themor – Shorn's home planet.

Thrikyl – coastal city whose inhabitants mostly killed themselves to avoid being killed by the Children.

Treylen – Sounder who saved the city when the Children tried to come in under the wall. He is the same man from *Landsend Plateau* who mourned the giant sea creature killed by the Tenders after it came over the wall into Qarath.

Truebane Mountains – home to Ankha del'Ath, ancestral home of the Takare.

trunk lines – the huge flows of LifeSong that branch directly off the River. From the trunk lines the feeder lines branch off, and off the feeder lines come the individual flows that directly sustain every living thing.

Tu Sinar – one of the Eight, who lived under the Landsend Plateau and was the first Shaper destroyed by the *ingerlings*.

Velma – Tender that Nalene leaves in charge when she leaves with the army.

Werthin – young Takare man who carries Shakre off the Plateau and keeps an eye on her.

Windcaller – men reputed to be able to call things in the wind. They are considered blasphemers by the Tenders.

Windrider – name given by the Takare to Shakre after she rides the wind to save the people of Bent Tree Shelter when the Plateau is tearing itself apart.

Wreckers Gate – the name of the main gate at Ankha del'Ath, ancestral home of the Takare. It was made by the *ronhym*.

Wulf Rome – leader of Qarath.

Xochitl (so-SHEEL) – the deity worshipped by the Tenders. She is a Nipashanti of the First Ring and was a Shaper of the Sphere of Stone before moving to Life.

Ya'Shi – Lementh'kal who abducted Netra and Shorn to save them from the *zhoulin*.

Yelvin – name of the two Insect Tenders who accompany Ricarn.

Youlin – (YOU-lin) young Pastwalker from Mad River Shelter. She awakens the Takare warriors to their past lives and calls in the old spirits.

zhoulin – powerful, deadly creature that Golgath sent to kill the Ominati when they began to meddle with Sea force.

ABOUT THE AUTHOR

Born in 1965, I grew up on a working cattle ranch in the desert thirty miles from Wickenburg, Arizona, which at that time was exactly the middle of nowhere. Work, cactus and heat were plentiful, forms of recreation were not. The TV got two channels when it wanted to, and only in the evening after someone hand cranked the balky diesel generator to life. All of which meant that my primary form of escape was reading.

At 18 I escaped to Tucson where I attended the University of Arizona. A number of fruitless attempts at productive majors followed, none of which stuck. Discovering I liked writing, I tried journalism two separate times, but had to drop it when I realized that I had no intention of conducting interviews with actual people but preferred simply making them up.

After graduating with a degree in Creative Writing in 1989, I backpacked Europe with a friend and caught the travel bug. With no meaningful job prospects, I hitchhiked around the U.S. for a while then went back to school to learn to be a high school English teacher. I got a teaching job right out of school in the middle of the year. The job lasted exactly one semester, or until I received my summer pay and realized I actually had money to continue backpacking.

The next stop was Australia, where I hoped to spend six months, working wherever I could, then a few months in New Zealand and the South Pacific Islands. However, my plans changed irrevocably when I met a lovely Swiss woman, Claudia, in Alice Springs. Undoubtedly swept away by my lack of a job or real future, she agreed to allow me to follow her back to Switzerland where, a few months later, she gave up her job to continue traveling with me. Over the next couple years we backpacked the U.S., Eastern Europe and Australia/New Zealand, before marrying and settling in the mountains of Colorado, in a small town called Salida.

In Colorado we started our own electronics business (because, you know, my Creative Writing background totally prepared me for installing home theater systems), and had a couple of sons, Dylan and Daniel. In 2005 we shut the business down and moved back to Tucson where we currently live.

Made in the USA
Monee, IL
03 November 2023

45710467R00226